HIDE
AND
SEEK

Also by Chris Carter

The Robert Hunter Series

The Crucifix Killer
The Executioner
The Night Stalker
The Death Sculptor
One by One
An Evil Mind
I Am Death
The Caller
Gallery of the Dead
Hunting Evil
Written in Blood
Genesis
The Death Watcher

CHRIS CARTER

HIDE AND SEEK

SIMON & SCHUSTER

London · New York · Amsterdam/Antwerp · Sydney/Melbourne · Toronto · New Delhi

First published in Great Britain by Simon & Schuster UK Ltd, 2026

1 3 5 7 9 10 8 6 4 2

Simon & Schuster UK Ltd, 7th Floor
199 Bishopsgate, London, EC2M 3TY

Simon & Schuster Australia, Sydney
Simon & Schuster India, New Delhi

www.simonandschuster.co.uk
www.simonandschuster.com.au
www.simonandschuster.co.in

The authorised representative in the EEA is Simon & Schuster Netherlands BV, Herculesplein 96, 3584 AA Utrecht, Netherlands. info@simonandschuster.nl

A CIP catalogue record for this book is available from the British Library

Hardback ISBN: 978-1-3985-5630-0
Trade Paperback ISBN: 978-1-3985-5631-7
eBook ISBN: 978-1-3985-5632-4
Audio ISBN: 978-1-3985-5633-1

Typeset in the UK by M Rules
Printed and Bound in the UK using 100% Renewable Electricity
at CPI Group (UK) Ltd

HIDE AND SEEK

One

From the defendant's chair, Nelson Stewart watched the twelve jurors – six male, six female – file back into the courtroom, their different heels clacking against the wooden floorboards at odd intervals, creating an ominous march that reverberated across the courtroom like an anthem. Despite none of them even glancing in his direction, as each juror took their respective seats back inside the box, Nelson tried his best to read his fate in their blank expressions.

For the past six days, those twelve jurors had listened to every account ... every word ... every detail that had been exposed to them by the prosecution, the defense, and all the thirteen witnesses that had been called to testify.

For the past six days, as the trial slowly unraveled, Nelson observed as those twelve jurors kept on sporadically gazing his way, searching his expressions, his body language for any signs of guilt – uncomfortably shifting on his chair, fidgeting, anxious scratching of the hands, dry swallowing, excessive blinking ... anything that could give up his game – but Nelson had followed Tenor Bryant, his defense attorney's, instructions to perfection.

'Nelson,' Bryant had said during their last pre-trial meeting, seven days ago. 'I need you to listen to me very carefully because this is very important. Once this thing starts tomorrow, I want you to show no emotions at all ... and I mean *nothing*. I've been doing this for long enough to know that every expression you make, every reaction you show, will be interpreted against you, not in your favor, regardless of how truthful those expressions and reactions really are. If you cry, even a single tear, they'll think you're faking it. If you smile, they'll say that you're not taking this seriously. If you fidget, they'll think it's because you're guilty. In a trial, they won't only be listening to the words that'll be said by everyone. They'll be looking at you . . . all the time . . . and they'll be doing so very carefully, especially the judge, Rebecca Reeves, who can be an absolute bitch when presiding over cases that deal directly with violence against women, but most important of all – as the prosecution puts their case forward . . . as you listen to what some of the witnesses will say against you, no matter how much of a lie you think they are telling, you *cannot* show any signs of anger – no outbursts, no fists against the table, no grinding of the teeth . . . nothing. If you show any anger whatsoever, it will bury our case.'

From day one, just like Bryant had asked him to, Nelson Stewart had sat at the defendant's table as still as a potted plant, giving absolutely nothing away, until three days ago, when his wife, Samantha Stewart, took the stand to give evidence for the prosecution, as their first key witness.

Nelson hadn't seen Sam in nine weeks, since he was arrested for allegedly severely beating her up and leaving her handcuffed to the pipework inside their bathroom, while he went out to his weekly poker game with the boys.

As Sam entered the courtroom, Nelson was shocked. She looked tired and frail, having seemingly aged several years in just over two months. Her weight had plummeted, her skin seemed sallow and dry, and her hair looked bristled and uncared for, something that Nelson had never seen in two years of marriage. Despite all that, her astonishing beauty still managed to somehow shine through.

When Sam took the witness stand, she almost immediately began crying, as she gave the court a thorough account of how quickly their marriage had become completely toxic. Under the watchful eyes and attentive ears of everyone inside courtroom one, Samantha Stewart, with the help of several photograph exhibits provided by the prosecution, all of them Polaroids, explained that to her, the fairytale of a perfect marriage had lasted just a little over three months. That was when everything started to change – their rows got louder and more heated . . . their nights apart more common . . . and Nelson's temper gradually more aggressive, until the night that he finally snapped and slapped her across the face for the very first time.

Sam went on to detail how, throughout the next nineteen months, the beatings that she received from her husband became more and more frequent and increasingly more violent, until the point at which she'd become terrified for her life. She told the court that the night that her husband was arrested hadn't been the first time that she'd been handcuffed to the bathroom pipework in their house in Woburn, Massachusetts. No, the shackling to the pipework had happened several times before, and that was why she had hidden a pre-paid cellphone inside the towel drawer in the bathroom.

After Nelson locked the door behind him, leaving Sam bleeding, bruised, and cuffed under the sink, she waited for five minutes to make sure that he wasn't coming back. Once she was sure that her husband was really gone, Samantha Stewart reached for the hidden cellphone and finally called the police.

The prosecution, knowing fully well how effective this was in a trial, petitioned the recorded 911 call so that it could be played in court. They wanted the jury to hear the desperation in Samantha Stewart's voice.

(Female emergency operator) *'911, what's your emergency?'*

(Sam's voice came through in a whisper.) 'I . . . I'm being

held prisoner in my house by my husband. He's . . . a very violent man. I'm . . . really scared.'

'What's your name, darling?'

'Samantha . . . Samantha Stewart . . . Sam.'

'What's your husband's name, Sam?'

'It's Nelson Stewart.'

'Sam, are you whispering because you are in danger? Is your husband in the house with you at the moment?'

(Still in a whisper) 'No. He went out, but I don't know how long he'll be gone for. Please help me. I'm so scared.' Emotion started to strangle Sam's already weak voice. 'I am chained to the pipes in the bathroom. I can't get out.'

'You are "chained" to the pipework inside your bathroom?' There was a tone of disbelief in the operator's voice.

'Yes.'

'What's your address, Sam?'

As Sam dictated her address, the court could hear the sound of hurried keyboard clicks coming from the other end of the line.

'Sam, are you hurt?'

'Yes.'

'How bad are you hurt? Are you bleeding? Have you sustained any life-threatening injuries?'

'No. I'm not bleeding anymore. I'm just bruised. My lip and eye are swollen.'

'OK, Sam, officers are on their way to you now, but I'll stay on the line with you until they get there, in case your husband comes back. The officers are less than three minutes from your house.'

'I . . . I can't get to the door. And they won't be able to hear me. I'm chained in the bathroom inside our room, right at the back of the house.'

'It's OK, Sam, I'll instruct the officers to break and enter.

They won't need a warrant because you are being imprisoned in the house and there's fear for life. They will get to you. Trust me. Is the house alarmed?'

'Yes.'

'Do you know the code?'

'Yes, it's . . . 071421.' More strain in her voice. 'Please hurry.'

'They're almost there, Sam. Where exactly in the house are you?'

'I'm in the bathroom, inside our bedroom. It's up the stairs, second floor – last door, right at the end of the corridor. The bathroom door is locked. I'm not sure if the bedroom door is locked as well, but it probably will be.'

'It's OK, Sam, they'll break it down.'

There was a momentary pause.

'OK, Sam, officers are at your door right now. Just hold on tight and they'll be right with you. You don't have to be scared anymore, you hear?'

'Thank you . . . thank you so much.' Those words came in between sobs.

The call ended.

It was during Sam's testimony, just as she told the court about the first time that Nelson had left her bruised and shackled inside a locked bathroom, that Nelson lost his composure.

'You're a fucking liar, you *fucking bitch*,' he jumped up from the defendant's table, immediately prompting the judge to slam down her gavel and demand order in her court.

'Counsel,' Judge Reeves called, pinning Tenor Bryant with a stare that could've vaporized diamonds. 'If you cannot keep your client on a leash, I'll have *you* charged with contempt of court and your client removed from court. Is that clear?'

'Yes, Your Honor. I'm sorry.' Bryant quickly apologized, placing a firm hand on Nelson's shoulder. 'It won't happen again.'

'It better not.'

'What the hell are you doing?' Bryant asked Nelson in a hushed voice, his eyes wide.

'She's a fucking liar,' Nelson replied through gritted teeth, anger practically dripping through the corners of his mouth like snake venom.

'She might be,' Bryant agreed. 'But that little outburst of yours might've just cost us the damn case, Nelson. Jesus Christ, do you want to go to prison? From now on, I need you to stay as still as toilet water, you hear? No matter what she, or anyone else says – you don't move … you don't say anything. Do you understand what I'm saying?'

Nelson clenched his teeth until pain licked at his jaw.

After Samantha's testimony, the prosecution called their second and final key witness to the stand, Dr. Louise Steinmann.

Dr. Steinmann was a well-known and very reputable psychotherapist, whose private practice was located in Boston, nine miles south of Woburn. In her testimony, Dr. Steinmann confirmed that Samantha Stewart had been one of her clients for the past twenty-five months. She testified that on average, Samantha attended two sessions a week. After about nine months of therapy, she started noticing bruises on Samantha's body. Despite Sam telling Dr. Steinmann that she was a very clumsy person and that she bruised easily, Dr. Steinmann testified that she had enough experience with domestic violence victims to know that those bruises came from physical aggression, not from bumping into furniture.

Throughout the rest of the trial, including the whole of Dr. Steinmann's testimony, Nelson Stewart kept his promise, sitting as still and as quiet as he possibly could … until yesterday mid-afternoon, when the prosecution dropped a surprise nuclear bomb right on the defense's lap.

Two

The Day Before

After five long and exhaustive days in court, both the prosecution and the defense looked to have fully finished presenting their cases before the jury. Together, they had called a total of twelve witnesses, each of which had been extensively examined, cross-examined, and some even re-directed. What would follow, the next the morning, after the prosecution and the defense had finally rested and Judge Reeves had adjourned proceedings for the day, would be the closing arguments from both sides. The prosecution would go first. Once the closing arguments were done, the jury would be instructed to retire to the jury room so that the deliberation process could begin.

At three-thirty in the afternoon, as the final defense witness stepped down from the witness stand, Tenor Bryant was just about ready to finally rest the defense's case when Leonard Sutton pulled open the courtroom door and rushed towards the bar just behind the prosecution's table.

Sutton was the main investigator for the DA's office in Woburn, and an expert in tracking down missing witnesses. As he entered the courtroom and hurried down the center aisle, a barrage of intrigued and expectant eyes moved to him, none more so than Judge Reeves'.

'What's happening in my courtroom?' she asked, even before Sutton had reached the bar.

The prosecutor, George Oakfield, who was also the District Attorney for the district of Middlesex in Massachusetts, had to fully swivel his chair round so that he could look behind him. He was truly a larger-than-life man . . . too large to be able to simply twist his body at the waist.

'Umm . . . just a minute, if I may, Your Honor,' Oakfield said in return, lifting a tentative finger at the judge.

Sutton got to the bar and handed Oakfield a piece of paper before whispering something into his ear.

'Mr. Oakfield,' the judge pushed. 'My courtroom isn't a cocktail lounge.'

'Yes, Your Honor,' the DA replied, finally swiveling his chair back to face the court again. 'I sincerely apologize for the interruption.'

From the defense's table, Nelson and Bryant stared back at Oakfield, worryingly.

'What the hell is going on?' Nelson asked, his eyebrows angling awkwardly at his attorney.

'I'm not sure,' Bryant replied, with a subtle headshake. 'But if Leo came running into the courtroom just before I was able to rest our case, it's probably something bad . . . for us.'

'Who the fuck is Leo?'

Before Bryant could reply, Oakfield wiggled the piece of paper that Sutton had handed him at Judge Reeves.

'Your Honor, if it pleases the court . . . may we approach?' His gaze pinged to Tenor Bryant at the defense's table, who looked death back at him.

Judge Reeves didn't look happy either, but she still gestured both counsels towards her bench.

'What's happening here?' she immediately asked Oakfield, cupping a hand over the courtroom microphone on her desk.

Oakfield used a handkerchief to dab his neck and forehead, which were covered in beads of sweat. His cheeks were constantly a light shade of pink, regardless of how hot or cold it was, and he always seemed to be about two breaths away from needing an oxygen tank. In all honesty, Oakfield looked nothing like the ruthless prosecutor that he was.

'Your Honor,' he began. 'I know that this is as late in a trial as it can possibly be, but since neither the prosecution nor the defense have officially rested our cases, I was wondering if you would allow me one final witness before you adjourn proceedings for the day.'

Bryant's jaw nearly hit the floor. '*What?* A witness? You have *got* to be kidding me, right?' His desperate gaze moved to Judge Reeves. 'Your Honor, you can't possibly even entertain the idea of allowing the prosecution to call an extra witness this late in the trial. According to the official list of witnesses that was provided during "Discovery", all witnesses from prosecution and defense have testified. Both arguments have been presented and exhausted before the court. We were both just about to rest our cases.'

'But we haven't yet,' Oakfield cut in. His voice was an odd combination of gravel and velvet all in one.

'This is unacceptable, Your Honor,' Bryant shot back, the large vein on his neck just about to burst. 'The prosecution is clearly reverting to ambush tactics here. This witness, whoever he/she is, wasn't even disclosed at "Discovery", which means that we have no idea who this witness is. Which in turn means that we haven't prepared a line of questioning. This isn't only unethical, it's a below-the-belt punch by the prosecution and you simply can't allow them to get away with it. My client's freedom is at stake here and—'

Judge Reeves shushed Bryant with a hand gesture, before addressing Oakfield. 'Counsel, I'm inclined to agree with the defense here. This looks like ambush tactics . . . and quite late in the day, I might add. Who is this witness that you want to bring into my courtroom? Why haven't you mentioned this witness before? And why wasn't the witness on the witnesses list that was provided in "Discovery"?'

'Because we had no idea this witness existed until yesterday, Your Honor.'

'Oh bull-*fucking*-shit, George,' Bryant said, pulling a face at Oakfield. 'Your Honor, the prosecution is clearly trying to make a mockery of this court. You must not allow this to happen.'

'It's true, Your Honor.' Oakfield lifted both hands in surrender. 'I swear that we only heard about her yesterday, at around ten in the morning.' His head tilted right, towards the prosecution's table. 'That was when I got Leonard Sutton, our top investigator, to try to track her down. I, myself, had completely given up on us finding her.' He looked at Bryant. 'And you're right, Tenor, I was ready to rest the prosecution's case, but we found her and she's here.'

'She's what?' Judge Reeves asked, her eyes moving to the courtroom doors.

'She's here, Your Honor,' Oakfield repeated it. 'Just outside the courtroom, and if you allow her on the stand, you will hear a shocking testimony that could completely change the outcome of this trial.' He handed her the same piece of paper that Sutton had handed him moments earlier.

'Your Honor, I strongly object to this sabotage,' Bryant said, making no effort to keep the anger out of his tone of voice. 'If the prosecution knew about the possibility of a new witness since yesterday morning, why didn't they mention that possibility yesterday . . . or even today, at the start of proceedings? No, they waited until the last second to bring her in? C'mon, Your Honor, you can't possibly fall for such a cheap trick.'

Once again, Judge Reeves lifted a hand at Bryant to shut him up, while she read through the information on the piece of paper that Oakfield had handed her. Once she was done, she paused, her expression pensive and serious in equal measures.

Both counsels waited.

Judge Reeves consulted her watch.

'OK,' she finally said, addressing Bryant. 'We'll take a forty-five-minute recess so that you can prepare a line of questioning.' Her stare moved to Oakfield. 'I'll allow your witness to testify because the jury needs to hear about this, but don't you ever try this trick again in my courtroom, are we clear?'

'You can't be serious, Your Honor!' Bryant exclaimed, his eyes widening at the judge. 'You can't allow the prosecution to ambush us like this. This is preposterous. How can this ever be called a fair trial when the plaintiff can do as they please?'

'Are you saying that I'm unfair as a judge, counsel?' Judge Reeves volleyed back. She was a large, fifty-seven-year-old African American woman, who had graduated from Princeton University twenty-four years ago and had, for the next twenty years, worked her butt off to become a judge. She had experience in both sides of the criminal law – prosecution and defense – and her win record, regardless of side, was nothing shy of impressive. Despite having been a judge for only four years, Rebecca Reeves had already gained a reputation for being as tough as nails, but an incredibly fair judge. Her questioning eyes settled on Tenor Bryant's face.

'That's not what I said, Your Honor, but just a moment ago you agreed that my client's defense was being ambushed by the prosecution's team, but now you're going to allow it? I must strenuously object to this decision, Your Honor.'

'Your "strenuous" objection is noted, counsel,' Judge Reeves said, scribbling something down on her pad. 'But my decision is made. You have forty-five minutes to prepare a line of questioning.'

Bryant shook his head in disbelief. 'How can I possibly prepare a line of questioning when I don't even know who this witness is, Your Honor.'

'Her name is Candice Logan.' The answer came from Oakfield. 'And if you really want to know who she is, I "strenuously" suggest you go ask your client.' He followed his advice with a smirk. 'He knows who she is.'

'What the fuck is going on?' Nelson asked, as Bryant got back to the defendant's table, shaking with concern and rage.

His reply was a new question. 'Who's Candice Logan?'

That was when Nelson's whole face melted. 'Oh *fuck*!'

Three

Tenor Bryant knew that the case that he and his team had built for the defense wasn't a strong one, and it became even more flimsy after the testimony of both prosecutions' key witnesses, Samantha Stewart and Dr. Louise Steinmann, but in the State of Massachusetts, domestic violence was a felony offense, punishable by up to five years in a state prison. Since it was a felony, for a conviction, the prosecution needed all twelve jurors to agree on a guilty verdict. If a single juror saw any reasonable doubt in the prosecution's case, the prosecution wouldn't get a conviction, and Bryant was sure that despite Samantha Stewart and Dr. Steinmann's testimonies, he had done enough to swing at least one juror into the 'reasonable doubt' camp. But he wasn't counting on a late, surprise witness, especially one that prompted Judge Reeves to comment: 'I'll allow your witness to testify because the jury needs to hear about this.'

And he was right to be worried.

Even with cross-examination and re-direction, Candice Logan's testimony lasted less than thirty minutes, and in those thirty minutes, she shredded any possibilities of 'reasonable doubt' for the defense.

Miss Logan, who was a striking woman in every sense of the word, with blonde hair and a figure that made even Judge Reeves slide her glasses to the tip of her nose so that she could have a better look, testified that she had started an affair with Nelson Stewart after meeting him at a cocktail lounge in Boston just over a year ago. The affair had lasted eleven months.

During their direct examination of their witness, the prosecution was easily able to establish that when it came to his marriage, Nelson Stewart was a gifted con artist, having weaved a perfect web of lies for almost a year to deceive his wife, with tales of late-night meetings, business trips and what have you.

The 'mistress' angle had been terribly damaging to the defense's case, but not as much as when George Oakfield surprised the entire courtroom with a simple line of questions.

'Miss Logan,' Oakfield said, pausing directly in front of the witness stand, his weaponized eyes aiming straight at the jury box. 'Can I ask you – why did your affair with the defendant, Mr. Nelson Stewart, end? Can you tell us? Was it because of remorse? Did he feel guilty because he was cheating on his wife?'

Candice Logan took a deep breath and allowed her stare to crawl over to the defendant's table. Nelson Stewart was looking back at her with murderous eyes.

'No,' she replied. 'That wasn't the reason.'

'Who ended the affair, Miss Logan?' Oakfield asked, already knowing the answer.

'I did.'

'And can you tell us why?'

Nelson Stewart was still looking at Candice Logan as if he was ready to strangle her, his whole demeanor screaming – 'don't do it . . . don't you fucking do it.'

That was when her eyes narrowed at him almost imperceptibly, just enough to send a clear message back Nelson's way – 'fuck you'.

'Because I simply couldn't take the beatings anymore.'

Four

After the closing arguments, the jury was instructed to retire to the jury room to deliberate. It took them under four hours to reach a verdict.

At the defendant's chair, Nelson could sense a pair of eyes burning a hole at the back of his head. He swiveled at the waist to look at the court audience just behind him. As he did, he immediately spotted Sam, sitting three rows behind the plaintiff's table. Her eyes were like laser beams aimed directly at him. This time, Nelson wasn't able to hold her stare. As far as he knew, yesterday had been the first time that Sam had heard about his affair with Candice, and even he had to admit that that was a horrible way to find out that your husband had cheated on you.

He turned to face the court again.

As the jurors took their seats, an air of excitement filled the room. The court clerk took his place and faced the jury box. The jury's foreperson stood up. Her name was Martha and she was an average woman in just about everything – height, body type, hair, looks . . . but to Nelson, she looked like a typical Karen – the kind of woman that would pick a fight in a grocery store over two cents just for the hell of it. As she stood up, her anxious gaze pinged to Nelson for a fraction of a second before moving back to the clerk.

After the clerk recited the customary introduction to a verdict, naming the state, the county and the court that they were in, followed by the defendant's name and the case number, he addressed the jury's foreperson.

'Has the jury reached a verdict upon which you have all agreed?'

Silence settled over the room like a heavy morning fog.

Oakfield and Bryant both sat up taller in their seats, their breaths held in their chests as if they were professional free divers.

Right then, for the first time since the trial had started six days ago, Nelson was overcome by fear – the kind of fear that rattled a person's core and paralyzed them in place. Despite everything that had happened until then, there was a tiny part of Nelson's brain that still refused to accept the past nine weeks as reality, telling him that things would turn out fine, just like they always did. But that tiny part of his brain had finally been overruled.

From the defendant's chair, Nelson heard Martha lightly clear her throat before straightening up her shoulders. Every pair of eyes in that courtroom was on her, and she knew it.

'Yes, we have,' she replied. The nod that she gave the courtroom was anxious, but firm.

'On count one,' the clerk asked. 'Criminal domestic violence, and physical abuse against Samantha Stewart – how do you find the defendant?'

For Nelson, time seemed to slow down to an absolute crawl. He knew that Martha's next word would be life changing for him ... and he knew what that word would be even before it left her lips.

'Guilty,' Martha replied, her voice loud and clear.

And there it was – six letters ... two syllables ... one word – a word that would tarnish Nelson's past, change his present and destroy his future.

The entire courtroom seemed to shift in place, with shouts and comments coming from every corner. Nelson, on the other hand, stood silent and completely still . . . his eyes straight ahead . . . his heart beating at the bottom of his throat, as he watched his whole life starting to collapse right in front of him.

The clerk waited until the room had quietened down again before he asked the foreperson his second and final question.

'On count two – false imprisonment and captivity of Samantha Stewart – how do you find the defendant?'

Nelson wasn't listening anymore, but it wasn't out of choice. This was a defense mechanism move by his brain to try to shut out any new aggressors that could hurt him further. Sounds became muffled, as if Nelson was underwater . . . but it didn't matter. Nelson saw Martha's lips move, and even without hearing a sound . . . even without being a lip reader . . . he knew what she had said – one word . . . not two.

Life collapse successfully completed.

The room erupted in shouts and hushed voices.

Nelson closed his eyes for a moment, while Judge Reeves restored order in her courtroom. That done, she informed the attorneys and the defendant that sentencing would take place in two weeks' time – directly after the pre-sentencing investigation. She then instructed the court marshals to take Nelson into custody, but before they got to him, Nelson had a chance to turn around and face the court audience one last time, and this time, it was his eyes that lasered in on Samantha . . . and they were full of rage.

'You fucking bitch,' he shouted, his voice booming across the courtroom. 'If you think that this is the last that you'll see of me, then you've got another think coming. I know everything about you . . . everything . . . and no matter where you go, someday, I *will* find you. I can promise you that. I will haunt your fucking dreams, you bitch. Good luck looking over your shoulder for the rest of your life.'

The two court marshals finally managed to restrain Nelson

and drag him away, but as the audience trickled out of the courtroom, Samantha stayed behind, her breathing erratic and out of sync . . . her legs just a little unsteady because if there was one thing she knew for sure, it was that Nelson Stewart didn't make empty promises.

Five

'Congratulations,' Oakfield said, as he and Samantha met in the corridor, just outside the courtroom. The smile on his face was almost as large as he was. 'Thanks to you, we just put another creep in prison.'

Samantha stayed quiet, her gaze moving from Oakfield's round face down to her Gucci shoes.

'You look tense and worried, Sam,' Oakfield said, noticing how red her eyes were. She had definitely been crying. 'Aren't you happy with the outcome of the trial?'

'Wouldn't you be worried?' she finally replied, her voice lacking strength. 'Did you hear what Nelson said to me just before he was taken away?'

Oakfield scoffed. 'I did, and that was a huge mistake on his part. As you know, sentencing hasn't been passed yet. Judge Reeves will announce it in two weeks' time, and the reason for that is because during the next two weeks there will be a pre-sentencing investigation, which is carried out by probation officers. They'll scrutinize Nelson's whole life before reporting back to the judge. That investigation will help Judge Reeves determine the appropriate sentence for Nelson.' He smiled again. 'Now here's what we have so far: Nelson received a "guilty" verdict on count one – "criminal domestic violence against you". The maximum penalty for that is five years in prison, and I'll be very surprised if Judge Reeves doesn't go for the full five years here.'

Samantha shifted her weight from one foot to the other.

'He also received a "guilty" verdict on count two,' Oakfield continued. '"False imprisonment and captivity of a spouse", and that, when coupled together with criminal domestic violence, carries a maximum penalty of *ten* years in prison.' He used his handkerchief to dab his neck and forehead again. 'Judge Reeves might not go for the full ten years here, but he isn't getting less than six or seven, I'm pretty sure of that. Which already brings us to eleven, maybe twelve years of incarceration.' He lifted a finger at Sam. 'Then we have that little stunt that Nelson pulled after the verdict was read. That verbal threat to you will constitute aggravating circumstances.'

'And what does that mean?'

'It means that it's a direct verbal threat against you,' Oakfield explained. 'After two guilty verdicts, that will weigh heavily against Nelson, and Judge Reeves will certainly take that into consideration when determining the appropriate sentence for his crimes.'

He paused, and from the look on Sam's face he knew that she still wasn't getting it.

'In short,' Oakfield tried again, 'Judge Reeves might add an extra year or two to the sentence, just for what Nelson said to you.' He placed a hand on Sam's shoulder. 'Sam, relax. Nelson Stewart will not be seeing the outside of a prison cell for at least twelve years. I can guarantee you that. He's done. He's no threat to you. What happened in there,' his head dipped right, in the direction of the courtroom, 'was angry bravado from a scumbag who had just realized that his game was up, nothing more. He can't touch you, Sam.'

Sam dug at the red and raggedy cuticle on her left thumb. 'You don't really know Nelson, do you?'

'I don't have to know Nelson, Sam,' Oakfield came back. 'I know the law, and I know that he'll be behind bars for over a decade.'

Sam's cuticle started to bleed, as she chuckled nervously. 'If you think his reach won't go beyond prison walls just because he's behind bars, then you really don't know Nelson Stewart.'

Oakfield consulted his watch before looking round at the busy corridor that they were in. 'Do you have time to go get a coffee . . . or a drink somewhere, away from the courthouse. There's something I want to talk to you about – something that I'm sure will change the way you're thinking.'

Six

The city of Cambridge, in Massachusetts, was located a mere ten miles away from Woburn and the courthouse where Nelson's trial had taken place. It was home to Harvard University, one of the most prestigious and well-known universities in the world, and that was exactly where Oakfield had suggested that he and Sam went for a drink – not to the university itself but to Harvard Square, which funnily enough was actually triangular in shape and located outside the university campus. The square, which was a favorite among students and professors alike, offered an abundance of coffee shops, restaurants, bars and, obviously, bookshops.

Oakfield and Sam each drove their own cars – Oakfield leading and Sam following – and he guided her to a stylish and sleek cocktail bar right at the western end of the square called The Longfellow.

The time was just coming up to five-thirty in the afternoon, and despite being only Wednesday, the place was almost packed to capacity. The waitress at the entrance explained that she had no booths available at that time, but they could either sit at the bar, or take one of the outside tables, under a heater.

Oakfield and Sam opted for the outside table.

Sam ordered a Cosmopolitan, while Oakfield went for a single malt on the rocks.

'Have you filed for divorce yet?' Oakfield asked, once the waitress was out of earshot.

'I wanted to, but my divorce lawyer told me that we should wait for the criminal court verdict.'

'Who's your divorce lawyer?'

'Kristin Miller.'

'Oh, she's great.' Oakfield nodded his approval, while he sipped his Scotch. 'Actually, she's one of the best. And she's one hundred percent right – the criminal court verdict will make a world of difference. Was Kristin in court today? I didn't see her.'

'No, she wasn't.'

'Does she know the outcome of the trial?'

'Yes, we spoke briefly on the phone right after the verdict.'

'So she's probably already told you that it will be even better if you wait for Judge Reeves to pass sentence first before filing the divorce petition.'

'Yes,' Sam confirmed.

Oakfield paused and studied Sam for a few seconds. Despite what the stress of the past couple of months had done to her, she was still a very beautiful woman, there was no doubt about that, but right then, she looked more like a scared little child than a woman who was just about to become a millionaire.

'Do you mind if I smoke?' Oakfield asked.

Sam shook her head.

Oakfield lit up a cigarette and took a deep drag.

'Actually,' Sam said, nodding at the packet on the table. 'Could I have one of those as well?'

'Of course.' Oakfield tapped a new cigarette out of the packet before lighting it up for her. 'I didn't know you smoke.'

'I stopped about two years ago. Nelson forced me to, but since this whole thing began . . .' Sam allowed the unfinished sentence to dance away in the air, just like the smoke that she blew out of the corner of her mouth.

Oakfield nodded, sympathetically. He knew that for Sam, going back to smoking was much more than just giving in to the crave. It was a way for her to get back at Nelson. The fact that she had just sent him to prison didn't matter. What mattered was that she was doing something that he had specifically stopped her from doing. Psychologically, going back to smoking symbolized "taking back control" of her actions and of her life.

'I'm guessing that you want to get as much out of this shitty deal as you can, right?' Oakfield asked.

Sam had a sip of her cocktail. 'What do you mean?'

'Well. You were married to a millionaire, who turned out to be a narcissistic scumbag. In a regular divorce litigation, you would easily be able to walk away with at least half of what he had – properties, cars, money ... even his wardrobe, if you so wished to.'

'Nelson isn't as wealthy as you might think,' Sam quickly added.

'Maybe not when compared to some of the fortunes around Woburn,' Oakfield accepted it. 'But he was still pretty wealthy by most people's standards. Just the house that you lived in together is worth what – five ... six mil?'

Sam's reply was a shy movement, trying to tuck a lock of bristly hair behind her right ear.

'So, this is what I'm trying to tell you,' Oakfield carried on. 'If this was a normal divorce case – you and your husband deciding that it just wasn't working out anymore and it was time for both of you to go your separate ways – any a-dime-an-hour lawyer could've gotten you fifty percent of everything.' He dipped his head sideways and gave Sam a wink that came across a lot slimier than he would've wanted. 'But now, your soon-to-be ex-husband is an adulterous and convicted "wife-beater" – someone who caused you a world of pain, both physically and psychologically.' Oakfield shook his head, as he took another long drag of his cigarette. 'You can't put a price on what he did to you, Sam. You can't put a price on how much he made you suffer, and a good divorce lawyer knows that.' He lifted his finger at Sam to halt her before she could say anything. 'A great divorce lawyer, like Kristin, can bleed that motherfucker dry. You can walk away with everything, Sam, leaving behind nothing but a huge "fuck you, Nelson".'

Sam's anxious gaze darted away for a split second before coming back to Oakfield. 'I don't want to bleed him dry. That's just going to make him even angrier. All I want is to get my life back, you know? I want to be able to wake up and not feel scared from the moment I open my eyes. I don't want money, especially his money.' Sam's voice faltered, as tears began welling up in her eyes.

Oakfield stubbed out his cigarette. 'Do you intend to move on with your life in Woburn? Do you have friends and family there?'

'God, no.' Sam chuckled the words at Oakfield. 'I have maybe a couple of people I can call friends, but that's all. Nelson was way too controlling to allow me to have friends of my own.'

'Where are you from . . . originally?'

'Missouri, but I ain't going back there either.'

Oakfield detected a different kind of pain in the curves of Sam's words. Something that hinted that maybe her relationship with her family wasn't a great one. He decided not to ask.

'Do you have some place in mind? Some place you'd like to go to start over?'

Sam's headshake was a tense one. 'Maybe this whole thing was a mistake, you know? I shouldn't have done this. I should've just packed what I had and left. I shouldn't have taken him to court. Now, Nelson will come for me. I know he will. Maybe not now . . . maybe not in a year . . . or two . . . or five, but he'll come for me, and when he does, he won't just slap me about and handcuff me to the pipework.'

'He might come for you, sure,' Oakfield agreed, to Sam's surprise, but it was what he said next that really seemed to catch her attention. 'But he won't be able to do anything if he can't find you, will he?'

Sam used a paper napkin to dab the tears from her cheeks. 'What do you mean?'

Oakfield finished his Scotch and signaled the waitress for a new one. 'Would you like another Cosmo?'

'No, I'm OK for now, thank you. What are you talking about? Nelson not finding me?'

Oakfield lit up a new cigarette. 'Like I said, your soon-to-be ex-husband is now a convicted wife-beater . . . not to mention a cheater, and that will only make things easier for you.'

'How so?'

'Two reasons. One – it will completely expedite the divorce process,' Oakfield explained. 'I'll be surprised if Kristin doesn't have everything finalized a week after sentencing.'

Sam's eyebrows arched, but in a positive way.

'And two,' Oakfield continued. 'That little threatening stunt that Nelson pulled at the end.' He lifted a finger for emphasis. 'Right in front of Judge Reeves, will give Kristin plenty of grounds to initiate a process for an identity change.'

'Excuse me?' Sam's head angled slightly to the left.

'Sam, you're still so young. You have your whole life ahead of you. Please don't allow the two years that you spent with that scumbag to destroy the rest of your life.'

'I'm thirty-four years old,' Sam said back, as if thirty-four was the age of ancient gods. 'I'm not that young.'

Oakfield threw his head back as he laughed. 'Trust me, Sam, you're still so very young.'

The waitress brought Oakfield a new Scotch on the rocks.

'You said that all you wanted was to put this whole thing behind you and move on with your life, right?'

Sam nodded, as she also finished her cigarette.

'Well, believe it or not, this is the perfect opportunity,' Oakfield explained, leaning forward and resting his elbows on the table. 'I know that this is a cliché sentence, used by many lawyers, but in your case, this is one hundred percent true.'

Sam frowned at Oakfield. 'What sentence?'

'The one that goes – "This is the first day of the rest of your life".'

Sam chewed on her bottom lip.

'And I'm talking about your brand-new life,' Oakfield continued. 'Everything that was said in that courtroom from day one has been recorded and noted down by the court reporters and the stenographers. And I mean every ... single ... word, including Nelson's outbursts. All you need to do is tell Kristin that after the events of today, you would like to file for a change of identity on the grounds of personal safety.'

Sam's eyes narrowed at Oakfield, who gave her a new smile.

'And this is part two of why it was such a huge mistake for Nelson to have threatened you the way he did.' Oakfield sat back on his chair, with a triumphant air about him. 'There is no judge in the country who won't sign off on the papers for an identity change after reading today's trial transcripts.' He paused for a second to allow Sam to grasp what he was really saying. 'You'll be able to pick a new name for yourself, Sam ... any name you like ... and that name will come with a whole new batch of documents – driver's license, passport, social security – the whole nine yards. You'll be able move anywhere you want – some place where no one will know who you are.' Oakfield sipped his Scotch and gave Sam a renewed smile. 'You can move to Europe if you like – London, Paris, Berlin – the choice is yours.'

Sam held her breath for a moment.

'How is that for starting again away from Nelson?'

Sam's silence was thoughtful and heavy, a ghost of a smile haunting her lips.

'Still thinking twice about bleeding that scumbag dry?' Oakfield added.

Seven

Two weeks after Nelson's guilty verdict, the court reconvened so that Judge Reeves could finally pass sentence on Nelson Stewart, and she wasn't at all lenient.

That evening at The Longfellow, on Harvard Square, George Oakfield had predicted that Nelson wouldn't get less that twelve years in prison for what he'd done, and the DA had perfectly hit the mark with his first prediction. Judge Reeves initially sentenced Nelson to twelve years of incarceration – five for the crime of criminal domestic violence and seven for the crime of false imprisonment and captivity – but Nelson's threatening outburst at the end of court proceedings had really angered Judge Reeves, and for that she had added another full year to her ruling, giving Nelson a total of thirteen years behind bars.

To everyone's surprise, as Judge Reeves read the final sentencing out loud, Nelson stood completely still and totally silent – no angry outbursts ... no offensive gestures either. He didn't even look up at the judge as she brought gavel to lectern to finally conclude proceedings. No, Nelson simply kept his eyes low ... lost in thought ... deep in anger.

The next prediction that Oakfield got right was with regards to Samantha and Nelson's divorce process, which was completely expedited by the outcome of the trial, and nine days after the guilty verdict, Sam legally ceased to be Samantha Stewart, reverting back to her maiden name – Samantha Chambers.

With Sam and Nelson's divorce process completely finalized, Samantha's lawyer, Kristin Miller, had all the ammunition she needed to finally file a petition for the identity change process. Kristin cited 'fear for personal safety and endangerment to life' as the main grounds for the requisition, but she didn't even need to. As luck would have it, the application for the identity change ended up on Judge Reeves' desk, and she didn't have to read the trial transcripts to approve the petition.

And just like that, a mere three and a half weeks after Nelson had been officially sentenced to thirteen years in a correctional institution, Samantha Stewart, aka Samantha Chambers, was ready to simply vanish from the face of the earth. With a simple signature from a court judge, she was free to reinvent herself and pick whatever new name she wanted to, and it didn't take her long to decide on one – less than a day, actually. All she had to do was weigh her choices, and once again, George Oakfield had given her some very sound advice.

Eight

'Once the identity change process is approved,' Oakfield said, while they were still sitting at The Longfellow, 'you'll be able to pick any name you like, but please allow me to give you a few pointers here.'

'Please do.'

'First let me explain the difference between a "name" change and an "identity" change.'

Sam looked back at Oakfield a little sideways.

'Anyone in the land can initiate a process for a name change. A lot of people do it once they get married, or divorced . . . artists and celebrities do it to make their artistic names official . . . some people do it because they don't want anything to do with their families anymore.' He shrugged. 'It's not an uncommon process. All someone needs to do is file a petition, pay the fee, and notify several federal and state agencies. That's it. In all honesty, the process is really quite simple and very straightforward.' Oakfield emphasized his next point with a head nod. 'Now, to avoid con artists trying to run away from financial commitments by simply changing their names and moving somewhere else, name-changing processes are completely transparent to everyone. And what I mean by that is – if anybody wants to find out what Joe Blog's new name is, all they need to do is ask the County Court. Name-changing records are public files, and *that* is the difference between a "name change" and an "identity" change.'

'An identity change isn't public?' Sam asked.

'No,' Oakfield confirmed. 'That's why when you file a petition for an "identity" change, you also need to file a document called "Order to Show Cause". Kristin will do all that for you, and it's in the "Order to Show Cause" document that she'll cite "fear for personal safety and endangerment to life". Since the reason behind your name and identity change is to safeguard your well-being, those records will be flagged as confidential and access to them becomes extremely difficult.'

Right then, Sam's eyes darted away, as if she was mulling over different options.

Oakfield gave her another second before clarifying. 'They'll become hard to get to, but not impossible. And what I mean here is – there are legal and illegal ways of obtaining the information on those records.'

The concerned look returned to Sam's face.

'And here are the two biggest pointers I can give you for your identity change. One – go for a common name. Two – when you move, don't pick a tiny town.'

Sam squinted at Oakfield. 'Go for a common name?'

Oakfield nodded. 'And here's why – if Nelson really decides to come after you and he somehow manages to find out your new identify – a common name and a not so small town will play to your advantage.'

'In which way?'

'Think about it,' Oakfield urged Sam. 'Let's say you picked an unusual name, something like Anuska Clissold.'

Sam frowned at him.

'I just made that up,' Oakfield explained, giving Sam a shrug. 'Anyway, what I'm trying to tell you here is – let's say that Nelson has managed to find out that your new name is Anuska Clissold.

Now he needs to find your location. There are several specific search engines out there that'll search for names and addresses up and down the country.'

Sam finally caught up with Oakfield's train of thought. 'A more common name should give him a longer result list on a name search.'

'Exactly. Now let's say that somehow, Nelson went a step further and managed to find out not only your new name, but also the city you picked to restart your life. So now all he needs is the address.'

Sam caught up with Oakfield yet again. 'Chances are that a more common name will return several different addresses in a bigger city.'

'As opposed to just a couple in a tiny town,' Oakfield confirmed. 'What you'll be doing is tipping the odds in your favor . . . amplifying the playing field and making it harder for anyone to pinpoint you.'

'I never thought of that,' Sam admitted.

'Most people don't.' Oakfield paused and once again dabbed the sweat from his forehead with a handkerchief. 'But if you really prefer to live in a smaller town, instead of a bigger city, here's another valid trick: once you get your new identity, move to any city you like – big or small – it doesn't matter because this first move won't be your permanent address.'

Sam gave Oakfield a single eyebrow lift.

'In fact,' the DA continued. 'If I were you, I'd place all my belongings in storage and simply rent an already furnished place somewhere. Go for a short-term contract – a year, maximum – at the end of which, you move again. This time you can go for a permanent address, or, if you really want to be on the safe side, go for another one-year contract some place else – different city, different state even. After that, I'm sure you'll be OK to finally settle down into a permanent address.'

Sam drummed her fingers on the table.

'It's a lot of fuss,' Oakfield admitted. 'But the more you move around, the more tangled the web gets for anyone trying to find you.'

Sam still looked a little uncertain.

'Your new name will go on file, Sam,' Oakfield informed her. 'But not your address. You're not entering a government witness protection program. You're simply getting a new identity, that's all. You don't have to inform the court of a new address every time you move. So even if someone manages to find out about your new name, finding your location is a whole new cat and mouse game for them. If you move around a couple of times, you'll make that game one hundred times harder.' This time, the wink he gave Sam didn't come across so sleazy. 'Tipping the odds in your favor, remember?'

Sam smiled back.

But Oakfield wasn't done yet. 'Now, here's my most important piece of advice regarding your identity change.'

Sam locked eyes with the DA and waited.

'You just said that you're thirty-four years old right?'

Sam nodded, stretching her mouth in a sad manner, as if being thirty-four was a sin.

'But on looks,' Oakfield continued, 'you can easily pass for twenty-six . . . twenty-five even.' The pause was deliberate just to hold the suspense for a little longer. 'Well . . . here's your chance.'

Sam bit her bottom lip. 'Are you saying what I think you're saying? I can alter my date of birth?'

'It's not so much that you *can* alter your date of birth,' the DA told her. 'It's more a case of you *should* alter your date of birth.'

Sam's smile was one hundred percent genuine.

'Within the realms of reality, of course,' Oakfield added.

'Of course,' Sam agreed.

'And the reason why I told you that this is my most important piece of advice, is because if Nelson manages to find out which new name you went for, the one searching parameter he will have to try to narrow down the number of results for location is . . .'

'My date of birth.' Sam was, once again, late to the party, but she got there eventually.

Oakfield lit up another cigarette. 'Pick a different day . . . a different month . . . a different year and Nelson will be dead in the water.'

Sam's shoulders relaxed ever so slightly, as if a huge weight was finally being lifted off of them.

'I bet you never thought of that either, right?' Oakfield asked.

Sam shook her head. 'No, but it all makes perfect sense. And I'll be able to pick any date I want?'

'Of course,' Oakfield confirmed.

Sam's smile reached her eyes. 'That's amazing, because I've always hated being a Cancerian.'

Oakfield laughed. 'One more piece of advice, if I may.'

'Please, by all means,' Sam replied. 'I need all the advice I can get.'

'This is regarding the money you will get from Nelson, because there's no doubt that you will get it.'

'OK.'

Oakfield leaned forward, placing his elbows on the table.

Sam did the same.

Oakfield spoke in a much quieter voice. 'Your divorce settlement will come through before your identity change is finalized. That's a fact. Once the divorce settlement is finally completed, however much money you are awarded by the courts, it will all be electronically transferred straight into your existing bank account. You won't get a cheque for a deposit.'

'I didn't think I would either,' Sam commented.

'OK,' Oakfield continued. 'So, here's my advice – once the money hits your account, just sit tight and wait until the identity change process is concluded. It won't take that much longer after the divorce – a few days probably.'

'Alright.'

'Now, before you swap identities.' Oakfield lifted a finger at Sam. 'And I mean either the day before, or on the day that you are supposed to go pick up your new documents, go to your bank and clear out the account. Withdraw everything . . . in cash. Do not transfer it to a new account.'

'Withdraw the whole lot in cash?' Sam looked back at Oakfield as if he was joking.

Oakfield nodded. 'I know that with the amount that you'll probably get, this sounds like a crazy thing to do, but Nelson worked with hedge funds and finance, am I right? So, I'm sure that despite being behind bars, he'll probably still be very well connected with people in the financial sector.'

Sam gave Oakfield a subtle nod of acceptance.

'So, my guess is that if Nelson really tries to track you down,' he continued, 'that is exactly where he'll look first. He'll look for a financial transaction between your old account and any new ones.' He shrugged. 'He'll want to know where his money went, and if he finds a transfer document from your bank, your new name will no doubt be attached to it.'

Sam's jaw tensed.

'By withdrawing the funds in cash,' Oakfield explained, 'what you'll actually be doing is avoiding creating an electronic money transfer trail.'

'So, what do I do with the money? Put it inside my mattress?'

'No. After you take all the money out of your bank, you get your new identity, and you open new bank accounts . . . and I mean accounts – more than one. And if you want to play it really safe – use different banks . . . spread your money around.'

Sam took a second. 'You mean – by walking into a bank carrying a suitcase full of cash and dumping it on the counter?'

'Pretty much,' Oakfield agreed.

Sam pulled a face at the District Attorney. 'I don't think that nowadays banks allow you to make a large cash deposit without bombarding you with questions.'

'And you're right,' Oakfield confirmed. 'They don't.' He gave Sam a conman kind of smile. 'And they would bombard you with questions if you didn't have a legal document, signed by a court judge, explaining the reason why you are making such a large cash deposit. With that, they won't ask you a single question, and they will take as much cash as you can dump on their counter.'

Nine

It was as if George Oakfield had some sort of magic crystal ball, because all of his predictions came true.

On the same day that Judge Reeves sentenced Nelson to a term of thirteen years, Kristin Miller, Sam's divorce attorney, started the process to do exactly what Oakfield had said that she and Sam should do – bleed Nelson Stewart dry – and since Sam had been the victim of domestic violence and unlawful imprisonment by an adulterous and violent husband, it didn't take Kristin long to get the whole process signed off and authorized by the court.

So, just a few days after Nelson took residency at MCI-Cedar Junction, Samantha Chambers was awarded over fifty percent of Nelson's fortune through the divorce litigation, plus an extra forty percent in punitive damages for what he'd put her through. In short, Samantha Chambers walked away with pretty much everything Nelson had, including property, jewelry, stocks and shares. The judge also awarded Sam both of Nelson's prize possessions – a cherry red Lamborghini Huracan, the value of which exceeded three hundred thousand dollars, and a rapid blue, souped-up to the teeth, Corvette Stingray Z51, which had cost him over one hundred thousand dollars. Most of the funds in Nelson's current and safety accounts were also seized and transferred to his ex-wife's account.

Kristin and her law firm had been over the moon with the

results of the divorce litigation. In their books, that had been a stupendous win, but Sam didn't really care to keep almost anything of what she was awarded – the cars, the properties, the furniture, the investments, the jewelry ... in fact, she wanted absolutely nothing that could remind her of Nelson Stewart and of her time in Woburn. With that in mind, on the same day that Kristin managed to bleed Nelson dry, Sam instructed her to liquidate everything as fast as she possibly could. Just a few weeks after that, Samantha Chambers was officially a millionaire ... several times over.

Ten

When it came to choosing her new name, the woman once known as Samantha Chambers took Oakfield's advice to the letter. After a quick Internet search, she found out that the three most common last names in America were: Smith, Johnson, and Williams – each of them with over 1.5 million individuals around the USA. The three most common female first-names were: Mary, Patricia and Jennifer – with Mary having a count of over three million hits, practically double the number of Patricia's and Jennifer's living in the US.

Sam's priority wasn't to have a new, cool-sounding name. She truly didn't care for any of that. Her priority was to make the process of finding her as difficult as possible to anyone who ever tried to, if anyone ever did.

So, with that in mind, a day after Samantha Chambers was granted the right to a new identity, she picked the name combination that would return the largest number of results through a name search – Mary Smith.

'It actually doesn't sound that bad,' she said to her reflection in the mirror, after repeating the name out loud a handful of times.

The next field on the identity change form was 'Date of Birth', and she once again took Oakfield's advice – different day, different month, different year.

It felt good to be twenty-six again.

As for the date, Mary Smith could think of no better date than October thirtieth, because what that meant was that every year, from then on, she would be celebrating her birthday a day before Halloween – by far her favorite holiday season.

With her new name and date of birth finally chosen, all that Mary needed to do to complete the identity change form was to enter her parents' names and the city in which Mary Smith had been born.

For her father's name, she simply decided to follow the same rule that she'd used to create her own.

After another quick Internet search, she discovered that the three most common male first names in the USA were: James, Robert and John.

This time, Sam decided to go with the second most popular male first name in America, Robert, and the main reason for that was because since she would soon become Mary Smith, her father would then be Robert Smith, which was also the name of the lead singer in one of her favorite bands – The Cure.

For her mother, she picked a completely different name – Heather. She did think about going with either Patricia or Jennifer – second and third most popular female names in the US – but having a whole family made out of the three most common names in America would be a bit much. Heather was also the name of her real mother's best friend, which made Sam believe that it was a suitable choice.

Now, Sam had only one decision left to make to complete the identity change process – Mary Smith's original birthplace. Here, Sam wanted to go with a very large city – Los Angeles, Chicago, Washington DC, New York City, etc. She blew hot and cold over a few of them for a while, but in the end she chose New York City, and the thinking behind that decision was based on one simple thing: Sam knew for a fact that the smaller the place, the more people tended to show interest in their local communities, and what that ultimately translated into was "nosy neighbors". People knew more about each other's lives in smaller towns than in bigger cities, and they were usually happy to answer questions if anyone came asking. The Big Apple, on the other hand, was famous for many things, and one of them was the fact that people were usually too busy with their own lives and problems to nose into anybody else's business. New Yorkers had a reputation for keeping themselves to themselves, many not even knowing the name of their next-door neighbor after living in the same neighborhood for years.

And that was it. It had really been that simple. With the identity change petition already approved and signed off by Judge Reeves, all that Mary's lawyers had to do was hand in all the documentation that the courts had asked for, which Kristin did on the very same day that she received the form with Sam's choices – a form that had been delivered to her in a sealed envelope, so that not even Kristin knew what Sam's new identity would be. A short week after that, a whole new batch of documents – also in a sealed envelope – was delivered to Kristin Miller's office.

So, on a warm and sunny afternoon in late May, a battered and broken Samantha Chambers was no more. In her place, a shy, but very happy Mary Smith, stepped out of Kristin Miller's law office, slid her Carrera sunglasses back on, jumped into her rented car, and simply disappeared into the world.

Eleven

Two Days Later

If there was one thing that Mary Smith knew right from the start – something she knew even before she was granted the right to an identity change – was that as soon as she was free from that whole court circus, she would be getting the hell out of Woburn. In fact, Mary was certain that she'd be getting the hell out of Massachusetts too. All she needed to do was pick a new place to start over, and for that, once again, she decided to follow Oakfield's advice as best as she could and 'tip the odds in her favor'.

'If I were you,' he had said. *'I'd place all my belongings in storage and simply rent an already furnished place somewhere.'*

Despite being a millionaire, at that exact point in time, Mary Smith had very few belongings of her own. As soon as her divorce settlement came through, she had instructed her lawyers to liquidate whatever they could, as fast as they could, and since then, they had marketed and sold over ninety-five percent of everything that the court had awarded her. All that she'd kept for herself were a few wardrobe items, but not many.

Something else that Mary had decided on was that she would completely reinvent herself – from top to bottom. She would walk, talk, look and dress in a completely different way to Samantha

Stewart, and the lack of earthly possessions, at least right then, wasn't such a bad thing. It actually meant that Mary was free to move around as much as she wanted to, without needing to put anything into storage. And for her 'move around' phase, she had her own little trick to add to Oakfield's advice – her own little way of tipping the odds in her favor.

After yet another Internet search, Mary found out that in America, the largest concentration of women whose first name was Mary lived inside what was known as the 'Bible Belt' – a very large area of land that included almost all of Southeastern USA, running from Virginia down to Northern Florida, while also stretching west all the way to Oklahoma and part of Texas. And what better way to hide someone called Mary other than right among thousands of other Mary's.

With that as her starting point, Mary decided that she would spend the first six months – maybe even the first year of her new life – somewhere inside the 'Bible Belt', but there was one problem – the same problem that she faced when deciding where Mary Smith had originally come from: small American towns – and the ones inside the 'Bible Belt' – were famous for how everyone tended to stick their noses into everybody else's business. They were also famous for people being more concerned with your past than your present: where did you come from? Why did you decide to move into their town? How come at your age you're unmarried with no kids . . . and so on.

Privacy, or better yet, other people's privacy, wasn't something that many folks over in the 'Bible Belt' cared too much for. But as far as Mary was concerned, as long as she kept herself to herself and stuck to a large city – where theoretically, the 'Belt' should lose some of its grip – she couldn't see any real problems. This was only a temporary tactical move anyway – a decoy, just like Oakfield had suggested – and out of all the large cities that sat within the 'Belt', one certainly appealed to Mary a lot more than all the others. A place that she'd always wanted to visit but never really had a chance to – Nashville, Tennessee.

From a very early age, music had been Mary's safe haven from just about everything – pain, bullying, anxiety, loneliness, anger, betrayal – anything and everything that had ever made her feel sad or distressed. It had been the one thing she knew she could count on at any time. All she needed to do was click a button and the notes ... the melody ... the harmonies ... would whisper comfort directly into her ear. But music hadn't only been there for her during sad times. In fact, for as long as she could remember, music had been the only constant presence in her life – and Nashville wasn't known as the 'Music City' for nothing. There was no place in the world as legendary as Nashville when it came to country music and live performance venues.

Fine, country music wasn't exactly Mary's preferred choice, but she did like some of it, and since the idea was to reinvent herself from top to bottom, why not start with her taste in music?

Twelve

Five Months Later

Nashville, Tennessee

Mary would be lying if she didn't admit that even she was surprised by how quickly and well she had taken to the city of Nashville.

She'd heard plenty about the'Music City' in the past, about the famous sights, the legendary music venues, the museums, the art scene, the fantastic nightlife, all of it, but she wasn't expecting the city, especially one right at the heart of the 'Bible Belt', to be so laidback and welcoming – but maybe that was because Mary had played a very smart card when it came to choosing her neighborhood.

On her first trip to Nashville, Mary visited three out of the seven most exclusive neighborhoods – Forrest Hills, West Mead and Sylvan Park. They were certainly luxurious, with the average monthly rent starting at around two thousand dollars for a one-bedroom apartment, but Mary was also intelligent enough to know that flashing money around was a quick-fire way to get noticed, especially for a woman on her own, and that had been Mary's smart card.

Nashville was undoubtedly a very artistic city – and just like every artistic city on the planet, it had what was commonly known as 'the arts district' – a section of the city where many of its artists lived and hung out – usually the struggling ones – and for that reason, rent tended to be a lot more affordable. But that hadn't been why Mary had chosen to move into Nashville's art district. Her reasoning was that art districts, all around the world, also tended to attract a very diverse group of people. Artists from other cities, other states, other countries even, flocked to well-known 'artistic hubs' to try their luck – actors and actresses flocked to Los Angeles, dancers flocked to New York, jazz and blues musicians flocked to New Orleans, and country artists flocked to Nashville – it was a fact – and artists, of any kind, were well known all over the world for being laidback. In Mary's case, that was advantage number one. Advantage number two was that many of the artists living in Nashville didn't come from within the 'Bible Belt', and what that meant was that the 'belt grip', at least in and around the arts district, was pretty damn loose – nobody stuck their noses into anybody else's business. People didn't even care if you were religious or not.

After reading several articles about Nashville's arts district, Mary picked a small but very comfortable one-bedroom apartment in Hillsborough Village – a very popular area amongst young artists and students alike. The village was sandwiched between Vanderbilt University and Belmont University, with plenty of shops, coffee houses, saloons and live music venues to keep anyone busy every day and night of the week. But that evening, Mary was about three miles away from H Village, just leisurely strolling down the famous Broadway by the Cumberland River, when she was approached by a young-looking man.

'Good evening, ma'am,' the man said, his tone pleasant, excited, even. 'How're you doing today?' He offered her a bright, but somewhat timid smile, holding out a homemade flyer in her direction. 'How about a really good acoustic gig tonight?'

Mary didn't take the flyer. 'No, thanks,' she replied without even making eye contact with the man. 'I'm good.'

The Broadway was famous for its numerous bars and live music venues. Young musicians and venue employees were always around in the evenings, flyers in hand, doing their best to attract passers-by into their bars. Right then, they were standing just outside The Whiskey Bent Saloon – a small live music venue that was considered a hidden gem by most country music lovers.

'It's only five bucks to get in, ma'am,' the man tried again, doing his best to catch Mary's dark brown eyes. His southern accent wasn't exactly pronounced, but Mary couldn't miss it either. 'Drinks are cheap, the music is great, and your five bucks will go to a very good cause. Have you been to The Whiskey Bent Saloon before?' He threw his right thumb over his shoulder to indicate the venue just behind him.

Something in the man's enthusiastic tone of voice made Mary pause and look up at the spinning neon sign just above the entry door. She'd walked past that bar tens of times in the past five months, but she'd never set foot inside it. Her gaze finally came down and rested on the man standing before her. He was still holding out his homemade flyer.

Mary blinked once.

The man looked to be in his early to mid-twenties, tall and well built, with a strong jawline that was nicely accentuated by a dark five o'clock shadow. His long black hair was pulled back into a messy ponytail, which added an extra degree of charm to his already attractive diamond-shaped face. He was wearing blue jeans – ripped at both knees – white sneakers, and a tight, dark-blue t-shirt that hinted at his toned body and exposed his fully tattooed arms – flowers and skulls mostly. The smile on his lips seemed genuine, and there was a certain intensity inside his hazel eyes that intrigued Mary somewhat.

'No, I've never been in there,' she replied. Her eyes stayed on the man. 'I've walked past it many times, but I've never walked in.'

The man's eyebrows arched ever so slightly. 'Ma'am, then you have to. This place is a must if you're visiting Nashville. It's small and cozy, almost like a private bar, but it has the vibe of an arena. All the greats have been on that stage. You like country music, right?'

'What makes you so sure that I'm visiting?'

The man hesitated for a second, unsure. 'Ma'am?'

'You said that this place is a must if you're visiting Nashville. What makes you so sure that I'm visiting?' Mary's tone took a defensive edge that the man clearly noticed.

'Umm . . . just a guess, ma'am. Didn't mean nothing by it.'

'A guess based on what?' Mary pushed, her tone a touch softer than a moment ago, but still defensive.

The man gave Mary a sheepish, but sincere smile. 'I was born and bred in Huntsville, Alabama, ma'am,' he explained, before pausing and chewing on the side of his bottom lip for an instant. 'When you grow up in a place like Huntsville – big city with a small-town feel – spotting people who were either born or grew up in the south is practically part of our DNA. We talk a certain way . . . we walk a certain way . . . we drink a certain way.' He turned his neck to look back at The Whiskey Bent Saloon. 'And we certainly play music a certain way.' His chin dropped a fraction, his tone apologetic. 'Nashville is a fantastic place, and we get people visiting from all over . . . every day of the year. I just meant to say that you don't look to be from round here, ma'am. That's all. I meant to cause no offense.'

Mary found the man's embarrassment quite charming. 'You didn't.' She finally smiled back at him. 'And you're right. I'm not from around here. But I'm not visiting either.'

'You live here?' The man's surprise didn't seem faked.

Mary nodded. 'For now.'

'Really?' This time, the man smiled with his eyes. 'Whereabouts?'

Mary's head tilted slightly to the right and her eyebrows tightened as she gave the man a 'you're doing it again' look.

The man read it like a flashing billboard. 'So terribly sorry, ma'am. I guess this is something else that's embedded in southern folks' DNA.'

'You mean – being nosy?'

'I believe that's the correct term, ma'am . . . yeah.'

Mary's new smile was a relaxed one. 'So . . . who's playing tonight?'

The man's face seemed to light up. He offered her a flyer once again.

This time, Mary took it. It was a simple piece of white paper, rectangular in shape, and printed in black and white. The photo showed the artist standing with his back pressed against a brick wall, his right leg bent at the knee . . . the sole of his right cowboy boot flat against that same wall. He was holding an acoustic guitar across his body, as if he was just about to start playing. His cowboy hat was tipped down at the front, but not enough to cover his face, while his long, straight black hair fell just past his shoulders. Mary recognized him straight away. It was the same man who was standing right in front of her.

'Luke Jenkins,' Mary read the name across the top of the flyer, before her gaze returned to the man. 'It's got a good sound to it. Is that your real name?'

The man nodded. 'Luke Jenkins. Baptized and dipped in a bucket of holy water, ma'am.' He offered her his hand. 'Pleasure to make your acquaintance.'

Mary shook it. 'Mary. Nice to meet you, Luke.' Her chin jerked at the flyer. 'Are you any good?'

'I'm always trying to be better, ma'am,' Luke replied. 'But I can get a crowd going . . . the southern way.'

Mary looked back at The Whiskey Bent Saloon. 'It doesn't look too busy in there. Not much of a crowd to get going.'

'Monday evenings are always slow,' Luke explained. 'That's why most small venues, like The Whiskey, will book new, less-known acts on Monday nights. Artists starting out, like myself. The management then checks you out to see how good you are. If they like you, they might book you on a few more Mondays before giving you a shot at busier nights and bigger crowds.'

'I see.' Mary nodded. 'Is this your first Monday playing here?'

'No, ma'am. This is my second time playing The Whiskey. I was here last Monday too.'

'So, they liked you.'

Luke gave Mary a cowboy nod. 'It appears so, ma'am.'

Their stares locked and Luke smiled again, but this time it wasn't shy or timid. It was just a smile – as genuine as before, but brighter. 'So, what do you say, ma'am? Give a new artist a chance?'

Mary looked down at the flyer again. 'Five bucks?'

'It's for a good cause, ma'am.'

'And that cause would be?'

Luke pressed his lips tight together. The embarrassment was back in his tone. 'Umm . . . food and board, ma'am. Nashville ain't as cheap as Huntsville.'

Mary found Luke's honesty to be quite attractive.

'But I'm sure that I can get you on some sort of guest list, if you like. I get a free "plus one" that I don't use.'

'No, it's OK,' Mary nodded. 'I think I can afford five bucks tonight, but on one condition.'

Luke bit back on a pleased smile. 'And what's that, ma'am.'

'You've got to stop calling me ma'am. You're making me feel old. Call me Mary . . . OK?'

'Mary it is,' Luke said, giving her another cowboy nod and gesturing towards the door to The Whiskey Bent Saloon. 'And thank you very much. You ain't gonna regret it.'

Thirteen

Luke was right – Mary did not regret stepping into The Whiskey Bent Salon for the very first time that evening, not even for a second. The decoration was maybe a little too 'huntsmen' for her liking, with a full-sized stuffed bear and a variety of animal heads mounted high on the walls amongst the many neon lights, but the atmosphere inside the venue was simply electric. Country music played through the ceiling speakers, while laughter and animated talk could be heard coming from just about every corner of The Whiskey. Two bartenders – both of them female – looked to be rushed off their feet, as they expertly mixed colorful cocktails and served beer and whiskey to a pretty busy bar. Mary simply couldn't help being sucked into the party mood that lingered in the air.

'Wow,' she said, as she allowed her eyes to circle the room. 'I was definitely wrong. It's a lot busier than I thought.'

Luke smiled proudly. 'Let me get you a drink,' he said, leading the way to the bar. 'Beer?'

'No, please,' Mary replied, as they got to the varnished wood counter. 'Let *me* get *you* a drink. Whiskey?'

Luke's head angled slightly to one side. 'That would be correct, ma' . . . . . . ry, but I never drink before a gig.'

Mary's eyebrows arched. 'What, really? Not even to settle the nerves?'

'Specially not to settle the nerves,' Luke replied. 'Playing and singing is what I love doing . . . it's what I was born to do. I love the excitement of it all and the nerves are simply part of it. They also keep me in check so that I always try to better myself.'

Mary was impressed by Luke's answer, but she kept her cool.

'But please,' Luke insisted. 'Let me get you a beer or something.' He broadly gestured at the packed floor. 'It'll be like a welcome to The Whiskey gift.' The wink he sent Mary's way was so subtle that she wouldn't have noticed it if she hadn't been looking straight into his eyes.

Luke lifted his hand at one of the two women behind the bar.

'Hey, Luke.' The short-haired brunette bartender greeted him with a flirtatious smile. 'Are you playing the same set as last Monday?'

'Hey Josie.' Luke smiled back at her. 'Not the exact same. I'm adding a few new tunes, and a couple of original ones as well.'

'Really? Wow, I can't wait to hear them.' The flirtatious smile stayed exactly where it was. 'So, what can I get you tonight?'

'Can I get a bottle of beer for my friend Mary here. It's her first time at The Whiskey.'

Josie's eyes moved to Mary. 'Is that a fact?'

Mary nodded. 'Walked past it many times, but this is my first time inside.'

'In that case,' Josie said. 'We need to pop your cherry.' She reached for the glass-door fridge behind her, grabbed a beer, twisted the cap off, and placed it on the bar in front of Mary. 'Glass?'

Mary shook her head. 'Nah, it tastes better from the bottle.'

'Amen to that, sister,' Josie replied, with a nod.

Mary reached for her beer, but Josie lifted a hand at her. 'Hold on, we've gotta do this The Whiskey way.' She grabbed a bottle of bourbon from one of the shelves behind her and poured it into a couple of shot glasses before addressing Luke. 'I'm not pouring you one because you told me you don't drink before a gig.'

'That's right,' Luke confirmed, his gaze pinging to Mary for a split second. 'But you can keep mine behind the bar and we can have a round once I'm done.'

'We can certainly do that,' Josie replied, the flirtatious smile back on her lips.

Mary nodded her agreement.

'Talking about gigging,' Luke said. 'I better go get ready. I'm on in five.'

'Yes, you are,' Josie confirmed, quickly checking her watch.

'So, let me get these,' Luke said, nodding at the drinks before reaching into his pocket.

What he got in return was a resounding 'No' coming from both Mary and Josie.

'I'll get these,' Mary tried.

'That's a "no" for you too,' Josie stopped her as well. 'This is your first time at The Whiskey, so this one is on us.' She grabbed her shot of bourbon and raised it at Mary. 'Welcome to the best little bar in town.'

Mary did the same and they touched glasses.

'Thank you.' Her gaze moved to Luke. 'To a good gig. Break a leg, Luke.'

'I'll do my best.' Luke smiled. 'OK, I've got to go. You can come closer to the stage if you like.'

'I'm good here, thanks,' Mary replied, leaning back against the bar before pointing at the stage. 'You go do your thing.'

'Will you stay until the end?' Luke asked. 'We've gotta have that shot together.'

'My staying is directly dependent on how good you are.' Mary said back, a quirky smile on her lips.

Luke smiled back before turning on the balls of his feet and disappearing into a door to the left of the small stage.

'Can we finally do this now?' Josie said, still holding her shot up at Mary.

'Yep. Sorry about that.'

Mary and Josie touched glasses again before knocking back their shots and slamming the empty glasses upside down on the bar counter.

Mary nodded at Josie. 'Wow, nice bourbon.'

'Angel's Envy,' Josie told her. 'From Kentucky. Mellow and smooth.'

'Definitely smooth,' Mary agreed.

'And you'll stay,' Josie said.

'Sorry?' Mary frowned at her.

'If you're staying here is directly dependent on how good Luke is,' Josie explained, 'then you'll stay.' She nodded confidently. 'He's fucking great.'

'Is he?'

'You'll see.'

As Josie walked away to go serve a new customer at the other end of the bar, Mary turned to face the stage. She was in a good spot. Despite being at an angle, she could see the stage very clearly.

A short man, with a quite pronounced beer belly and a cowboy hat, got up on the stage just as the lights inside The Whiskey dimmed a touch.

Mary sipped her beer.

'Is this thing on?' the man on stage said, tapping the microphone a couple of times with his index finger.

The loud chatter simmered down, and the crowd turned to face the stage.

'OK,' the cowboy continued. 'Welcome everyone to Monday Nights at The Whiskey.' That sentence was greeted with a chorus of 'woo-hoos', 'yee-haws' and cheerful applause. 'As most of you know – and I guess that's why you're all here tonight – Monday nights is when we open the stage to new acts – bands, solo artists, duos . . . whoever wants to showcase their talent, right here, at the heart of the 'Music City'. And I am very proud to say that many ... many country music superstars out there today have started their journey to stardom right here, on this very stage.'

More 'woo-hoos' and 'yee-haws'.

'And I've got a feeling that this next act is well on his way to the top. Last Monday he played his first gig here at The Whiskey and boy, was he a hit.' The man pointed at the first row of people right in front of the stage. 'Specially with the ladies, right here.'

That front row was made up entirely of young women, who right then, cheered loudly, raising bottles of beer and whiskey glasses up in the air.

'Looks like you've got some stiff competition,' Josie said, leaning her elbows on the bar.

Mary hadn't even noticed that Josie was standing right behind her.

'What?'

Josie nodded at all the excited women on the front row. 'G.R.I.T.S. And they are ferocious.'

'Grits?' Mary questioned, resting her bottle on the bar counter. 'Like cornmeal porridge?'

Josie laughed. 'Nope. Much worse,' she explained. 'It stands for – girls raised in the south. You never heard that term before?'

Mary's turn to laugh. 'No. Never.'

'Yep,' Josie confirmed. 'G.R.I.T.S – mean as hell and sweet as honey. We act all innocent and naive, but we play dirty – the kind of dirty that men love.' She indicated the front row once again. 'And those girls right there, they'll snap like gators and bite like rattlesnakes. They're basically Jersey Shore on steroids.'

'Hold on,' Mary said, her stare bouncing between the stage and Josie. 'You think that Luke and I are like ...' Instead of finishing her sentence, Mary widened her eyes at the bartender.

'Girl,' Josie said in return, her eyebrows lifting at the center. 'I saw the way you were looking at him ... and I don't blame you – that boy is a barn burner.'

'So,' the cowboy on stage announced. 'Before these beautiful ladies over here lynch me off the stage, here he is again – ladies and gentlemen – to delight us all with another incredible acoustic set – Luke Jenkins.'

The entire place erupted in applause and cheers.

Luke cleared the back curtains and stepped on stage – a spotlight following him – and he looked like a rock star. The ripped trousers were gone, substituted by a pair of stonewashed, bootcut jeans. The t-shirt had also been swapped for a black, western button-up shirt, with the sleeves rolled up to his elbows. Instead of white sneakers, he was wearing black cowboy boots, with silver metal tips. His hair had also been let loose, under a dark-brown cowboy hat. His acoustic guitar hung from his neck – Elvis Presley style.

'Good evening, y'all,' he said, as he reached the microphone. 'Thank y'all so much for coming out tonight. Your support and love is very much appreciated.'

More cheers and screams, especially from the front row.

Right then, Luke's eyes moved left, in the direction of the bar. They stopped when they reached Mary. 'It's nice to see you here.' The sentence was delivered with a coy smile.

Without noticing it, Mary bit her bottom lip. *Damn, that boy was one smooth operator.*

'The good news for you over all those G.R.I.T.S,' Josie said, pouring another shot of bourbon for her and Mary, 'is that it looks like Luke likes you too.'

Mary felt a giddy smile start to blossom on her lips, but she was able to keep her poker face solid. 'This one is on me,' she said, nodding at the shots before placing a twenty-dollar bill on the counter. They clinked glasses again and downed the shots in one.

On stage, Luke tapped his foot to a count of four before the sound of his guitar took over, soon followed by his voice. Mary turned to face him again and as she did, she felt her entire core shake. Josie was right – Luke Jenkins wasn't just good . . . he was fucking great.

Fourteen

'Thank you all so much,' Luke said, raising his right arm up in the air, as if he'd just finished playing Madison Square Garden . . . and from the crowd's almost hysterical reaction, one would be forgiven for thinking that he had.

His set was fantastic. Mary couldn't argue with that. Not only did Luke's voice sounded perfect, but he was also a very accomplished guitar player. The icing on the cake had been his charisma. He hadn't lied when he'd told Mary that he knew how to get a crowd going. Despite being a small stage, Luke had owned it as if he'd been born on one, a total natural. The cherry on top of the icing had been his original songs. They were definitely catchy with 'hit' written all over most of them.

'If anyone is interested,' he continued, 'I have a few CDs that you can take home today. I've recorded fourteen original songs, including all the ones I've played in tonight's gig. They're only ten bucks a piece and your support will be very much appreciated.'

More applause and woo-hoos.

'Thank you all so much again and . . .' He gave the crowd one of his sexy winks. 'I'll see you at the bar. Please come say "howdy".'

As Luke disappeared backstage, Mary had another sip of her beer, trying to decide if she should wait for him, or simply make her way home. From all the women on the front row, she had already identified at least three who truly seemed to snap like gators and bite like rattlesnakes – and they were already heading towards the bar.

'G.R.I.T.S,' Mary whispered to herself, while shaking her head. 'You learn something new every day, I guess.' She finished her second beer of the evening and right then, decided that her best move was to go home. Luke had more than enough company for tonight. She just needed to visit the ladies' room first.

What an unexpected evening, she thought, as she slipped into one of the five cubicles in the 'Cowgirl's' bathroom. But despite unexpected, Mary had to admit that she had thoroughly enjoyed her night out. Since she'd moved to Nashville, she hadn't really talked to many people. That was the idea, anyway – keep herself to herself, spend six months to a year living in Tennessee, and then relocate somewhere else – but Mary did miss socializing ... she missed having friends with whom she could go out for a meal ... share a beer or a bottle of wine ... watch a gig ... all the common things that friends did together.

As she left her apartment earlier that evening, thinking that she would just spend some time walking by the Cumberland River on another mundane Monday night, Mary never expected the evening to be the best she'd had in quite a while. Frankly, she couldn't even remember the last time that she'd had that much fun. She'd even flirted with someone, and that hadn't happened in years. Luke was definitely cute, sexy and very talented – too bad that she couldn't really let her guard down ... or could she? For one night only?

Right then, Mary heard the bathroom door being pushed open, followed by a high-pitched and overexcited voice. 'So, is he hot, or is he lava?'

'Damn! I wasn't expecting that,' a second woman replied. 'That boy is about ninety in the shade ... and then some ... and I'm not even talking about how good he was on stage. Seriously, I'd ride him like a bronco.'

'Well, get in line, Pam,' the first woman said back.

'And it will soon be a very long line,' Mary heard Pam reply. 'Cause he's not just hot, he's also fucking good. With that voice? He's gonna make it big. It's just a matter of time.'

'Well, if I have my way tonight, that boy is waking up in my bed tomorrow morning.'

Definitely time to go home, Mary thought, as she stood up and flushed the toilet. *Before I'm forced to witness one of the G.R.I.T.S dry-humping Luke's leg at the bar.*

She stepped out of the cubicle and approached the sinks.

The two women were retouching their makeup in the mirror.

Mary made light eye contact through her reflection and gave them both a very polite and cordial smile.

'That's a very nice shade of red,' she said, nodding at the lipstick that one of them was applying.

'Right?' the woman said back, her high-pitched voice seeming to find a new octave.

She looked to be around twenty-five years old, with wavy blonde hair that just touched her shoulders. She was definitely attractive, in a 'girl-next-door' way. Mary had noticed her earlier, in the front row, by the stage. She was one of the three women that Mary had imagined would snap and bite.

'It's called Showstopper,' she told Mary. 'It's from Bobbi Brown.'

Mary smiled again. 'It really suits you.'

'Oh, thanks, hun.' The blonde woman stretched out her arm. 'I'm Vicky.'

'Mary, nice to meet you.' Mary dried her hands before shaking Vicky's.

'I'm Pam,' the other woman said, also offering her hand. She was at least a couple of inches taller than Vicky, with long black hair, twisted sideways and thrown over her left shoulder – mermaid style. She too was very attractive, but in a more conventional way – high cheekbones, full lips, light-brown eyes, incredible skin, and a killer smile.

'It's nice to meet you both,' Mary said.

'I can tell from your accent that you're not from round here,' Pam said.

'New York, actually.'

'Oh,' Vicky sounded genuinely surprised. 'So, what brings you to Nashville?' She immediately paused and raised a hand at Mary. 'Scrap that question. The answer is always the same – music, right? Music is what brings everyone to Nashville.'

Mary found it easier to simply agree. 'What else?' She smiled again, this time, shyly. 'Anyway . . . enjoy the rest of your evening.'

'You're not staying?' Vicky asked, as she pressed her lips together before blowing out the letter 'P' a couple of times at the mirror. 'Come hang out with us. Now the dancing starts. This is when it gets real good.'

'Tempting,' Mary replied, doing her best to keep the sarcasm off her tone. 'But I've really got to get going. It's only Monday and I've got quite a few things to do tomorrow morning,' she lied.

'Aww, pity,' Pam commented. 'But in that case, you've gotta come back here either Friday or Saturday. That's when The Whiskey goes ballistic.'

'Yes, I've heard,' Mary lied again. 'I'll try to make it this weekend.'

'We'll be here,' Vicky said in reply. 'We can hang out and I'll introduce you around. Seriously, you won't regret it.'

That was the second time that Mary had heard that phrase tonight.

She nodded goodbye at the girls and stepped out of the bathroom.

'Mary,' Luke called from the bar, waving at her. He was already surrounded by G.R.I.T.S.

Mary waved back and gestured towards the front door. 'I've

got to go,' she mouthed the words, while zigzagging through the crowd.

Luke's disappointment was clearly visible in his frown. 'What?' he mouthed back, before excusing himself from the group of drooling women that surrounded him and quickly making his way towards Mary. 'What do you mean you've gotta go?' he asked, as he intercepted her halfway between the bar and the door.

'I've got things I've got to do tomorrow morning,' Mary lied again.

'But we didn't even have our shot together,' Luke tried.

Mary's gaze skipped to the bar. The G.R.I.T.S were all looking back at her with fire in their eyes. Vicky and Pam had just joined the group.

'I think that if I do have that shot with you tonight,' Mary replied, 'I might be eaten alive by your fan club.'

'Fan club?' Luke's eyes widened at her. 'I don't have a fan club.'

'Evidence to the contrary,' Mary said, nodding in the direction of the bar.

Luke turned to follow Mary's gaze. At the bar, the G.R.I.T.S looked like a firing squad and Mary was clearly the one at the end of their scopes.

'They certainly look like they'll have more than a shot with you tonight.' Mary smiled before giving Luke a kiss on the cheek. 'It was a pleasure meeting you, Luke. Have fun.' She swerved past him.

'Mary,' Luke called again.

She turned to look back at him.

'Did you at least enjoy the gig? What did you think?'

Mary nodded. 'I did, very much so. You were great on stage, Luke. You're going to be a star. Just keep on doing what you're doing. It's just a matter of time.' It was Mary's turn to send a disarming wink Luke's way.

'Hold on,' he paused her again, before she had a chance to

walk away. 'Umm . . . ' Luke scratched his forehead. He seemed like he was having a hard time finding the right words. 'Would you . . . like to meet up again sometime? Maybe for a coffee, or . . . a walk in the afternoon? I know some pretty amazing places around town.'

Mary held Luke's stare for a couple of moments longer than she would've normally, just enough time for butterflies to start gathering momentum inside her stomach, but her resolve was unflinching, and she was able to curb them way before they started flying.

Sure, Luke Jenkins was a hell of an attractive guy, talented too, but despite missing the pleasures of having sex, Mary wasn't really looking for a quick hook-up, and she sure as hell wasn't looking to get into a relationship with anyone that early in her new life. Her reply to Luke's question was a meager slight tilting of the head, accompanied by a feeble smile that clearly said – 'I'm sorry.'

Without saying another word, Mary turned, cleared the crowd, and walked out of The Whiskey Bent Saloon.

Outside, she paused and took in a deep breath. It was a warm evening, but the breeze blowing in from the Cumberland River felt cool and refreshing against her skin.

As she started walking in the direction of the bus stop, she paused for a second, reflecting on how silly she felt right then. She should've been a bit nicer. She should've given Luke a verbal response, some sort of decent excuse, instead of simply walking away in silence like a diva. She was just beginning to ponder the thought of going back inside when she saw him for the first time – directly across the road from where she was standing – leaning back against the wall by the door to the Broadway Brewhouse. And the sight of him made Mary's core rattle for the second time that evening – only this time it wasn't out of excitement, it was out of pure fear.

Fifteen

Tall, clean-shaven, with short dark hair and a strong frame, the man standing across the road from Mary looked to be around her real age, give or take a year or two. He was wearing a dark gray suit that seemed to have come straight out of a gangster movie. His posture was calm and relaxed, with one hand tucked into his trouser pocket, matter-of-factly, and the other holding a lit cigarette.

In all fairness, there wasn't really anything about the man standing across the road that could scare anyone, except for the fact that to Mary he looked familiar . . . too familiar, in fact.

The man's eyes moved up and for the briefest of instants their stares met. Right then, it seemed like the whole world had frozen in place. His unblinking dark eyes, like two black holes, seemed to be staring straight into Mary's soul, as if he could see past her disguise . . . as if he knew who she really was.

Mary's heart stuttered. She was certain that she had seen that face and those eyes before . . . but when? And where?

The man casually turned to face the other way, taking another drag of his cigarette, but Mary found herself unable to drag her eyes away from him, as if spellbound. The harder she stared at him, the faster the gears inside her brain turned – the faster they turned, the more that she was certain that the memory of him hadn't been created in Nashville. She hadn't seen him during one of her many walks by the Cumberland River or sitting outside one of the many bars and saloons along the Broadway. She hadn't seen him at any of the cafes in Hillsborough Village either. No, Mary was almost certain that she had seen him somewhere else, before she made it to Nashville.

'Mary.' A voice called from behind her.

She didn't move.

'Mary . . . wait.' A hand fell over her left shoulder.

Spell broken.

She turned around to find herself face to face with Luke one more time. 'Hi.' The word came out as a whisper, riding on the waves of a deep breath.

'Sorry,' Luke said, his embarrassment palpable. 'Did I scare you?'

'What?'

'You seem spooked. Did I scare you? I'm sorry.'

Mary turned her neck to look behind her. The man was still there. This time, he seemed to be looking into the Broadway Brewhouse through the front door and waving at someone.

'Mary, are you OK?'

'No,' she finally replied. 'You didn't scare me. I was just . . . looking at the lights.'

Luke smiled shyly as he offered her the CD that he was holding in his right hand. 'You said that you enjoyed the gig, so I wanted to give you this. Just . . . something to remember the night, you know? Maybe you'll come back again.'

'Oh my God,' Mary said, shaking her head as if snapping out of a dream. 'I completely forgot. I wanted to get one of your CDs anyway. And yes, I loved the gig. I just . . . forgot, really.' She reached into her handbag and came out with a ten-dollar bill. 'They're ten bucks a piece, right?'

'Oh no, please,' Luke said, shaking his index finger at the money. 'It's a gift.'

Mary peeked behind her again. The man dropped his cigarette on the ground and stubbed it out with the tip of his shoe.

'Do you know what?' Mary said, hooking her arm through Luke's. 'I've changed my mind. How about we go have that shot . . . right now. What do you say?'

Luke perked up. 'What? Really?'

Mary nodded.

'I say – hell yeah.'

'But only if you let me pay for the CD,' Mary said, catching Luke's eyes. 'It's for a good cause, remember?'

Luke chewed on his smile as he hesitated for a second.

'And you've got to sign it for me too.'

'OK,' Luke finally gave in. 'Deal.'

As they started walking back to The Whiskey, Mary turned to check behind her one last time – gangster-suit man was all but gone. She checked left then right, but he was nowhere to be seen, as if he'd just vanished into thin air, like cigarette smoke.

Sixteen

Back inside The Whiskey, everyone was already dancing away, including all the G.R.I.T.S. Luke brought Mary back to the same end of the bar from where she had watched his gig. Josie was also dancing, but on the inside of the bar, and she had some moves.

'Hey, you're back,' she said, approaching Mary and Luke. 'Couldn't stay away, huh?' She winked at Mary.

'I think that we're ready for that shot now, Josie,' Luke said. 'And could I please borrow a pen.' He placed the CD on the bar counter.

'Shots coming right up.' Josie grabbed a pen from behind the bar and placed it on the counter, by the CD case.

Luke wrote a dedication, signed it, closed the CD case and handed it to Mary. 'I really hope you enjoy it.'

'I'm very sure I will,' she said, placing a ten-dollar bill on the counter.

'No, c'mon, Mary, seriously. It's a gift.'

'Nope.' Mary shook her head. 'You agreed. Don't tell me you're one of those who goes back on a deal.'

Touché – to a southern cowboy, questioning if he was a man of his word or not was worse than a punch to the face. Luke lifted his hands in surrender before reluctantly taking the cash. 'You sure drive a hard bargain.'

'And here we go,' Josie came back with three shot glasses and placed them on the counter. 'Angel's Envy all round.'

They all reached for a shot and raised them up in the air.

'To new friends,' Luke said.

'To new friends,' Mary and Josie repeated it in unison. 'And to your success,' Mary added, as she touched her glass against Luke's.

Toast done, they knocked back their shots. As Mary downed hers, her stare returned to the door – no gangster-suit man. Was he gone, or was he waiting for Mary outside like earlier? And was he really waiting for her, or was she being paranoid?

That whole time, since Mary had spotted the stranger outside, her brain had been working flat out to try to match his face against a memory. She thought back to the many parties that she had attended with Nelson in Woburn. She thought back to the ones that they used to throw at their house. She thought back to the holiday trips to the Hamptons, the ones where Nelson's group of buddies would always turn up, but no, none of it brought back any recollections of the stranger's face, and that made Mary begin to doubt herself. Had she really seen him before? Or did he just have one of those overly common faces – the ones that got strangers squinting at them from afar, trying to place them in their cloudy memories.

The more Mary thought about it, the more she convinced herself that had to be it – the man from outside simply had one of those common faces – because Mary couldn't understand how anyone would've recognized her from her previous life. Mary Smith looked absolutely nothing like Samantha Stewart.

Sam used to have long, wavy sandy-blonde hair, ocean-blue eyes, flawless skin, and a figure that could cause traffic accidents. Nelson had told her numerous times that she could easily pass herself as Taylor Swift, if she ever wanted to, as long as she didn't actually sing.

Mary, on the other hand, had undergone an incredible transformation from her previous self. The first thing she did before moving to Nashville was to have her hair cut short and dyed raven black. With the help of vanity contact lenses, her eyes were now almost as dark as her hair, a look that despite all odds, actually suited her. Her eyebrows were also different – drawn on instead of natural. To complete her transformation from Samantha to Mary, she had not only stopped exercising, but also fully dropped her usual strict diet – a move that after just a couple of months saw her gaining almost thirty pounds – her face was plumper, her cheeks chubbier, and her waist a lot rounder than it ever was. All in all, she looked so different that not even her mother would've recognized her.

Mary hated her new weight, her chubby cheeks, and the new curves showing all around her body – way too many, if you asked her – but she knew that they were just temporary. When she moved again to somewhere permanent, she'd change her look once more.

'Mary?' Luke called.

She blinked twice before her attention finally landed back on him.

'Are you alright?' he asked. 'You spaced out there for a moment.'

'Sorry. I do that sometimes.'

'So, do you wanna dance?'

Mary coughed a laugh. 'Ha … no … I'm really bad at it,' she lied.

'It's OK,' Luke volleyed back. 'So am I. And in here, no one will notice.'

'No, seriously,' Mary stepped back as Luke tried to grab her hand. 'Not a good idea.'

'Oh, c'mon,' Luke insisted. 'You know what they say, right? Dance as if no one is watching.'

'Haha!' Mary laughed before her tone went back to serious. 'Yeah, I tried that last time. The problem was – somebody *was* watching, and they called an ambulance because they thought I was having a stroke.'

That made Luke laugh out loud. 'We might have very similar dance moves then.'

Gosh, Mary thought. *Even his laugh is kind of sexy.*

All of a sudden Mary went rigid, her muscles tightening to almost the point of spasms. The stranger's face . . . his eyes. She had been looking in the wrong corners of her mind. The feeling that she had seen that man before was all too real, but the memory didn't come from a party or from a holiday somewhere, it came from court. He was there on the day that she testified, sitting somewhere towards the back. That day, while giving her account to the court, her gaze had landed on him at least a couple of times – those same black-hole eyes staring straight at her, sizing her up.

And he was there again on the day of the verdict. As she stood up to leave, once the court had been adjourned by Judge Reeves, Mary saw him again, standing at the back of the courtroom, hands tucked into his trouser pockets, head low, as if he was trying hard not to be noticed.

Standing at the bar inside The Whiskey Bent Saloon, Mary felt her core rattle for the third time that evening. That man – the same man that she had seen in court almost seven months earlier – didn't just happen to be in Nashville, he didn't just happen to bump into her while strolling down the Broadway. This wasn't some freaky coincidence, it couldn't be. That man, whoever he was, had been looking for her . . . and somehow, despite all of Mary's efforts, he had managed to find her.

Seventeen

The music inside The Whiskey went from country rock to country ballad. Some of the crowd began dispersing from the dance floor, but the majority stayed, pairing themselves up into couples.

Mary's eyes, once again, moved past Luke to refocus on the door.

Nothing. No sign of the man from outside.

Her gaze moved to the crowd, in case he had managed to slip into The Whiskey without her noticing it.

Still nothing. She couldn't see him anywhere. What she did see were the G.R.I.T.S, including Vicky and Pam, making their way back to the bar, and they were all staring death at Mary.

'OK, now you have no excuse,' Luke said, bringing Mary's attention back to him, as he once again offered her his hand. 'We've gotta go dance.'

'To a slow song?' Mary's chin dipped, as she asked the question.

'Why not?'

'I'll dance with you.' The comment came from Vicky, who had finally reached the bar, along with the other G.R.I.T.S. She then turned to address Mary. 'You're still here? I thought you were leaving.'

'Do you know each other?' Luke asked.

'We met in the bathroom earlier,' Vicky explained. 'She said that she was just leaving. Did you get lost, honey?'

Mary could feel a barbed reply lodging itself right at the back of her throat, but she took a second and swallowed it back down. The last thing she needed right then was to pick a silly fight with a local. What she needed to do was think and come up with a plan of action, which was hard to do with loud music blasting in her ears and bitching women surrounding her. Mary quickly checked the door and the crowd one last time – still no sign from gangster-suit man. She reached for the CD that Luke had signed for her and placed it inside her handbag.

'I need the bathroom again,' she said, indicating the dance floor. 'You guys should go dance.'

'Oh, we will,' Vicky said, grabbing Luke's hand and dragging him over to the floor with her. 'Don't you get lost again, you hear?'

Mary zigzagged through some of the dancing couples, and returned to the bathroom, where she quickly locked herself into one of the cubicles.

Think, Mary, think, she urged herself, shaking her arms by her side to try to relax. *How the fuck did that guy find you here?* As soon as she asked herself that question, a second voice inside her head immediately shut the door on it. *Who cares how he found you? The fact is that he did. You can think of how, or where you went wrong later. Right now, you need to think of what to do so he doesn't get to you.*

Mary opened her handbag and checked its contents – house keys, her purse, sunglasses, two cellphones – her main one and a burner phone – Luke's CD, a mini perfume bottle and a small makeup bag. She unzipped her purse to check what was inside it – a futile exercise, done just to calm her nerves, because she knew exactly what she had in that purse – cash, four different credit cards, four different bankcards, her ID card, and her Medicaid photo card.

From her very first day as Mary Smith, she had stuck to her plan like white on rice. Her first and most important rule was – wherever she went, her purse went with her. If she ever found herself in trouble, the kind of trouble that required her to drop everything at the blink of an eye and disappear, her purse contained everything she needed to do exactly that.

The suggestion had, once again, come from George Oakfield, but Mary had seen it before in several spy movies. They called it a 'go-bag' – a bag or suitcase that was usually tucked away at a secure location and it would contain whatever the spy deemed necessary to escape a dangerous situation with minimum or no time to spare. Mary had created her own watered-down version of the go-bag, which she kept with her at all times. Sure, she knew that in America, there was always the risk of her purse being snatched, and that was why her passport, together with a second driver's license, another burner phone, and ten thousand dollars in cash were tucked away in a safety deposit box in a bank far away from Nashville. The box was identified only by a number – no names – and it was only opened by the use of double thumbprint – no keys. But in all honesty, never in her wildest dreams did Mary truly believe that her 'spy' plan would need to be put into action. She had been extremely careful in her choice of identity, looks and temporary location, and she had told absolutely no one about any of it.

After confirming that she had everything she needed inside her handbag and purse, Mary sat down on the toilet and took a second or two to try to calm the rapid beating of her heart, waiting patiently until she could feel the rate settle, slowly.

You can't go home, the voice told her. *If that guy found you here, in Nashville, then chances are that he has your address, and that's probably why he never came into The Whiskey after you spotted him outside. He probably figured out that his best chance would be to wait for you back at your place.'*

'Fuck!' Mary whispered, as she leaned forward, rested her elbows onto her knees and buried her head in her hands. She was just starting to really like Nashville, but because she had followed her plan step-by-step, with no deviations whatsoever, she could get up, walk straight out of The Whiskey, and simply disappear without even needing to go back home.

Other than the go-bag and the safety deposit box in a completely different city, Mary had also rented a small, furnished, one-bedroom apartment, which she had paid for in cash and six months in advance. When it came to earthly possessions, especially her wardrobe, Mary had made the biggest sacrifice of them all, filling it with just a few basic pieces that she could leave behind at any time without worrying about any of it.

Truth be told – going from over two hundred designer pieces in her fourteen-feet by fourteen-feet walk-in wardrobe back in Woburn, to just a few budget ones in a closet the size of a cupboard, was to Mary what going 'cold turkey' was to a heroin junkie – it took her an effort of will not go on some mad shopping sprees.

'So, what do we do now?' Mary murmured, engaging herself in another internal monologue.

Well, we don't have that many options, do we, her mental voice replied. *Going back home is too much of a risk.*

So, where the fuck do we go? We've got to go somewhere. We can't be sitting in here all night.

She checked her watch. It was just coming up to eleven-thirty. The place would probably be closing soon.

Well, for tonight we could go home with Mr. 'soon-to-be-a-country-music-star, sexy-tattooed-cowboy' Luke Jenkins. We get to avoid going back home, which is the main idea, and as a bonus, we'll get laid ... something that hasn't happened for a while, I might add.

Mary sat up straight, her eyes widening at her own thoughts. 'You have got to be fucking kidding, right?' she argued with herself. 'Like I fucking need that kind of headache right about now.

Not to mention the G.R.I.T.S. If they find out that I went home with Luke, they'll probably camp outside his house and shoot me in the head when they see me leaving in the morning. I bet they all carry guns.'

Mary shook her head at nothing, taking a moment to think. She didn't really have to stay the night in Nashville and get out in the morning. She had everything she needed, and the Greyhound bus station was just a few blocks away, with buses leaving every fifteen to thirty minutes. The train station was about the same distance. She'd need a cab to get to the airport, but at this hour, she wasn't sure she'd be able to make any flights.

Mary took a deep breath. Maybe getting the fuck out of Nashville even before sunrise really was the right call. Anywhere would do for tonight, as long as it wasn't here. She could think of a better temporary location tomorrow.

To Mary, that did sound like a much better option than going home with Luke ... probably a better option than getting a room in some seedy hotel somewhere in town too. Knowing that gangster-suit man was still in Nashville while she was already somewhere else would at least make her sleep better.

Decision made.

The only problem now was getting out of The Whiskey, because what if she was wrong? What if gangster-suit man hadn't gone anywhere? What if he was just waiting across the road, like before? In fact, that would've made more sense than him waiting for Mary somewhere outside her apartment – if he did know where she lived.

Well, this is a drinking den with a kitchen, the voice inside her head reminded her. *They will have a back door ... a kitchen door ... a fire exit door ... something.*

The fire exit door was out of the question – Mary had clocked it earlier – alarmed and located on the main floor, at the opposite end of the bar from where she'd been standing with Luke, but she had walked past the entrance to the kitchen on her way to the bathroom – it was completely out of sight from the main floor. Down the corridor, past the restrooms, there was no other door, so the back door had to be through the kitchen.

She stood up, slung her handbag over her right shoulder, took a deep breath, and finally exited the bathroom. Just before the door that would lead her back to the main floor at The Whiskey, Mary turned right and entered the kitchen. It looked like she'd been right in her assumption – at least the kitchen at The Whiskey looked to be already closing.

At that time, there were only two people in the kitchen – the chef and the porter. The chef was dressed in a typical white chef's uniform, and the porter was dressed in normal clothes, with a long waterproof apron slung over his neck and tied around at his waist. They were both busy cleaning surfaces, stacking pans and pots back on shelves, and emptying and reloading the industrial dishwasher at the far end of a double sink.

'If you're looking for the bathroom,' the chef said, indicating the door. His southern drawl was heavy. 'Keep on going down the corridor and turn left. It will be the second door on your right.'

From where she was standing, Mary spotted the back door, right at the far end of the kitchen, just past the two large chest freezers by the east wall.

'I'm actually looking for the rear exit,' she replied, as she pointed at the door.

The chef and the porter exchanged a curious look.

'Is someone out there bothering you, miss?' the chef asked. He was a large man who, judging by the size of his waist, clearly enjoyed the food he cooked. 'If you show me who he is, I can go and have a word. We don't allow that kind of behavior in here.'

Mary smiled back at the chef. 'Thank you, that's very kind of you to offer, but it really isn't necessary. I know him from work. He's an OK guy, but sometimes, when he's had a few too many, he can get a little too insistent, you know what I mean? I find it easier to just avoid it. He probably won't remember any of it tomorrow.' She indicated the door again. 'Do you mind if I leave through the back?'

The large chef shrugged. 'Sure. Be my guest, but don't make a habit of it, OK?'

'I won't,' Mary said, as she crossed the kitchen in fast strides. 'You're a lifesaver. Thank you again.' She pushed the door open and finally stepped out into the night.

Eighteen

'I can see that you're not only a talented musician,' Vicky said, as Luke swirled her around before bringing her back closer to him. 'You can also certainly lead on the dance floor.' She pressed her hips tighter against his body.

Luke half blushed.

She moved her lips closer to his ear. 'I wonder what else you're good at.'

Luke replied with a subtle 'who knows' movement of the head, while his eyes moved over Vicky's shoulder to look in the direction of the door that led to the bathrooms. Mary still hadn't come back.

The song that they were dancing to came to an end and it was smoothly mixed into the next track – another slow song. Luke let go of Vicky's body, but she quickly pulled him back towards her.

'Oh, c'mon,' she said, locking eyes with him. 'This is a great song. You're not going to just leave me here on the dance floor all by myself, are you?'

Luke glanced back in the direction of the bathrooms – still no Mary. He began wondering if maybe there was something wrong. She *was* acting a little different since they walked back into The Whiskey. Maybe she wasn't feeling too well . . . or maybe she was trying to avoid him.

'C'mon,' Vicky insisted. 'One more dance?' She batted her eyelids like Betty Boop.

Luke finally smiled back at her. 'Sure.'

Throughout the whole song, every chance he got, Luke's stare would ping back to the door leading to the bathrooms.

No Mary.

As the song drew to an end, Luke nodded at Vicky. 'Let's go back to the bar, let me get you one last drink before they shut for the night.'

'Yeah,' Vicky replied. 'I'd like that.'

All the G.R.I.T.S had already left, except for Pam.

'My turn,' she said, reaching for Luke's hand, just as they got to the bar.

Luke clearly wasn't expecting that.

'Umm . . . how about we get a beer first? I think they'll be closing soon.' He raised a hand at Josie.

Pam looked a little disappointed, but she agreed to the beer.

'Last orders, y'all,' Josie announced, getting to their end of the bar. 'We'll be closing in five, OK?'

Luke ordered three bottles of beer and as he did, he leaned over the bar and whispered something in Josie's ear.

Josie nodded back at him before serving them three bottles of Bud. She then walked out and around the bar and disappeared through the door that led to the bathrooms. Less than a minute later, she was back.

'She's not in the bathroom, Luke,' she told him, as she began wiping down the bar counter.

Luke frowned back at Josie. 'Did you see her leave at all?' he asked, turning around to check the dance floor.

'I didn't, no,' Josie replied, with a shake of the head. 'But I was busy with customers. She might have.'

'Something wrong?' Vicky asked.

'Mary,' Luke replied. 'I think she might've left. I'm not sure. I didn't see her leave. Did you?' he addressed Pam.

'I didn't see her, either,' Pam replied. 'And I was standing here the whole time. If she did, she didn't walk past me.'

'That's quite rude of her, don't you think?' Vicky commented, her tone like shards of glass. 'She could've at least said goodbye.'

Pam nodded in agreement.

'I think she wasn't feeling too well,' Luke said before raising a hand at the two G.R.I.T.S. 'Give me a sec.' He had a swig of his beer. 'Let me go check outside real quick.'

As Luke turned around and quickly exited The Whiskey, Vicky shook her head at Pam. 'What the fuck does he see in her? She's a bit chubby.'

'That she is,' Pam agreed.

Back out on the Broadway, Luke looked left then right, checking the small group of people spilling out of The Whiskey and walking up and down the boulevard.

No Mary.

He walked a little to his right before getting onto the tips of his toes and looking again.

Mary was nowhere to be seen.

He checked across the street.

Nothing.

'Fuck!' Luke said, as he finally gave up and returned to The Whiskey.

Nineteen

Across the road, the stranger in the gangster suit watched as Luke came running out of The Whiskey with a concerned look on his face.

The stranger's eyes narrowed to slits.

He recognized Luke from earlier. He was the guy who had come out to talk to Mary – the same guy who Mary had locked arms with before walking back into the bar.

The stranger straightened up his body and watched as Luke looked to one side then the other, clearly searching for someone.

That can't be good, the stranger thought, walking out of the shadows and up to the edge of the curb.

Luke got on his tiptoes, searching further down the street.

Is he looking for Mary? the stranger asked himself. Instinctively, he too began searching the crowd of streetwalkers, but he hadn't seen Mary walk out of the bar. Since she and the guy across the road had walked back into The Whiskey Bent Saloon arm-in-arm, he had kept a close watch on that door. Mary had not walked out of it – at least not through the front door.

'Fuck!' The word came out through gritted teeth.

The stranger's eyes searched the Broadway a little more urgently.

No Mary anywhere.

'Fuck, fuck, fuck ... back door,' the man said, as he rushed across the Broadway in a stop-and-start motion, to avoid being hit by oncoming traffic, but he didn't rush towards The Whiskey Bent Saloon – he ran towards the side street to its right, which he knew would allow him to get to the back alley, directly behind that particular row of bars and restaurants. It took him just a few seconds to reach it.

From that end of the alleyway, The Whiskey was the third building along. The back alley was badly lit, and the air was saturated with the smell of stale alcohol and of food gone bad.

No sign of Mary anywhere.

He ran past two large food dumpsters, and just as he was getting to the third back door on his left, it was pushed open by a tall Hispanic-looking man, wearing a waterproof apron and carrying a large bag full of food waste. The Hispanic man paused as he saw the stranger slow down to a walking pace. He certainly didn't look like any of the regular food scavengers.

'Hi there,' the stranger said, catching his breath. 'You work at The Whiskey Bent Saloon?' He spoke with a clear Texan drawl.

The kitchen porter swung the food bag into one of the large dumpsters before turning to face the stranger.

'That's right.'

'Did you, by any chance,' the stranger asked, gesticulating while he spoke, 'happen to see a woman . . . about my height . . . short black hair . . . blue jeans . . . dark jacket . . . black cowboy boots . . . leave through that back door not so long ago?'

The porter stared back at the stranger with more than just a question in his eyes.

'I was just in there with a friend,' the stranger tried to explain. 'And unfortunately, she had one too many. You know how it goes sometimes, right? Towards the end, I don't think that she was feeling too well. She went into the bathroom a few minutes ago and simply disappeared. I can't find her anywhere.'

'Um-hum.' The porter didn't look like he was buying any of it.

'So, I thought that maybe,' gangster-suit man continued, 'in her drunken state, she came out of the bathroom and used the wrong door.'

'This is the kitchen door, ese,' the porter explained. 'Not a back exit. No one has left through here.'

'Umm . . . are you sure?'

The porter's look could've started a fire on wet grass.

'Is there a back door to this bar, then?'

The porter shook his head. 'There's a fire exit door that drops you back on the Broadway, but that door is alarmed, and the alarm hasn't gone off.'

'And no one came through the kitchen?'

The porter wiped his hands on his apron. 'Nope.'

Gangster-suit man held the porter's stare for a second before reaching for his wallet.

'How positive are you about that?' He pulled out two twenty-dollar bills.

This time, it was the porter who hesitated. 'Umm . . . well . . . quite positive.'

Gangster-suit man nodded slowly, understanding the bargain. 'I see.' He took out another twenty-dollar bill. 'How about now?'

The porter motioned gangster-suit man to hand him the sixty dollars.

He did, but didn't let go of the money, holding the bills at one end, while the porter grabbed them at the other.

'She left about a minute before you got here,' the porter said. 'You really just missed her.'

'Do you know which way she went?'

The porter pulled harder on the money.

Gangster-suit man finally let go of it.

'I don't know, ese,' the porter replied, taking the money and placing it in his back pocket. 'She just opened the door and she was gone. I didn't come out with her. But I ain't joking when I said that you just missed her. So, if you came from that way . . .'

His head tilted right, in the direction that gangster-suit man had surfaced, 'and you didn't see her, then she probably went the other way.' His head jerked left.

'Thank you.' Gangster-suit man nodded at the porter before taking off like a rocket down the alleyway. As he finally reached the street at the other end of it, he looked right then left. He couldn't see Mary anywhere.

The man took a second, pondering his options. If he turned left, the street would take him back to The Broadway, dropping him right at the opposite end of the same block where The Whiskey was located. He doubted that if Mary was trying to get away from him – which he was pretty certain that she was – she would've tracked back to The Broadway. Too risky. So, using logic, she must've turned right, but he was standing right on 4th Avenue North, which was a very long avenue, intersected by a multitude of different streets. Mary could've easily turned off on any of them and simply disappeared.

Gangster-suit man breathed out in frustration. Turning right and running down the avenue would be a pointless exercise. There was no way that he'd be able to find her now.

'Fuck!' he said as he reached for his cellphone and pressed 'redial' on the last number he had called.

The call was answered after the second ring.

'I've lost her,' he said, looking down at his shiny shoes.

There was a long, slow exhale ... a second later, the line went dead.

Twenty

Less Than Five Minutes Earlier

The kitchen door at The Whiskey led Mary straight onto a smelly alleyway filled with large restaurant dumpsters. Two lampposts bathed the narrow street in a weak orange glow, reminiscent of old 1950s horror films. Mary hesitated for a second, but she knew exactly where she was. No need to consult the map application on her phone. She could see the thirty-three-story-high AT&T building directly in front of her, just past another row of shops.

She looked left then right. The alleyway looked deserted – there was no sign of gangster-suit man.

Mary veered right, took three steps in that direction and then paused, her brain half disagreeing with her move.

The alleyway wasn't exactly a long one. It ran parallel to the Broadway, behind that particular row of shops, bars and restaurants – ten in total. The Whiskey Bent Saloon was the third building from the right, but the seventh from the left, which meant that the run to the side street was much shorter for Mary if she went right instead of left. The problem was, it would also be a considerably shorter run for the stranger coming from across the road from The Whiskey, which Mary had no doubt he would do, as soon as he figured out that she must've fled through a back door – and the last thing that Mary wanted was to bump into gangster-suit man as she got to the side street.

Run against the tide, the voice in her head told her. *Do the unexpected.*

Mary turned left and ran as fast as her cowboy boots would allow her. As she got to the side street – 4th Avenue North – she paused again. Turning left would take her back to The Broadway – opposite end of the block from where The Whiskey was – turning right would take her north, past the AT&T building, with several intersecting streets crossing the long avenue, giving her a lot more escape options. That was clearly the obvious choice.

Run against the tide. Do the unexpected.

Mary turned left and quickly made her way back to The Broadway, but before doing so, she opened her handbag, reached for her cellphone, and dropped it inside the dumpster to her right – just in case, somehow, the stranger was using the GPS on her cellphone to track her.

Despite being a Monday night, there was still a considerable number of people walking up and down that stretch of the boulevard – too many for Mary to be able to spot gangster-suit man – and if Mary couldn't spot the stranger, then he wouldn't be able to spot her either.

But luck also seemed to be on Mary's side that evening. After quickly checking The Broadway, she turned right, moving away from The Whiskey. She had only taken a couple of steps when she saw a cab pull up by the sidewalk to drop a passenger. She quickly walked up to the passenger's window and gave it a quick knuckle knock.

'Are you ending for the night,' she asked, as the driver rolled down the window. 'Or can you take one more fare?'

'I've actually just started, ma'am,' the cab driver replied. He was a slim man with kind eyes, wearing a cowboy hat and sporting a thick, peppery horseshoe mustache. 'I'll be going until morning. Hop in.'

Mary quickly got into the back seat.

'Where to?'

'Greyhound bus station please.'

'Sure.' The driver switched on the taximeter, indicated left and pulled out onto The Broadway, heading southwest. According to his ID information displayed on the dashboard, his name was Travis Anderson.

As the cab pulled away, Mary saw a man wearing what looked like a marching-band military jacket, walking along The Broadway. That was when she had a brand-new idea.

When the estate realtor showed her the first few properties around Nashville, he mentioned a few touristic attractions not only in Nashville, but in some of the nearby towns as well. One of his top recommendations was the city of Franklin, a mere twenty miles away. Franklin, the realtor had explained, had been a key site of the American Civil War, and all throughout the year, with its antebellum plantation homes and civil war-era wooden houses, the city attracted a diverse multitude of tourists.

Mary sat back on her seat and began pondering an alternative. She hadn't really had time to check which buses she would be able catch from the Greyhound station at that time of night. And the one thing that she didn't want to do was hang around the station for too long, waiting for the next bus. However small, there was always the possibility that gangster-suit man could come looking.

'Excuse me,' Mary said, leaning forward on her seat. 'How long would it take for you to drive me to Franklin instead?'

The driver looked at Mary through the rear-view mirror before checking the dashboard clock. 'At this time at night, ma'am, not long at all. Less than half an hour, for sure.'

Mary took another second to think about it. She didn't need to ask about the fare price. She had almost seven hundred dollars in cash in her wallet – more than enough to cover the trip and a one-night stay at any hotel in Franklin. The advantage was that in the morning, she wouldn't have to rush. She could take her time and pick a better city to travel to, without having to worry about the stranger tracking her down again.

'Is it easy to find a hotel there? Do you know?'

'In Franklin?' The driver, once again, checked Mary through the rear-view mirror. 'Oh yeah, for sure, ma'am. Franklin is almost as touristic as Nashville itself. It's a great little town. You can even get a room in an old-style plantation house, if you want.'

'Do you know any good ones . . . hotels, I mean. Not plantation houses.'

The driver smiled at Mary. 'I sure do, ma'am. I know a couple of great little boutique hotels, but the choice is plenty. The I-65 cuts right through Franklin, and honestly, that's like a hotel boulevard. You look left . . . you look right . . . all you see are hotels, ma'am – from cheap ones to living in high cotton.'

Mary nodded at the driver's eyes on the mirror. 'Do you mind driving me there instead of the bus station. I can pay cash.'

'I'll drive you wherever you'd like me to, ma'am.' He touched the tip of his hat, as he gave Mary a cowboy nod. 'It's my job.'

The driver was right. The ride from The Broadway all the way to Franklin, just south of Nashville, took him no longer than twenty-five minutes. Once there, Mary decided to go for a simple three-star hotel – The Comfort Inn – just off the I-65, like the cab driver had told her.

It was true that the Covid pandemic changed the world in many ways, including how customers paid for goods and services all around the planet. Credit cards and phone pays have become the norm, with many establishments accepting no other form of payment, but in the USA, you could still find plenty of places where cash was king, especially in the Deep South. At The Comfort Inn, Mary had no problems getting the female desk clerk to accept cash instead of a credit card. There was no need to create a digital trail.

'I need to ask you for a huge favor,' Mary said, as she handed the clerk her ID card. Her voice was sad and pleading. 'Could you please register me under a different name.'

The clerk, an older lady with curly blonde hair and a gentle smile, paused and looked back at Mary curiously.

'I know that artists do that sometimes,' Mary explained. 'To avoid fan calls, journalists . . . things like that, you know?'

'Oh,' the clerk's eyes narrowed at Mary, as if trying to place her. 'Are you . . .'

'No,' Mary responded with a shake of the head. 'I'm not an artist. I'm not famous or anything like that either.' The sadness in her tone became a little more prominent. 'But I finally got the courage to run away from a very abusive and toxic relationship. I'm doing this all by myself and to be honest, I'm terrified. I'm not really sure what I'm doing . . . I don't really know where I'm going. I didn't even get a chance to pack a bag or anything.' She lifted her hands to indicate that all she had with her was her handbag. 'But I know that he and his buddies will be searching for me.' Mary shook her head, as tears glassed her eyes. 'I can't go back, you know? I just can't.'

'Heavens to Betsy, honey,' the clerk said, her tone tender. 'Bless your heart, and good for you that you decided to finally leave.' She gave Mary a kind and understanding smile. 'And of course I can put you down in the books under a different name. No one will find you here, honey. Don't you worry about that, you hear?' She handed Mary back her ID card. 'Do you have a name in mind?'

'Oh, thank you so much.' Mary's tone was sincere. 'Right now, I need all the help I can get, you know?'

'Of course, honey.'

Mary took a second. 'How about Vicky . . .' She thought about giving Vicky the surname 'Grit', but Vicky Grit sounded like too odd of a name. She decided that it would be better to go with something more traditional. That was when the cab driver's name came back to her. 'How about Vicky Anderson?'

The clerk nodded, as she typed the name into her computer. 'Vicky Anderson it is.' She gave Mary a renewed smile. 'And I'll tell you what – I think you've been through enough for one night, so I'm going to upgrade you to one of our suites, for no extra cost.' She carried on typing into her computer. 'It's a larger and more comfortable room, with a separate living area, a balcony and a super king-sized bed. I'm sure that you must be worn slap out. And the room comes with a complimentary bottle of white wine, which you'll find in the minibar.'

'Aw, thank you so much. That's so very kind of you.' Mary's eyes glassed over again. 'And you're right, I really am exhausted.'

'I'm sure you are, honey.' The clerk handed Mary a keycard. 'Room 410, on the top floor. The lifts are just over there.' She indicated just ahead and to the right of the reception counter.

Mary took the card and thanked the clerk once again.

'Miss Anderson?' the clerk called, just as Mary got to the lifts. 'I hope everything turns out just fine for you. You deserve better, honey. You're doing the right thing.'

Up on the fourth floor, it was only when Mary touched the keycard against the lock pad on the door that she realized how much she was shaking. Inside the large and nicely decorated suite, as the door finally closed behind her, Mary dropped to her knees and broke down in desperate sobs.

Twenty-One

Despite managing to evade gangster-suit man back at The Whiskey Bent Saloon, Mary barely got any sleep that night. First, she took a long, warm shower, allowing the strong water jet to massage her stiff neck muscles for almost ten minutes, before opening the bottle of wine from the minibar and spending most of the night sitting awake in bed, rethinking her plan, and trying to figure out where she went wrong – how had he managed to track her down all the way to Nashville?

Mary thought back to every step she had taken after she was granted her identity change, and she just couldn't pinpoint where her mistake had come from. She hadn't told a soul about her new name, not even her lawyer, and the only document she had signed that attested to her name change had been the one at the courthouse, which was a mandatory step to finalize the identity change process – a document that she was told would be kept under lock and key – and that was when Mary remembered what George Oakfield had told her, while explaining the intricacies of the process:

'*Once an identity change is granted and finalized, the documentation for the whole process goes into "lock and key" mode – very, very hard for anyone to get to – but not impossible. And what I mean here is – there are legal and illegal ways of obtaining the information on those records. This is America, where money talks and bullshit walks. And people can be easily bribed.'*

'That must've been it,' Mary said to herself, as she stared out of her hotel room window, down at a completely empty street. 'One of Nelson's buddies must've managed to bribe someone in the courthouse. But even so . . .' she breathed out frustration, '. . .all that anyone would've obtained from the courthouse documents would've been my new name – Mary Smith – nothing else. So how did that guy find me in Nashville?'

When it came to her money and her bank accounts, Mary had once again followed Oakfield's advice to the letter. Once the divorce settlement money hit her old account, she had sat tight and waited until her identity change process was concluded. That same day, just hours before she had to sign the courthouse papers, finalizing the entire identity change process, Sam walked into her bank in downtown Boston and, to the total disbelief of the bank manager, withdrew everything she had . . . to the last penny . . . and all in cash. Minutes after Samantha Chambers had legally ceased to exist, with a trunkful of money, a newly born Mary Smith drove straight out of Boston and into the city of New York. Her first stop was the JPMorgan Chase & Co. bank on Park Avenue, where she deposited some of the money that she had with her. During the next couple of days, Mary travelled to Pennsylvania, Washington DC, and West Virginia, where she opened three other bank accounts, in three completely different banks. Each deposit was for a different amount, and once again, George Oakfield had been right on the money.

As Sam signed the court documents to become Mary Smith, she was also given a letter, signed by a District Judge, instructing any bank she chose to accept whatever large cash deposit she offered them – no questions asked.

As for the address registered against her bank accounts, Mary had used a different nameless PO Box for each of them.

She thought about it for a while, and the only conclusion that she could come to was that there really was no feasible way that anyone could've tracked her down by following the money.

So how had she been found?

Right then, as Mary had another sip of her wine, she heard the sound of a commercial plane crossing the sky high above the hotel. She looked up and saw its lights blinking against the night clouds.

Two seconds later, her brain engaged, making her heart stutter inside her chest.

'Oh fuck!' she said in a whisper. 'But of course – Kyle fucking Doyle.'

Kyle Doyle was one of Nelson's best friends and a mammoth of a man – greasy hair, chubby cheeks, and always hiking up his trousers, the ones that every couple of minutes or so would slip down below the pouch of his belly, well fed, as it was, from a daily serving of beer and fried food from one of the many junk food outlets at Logan International Airport in Boston, where he worked. Doyle was an Assistant Director for the US Federal Air Marshall Service in Massachusetts – a position that would grant him easy access to any national or international flight manifest from any airline flying inside US territory.

And that had been Mary's mistake.

Just a few days after her identity change process was finalized, once she had secured all four of her new bank accounts, Mary had purchased an airline ticket to Nashville, with the booking being made under her new name – Mary Smith. She flew out from JFK airport in New York City, not Logan International in Boston, but even so, armed with her new name, Doyle could've easily done a search through all the flight manifests from aircrafts flying out of any US airport, starting with all the ones in Massachusetts before branching out to adjacent estates – and New York City was just 230 miles south of Boston.

It had clearly taken Doyle a while to properly narrow the result list down. There was no telling how many other Mary Smiths would've shown up on those flight manifests, but in the days following her first-ever flight to Nashville, Mary flew back and forth between Nashville and New York City twice more, with the second time being the final move. That must've been what had alerted Doyle because five months later, gangster-suit man had finally found her.

Mary walked over to the minibar and poured herself another glass of wine. From her handbag, she retrieved her burner smartphone and connected to the hotel's Wi-Fi. She knew that she needed to start again – find a brand-new city to move to – and since she was sure that she had lost gangster-suit man once she left The Whiskey Bent Saloon through its kitchen door, he too would have to start again, but this time, he would have no passenger manifest to follow because Mary wasn't about to make the same mistake twice.

She sipped her wine and stepped out onto the room's balcony. Despite also being a touristic city, Franklin was, without a doubt, a much quieter town than Nashville. At that time of night, the streets surrounding The Comfort Inn hotel seemed deserted – no vehicles driving by . . . no pedestrians walking around anywhere.

Mary welcomed the cooling night breeze that kissed her skin and brushed at her hair, before thinking back to the man outside The Whiskey. She tried to imagine what he had done after he'd realized that he'd lost her. The most probable move would've been to stake out her apartment, hoping that Mary would turn up to collect a few things before making a run for it. Going straight from The Broadway to the bus station, the train station, or even the airport, were also possibilities, albeit unlikely. For that, gangster-suit man would've had to have anticipated that after spotting him outside The Whiskey, Mary was not only prepared, but also all set up to get the hell out of Nashville at the blink of an eye – CIA spy style – and the chances of him having predicted that were very slim, to say the least.

As crazy as it might've sounded at the time, Mary's go-bag plan seemed to have already paid off . . . and with dividends, because while she was already on the move, gangster-suit man was back in Nashville, wondering where the hell she was.

Mary returned to the room, refilled her wine glass and opened up the browser on her cellphone. After a lot of pondering and a lot of Internet searching, she decided to stick to her original plan and for now, stay within the 'Bible Belt', where the biggest concentration of women whose first name was 'Mary' resided. She also decided to stick with the idea of relocating to a large city, instead of a smaller one, for the same reasons as before, but this time she picked a place even larger than Nashville – the fourth largest and most populated city in the USA: Houston, Texas.

Twenty-Two

There was no doubt in Mary's mind that she had figured out exactly how Nelson had managed to track her down all the way in Nashville – Kyle Doyle, with the help of the flight manifest. There was no other explanation, so the first item on Mary's new 'no go' list was air travel – at least not for a while. She'd also decided that for good measure, she would bounce from city to city for a bit before finally reaching her desired destination of Houston. The bouncing around had been something else that she had picked up from spy movies, and since she was in no hurry to get to Texas and she certainly had the means to afford as many hotel nights as she wished, bouncing around sounded just like the kind of distraction she needed – but her first priority was to get out of Franklin ... pronto. It was too close to Nashville, and despite having managed to give gangster-suit man the slip, Mary had this nagging feeling that she was still far from safe. The faster she got out of town, or better yet, the faster she got out of Tennessee, the better.

George Oakfield's cliché sentence came back to her – 'This is the first day of the rest of your life.'

With that in mind, just a few hours later, as the night sky began morphing itself into a bright-blue and cloudless morning, Mary took the first bus out of Franklin Transit Center bus station, heading south. The bus she hopped on was half empty and heading to Birmingham, Alabama. It was just a short three-hour trip, but it got her across the state line, and as soon as she got out of Tennessee, Mary could feel her heartbeat finally starting to settle into a steady rhythm.

Twenty-Three

The man in the gangster suit scratched his chin, as he watched the CCTV camera footage from the Transit Center bus station in Franklin, Tennessee. He'd been doing so for less than five minutes when he finally spotted her, boarding an early bus to Birmingham, Alabama.

'And there you are,' he whispered to himself, freezing the image on the screen, with the touch of a button. 'You really are a clever one, aren't you, *Miss* Mary Smith? I have to give you that. And very well prepared too.'

In the footage, Mary looked a little different than she had the night before, at The Whiskey Bent Saloon – certainly a lot less glamorous. Her hair was tucked under a baseball cap that she had clearly purchased from the hotel in which she had spent the night. Her jacket was zipped up to her neck, and she kept her hands firmly tucked into its pockets. She had no carry-on luggage with her, except for her handbag, which was slung over her shoulder. As she boarded the bus, Mary had kept her head low – eyes on the ground – so that the CCTV camera wouldn't capture her face, but the man had no doubt that it was her – she was wearing the exact same outfit as last night – which wasn't exactly surprising, given that she'd never gone back to her apartment in Nashville to pack a bag. The man in the gangster suit knew that because he had waited for her there the entire night.

After he had placed the call to his employer to inform him that he had lost Mary, he tried to anticipate what her next move would be, and the most obvious one would be for her to return to her flat to at least pack a bag before hitting the road again, but that was not what she did.

The man had been given a lot of information on Mary, including that she was a very smart woman, but what he was never told was that she either had some kind of photographic memory, or an incredible talent when it came to remembering faces.

At Nelson Stewart's trial, just over seven months ago, gangster-suit man had sat as far back as he possibly could – last row – last seat on the far left. During Samantha Stewart's testimony, her eyes had circled the courtroom, like a teacher's during a lecture, trying to make sure that every student's attention was on her, but it was a large courtroom, with one hundred and twenty-five seats, and most of them were taken. There was no way that six months later she could still remember every face in that room, unless she had an eidetic memory or a gift when it came to remembering faces. But last night, outside The Whiskey, Mary Smith had done just that – recognized him – even though their eyes had met for just a fraction of a second. Why else would she have fled the way she did?

This morning, as the sun cracked through the horizon line, the man, who had been sitting in his car all night, hidden away, but with a clear view to the entrance door to Mary's apartment building, knew that he'd anticipated the wrong move from her. Mary wasn't coming back to her flat to pack a bag, grab some money, or anything else. She was already gone, but the worst of it was that now, she also had at least a five-hour head start on him.

'She jumped into a cab last night,' the man had finally concluded, angry with himself for not thinking of that earlier. Every other possibility would've been too risky for anybody who knew that they had just been tracked down. Survival instinct would tell anyone in that situation to get away . . . fast . . . not wait for a bus, order an Uber, or try to get away on foot – but if Mary didn't go back to her flat, then where did she go at that time of night with nothing but her handbag? A hotel? A friend's house? Where?

He knew that right then, only two people would have the answer to that question – Mary herself and the cab driver who had picked her up.

Now the race was on to find the cab driver, which despite having a precise five to ten minute window – from the time that Mary had spotted him across the road, until the time that guitar man had come out again looking for her – it still took gangster-suit man almost two and a half hours to find out which cab companies had picked up a single female passenger around The Whiskey Bent Saloon area at that exact time last night. Four different drivers made the list, but only one had had a female passenger who matched Mary's description. The driver had dropped her off at The Comfort Inn Hotel, in Franklin – just off the I-65.

At the hotel, all that gangster-suit man had to do was flash his fake FBI ID to find out that they had only one guest who had checked in late last night – Vicky Anderson. She had also checked out first thing this morning – before 6:00 a.m. And that was how he came to be sitting inside the control room at the Transit Center bus station in Franklin, going over all the CCTV camera footage from every bus leaving the station early that morning. Mary had jumped onto a Greyhound bus that had left at 6:25 a.m., heading towards the city of Birmingham, in Alabama.

The man checked his watch – 10:55 a.m. Mary would've already arrived, as the trip from Franklin to Birmingham took around three hours. He could make it in just under two-and-a-half, depending on traffic, but he had to leave pronto.

The man reached for his car keys and rushed out of the control room.

This cat and mouse game was turning out to be a lot harder that he had anticipated.

Twenty-Four

Traffic wasn't exactly what gangster-suit man had hoped for. A broken-down truck, just past Athens in Alabama, added at least another forty minutes to his journey, which meant that with one stop for coffee, food and a quick trip to the bathroom, he arrived in Birmingham at around 3:00 p.m. – five and a half hours after Mary. He was in desperate need of a shower and at least a couple of hours of sleep, and if he was tracking just about anyone else he would've probably gone for it, but Mary had already proven to be a hell of a lot smarter than the average Joe that he was usually hired to track down, so for the time being, he would have to make do with strong coffee, energy drinks and some deodorant.

In Birmingham, his first stop had been the Greyhound bus station on Morris Avenue. He needed to gain access to their CCTV camera footage and check if Mary had come out of the bus in Birmingham or not. If not, it meant that she had probably asked the driver to stop somewhere along the way and let her off. She could've given him the old 'feeling sick' excuse, and the driver would've had to stop. With no luggage to retrieve from the luggage compartment, it would've taken the driver all of ten seconds to pull up to a gas station along the way, or even the side of the road, and allow Mary to jump off the bus.

Just like he'd done at the hotel in Franklin that morning,

gangster-suit man simply used his fake FBI ID as he requested the footage from the bus station security room. No one questioned him because no one really wanted to get between the federal government and a 'wanted fugitive' – on the contrary, most people would do anything to help.

'And there you are again, Miss Smith,' he said to himself, breathing out relief, as he watched Mary step off the bus at 9:31 that morning.

If Mary had exited the bus anywhere along the way between Franklin and Birmingham, it would practically be game over for him. The five-hour headstart that Mary already had on him would've easily turned into ten plus, and the chances of him finding her again would decrease by the minute ... but now he knew that Mary *was* in Birmingham – at least for the time being. If she was clever – and he already knew that she was – now that she knew she was being tracked, she'd want to put as much distance and as many different cities ... even states ... between her and the person tracking her. Birmingham hadn't been a planned destination for Mary. It simply happened to be the first bus out of Franklin that morning, so yes, Mary was in Birmingham, but she wouldn't stay long. He was pretty certain of that.

With the image of Mary stepping off the bus still frozen on the screen, the man in the gangster suit finished his donut and drank the rest of his coffee in large gulps, his brain grinding through the possibilities.

Would Mary stay in Birmingham for a day or more, or would she stay just a matter of hours before hitting the road again?

The man figured that Mary was probably just as tired as he was, perhaps even more. Despite taking the room at the hotel in Franklin, it was very doubtful that she'd managed to get any sort of sleep. Adrenaline would've flooded her system, causing tremendous anxiety, not to mention the absolute necessity of plotting an escape route in just a few hours. Maybe she got an hour or so of shuteye in the bus, on her way to Birmingham, but that would've been it.

'She's not a bank robber or a terrorist,' the man told himself, once again, trying to anticipate Mary's next move. 'She's just a woman who doesn't want her ex-husband to know where she is, that's all. Yes, she's smart, but she's not a spy. She doesn't know the tricks of the trade. She's tired ... she's anxious ... and she's certainly scared ... but she probably believes that at least for the time being – a day, maybe two – she's done enough to lose me, which means that she might let her guard down and take a breather.' The man had another gulp of his coffee.

'What would I do if I were you?' he asked himself, leaning closer to the monitor.

'Well, you definitely need some new clothes because you didn't even go back to your apartment to grab a bag, did you? And that translates to you being a well-prepared woman. You were ready to drop Nashville and just go at the blink of an eye.' He scratched the underside of his chin. 'You're truly terrified of your ex-husband, aren't you? Also ...' He pointed first at the monitor, then at himself. 'You know that I know what you're wearing, so a change of clothes would be a big, big priority here.'

He pinched his bottom lip, as he pondered.

'So, if I were you, I'd get a hotel for one night ... somewhere close by, and then go shopping ... something quick ... nothing extravagant ... just something that would make me look a little different than this.' He pointed at the screen again. 'That's what you did, isn't it? You're somewhere not that far from the station.'

He smiled proudly before reaching for his jacket. Time to go flash his FBI badge at all the hotels within walking distance of the bus station. But as he got to his feet, an odd feeling started to creep on in and he paused.

'Did you get what you needed?' the Greyhound employee who managed the control room at the station asked. He was a man of average height, who looked to be in his early sixties, with a belly that was severely testing the strength of the lower buttons on his shirt.

Gangster-suit man didn't reply. Instead, he simply turned to look at the monitor again.

'Hello?'

Gangster-suit man lifted a hand at the Greyhound employee, his brain, once again, grinding through the possibilities.

Back in Nashville, he had anticipated the wrong move from Mary. He thought that she'd go back to her apartment, but she never did. What if he was making the same mistake here? What if he was anticipating the wrong move? What if Mary got to Birmingham that morning, walked straight into a clothes shop nearby, purchased a simple change of clothes, and immediately jumped back on a bus? Or maybe a train?

Like he had already determined – now that she knew that she was being tracked, Mary would want to put as much distance as possible between her and the person tracking her. Birmingham wasn't in her plans, but she could easily use it as a springboard – adding one extra tangled twist to the web. *That* would've been a clever move – and Mary sure was clever.

'Maybe not yet,' he finally replied to the employee's original question, getting back to the seat in front of the monitors. 'Can you load up the footage of every bus that has left the station since 9:40 this morning?'

'Every bus?'

The man in the gangster suit nodded. 'All I need is to see the boarding footage, that's all.'

'Sure,' the employee replied, using the mouse on the desk to click away on the screen before typing a few parameters into a couple of search boxes. A minute later, on the left of the screen, he had created a list of buses, showing their route number and the destination. 'There you go. Just double click on the bus and the footage will load right here.' He indicated the right side of the screen.

'Much appreciated.'

'Would you like another cup of coffee?'

Gangster-suit man smiled at the employee. 'I'd absolutely love another cup of coffee.'

'I'll get it for you.'

As the employee left the room, he began at the top of the list.

'I'll be dipped in shit!' he said, sitting up on his chair and once again, leaning closer to the monitor. He rewound the footage on the screen a couple of seconds and played it again before hitting the pause button. The screen froze at the same time that a smile parted his lips.

'You clever little thing,' he said before having a sip of the coffee that the Greyhound employee had brought him just a few minutes ago. 'I almost got you wrong again, didn't I? You didn't even go for a change of clothes.'

On the screen, the same Mary that he had seen board the bus back in Franklin, then step out of that same bus in Birmingham that morning, was just boarding a new bus – twenty-nine minutes after arriving in Birmingham. There had been no change of clothes. She was still wearing the same baseball cap that she had purchased at the hotel, the same jacket, the same blue jeans, and the same cowboy boots. Just as she did in Franklin and when arriving in Birmingham, she kept her hands firmly tucked into her jacket pockets and her head low, eyes on the ground, so that the CCTV camera wouldn't capture her face.

The man checked the list on the left of his screen. He was watching the footage from the seventh bus on that list – destined for Milwaukee, in Wisconsin. That was a long trip – eleven and a half hours. Arrival in Milwaukee was scheduled for 10:35 that evening.

He checked his watch – 3:40 p.m. There was no way that he

could jump straight back into his car and drive to Milwaukee. He needed to catch some sleep before he was able to do anything else. He reached for his smartphone and performed a quick Internet search. A flight from Birmingham to Milwaukee would get him there in three hours and forty-five minutes.

Another quick search.

There was a flight leaving Birmingham-Shuttlesworth International Airport at 5:45 p.m., arriving in Milwaukee at 9:30 that evening – a full hour before Mary was due to get there. He could get a few hours of sleep in the plane, hire a car at the airport when he landed, and be at the Greyhound bus station in Milwaukee with a few minutes to spare to watch Mary step out of the bus.

'You might not be a spy, Miss Mary Smith,' the man murmured to himself, 'but you certainly can think out of the box. Very smart.' On his phone, he began the process of purchasing an airline ticket. 'But I'm smarter. I'll see you in Milwaukee.'

Twenty-Five

Mary had come up with the idea while still at the hotel in Franklin. Her train of thought had been simple: if gangster-suit man had managed to track her down in Nashville, it meant that he was good at what he did. It would be just a matter of time before he figured out that she had jumped into a cab and that she wasn't going back to her apartment. From there, it wouldn't take him long to find out about the hotel in Franklin and the early bus heading towards Birmingham.

Unlike airlines, bus companies did not have a passenger manifest, so the only way for gangster-suit man to confirm if Mary had boarded the bus in Franklin, then debarked it in Birmingham, would be by watching the CCTV camera footage at the bus stations. Sure, she had kept her head low so that the camera wouldn't capture her face, but that wouldn't really keep gangster-suit man from recognizing her. So, Mary's plan had been to simply fake it – make him believe that she had used Birmingham as a springboard destination, boarding another bus shortly after arriving in town, but this time the bus would be heading somewhere far, somewhere where he couldn't drive to so easily – a clear indication that she was trying to put as much distance between her and him as she possibly could. Another trick that she had picked up from spy films.

With that in mind, after arriving in Birmingham, Mary

checked the departures' board at the station. In less than half an hour there was a bus departing to Milwaukee, in Wisconsin. That was certainly far enough, and the timing was absolutely perfect.

Mary walked up to the teller window and used her credit card to purchase a ticket. She knew that that would leave a trail, but that had been exactly why she did it – in case, somehow, gangster-suit man had a way of tracking her credit card activity.

Minutes later, Mary boarded the bus, heading towards Milwaukee, with all the other passengers. Once again, for the sake of the CCTV camera, she kept her head low and her hands firmly tucked into her jacket pockets – fugitive style.

The bus departed exactly on time, but just a minute after that, as it veered right and came to a stop at a red traffic light, Mary asked the driver to open the door and let her out. The driver frowned at her, not really understanding what was going on. She simply told him that she had changed her mind about going to Wisconsin. With no luggage for her to retrieve from the luggage compartment, it would cause the driver no delay at all to let her out.

'There are no refunds,' the driver had said, in a heavy Alabama accent. 'You know that, right?'

'Yep. No problem.'

'Fine, it's your money lady,' the driver had commented, before pressing the button to release the door.

As she stepped out of the bus, Mary didn't know if gangster-suit man would end up in Milwaukee or not. Either way, with her little 'hop-on hop-off' trick, she was pretty sure that she would never see him again.

Twenty-Six

For the next seven weeks, Mary traveled through the Deep South like a tourist on holiday – sixteen cities across six different states – tangling the trail web behind her so thickly that even a spider wouldn't be able to properly navigate it. But before leaving Birmingham, in Alabama, Mary decided to reinvent her look yet again. If gangster-suit man had managed to track her down, chances were that he had also managed to photograph her, and that would be what he, or whoever else took over from him, would use to try to pick up her trail again.

Mary's hair stayed the same – short and raven black – but the reason for that was because short hair was easier to manage when wearing a wig.

This time, Mary decided to go with shoulder length, straight brown hair – a look that she could easily pull. At the opticians, she purchased a whole new batch of daily contact lenses – still brown in color, but a couple of shades lighter than the ones she'd been wearing for the past six months. She had checked the statistics on the Internet – the probability of a female in the USA being born with brown hair and brown eyes was one in every two – the most common eye/hair color combination in the land.

Mary was also extremely glad that she could now go back into a proper diet and exercise routine and lose all of the weight that she had put on since she'd left Massachusetts, and she couldn't wait to get rid of her plump cheeks and her muffin top.

'Goodbye burgers and fried food,' she told herself, smiling at the mirror, on the same day that she left Birmingham.

The plan was to simply travel around – no specific place in mind . . . no exact number of days to spend anywhere. All that Mary really wanted to do was put as many cities and states in between her Nashville address and her new one – somewhere in Houston.

There was only one state in the Deep South that Mary had to visit before she settled down in Texas, and that state was Louisiana. The reason why she just couldn't wait to visit the Pelican State was rather silly, but very personal.

Something that went back to her teenage years.

Something very few people ever knew about her.

What Mary had forgotten was that Nelson Stewart was one of those few.

Twenty-Seven

At the tender age of thirteen, Mary began developing a somewhat platonic love affair with the state of Louisiana, and it was all thanks to a vampire TV show that had aired its pilot episode in September 2004, called *Vamp Blood*.

The show took place in a fictional town called St. Veeds, located right in the heart of the Pelican State. Despite being fictional, most of the episodes in the first two seasons – considered by many to be the show's best era – were shot in actual locations in Louisiana, not inside a studio in Hollywood. Mary had fallen in love not only with the show's characters and plot, but also with the whole dark, swampy and moody backdrop that was used as a base for the series. From 2004 to 2010, seven seasons and a total of eighty episodes were aired, and Mary had watched every single one of them.

By the end of the show's first season Mary was completely hooked, and while still only a young teenager, she had promised herself that she would, one day, visit Louisiana and some of its most iconic towns, especially the ones where she knew some episodes had been shot.

With that in mind, Mary created a list of five cities that she really wanted to visit inside the Pelican State – Baton Rouge, Monroe, Natchitoches, Lafayette and, of course, New Orleans.

Mary started her journey through Louisiana right at the top

of the state, in the city of Monroe. From there, she slowly worked her way down, leaving the most famous city – New Orleans, also known as 'The Big Easy', for last. She spent two weeks exploring the Pelican State and she loved every minute of it, despite the oppressive heat.

Every city that Mary visited in Louisiana had its unique calling card. Monroe with its many famous museums. Natchitoches with its national historic landmarks. Baton Rouge with its beauty and rich past. Lafayette with its incredible festivals and Cajun music, not to mention the food. And New Orleans with . . . well, New Orleans was a show apart – the wrought-iron balustrades, the sultry riffs of live jazz, the nightlife, the French Quarter – all of it was exactly like what Mary had always imagined it would be, simply spectacular. But not surprisingly, the place that she most wanted to visit in The Big Easy wasn't considered one of the city's main attractions. It was, in fact, just a tiny bar, tucked away right at the corner of Bourbon and St. Philip in the town's French Quarter. The bar was called Lafitte's Blacksmith Shop. The building itself had originally been used as a base of operations for pirates from around 1730 to 1795 – but that had absolutely nothing to do with why Mary wanted to go there so badly.

Through a social media fan group, Mary had found out that several bar scenes that appeared in the first two seasons of *Vamp Blood* had been shot inside Lafitte's. Of course, the bar's interior had been redecorated to better suit the series' vampire theme, but all of its original, century-old fixtures that had featured in those scenes were still there, and the teenager inside Mary just couldn't wait to go see them.

Mary spent three days in New Orleans where, of course, she chose a hotel in the famous French Quarter, the film location for many of the street scenes in *Vamp Blood*. The hotel she picked was just a couple of blocks away from Lafitte's, but she decided to keep the best for last, visiting all the other sites first, before, on her last day in 'The Big Easy', finally quenching a twenty-one-year-old thirst and visiting the vampire bar.

In the TV series, the bar was called The Black Shop, and as Mary got to the corner of Bourbon and St. Philip she paused, her eyes smiling just as much as her lips. The dilapidated building did indeed have a dark and somewhat Gothic mystique to it. If vampires really existed, Mary wouldn't be surprised if that was where they'd hang out.

With a smile that could've rivaled the Joker's, Mary crossed the road and finally, after so many years as a fan of the show, walked through the doors of The Black Shop. As she did, a rush of heat, mixed with the smell of alcohol, immediately washed over her and she paused, but not because of the heat or the smell – somehow, once inside Lafitte's, the place looked a lot more spacious than it did from the outside.

'Vampire magic, I guess,' Mary murmured, the teenager inside her giggling.

Up-tempo jazz played from the ceiling speakers, but the loud and animated chatter coming from just about everywhere, drowned it to nothing more than just background music.

The bar counter was straight ahead, L-shaped and made from stained bricks and mahogany wood. As soon as Mary's eyes settled on it, a happy avalanche of images flooded her memory.

'And there it is,' she said in a nostalgic whisper.

To her left, as the main floor gained a single step to create a split-level floor, she recognized another historic feature that had appeared in several episodes – a floor to ceiling stained-brick fireplace.

Mary's smile widened.

'Hey there,' one of the two bartenders behind the compact bar said, as he got to her. 'Welcome to Lafitte's Blacksmith Shop. What can I do for you tonight?' He was around fifty years old, with a bushy and peppery goatee that could've easily featured on a five-dollar bill.

Mary had never been one to truly appreciate bourbon, but since Nashville, she was beginning to get a taste for it.

'Umm, do you have any Angel's Envy?'

'Of course.' The bartender smiled. 'Would you like it as a shot, a drink, or a chaser?'

'A chaser would be great,' Mary replied. 'Any beer will do.'

As the bartender turned to fetch a beer from the fridge at the other end of the bar, Mary saw a corkboard to the right of the bar's back-wall bottle display . . . and the first picture that caught her eye was one of three *Vamp Blood* actors together – Mary's three favorite characters in the entire show, and the photo had been signed by all three actors.

The bartender came back to Mary, placed a bottle of beer on the counter, and poured her a full shot of Angel's Envy, Kentucky Straight bourbon. He also noticed the way that she was looking at the picture board.

'Were you a fan of the show?' he asked.

Mary nodded. 'I guess you could say that.' She paid the bartender in cash, leaving him a five-dollar tip.

'In that case, welcome to The Black Shop . . . and you should try one of our *Vamp Blood*-inspired cocktails.' He handed her a drinks menu before indicating a section right at the bottom of it. There were three cocktails listed in that particular section – 'Vamp Blood', 'Bluehouse' and 'Cliffhanger'. 'Years ago, we used to have a lot more,' the bartender explained, with a shrug. 'But it's an old show now. A lot of people who come in here have never even heard of it. Those three stayed on the menu because they're actually quite nice.'

'Thanks, I'll certainly try one later.'

The bartender indicated right, past the brick fireplace and into the upper deck of the split-level floor. 'Right on that corner, by that table over there, there's another picture board with loads more photos and some memorabilia. You should go check it out.'

'Oh, for sure. Thanks again.' Mary had a swig of her beer and raised the shot glass at the bartender, who nodded at her.

'To your health,' he said. 'Enjoy.'

She nodded back before downing her chaser in one and walking over to where the bartender had indicated.

Twenty-Eight

The picture board that the bartender had referred to was much larger than the one at the bar, glass-framed and hanging from the wall just behind a small round table that sat inside an alcove at the far end of the floor, and Mary's luck seemed to be in. The three guys who were sitting at that table had just finished their whiskeys and gotten to their feet when Mary rounded the corner.

'Vampire magic,' Mary whispered to herself again, and even before the last of the three men had stepped out of the alcove, Mary was already sliding herself into the seat at the opposite end of the table.

As the men walked away, Mary poured a couple of sips of beer into the whiskey tumblers that they had left behind, and spread them around the table. Now, it looked like she wasn't at the table by herself. Whoever she was there with, could be either at the bar or in the bathroom. A simple trick that more often than not, proved to be quite effective for a woman sitting alone.

Mary's eyes lit up, as her full attention moved from the tumblers to the large, square picture board on the wall. It held several behind-the-scenes photos, where she could see the cameras, the crew, the actors and the director – and she could easily remember most of the scenes depicted in those images. She could even remember some of the dialogues.

'I'm so sorry to bother you.' Mary heard someone call from behind her. 'But could I leave my drink at your table just while I quickly nip to the loo? I won't be long, I promise.'

Mary turned to face a woman who looked to be somewhere in her early thirties. She was a couple of inches taller than Mary, with wavy blonde hair that just touched her shoulders. Her nails had been professionally manicured and her eyebrows professionally plucked. Her eyes were blue and they seemed kind. Her summer dress accentuated her curvy body in a simple but elegant way. She spoke with a foreign accent that Mary couldn't quite place – somewhere in Europe, she thought, but not France. The woman was holding a medieval-looking wooden goblet in one hand and a tabloid paper on the other.

'Umm . . .' Mary looked at the tumblers spread around the table.

'I'll be really quick. I swear,' the woman said, fidget-shuffling from one foot to the other, as if she was getting pee-shivers.

'Yeah, sure,' Mary finally replied, a thin smile gracing her lips. 'Don't worry.'

'Thank you so much.' The woman's eyebrows curved up and in, making her eyes rounder. She placed her drink and the tabloid paper on the table, turned around, and dashed away in the direction of the ladies' bathroom.

Mary's attention was just about to return to the picture board when something floating inside the woman's drink caught her eye. She leaned forward to have a better look at it, before smiling.

The drink inside the goblet was dark in color, and floating around on its surface was a couple of vampire jelly teeth. That had to be one of the three *Vamp Blood* cocktails.

Mary's eyes lingered on the tabloid paper for a moment, before bouncing back to the board.

'Thank you so much,' Mary heard the woman say, as she

returned to the table to collect her drink. 'I really appreciate it.' She fanned herself with the tabloid paper. 'This heat makes me want to go to the loo all the time.'

'That's one of the *Vamp Blood* cocktails, right?' Mary asked, halting the woman as she was just about to walk away.

'I think so, yeah,' the woman replied, turning to face Mary again. 'This is called ... Cliffhanger. It's actually quite nice ... and you get a couple of jelly teeth with it.' She slightly tilted her goblet so that Mary could see them.

Mary smiled. 'Were you a fan of the show?'

'*Vamp Blood*?' The woman seemed to be debating her answer. 'I wouldn't class myself as a "fan". I never watched the whole series, but I did watch quite a few episodes ... maybe a couple of seasons worth?' She didn't sound too sure. 'But that was a long time ago. I was young.' She paused and had a sip of her cocktail. 'How about you? Were you a fan?'

'Pretty much so, yeah,' Mary replied with a half shy, half embarrassed smile.

'Yeah, the bartender told me that a lot of the show was filmed in here,' the woman said.

'It was indeed.' Mary indicated the board behind her.

The woman's eyes moved to it. 'Hold on – that bar fight scene, where one of the vampires – the really good-looking one – crawls along the ceiling and pretty much rips the other guy's head off. D'you remember that?'

'Of course. Season two.'

'Was that filmed in here?'

Mary smiled and nodded at the same time. 'Shot right there by the bar, I'm guessing.'

'Wow, how cool is that? I never knew. I walked in here because it looked like a cool bar from the outside.' She looked around for a quick moment. 'Now that I do, this whole place seems a little different. It's gained a little ... mystique, you know?'

'I know what you mean,' Mary agreed.

'Umm ... I'm Natálie, by the way,' the woman said, offering her hand.

Mary shook it. 'Mary, nice to meet you. So where are you from, originally, if you don't mind me asking? Your accent sounds European, but I can't exactly place it.'

Natálie smiled. 'I'm from Prague, in the Czech Republic, but I live in London, in the UK. This is my first trip to America.'

'Oh really? Business or pleasure?'

'Well ... more recharging than anything else.' Natálie shrugged. 'I just really needed a break from everything and everyone, you know? I was feeling a bit suffocated, so I thought – why not? I've always wanted to visit the US so ... here I am.'

Mary picked up an odd tone to Natálie's explanation – sadness perhaps – the kind of sadness that you didn't ask about. Instead, she indicated the seat across the table from her. 'Do you want to sit down?'

Natálie looked at the whiskey tumblers. 'Umm ... I don't want to intrude.'

'Oh no. There's no one sitting there.' Mary quickly explained her little trick.

Natálie chuckled. 'Good trick, but that wouldn't work where I live. In England, the men wouldn't care. They'd still come and bother you ... probably drink whatever is left in those glasses too.'

Mary smiled then shook her head. 'Not over here. America is a happy suing country. People are terrified of being sued by others for just about anything, really. It's crazy.' She pushed the tumbler away and indicated the seat again. 'Please, sit down.'

Natálie finally accepted the invite. 'Thank you.' As she sat down, her attention flicked over to the picture board. A moment later, she indicated another photo. 'I actually remember this love scene too.'

Mary nodded. 'And it looks like it was all shot right here, inside this little alcove.'

'Amazing.' Natálie looked around again. 'You know, thinking about it, this totally looks like a place where vampires could hang out.'

'I know, right?' Mary tipped her bottle in Natálie's direction, who tapped her goblet against it.

They chatted and drank together for the next two hours. Mary ended up trying all three *Vamp Blood* cocktails, and the bartender was right – they were all pretty good, but also pretty strong. As they finished their third cocktail, Mary and Natálie were both feeling positively tipsy. After another bathroom run, Natálie told Mary that she needed to get going.

'I have an early flight tomorrow,' Natálie explained. 'I'm flying into New York, before getting a connecting flight back to London in the afternoon. And I still haven't packed.'

'Oh, OK!' Mary said back, also getting to her feet. 'Well . . . it was really nice meeting you.'

'Same here,' Natálie said, with a firm nod. 'And I would love to stay in touch, if you like.' She reached inside her handbag for her cellphone. 'We could swap Instagrams, if you like?'

Mary's eyes darted away for an instant. When they came back to Natálie, they came accompanied by a subtle headshake. 'I don't have an Instagram account.'

'Really?' Natálie's eyebrows arched awkwardly, as if she had never met anyone without an Instagram account. 'OK, Facebook works too.'

Another shake of the head. Mary knew that sooner or later this would happen. In today's world, if you had a cellphone, you had to have social media. It was practically mandatory. Why else would you have a cellphone in the twenty-first century? People rarely called each other anymore, unless it was a real emergency.

Sure, Mary could tell her the truth. She could tell anyone she liked that she was actually running scared from an ex-husband, who she had sent to prison for thirteen years, but whose reach went far beyond those prison walls. She could tell anyone she liked that even though Nelson was sitting behind bars, she still didn't feel safe because she knew that someone was already trying to track her down, but that was Samantha Stewart's truth, not Mary Smith's. Nevertheless, Mary needed a plausible story to justify her lack of interest in social media because she knew that people would ask. The story that she came up with was also one hundred percent true . . . borrowed from an old friend. It was simple – not too many details – but it was the kind of story that people tended not to ask too many questions about.

'I had a horrible, very toxic experience with someone who I met through a social media site,' she explained, her eyes averting Natálie's. 'It started well, but very soon it turned into a living nightmare.' She gave Natálie a worried shake of the head before delivering the line that she knew would keep most people from asking any further questions. 'I'm not going to go into all the horrid details of how bad it actually got, but since then, I completely stepped away from social media . . . at least for the time being.'

'Oh God, I'm so, so sorry,' Natálie said, stepping forward and giving Mary a tight hug. 'I completely understand. Social media can be great sometimes, but it can also be absolute hell on earth. There are too many freaks out there.'

Natálie let go of the hug and reached into her handbag once again. This time, she retrieved a pen and the tabloid paper that she was reading earlier.

'Like I said,' she began, unfolding the paper and scribbling something onto it. 'I would really love to stay in touch . . . if you want.' She finished writing, tore the whole page out of the newspaper, folded it four times, and handed it to Mary. 'This is my number. Text or WhatsApp me any time you like. And if you ever want to visit London, just let me know. I'd love to show you around.'

'Thank you,' Mary said, taking the folded page. 'That's very kind of you. I'm going to keep this, and I might take you up on that offer sometime.'

'I really hope you do.'

They hugged each other again.

As Natálie left Lafitte's, Mary returned to her table and placed Natálie's number inside one of the outside pockets of her handbag.

Twenty-Nine

After she got back from Lafitte's, Mary sat alone on the balcony of her third-floor hotel room in the French Quarter. She had a glass of red wine on the coffee table in front of her and what seemed like a carnival of thoughts running rampant inside her head, but one thought was the leader of them all – her relocation to Texas.

The relocation was extremely necessary, that wasn't what Mary had been debating with herself. What she'd become not so sure about was her city choice, Houston – she wasn't so sold on the idea of staying inside the 'Bible Belt' anymore.

Mary's plan had always been to follow George Oakfield's advice of relocating to a different large city every six months and laying low for at least a year. After that, she'd be able to choose a place to be her permanent address and start getting on with her life.

The problem was, the first six months got scrapped because Nelson had, somehow, managed to track her down – and he'd done so inside the 'Bible Belt'. So maybe staying inside the belt wasn't such a great idea anymore. True, Houston was the fourth largest and most populated city in the USA, with over seven hundred Mary Smiths listed in the city's online phone directory, but maybe that was exactly what gangster-suit man and Nelson were expecting her to do – stay where the biggest concentration of Marys resided.

Of the sixteen different cities in the six different states – all of them inside the 'Bible Belt' – that she had visited, she had left almost no paper or digital trail in any one of them. She used cash everywhere, and she quickly figured out that, just like in Franklin, getting the hotel clerk at reception to sign her in using an alias instead of her real name wasn't actually that hard. Mary found out that the same story that she had weaved back at the hotel in Franklin tended to work like a charm. In the past seven weeks, Mary's name had appeared in none of the registers in any of the many hotels that she had stayed in, and if the voice inside her head wanted to call it 'paranoia', fine, but she had also never stopped being cautious. Every time she left her hotel, no matter the city, she would be on high alert, checking the streets for anyone following her . . . paying attention to strangers in restaurants, bars, hotel lobbies, busses, trams, boats . . . wherever . . . looking for gangster-suit man or a face . . . any face . . . that she had probably seen before, and in the past seven weeks, she had seen no signs of either.

In that same period of time, Mary had used her credit card only twice – in two different cities, across two separate states – but that had been all planned . . . just another trick that she had picked up from spy movies.

Mary had no idea if Nelson knew anyone who would be capable of tracking down credit card activities, but that was what they did in films, and if Nelson did know someone, the idea was to purposely leave behind a very thin digital trail, leading to cities that she would never return to.

It was for that reason that for the past hour, Mary had been looking at cities outside the 'Bible Belt', and since Massachusetts was all the way on the far east coast of America, she had concentrated her efforts right on the opposite side of the country – America's west coast – and after several searches and a lot of reading, Mary had decided on another city, which just like New

Orleans, she had always wanted to visit but never really had the chance to – San Francisco, California.

You do remember that we can't really jump on a plane, right? the voice in her head reminded her. *Not for a while. That was how gangster-suit man found us.*

'I know.'

And you do realize that it's over twenty-two hundred miles from New Orleans to San Francisco, right?

'I do.'

That's thirty-something hours in a bus.

'I know.' Mary tapped the 'buy' button on her cellphone screen. 'And we leave tomorrow.'

Thirty

Five Months Later

San Francisco, California

Mary poured herself another glass of wine and took a seat on the leather sofa that faced the large floor-to-ceiling window in her living room. The view wasn't exactly great. All that she could really see was the residential building directly across the road from hers, but the two-bedroom apartment that she had rented was cozy, comfortable and very stylishly decorated ... and she absolutely loved the neighborhood that she lived in.

Once she got to San Francisco, Mary decided to stick to the same thought process that had worked so well for her back in Nashville – look for a place in or around the city's art district. The most that artists would ask anyone about their past would be – 'so where are you from?' – and that was it. No FBI-style interrogation about their history, or how a person came to be there. Mary liked that, and the apartment that she had managed to rent was located right at the edge of the Dogpatch – the most artistic neighborhood in San Francisco – just a block away from the famous San Francisco Bay.

Mary checked her watch – 7:42 p.m. on a Thursday evening. She walked back into her kitchen and was just about ready to pour herself another glass of wine, when the voice inside her head interrupted her.

Umm . . . are we not getting ready?

'What?'

It took Mary just a split second to see it . . . right there, pinned to the fridge door by a pineapple-shaped magnet.

'Oh shit!' She put down her wine glass and checked the time again – 7:43 p.m. 'I completely forgot all about this.' She reached for the flyer that she had pinned to the fridge just over two weeks ago.

Indie art exhibition.
Over twenty emerging artists exhibiting their work for the very first time.
Free entry (donations welcome).
Please come and support your local Dogpatch artists.
One night only.

The gallery address followed.

The Dogpatch neighborhood had once been a very busy shipbuilding hub and signs of its heyday could still be seen just about everywhere. No ships were built around the Dogpatch anymore, but its dockside area had retained its old industrial vibe, with large warehouses and hangers, most of which had been transformed into art galleries, alternative shops, nightlife hangouts and very affordable residential lofts. The apartment that Mary lived in was in one of those lofts, and the art gallery that was putting up the indie exhibition was at the opposite end of the dockside – at least a twenty-five minute walk from her place . . . twenty if she pushed it.

Mary checked her watch for the third time – 7:47 p.m.

She had promised Betsy that she'd be there.

Since arriving in San Francisco, Mary had barely deviated from her plans – no splashing out on anything and keeping herself to herself – just as she'd done in Nashville, and the Golden Gate City had proved to be a paradise in disguise for those who wanted to keep themselves to themselves.

The city was like a clash of parallel universes, capable of being hectic and relaxing at the same time. It could be A-list elite and tremendously expensive at one end, or mega alternative and dirt-cheap at the other. There was so much to see and do that if Mary wanted to, she could go out every night for a couple of years and never visit the same place twice. The choices seemed to be almost infinite because San Francisco truly was a city that catered to everyone, no matter the style, no matter the taste, no matter the budget. Compared to the Deep South, San Francisco was a culture shock.

Despite all the choices, there was a place that Mary had been to more than once – Jolt N Bolt – a bakery and coffee shop that had the most amazing tarts in all of Dogpatch . . . maybe even in all of San Francisco . . . and it was just around the corner from her apartment.

Betsy was a very sweet, Goth-looking, twenty-four-year-old girl, who worked at Jolt N Bolt, usually at the till. Mary had never really spoken to her before, other than to place an order, until about a month ago. That afternoon, Mary had ordered a slice of her favorite tart – chocolate raspberry marquise – together with a regular cappuccino, but instead of having it all to go, as she usually did, Mary took a table by the window and simply sat there, people-watching for a while. She finished her tart and ordered a second cappuccino. Betsy was the one who brought it over to her table.

'Hi,' the Goth-looking girl said in a shy voice. 'I hope you don't mind, but I . . . drew you.' She placed the cappuccino down on the table in front of Mary, who looked up at her a little confused.

'You drew me?' She shook her head. 'What do you m—' Her eyes moved to the cappuccino cup on the table and she paused, her mouth dropping half open.

Using just milk, poured from a beaked jug, and chocolate dust, the girl had drawn Mary's face onto the cappuccino's surface, and it looked uncanny.

'Oh my god!' Mary's eyes bounced between the girl and the cappuccino. 'This is . . . incredible.'

'Oh, thank you.' The girl gave Mary a timid smile. 'I'm so glad you like it.' She turned to walk back to the counter, but Mary paused her.

'Seriously. I've seen a lot of cappuccino art all over the place. I guess it's a thing nowadays, but nothing like this . . . with this much detail. You're very talented.'

'Aww, thank you so much,' the girl said again, averting Mary's eyes. It was clear that she wasn't used to dealing with compliments. 'I really appreciate it.'

'Are you an artist?' Mary pushed. 'I mean . . . do you also draw on paper . . . paint on canvas . . . anything? Please tell me that cappuccino drawing isn't all that you use your talent for.'

The girl finally met Mary's eyes. 'Well . . . I'm trying . . . to be an artist, I mean. I've been drawing since I was a young girl, and yeah, I do both – draw on paper and I also paint on canvas – I love it. It's . . . what makes me happy.'

'And we've got to do what makes us happy, right?'

The girl nodded, her stare, once again, running away from Mary's. 'I guess so . . . like I said . . . I'm trying.'

This time, Mary picked up a terribly sad undertone to the Goth girl's words and movements. 'I'd love to see your work,' she said. 'Do you have any of it here . . . or any photos or anything?'

The girl's smile was coy, but genuine. 'I do have a few photos on my phone. Would you really like to see them?'

'I'd love to.'

'Betsy, we've got customers, girl,' someone called from behind the counter in a tone that sounded a lot angrier than the moment warranted.

Betsy's eyes blinked nervously a couple of times. 'I'm so sorry,' she said to Mary.

Mary's gaze scooted over to the counter. Standing behind it was a bald man of average height, with a really unflattering nose. His stare could've burned a hole at the back of Betsy's head.

'It's alright,' Mary replied. 'I'll be sitting here for a while. I'm Mary, by the way.' She offered her hand.

'Betsy.' She shook it. 'It's really nice to meet you.'

In the days and weeks that followed, Mary and Betsy struck up a somewhat cordial friendship. Every time Mary went back to Jolt N Bolt, they would talk for a while.

About two weeks ago, as Mary walked into the coffee shop to grab a cappuccino to go, Betsy gave her the widest smile Mary had ever seen grace the Goth girl's lips. 'I got a place at an exhibition,' she said, offering Mary a flyer, almost bouncing from one foot to the other out of excitement. 'I'm allowed to display up to five pieces.'

'Oh my god. That's amazing.' Mary took the flyer and gave Betsy a hug. 'Congratulations. I'm so happy for you.'

'Will you come?' Betsy asked with puppy eyes. 'Please … it would mean a lot if you did.'

'Of course I will.' Mary's smile was almost as happy as Betsy's. 'It will be an absolute pleasure.'

Mary rushed into her bedroom and swung open the wardrobe doors.

Just like she'd done back in Nashville, Mary had kept her private belongings down to a bare minimum. The apartment that she had rented came fully furnished, and though she'd been itching to add her own personal touches to the décor, she'd somehow managed to restrain herself from doing so. Her wardrobe was pitiful. It looked more like a disused cupboard than anything else, but there was a flipside – at least she never ended up spending an hour trying different outfits before going out.

Mary caught a glimpse of her reflection on the wardrobe door mirror. She was wearing black jeans and a blue-and-white striped, long-sleeved shirt.

'Yeah, this will do,' she said to herself, as her eyes darted to the window for an instant. There was no sign of rain, but the temperature outside was around 52°F – not exactly cold – but if she was to walk for twenty minutes by the Bay, she'd need more than just a jacket, and in her limited wardrobe, there was only one option – a knitted white sweater that she had bought a week or so after arriving in San Francisco. She reached for it, put it on, and rushed into the bathroom. Her makeup also wasn't that bad. All she needed was to reapply some lipstick, maybe a new coat of eyeliner, and put her contact lenses back in. Her hair had already grown long enough for her to not need her wig anymore . . . and she kept the style pretty much identical.

Makeup reapplied and look restored, Mary was ready to go. At the front door, she slipped into her black ankle boots, grabbed her leather jacket from one of the hooks on the wall, and checked the time one last time – 8:02 p.m.

The flyer said that the exhibition closed at 9:00 p.m.

Mary reached for her handbag and quickly checked its contents – the same as always – including her go-bag.

She locked the door behind her and hurried towards the stairs, completely oblivious that that night would give George Oakfield's old clichéd sentence – 'this is the first day of the rest of your life' – a brand-new meaning.

Thirty-One

Located inside an old warehouse, the art gallery where the exhibition was taking place was extremely spacious, with tall office-like partitions that had been arranged to create a labyrinth of corridors, leading to different rooms.

Mary made it to the warehouse with over half an hour to spare before the exhibition was due to close. The place seemed packed.

At the entry doors, she was greeted by the gallery owners, a charming gay couple in their early forties, who handed her a map of the labyrinth inside. According to the map, Betsy was sharing a small room with one other artist, located about halfway down the labyrinth. Mary unzipped her leather jacket and began making her way through the crowd and the corridors. She navigated past four different rooms before she finally got to the one where Betsy's pieces were being displayed.

'Oh my god, you made it,' Betsy said, as soon as she saw Mary appear at the door. Her entire face seemed to morph into a giant smile.

'Of course.' Mary smiled back, giving Betsy a hug. 'I told you I'd be here, didn't I? And wow . . .' She took a step back, allowing her eyes to look at Betsy from head to toe. 'You look fantastic.'

'Aww, thank you so much,' Betsy said, showing Mary inside. There were about ten people inside the small room. 'Have you seen the other rooms yet? There are some incredible artists displaying here tonight.'

'I haven't.' Mary came clean. 'I'm a little late. I just got here, so I came straight to your room.'

'I really am glad you came.' Betsy hugged Mary again. 'I'll leave you to look around on your own, it's better that way, but please come find me at the end, OK?'

'Of course.'

The lighting in the room was moody . . . almost somber, reflecting the theme of the art pieces displayed in it. As Betsy walked away, Mary turned to face the wall to her right, where three people had gathered, all attentively studying a painting that hung from it. Mary decided that that would be a good place to start.

The piece was a framed, 24 by 24 inches, spray-painted canvas. It was titled *Veils of Darkness*, by Judith Wallace – the other artist who was sharing the room with Betsy.

'Amazing, don't you think?' a dark-haired woman with a hawk nose and large dangling earrings commented, addressing the older gentleman standing to her right. His hair was cut short, exposing his ears, which seemed a little too large for his head.

Mary had paused just a step or so behind them.

'You can clearly see the veils through all that darkness if you angle your body just a little to either side,' the woman continued. 'It's all a question of perspective and contrast.' As she said those words, the woman swung her body a few inches to her left, paused for a second or two, then swung it over a few inches to her right, in a slow rocking motion.

Mary frowned, took a second, and then copied the woman's swinging motion – first left, then right. As she did, through the corner of her eye, she noticed that the man standing to her left was doing the exact same.

'Yeah, I see it,' the gentleman standing with the woman ahead of Mary said. He too was gently moving his body from left to right in front of the painting.

'And look.' The woman carried on. 'From this angle.' She stopped with the gentle rocking motion and tilted only her head to her right. 'In a standing still position, you can see a different effect – as if the veils were flailing in the wind.'

Mary's frown deepened, as she too paused her subtle swinging motion and once again, copied the woman's movement.

The man to Mary's left did the same. His frown was just as deep as hers.

'I love it,' the woman continued. 'What an incredible piece.'

'Absolutely phenomenal,' the gentleman with her said in agreement, but his words seemed to lack conviction.

As they walked away, Mary stood motionless, her eyes still on the painting on the wall in front of her, but the look on her face was one of total confusion. She repeated the swinging motion first, then the head movement.

'Was she joking?' the man who had been standing to Mary's left that whole time asked, in an almost monotone voice. 'Or can you actually see any of the things that that woman just said? Veils flailing in the wind and whatnot?' He was standing still, except for his head, which he kept on angling slightly right before straightening it back again, then repeating the movement.

'Not even close,' Mary replied, her eyes still on the painting. 'You?'

'Not a thing. Regardless of the angle, all I can see is a squared canvas sprayed black. That's all.'

Mary nodded because that was exactly what they'd been looking at for the past two minutes – a squared canvas that had been evenly sprayed with black paint. No matter how much they rocked their bodies or angled their heads, all they could see was a black canvas.

'Yeah, I'm going to have to agree with you here,' Mary said

back, finally allowing her eyes to move to the man. As she did, her breath got caught somewhere between her nostrils and her lungs.

He was around six-foot tall, give or take. His black hair was tousled carelessly, with some stray edges curling in and out in all different directions, which gave him a youthful, somewhat skater look, even though he appeared to be in his early thirties. His three o'clock shadow was naturally uniform, over skin that was a couple of shades away from olive. His body was slender but muscular, something that was clearly noticeable by how much his long-sleeved shirt stretched over his chest and biceps. His eyes, under strong eyebrows, were just as dark as his hair, adding a touch of mystery to a face that was certainly attractive, but not in a traditional sense. He wasn't movie star good-looking, but there was a certain quality about him that Mary found it hard to define – a weird sort of magnetism, perhaps. It was as if the more that she looked at him, the more everyone else in the room seemed to dim away, while he simply stood there . . . drawing all the light into his center.

'Well,' he said, this time locking eyes with Mary. 'The piece is called *Veils of Darkness*. I can definitely see the darkness, so I guess one out of two isn't so bad.'

Mary finally breathed out and smiled a smile that lingered for a couple of seconds longer than it should have. 'I guess so.'

'Sorry,' the man said, reaching for his cellphone that had just started vibrating inside his back pocket. He checked the screen, raised his eyebrows, and quickly exited the room, while bringing the phone to his ear.

Mary stood still for another couple of seconds, wondering where such incredible magnetism came from. Was it charm? Charisma? His looks? A combination of everything? Mary couldn't really tell, but it was obvious that she wasn't alone in her thoughts because as the man stepped outside the room, Mary saw at least two other women turn to follow him with their eyes.

She chuckled, before her eyes moved left to another art piece, this one a 42 by 30 inches, unframed, oil-on-canvas painting. The piece was titled “Reflection”. The artist – Betsy Fletcher.

As Mary’s eyes studied Betsy’s work, she felt goosebumps caress the back of her neck. This was nothing like *Veils of Darkness*.

The painting depicted a woman, who looked to be no older than twenty-four . . . maybe . . . standing inside a bathroom, staring at her reflection in the mirror. The only problem was, the two images – the woman in front of the mirror and her reflection – didn’t quite match each other.

The woman, who looked devastatingly attractive in the painting, was standing confidently and carefree . . . chin up . . . squared shoulders . . . vivid eyes fixed forward . . . flawless skin . . . and long, black shiny hair that seemed to belong to a Disney princess. The smile on her lips was so bright, it could’ve substituted a star up in the night sky.

Her reflection, on the other hand, showed none of those qualities. The breathtaking beauty had, somehow, withered away from her. The vivid eyes looked almost void of life and tremendously sad, with the white in them tinged yellow, and their veins looking like a map of tiny burst blood vessels. The smile had also vanished from her lips, and the impression that Mary got was that they looked to be quivering, but not from cold, or sadness . . . they were quivering from fear. Her posture had lost all of its confidence, with her shoulders slumped forward and her chin down, as if even at such a young age, life had already defeated her. The shine in her hair had turned dull, and her once flawless skin was blotchy, with a few odd thin lines showing on her forehead and left cheek, but they looked more like scars than wrinkles.

Despite it being a little disturbing, Mary really did like the painting. It was an impressive piece of art, created by a very talented artist, but what had truly touched Mary’s feelings was that that painting was clearly a self-portrait of Betsy – a girl who was trying her best to appear strong and happy, but who, at such a young age, seemed to have already been through so much. To put it in simple terms – the bright outside didn't reflect the hurt, nor the fear, or the darkness from the inside. But the most incredible aspect of that piece was that it didn't only reflect Betsy's life, it reflected a whole world of people out there – including Mary herself.

Thirty-Two

Mary spent just a little under five minutes looking through the remainder of Betsy's paintings that were being displayed inside that room – four extra pieces. They were all fantastic creations, but the one titled *Reflection* had truly grabbed her in a way that she wasn't expecting it to.

Mary had always loved art, especially dark-themed paintings and drawings, but not because she was a connoisseur or understood a lot about the subject – on the contrary, Mary knew very little about art. Her expertise came from the old tradition of looking at it. She either liked it or she didn't. It was that simple, but sometimes – and this was much rarer – she would get goosebumps, just like tonight, but tonight there was something else ... something that had never happened to her before. As Mary looked at Betsy's *Reflection* painting, she felt as if it was looking back at her. There was so much in that piece that Mary could relate to.

There was no red-dot sticker next to it, which meant that the painting hadn't been sold yet.

'Yeah, I'm getting it,' she said to herself with a firm nod, noting down the reference number.

Mary exited Betsy's exhibition room, but as she got to the end of the corridor and turned left, she almost bumped into the gallery owner, the same man who had handed her a map of the exhibition at the front door.

'Oh, hello,' she said, with a smile. 'I was just coming to find you.'

'Oh, wonderful.' His eyebrows arched at her. 'Have you seen something you like?'

'Yes, very much so.'

'Great!' He smiled back, showing perfectly aligned teeth. 'I'm so glad that you found something to your liking. If you give me just a minute, I'll be right with you. I'm just going into a room to mark a piece as sold and I'll be right back.' He indicated down the corridor. 'If you wait for me at the entrance to the exhibition, I'll meet you there and we can finalize everything.'

'Will do.'

But as the man walked away from Mary, she didn't move, instead, she followed him with her eyes. He walked past a room to his left before turning right and entering the same room that Mary had just walked out from.

'Oh no, no, no.' She rushed after him. As she got to the door, she saw the gallery owner pull a red-dot sticker from a booklet that he had brought with him and place it on the wall, right next to *Reflection.*

'Oh no.' She quickly caught up with him. 'You've got to be kidding. This is the one I wanted. The one that I was just rushing to you to go purchase.'

'Oh really?' The man sounded truly sorry as he looked back at the painting for a couple of seconds. 'It's a magnificent piece. You've got great taste.' His lips stretched into a thin line as his head angled slightly left. 'And I'm so sorry that you've missed it, but there are loads of other amazing pieces that are still available ... some in this very room. Isn't there anything else that you've seen that you liked?'

Mary shook her head. 'Not as much as this one, really.' She hadn't had time to look at any other piece outside that room, but she made it sound like she had. 'Are you sure this one's gone?' She gave the gallery owner her best 'puppy eye' look.

For the sake of politeness, the man checked the screen on the tablet that he had with him. 'Yeah, this is the one.' He nodded. 'Reflection ... room five ... Betsy Fletcher.' He then read out the same reference number that Mary had noted down moments earlier. 'I'm so sorry.'

'Can't we maybe negotiate?' Mary tried. 'I can offer over the asking price. Would that work?'

The smile the man gave Mary was a courteous one. 'Unfortunately, that's not how it works in these sorts of exhibitions. Tonight, it's not an auction. Each piece has a set price tag attached to it, and that's the price, not the highest bid. Once the piece has been purchased, it's gone. We keep them on the walls so that everyone can still appreciate them, but it's not available for purchase anymore.'

Mary pressed her lips together, her puppy eyes still in place.

'If you want,' the gallery owner said, being sympathetic to Mary's frustration, 'I can introduce you to the artist, Betsy Fletcher. She might have something similar in her studio, or you can commission something from her. I'm sure that she'll be ever so happy to oblige.'

'I know Betsy,' Mary replied. 'She was the one who invited me over tonight.'

'Oh, that's great,' the gallery owner sounded truly pleased. 'Have you spoken to her about this piece?'

'Not yet.' A subtle but sad shake of the head.

'You should.' He indicated the room. 'But she still has a few pieces available. Do have a look.' He quickly consulted his watch. 'Well, if you'd excuse me, I need to get back.'

'How about if you introduce me to the person who bought the painting?' Mary tried playing one last card. 'Maybe I can negotiate directly with the buyer.'

The man paused and turned to face Mary. 'Sorry, I didn't catch your name earlier.'

'Mary.'

'I'm Harvey Steiner. It's a pleasure to meet you.' He tucked his lips in for a split second. 'I can see that you really want that piece.'

Mary nodded once. 'I do.'

'I can also see that you're not very familiar with how exhibitions or art galleries work.' His tone was explanatory without sounding condescending. 'Unfortunately, no gallery owner, auctioneer, art broker, salesperson . . . whoever . . . reveals the names of their buyers. If we did, we wouldn't have a business. Believe me. Art is a very private matter to collectors.' He checked the time again. 'There's still around ten minutes before we close and there are so many amazing art pieces still available. Just look around, maybe you can find something else you like, or if you come visit us during regular hours, I'll gladly show you our vast portfolio of artists. You might find something you like then, but in regards to the "Reflection" piece, unfortunately it's gone.'

Mary could see that Steiner was being as diplomatic as he could.

As he walked away, Mary returned to the room to check Betsy's remaining pieces. Out of the five that were being displayed that evening, only two were still available.

Mary paused in front of the one that she liked the most out of those two – an 18 by 12 inches, unframed, oil-on-canvas portrait of a brunette woman. The woman had her hands up, almost to her face, but not quite. They were cupped together just by her chin, as if she was about to drink water from an open tap . . . but there was no water. That wasn't the reason why her hands were cupped together beneath her chin. They were there to try to collect the pieces of her own face that were dropping off like broken shards of glass. The painting was titled *Fragmented*.

'It seems like you really like this room.'

The man's voice came from Mary's left, catching her a little off guard. The surprise made her blink once, before turning to face the same man who, a few minutes earlier, had tried and failed to see any veils of darkness together with her. Mary blinked again before her lips parted, as if she was about to say something, but no words came out. All she did was study his face – the contour of his chin, the outline of his lips, the shape of his eyes . . . all of it.

It took only a couple of seconds for the silent 'facing each other' situation to become a little awkward.

'Did you . . .' his right index finger pointed to the piece that they were both looking at earlier. 'Manage to finally see any veils of darkness over there?' The question had clearly been asked because due to Mary's hesitation, the man thought that she probably couldn't remember who he was.

Mary finally smiled as she shook her head. 'No, I gave up.' And that was it – no follow up – she simply went quiet again, and just like that, they were right back to the awkward 'facing each other' situation.

The man paused for an instant, as if not sure of what to do next. His eyes dropped to the floor for a split second before darting away from Mary, a clear giveaway that he had interpreted Mary's short answer as a sign that she had no intentions of having a conversation with a total stranger, and her silence was a hint for him to leave her alone – and that was exactly what he was about to do when Mary surprised him.

'I'm Mary, by the way,' she said, offering her hand and a new smile that was shy, but inviting.

The man smiled back as he reached out for her hand. 'I'm Thomas. It's a pleasure to meet you.'

His handshake was firm, confident, but not in a businesslike way.

Mary's eyes, once again, stayed on Thomas' face for longer than she had intended, but this time, her forehead creased into a slight frown.

'Do . . .' Thomas gently touched his own face with the tips of his fingers. 'Do I have something on my face?'

'No,' Mary replied. 'Not at all . . . it's just that you don't look like a Thomas.'

It was Thomas' turn to frown. 'Don't I?' The frown was followed by a half smile. 'What would you say that I look like then?'

'I don't know,' Mary returned the smile. 'A Maximilian . . . or maybe an Ambrose?'

Thomas laughed, but paused a second or two later, as Mary held on to her poker face. 'What? You're serious? Ambrose? Really?'

Mary couldn't hold it any longer. The surprise in Thomas' face caused her to burst out into laughter.

There was a small delay before Thomas followed suit. 'Damn! You really had me there. I thought you were serious.'

'When I was a young girl, in school,' Mary explained, 'I had a teacher called Thomas . . . and you look nothing like him. Now, every time I hear the name Thomas, that's the image that forms in my mind. That's why I said you don't look like a Thomas. I meant no offense.'

'Oh, none taken. Don't worry . . . and that's a very common type of memory association,' Thomas admitted. 'We all do it on one level or another.' He paused for a quick second, as if considering what to say next. 'Did you like that teacher, Thomas, when you were in school?'

Mary pressed her lips tightly together for an instant. 'I hated him with all my might.'

They both broke into laughter for a second time.

Mary couldn't help thinking that Thomas truly did have an odd sort of magnetism that she was finding hard to fight. Even his voice carried a certain attractive quality with it – husky, but not excessively so – the kind of voice that wouldn't be out of place narrating a nature documentary.

'Did you like anything enough to buy it?' he asked, bringing the subject back to the exhibition they were in. '*Veils of Darkness*, perhaps?'

Another smile from Mary, this one accompanied by an eyebrow lift. 'I decided to skip that one.' She pointed to Betsy's *Reflection* painting on the wall to their right. 'But I did like this piece very much. Unfortunately, I missed it by minutes apparently. I tried to charm the gallery owner . . . even offered him over the asking price, but no – he wasn't having it.'

'Oh yeah,' Thomas agreed. 'I liked that one too . . . very complex.' He then indicated the piece that Mary was looking at when he approached her – *Fragmented*. 'This one is also very nice . . . very powerful.'

'Oh damn!' Mary said, consulting her watch. 'I was just thinking about getting this one, but I've got to rush before the exhibition closes.'

'Good choice.' Thomas also checked his watch. 'And yeah, this whole thing will close in just under five minutes, but there's no real rush. If the piece hasn't sold, they'll still sell it to you after the exhibition has closed.'

'Right.' Mary made no attempt to hide the sarcasm in the way she nodded. 'That's exactly how I missed out on that piece.' She pointed at the *Reflection* painting again.

'Point taken,' Thomas accepted.

'Mary,' Betsy called from the door to the room, grabbing Mary and Thomas' attention. They were the only two left in that room. 'I've been looking for you.' She joined them by her own painting. 'The exhibition is closing in about four minutes. Did you . . .' Her eyes moved to Thomas and she went quiet.

Awkward facing each other situation – take three.

'Betsy,' Mary said, noticing the odd moment and wondering if she had done the exact same thing earlier. 'This is Thomas.' Her attention skipped to him. 'Thomas, this is Betsy Fletcher.'

Thomas' head tilted slightly right, as he recognized the name. 'You're the artist.'

Betsy's smile was a little shy. 'I am. Yes.'

'Great pleasure to meet you,' Thomas said, shaking Betsy's hand. 'You're very talented. This was easily my favorite room tonight.'

'Betsy.' Mary interrupted the pleasantries. 'I'm going to really quickly go talk to the gallery owner before the exhibition closes.'

'Oh, OK,' Betsy finally peeled her eyes away from Thomas. 'I'll come with you. I need to talk to him about something as well.'

Are you going to ask Thomas for his number, or what? the voice inside Mary's head asked.

She completely ignored it. 'Well,' she said, facing him, 'it was nice to meet you, Thomas.' She gave him a polite head nod.

Betsy frowned ever so slightly.

'The pleasure was mine,' Thomas said back. This time, it was his eyes that lingered on Mary's face for longer than expected, as if he wanted to say something else, but decided against it.

'Bye,' Betsy said. Her wave was just as timid as her smile.

Mary and Betsy exited the room and started down the corridor.

'Wow!' Betsy said, her eyes widening at Mary, as they turned left then right. 'Did you just meet him tonight?'

Mary nodded. 'Just after I got here.'

'I've seen him before,' Betsy said. 'At different galleries and exhibitions around town. He must be a collector or something.'

'Maybe. I didn't ask.'

'But you got his number, right?'

I told you.

'No, I didn't.'

Betsy stopped walking.

Mary followed suit.

'Why not?' Betsy asked. 'He's hot . . . and clearly into you. Did you notice the way that he was looking at you when you said goodbye.'

'A little.' Once again, Mary did her best to sound breezy.

They started walking again.

'So why didn't you ask for his number?' Betsy pushed. 'Or at least exchanged Instagram, Facebook . . . something.'

They exited the labyrinth and walked past the bar, which was already shut.

'I don't know about me asking him for his phone number,' Mary said. 'Sounds too desperate, don't you think?'

Betsy chuckled. 'Where are we? Mid-1980s? That kind of taboo is long gone.'

Mary paused, her lips pursing to one side, as she thought about it for an extra moment. 'You don't think it sounds desperate?'

'Not at all.' Betsy's shake of the head seemed decisive. 'And do you know what else I think? That he was probably about to ask you for *your* number, but you didn't give him a chance. You shot out of that room like a bullet.'

Mary took another second. 'So, you think I should go back?'

Yes.

'Yes.'

For one thing, the voice in her head added. *We could really do with some real sex. Give that poor rabbit a rest, you know what I'm saying?'*

'Shut up,' Mary whispered.

'No, I'm serious,' Betsy replied, assuming that Mary was addressing her. 'Go.' She nodded in the direction of the labyrinth again. 'Seriously . . . go.'

'Alright.' Mary gave in, quickening her step to get back to the corridor – two minutes to closing time. She then turned left then right and finally got back to room five – Betsy's exhibition room.

It was empty.

Thomas was nowhere to be seen.

Annnnnd we're back to the rabbit.

Thirty-Three

Three Days Later

Mary had spent the day walking around the world-famous neighborhood of Haight-Ashbury – without a doubt the hippest neighborhood in the whole of San Francisco and the birthplace of the Summer of Love movement in 1967. Fast forward sixty-odd years and that peace and love, ultra-artistic and creative aspect of the hippie movement was still very much present all around Haight-Ashbury – and it was that tranquil, laid-back vibe that Mary loved so much.

On her way back home, Mary stopped by Jolt N Bolt to grab a coffee and a freshly made salad bowl for her dinner.

'Mary,' Betsy said, as soon as Mary stepped into the bakery. 'I've got a delivery for you.' Her eyes widened and the smile that she gave Mary was a little cryptic, but enthusiastic nonetheless.

Mary paused, her brow creasing at Betsy, as her entire demeanor became one huge question mark. 'A delivery? For me? What?'

Betsy nodded. 'Hold on. I'll go get it.'

As Betsy disappeared into the back of the shop, Mary felt her blood run cold, triggering an avalanche of questions inside her head. How was she getting a delivery if she hadn't ordered anything? From who? And why deliver it to a coffee shop? Had she been found again? Had Nelson managed to somehow track her down all the way to the west coast of the country? How was that possible?

Mary knew that she hadn't let her guard down, not once since gangster-suit man and Nashville. No matter where she went, she still always checked the streets for anyone following her, and she always did her best to pay attention to strangers, looking for anyone who might've been watching her. Not once, in over seven months, had she seen any signs of a shadow.

Betsy reappeared carrying a large rectangular package, which had been wrapped in brown paper. Mary's eyes narrowed for a second time, but this was intrigue, not apprehension. The package was large in size, but not exactly thick in volume.

'Betsy,' Mary asked, her head twisting right. 'Are you sure that's for me?'

Mary didn't want to say that no one really knew where she lived, with the exception of the realtor who she had rented her apartment from, but that was exactly what she was thinking – how could she get a package delivered to her if no one had her address?

Betsy nodded, sending a daring wink Mary's way. 'Oh, I'm sure it's for you.' She paused for effect. 'It's from Thomas.'

Mary's entire upper body angled back slightly, as if she'd just been hit by a strong gust of wind. 'Sorry . . . what?'

'It's from Thomas,' Betsy told her again, joining Mary by one of the tables and handing her the large package. 'He delivered it himself earlier this afternoon.'

'Thomas?' Mary shook her head, trying to understand what was happening. 'The guy from the exhibition? How did . . . ? How did he know to come here? To this coffee shop?' She placed the package on the table to her left.

'He saw us together, remember? At the end of the exhibition? I was looking for you – you were in the room with him? You even introduced me to him.'

'Yeah, of course I remember, but how did he know to come here to Jolt N Bolt?'

'Oh, I told him to,' Betsy replied.

'You . . .' Mary paused. This was getting confusing. 'I thought you said you didn't know him.'

'I don't . . . I didn't,' Betsy tried to clarify. 'Well, do you remember that little catalogue that you got at the exhibition last Thursday, the one naming the artists exhibiting that evening . . . the works . . . and with the map of that crazy labyrinth?'

Mary nodded. 'Yes, of course.'

'OK,' Betsy continued. 'Well, the contact details to all the artists displaying that evening was included in there, and since he saw us together at the exhibition, he figured that we were friends.'

Mary stayed silent while she thought about it for a moment.

'You must've left a great impression because he wanted to give you a present,' Betsy said, nodding at Mary and indicating the package on the table. 'But he had no idea of how to get in touch with you.'

'So, he figured that since we were friends,' Mary concluded, 'you'd probably know.'

'Exactly, but he was very diplomatic about it.'

'Diplomatic?' Mary frowned.

Betsy nodded. 'Yeah . . . he was very gentleman-like – he never asked me for your number or your address.' She shrugged. 'Which I don't have anyway, but even if I did, I would've never given it to *anyone* without clearing it with you first . . . and he sounded like he knew that. He knew that it would be inappropriate for him to ask *me* for *your* number, so he never did.'

Mary's eyebrows arched, showing surprise and interest in equal measures. 'So, what did he say?'

'He asked me if it would be OK for him to drop off something, so that I could pass it on to you.'

'Hum!' Mary's attention bounced over to the package for an instant before returning to Betsy.

'I told him "Yeah, no problem",' Betsy continued. 'So, I gave him the address of the bakery, and he turned up just after lunchtime with this.' Her chin jerked in the direction of the package. 'I'll be honest with you, when he said that he had a gift for you, I thought that he'd turn up with some flowers, or maybe a box of chocolates or something. I wasn't expecting a painting, which this clearly is. But it makes sense, since he met you at an art exhibition . . . but that's not all.' She lifted her left index finger at Mary while reaching into her back pocket. 'There's a card.' She retrieved a golden envelope – the size of a postcard – and handed it to Mary. There was nothing on the envelope except Mary's name handwritten in black ink across the front of it.

Mary took it and stared at it for several long and silent seconds.

'I told you that he was into you!' Betsy's smile seemed naughty.

Mary tore open the envelope and pulled out a folded white piece of paper, with a handwritten note on it.

I think this was the one you really liked.
Enjoy.
Thomas

It was clear to see that there was something else on the inside of the folded note – a loose piece of paper, rectangular in shape. Mary unfolded the note to find a printed invitation and second handwritten note.

I'm not sure if you're free this coming Wednesday, but if you are, this is an invite to the Grand Opening of a brand-new exhibition at the Legion of Honor. I think that this is something you might really enjoy . . . plus, it would be truly nice to see you again.

I hope you can make it.
Thomas

Mary turned the note over. That was it. There was nothing else written on the back of it – no email . . . no phone number . . . no real way of contacting Thomas.

Her attention moved to the stylish invitation. Its backdrop was a printed image showing the façade of the Legion of Honor – a magnificent open-hall, white-pillared building, with a grand, arched main entrance that could've easily belonged to Ancient Greece, or Julius Caesar's Rome. Printed over the image, in striking, embossed, silver lettering was the following message:

YOU ARE HEREBY CORDIALLY INVITED TO ATTEND THE GRAND OPENING OF THE 'DARK AMERICA EXHIBITION' – AN EXTRAORDINARY COLLECTION OF DARK THEMED AMERICAN ART DATING BACK TO THE CIVIL WAR.
WEDNESDAY, FEBRUARY 20TH – 19:00 –
AT THE LEGION OF HONOR.
INVITATION ONLY.

'Oh my god!' Betsy's eyes almost popped out of their sockets, as she indicated the invite in Mary's hand. 'That's an invitation for Dark America.'

Mary nodded without making eye contact. She certainly wasn't expecting this. She checked the reverse of the invitation – again – no email or phone number.

'That's going to be an amazing exhibition.' Betsy's excitement was palpable. 'I've been waiting for it for months, but it will only be open to the public from next Monday on. That, right there . . .' she, once again, pointed to the invitation that Mary was holding, '. . . is a hot, hot ticket. You really have to be in with the in-crowd, or very rich, to manage to get your hands on one of those.'

Mary nodded at nothing at all, just a reflexive acceptance gesture. She paused for a second, as if uncertain of what to do before returning the note and the invitation to the envelope and placing it inside her handbag.

'Aren't you gonna open it?' Betsy asked, her gaze bouncing from the package on the table back to Mary.

'I'm not sure,' Mary replied, staring at the wrapped painting and giving it an extra moment's thought. She was pretty sure that she knew exactly what painting that was. 'Probably not.' Her right hand came up to her neck and she allowed the tips of her fingers to lightly brush against her neck dimple.

'Really?' Betsy looked truly surprised. 'Why not?'

Mary bit her bottom lip, as her left shoulder came up ever so slightly. 'Because I'm not sure I'm going to keep it. If I don't, then I'd like to return the gift to him exactly how I got it.'

'Oh.' Betsy needed a second to think about what Mary had just said. 'Why wouldn't you keep it?'

'Like you said before,' Mary explained, 'I didn't get flowers, or even a box of chocolates. I got a painting . . . and an invite to a very exclusive party, by the looks of it.'

Betsy's eyes widened before she frowned. She was clearly struggling to see the problem.

'From someone who I met for the first time three days ago,' Mary continued. 'And who I chatted to for no more than . . . three minutes? Maybe?' She read the look on Betsy's face and decided to clarify. 'I wouldn't exactly call myself a feminist, but I'm not sure I'm OK with this. Trust me when I say that some men will simply take things for granted, Betsy.' She reached for the painting. 'And what I mean by that is – the bigger the gift, the more that they'll expect in return . . . and some men, if they don't get what they expect to get, they'll simply take it, as if it were their right, just because they gave you a gift, or paid for dinner or something.'

Betsy's eyebrows arched again, but this time it came with the pursing of her lips and a gentle head nod.

'I know nothing about Thomas.' Mary reached inside her handbag for the golden envelope and waved it at Betsy. 'Except for the fact that he seems to be well connected . . .' She thought about it for a beat. 'Or very rich . . .' She thought about it again. 'Or both.'

Betsy nodded. 'He's also very hot.'

This time, Mary laughed. 'Then there's that.' She picked up the wrapped painting and turned towards the door.

'Even if you don't keep the painting,' Betsy pushed, 'you gonna go to the Grand Opening, right? Seriously, you can't miss that.'

Mary's reply was a simple angling of the head.

'If you decide not to go,' Betsy called, as Mary got to the door, 'can I have that invite . . . please?'

'If I don't go,' Mary said, practically already out the door, 'it's all yours.'

Thirty-Four

Back in her apartment, Mary kept the living room lights dimmed, using a single corner lamp to give the spacious room just enough light so that she wouldn't bump into any furniture. She kicked off her shoes and placed the wrapped painting on the low coffee table at the center of the room before pouring herself a large glass of red wine. When she left Jolt N Bolt, just over five minutes ago, she completely forgot to get both the coffee and the salad bowl that she had originally gone there to get, but it didn't matter – her appetite was all but gone and right then, Mary needed wine much more that she needed coffee.

She walked back to the living room and paused by the coffee table and the painting.

There was no point in opening the package because Mary knew exactly what it was.

I think this was the one you really liked.

When talking to Thomas at the exhibition on Thursday evening, there had been only one painting she'd mentioned liking – Betsy's *Reflection* piece – the one that she really wanted to get. Sure, Mary had also mentioned liking a second piece from Betsy – *Fragmented* – but that one was hanging on the wall to her right. She had purchased it at the end of the exhibition.

But if that was Betsy's *Reflection*, how the hell did Thomas manage to get hold of it?

Mary had another sip of her wine, while she thought of a plausible answer. It took her only a few seconds to come up with two – either this Thomas fellow really was in with the in-crowd, or he was the one who had bought the painting in the first place. If option one was the winner, then Thomas must've had to pull a few strings to get his hands on that piece. What that indicated was that Betsy was right – Mary must've left a very good impression for Thomas to want to impress her like that. If option two was the correct one, then Betsy was more than right, because that meant that Thomas had purchased the "Reflection" piece before he'd even met Mary at the end of the exhibition, which in turn meant that he was giving up something that he'd actually wanted for himself just to please her.

I like option two, the voice inside Mary's head butt in. *That means that he really wants to get into your pants.*

'I know.'

I'd let him.

'Shut up.'

Just saying.

Mary rounded the sofa and finally sat down.

Outside, as the day faded into night, a few menacing clouds began gathering above the harbor. She observed them for a while, hoping that enough of them would cluster together to produce some rain, maybe even a heavy downpour.

Mary loved the rain. She had done so since she was a little kid. To her, it had always been easier to hide in the rain because her stepfather didn't like standing in it for too long, so he'd give up before he was able to find her . . . and if he couldn't find her, he couldn't hurt her.

But Mary had always loved standing in the rain. To her, it was like a magic coat that not only protected her from her stepfather, but it also washed away the blood, it rid her hair from his whiskey breath, it cleansed her skin from his awful smell, and it hid the tears that she always tried so hard not to cry. She also loved falling asleep to the sound of rain – thunder or no thunder. To Mary, the constant drumming of raindrops against windowsills, rooftops, trees, whatever, had an almost unearthly calming effect. Rain also helped her think, and that was exactly what she needed to do right then.

She stretched her legs, and put her feet up on the coffee table. She'd be lying if she said that she hadn't thought about Thomas since the exhibition on Thursday evening. She wasn't the only one who had left an impression that night.

Mary gazed at the note that came with the painting before allowing her eyes to settle on the invitation – no phone number, no email, no way of getting in touch with him.

'Smooth and clever,' she said to herself.

And you know what that means, right?

Mary finished her glass of wine.

That's right – we're going shopping.

Thirty-Five

Wednesday turned out to be a beautiful cloudless and sunny day, with the temperature reaching 60°F. That daytime beauty seeped into the evening, with a postcard star-filled sky and a bright full moon that reflected off the San Francisco Bay like a trail of diamonds.

Mary arrived at the Legion of Honor at 7:10 p.m., and as she stepped out of her cab, she had to pause for a moment to catch her breath. The Legion of Honor building looked like something out of a fairytale, with imposing Ancient Greece-style white pillars that flanked a grandiose arched entrance, reminiscent of the Arc de Triomphe. The large, round water fountain at the front of the building greeted every arrival with a kaleidoscope of colors that changed to the sound of Vivaldi's *The Four Seasons*.

'Wow, this really is something else,' Mary whispered to herself, as she started towards the building, which was tinted a beautiful shade of purple, via several spotlights that sprang out of the front garden. A red carpet guided every arrival up the long ramp that led to the arched entrance, where Mary was greeted by a young man in a white tux. He checked her invitation before offering her a glass of pink champagne and ushering her into the wide, open courtyard, where laser lights projected a show of images against the main building, this time, to the sound of Mussorgsky's *Night on Bald Mountain*. This was what Mary imagined arriving at the Oscars would be like.

The paintings and works of art were being exhibited inside the building, but there were several guests hanging around the courtyard, mingling, chatting, smoking and enjoying the laser show. Mary sipped her champagne while her eyes circled the small crowd outside; Thomas didn't seem to be amongst them.

'Canapé, ma'am?' a waitress asked, walking up to Mary with a tray full of colorful hors d'oeuvre.

'No, I'm alright for now, thank you.'

As the waitress walked away, a new group of guests walked through the arched entrance and into the open courtyard. That was when Mary finally realized that all the men seemed to be dressed in tuxedos, and all the women were in very expensive-looking evening dresses – some quite extravagant in style.

Mary had spent a whole day in town searching for dresses, and despite the urge to spend a small fortune on a couple of designer numbers, in the end, she decided on a front-of-the-store, bean-paste, split-thigh, double-shoulder strap dress that truly accentuated her now slender and toned body. For shoes, she picked a black pair of ankle-strap sandals, with stiletto heels and a stylish bow detail over her toes. She complemented the look with a satin shawl over her shoulders. Her jewelry was simple but classy, and her makeup had never been more on point.

'Wow,' Mary heard a male voice say from behind her. 'You look . . . breathtaking.'

Mary turned to face Thomas, who was also dressed in a black tuxedo that seemed tailor-made, not a rental, but with a red bowtie that matched the handkerchief that just peeked out of his breast pocket. His longish hair wasn't tousled carelessly like when they first met – it was slickly combed back over his ears. His eyes, as they met Mary's, also seemed a little different . . . brighter perhaps, as if right then they'd acquired a somewhat 'happy sparkle'. The bowtie, though, was slightly lopsided.

'Oh, hello,' Mary said, surprised. 'I didn't see you there.'

'I was just in the gents, trying to fix this ... thing ...' He pointed at his bowtie. 'No matter how many times I've tried, I just can't get it to stay straight. I've watched at least five YouTube videos on how to tie a bowtie and just look at this.' He pointed at his neck before shaking his head. 'I really have no idea of what I'm doing wrong.'

Mary smiled. 'Yeah, it's definitely not straight.'

Thomas breathed out a mixture of frustration and embarrassment. 'I knew I should've gotten one of those with an elastic band.'

'May I?' Mary asked, nodding at the bowtie.

'You know how to tie a bowtie?'

'I can give it a shot,' she replied, matter-of-factly, handing Thomas her champagne flute. 'Could you please hold this for me?'

Thomas took the flute as Mary stepped closer, lifting his collar and reaching for the bowtie. It was only then that she got a noseful of Thomas' cologne. He smelled like that cool blast of fragrances that would hit her every time she walked past a perfume shop on the high street, or through the corridors of a duty-free shop at the airport.

'Thank you for the compliment, by the way,' Mary said, as she pulled the bowtie knot undone and began again. 'But the invite you sent me said nothing about this being a gala evening. I feel seriously underdressed here.'

'Underdressed?' Thomas dipped his chin to look at Mary again. 'You're kidding, right? You look absolutely stunning, Mary. Hands down the most elegant and attractive woman here tonight.'

Mary's smile was genuine, but she'd been in that same spot before, way too many times, actually – men complimenting her looks, her hair, her dress sense, her shoes, her perfume, showering her with gifts, acting like true gentlemen at first – just to turn into something completely different, practically overnight. Mary had learned that sad truth the hard way, but right then, the sincerity in Thomas' voice was somewhat disarming, and she had to gather all of her willpower not to blush.

'For me to get this right,' she said, her tone steady, 'you need to stop moving.'

'Sorry.' Thomas did his best to stay as still as possible, though it seemed like he was having trouble keeping his eyes off Mary.

'And you're being too kind with your words, but thank you again.'

'Just being truthful.'

'There you go,' Mary said, as she gave his bowtie a final tug to set it in place before folding his collar back down and taking a step back to get the full picture. Thomas looked impeccable. All he needed was a British accent and he could easily audition for the next James Bond.

'Really?' Thomas handed Mary's champagne flute back to her before reaching into his inside pocket for his cellphone. 'That quick?' He unlocked the phone, entered camera mode, and quickly held it up in front of him like a mirror. 'Oh my god, how did you do that? It's perfect. Thank you.'

'My pleasure.' Mary nodded back at him. 'And you look great, yourself. Very gentleman-chic, I'd say.'

Thomas chuckled. 'Well, in that case,' he offered Mary his arm, 'may I guide you into the exhibition, madam?'

Mary smiled as she placed her arm through his. 'You may indeed.'

As Thomas guided Mary towards the first exhibition hall, she couldn't help thinking that talking to him felt both safe and dangerous at the same time. She just had no real idea of how dangerous yet.

Thirty-Six

The inside of the Legion of Honor was just as impressive as its outside. Each exhibition room differed from one another in size, wall color, lighting and, sometimes, its ceiling design. The floors were all varnished wood, with some rooms sporting heavy mahogany benches so that visitors could take their time as they appreciated some of the larger pieces.

The Dark America exhibition itself was comprised of over two hundred works of art, occupying five of the museum's twenty exhibition halls. The remaining fifteen rooms were closed to the public at that time.

'Wow, this place is simply amazing,' Mary said, as she allowed her eyes to take in the hall as a whole.

'Is this your first time at The Legion?' Thomas asked, as they paused by a large oil painting on the west wall. It depicted a band of Mohawk Indians brutally attacking a group of US soldiers.

'It is,' Mary replied.

'Well,' Thomas turned to face her. 'Prepare to be overwhelmed then. It's a beautiful museum . . . inside and out . . . and you've got to come back some other time and have a proper look around – when all the rooms are open to the public, I mean. The rooms alone are worth it, but some of the art pieces in here will blow your mind.'

'Well, this room is truly beautiful,' Mary said, looking

around before bringing her attention back to the Indians and soldiers painting. 'And this is just as realistic and as brutal as it gets, isn't it? If we step any closer, we'll probably get arterial spray.'

Thomas laughed. 'You're probably right.'

They slowly began moving from piece to piece, but Mary would be lying if she said that her full attention was focused on the exhibition. She was truly enjoying Thomas' company. Yes, he was attractive, very charming, incredibly charismatic, and terribly funny at times, but the more they chatted, the more Mary saw hints of a man who was as witty as he was intelligent and to her, that was the biggest aphrodisiac of all.

They moved from room one to room two, and from room two to room three, which, at least until then, became Mary's favorite room in the exhibition. The room was named 'The Witches Room', and rightly so. Every piece in room three, and there were at least thirty of them, including three bronze sculptures, had witches as their main theme. Some were light-hearted, in a lower-school Halloween way, some were a little more serious, some were downright scary, and some were terribly sad, but all of them were incredibly vivid.

Mary's favorite piece in that room was also the saddest one of them all – a very large six-foot wide by five-foot tall, oil painting of the five most famous American witches burning at the stake in Salem, Massachusetts. The piece was titled *Injustice* and the details that the artist had managed to convey with her brushstrokes gave Mary the chills.

Thomas seemed to look just as sad, as he studied the painting. 'You know what?' he said, searching the room for one of the waiters. 'I wouldn't mind another drink after looking at this one.'

'Yeah, me too,' Mary agreed, adjusting her shawl over her shoulders to help with the goosebumps.

A waiter with a tray full of Champagne flutes was standing just a couple of steps behind Thomas. He reached for two glasses before passing one to Mary.

Exhibition room number four was titled 'Scary' and it was by far the busiest one of them all. At the center of the room there was a life-size waxwork of a witch stirring something inside her smoking, copper caldron. Mary was sure that the smoke coming from inside the caldron was being created by a smoke machine, but it smelled like real food – meat and potato stew, actually – and the realism of the witch itself was mindboggling.

Mary looked back at Thomas. 'Is it only me or does this smell delicious?' She nodded at the caldron before leaning over slightly to get a better noseful.

'I was just about to say exactly that.'

Right then, catching both of them off guard, the witch, who in truth was a human statue performer, turned her head to look at Mary and Thomas before lifting her wooden spoon from the caldron.

'Would you like to taste it?' Her voice sounded exactly like what most people would expect a witch to sound like – gritty and squeaky.

'Jesus!' Mary jumped back, eyes wide, almost dropping her Champagne flute.

'Whoa! What the hell?' Thomas didn't drop his glass either, but he did spill most of his Champagne onto the floor.

Everyone else who was in the room started applauding and laughing. A museum employee, who was standing on the corner armed with a wheeled bucket and a mop quickly made his way towards them. The museum clearly was expecting a lot of drink spillage by that witch.

'Sorry,' the witch apologized before going back to her initial position, ready to prank someone else.

'And now I understand why this is in the "scary" room,'

Mary said, her left hand resting on her chest. 'Instead of in the "witches" one.'

'Exactly,' the witch whispered through the corner of her mouth.

'I think I can actually taste my heart,' Thomas said, pointing to his throat. 'Because it's beating right here.' He finished what was left of his Champagne in one gulp.

Mary did the same.

They paused by the door to room five, the final exhibition room, and smiled at each other.

'That was brilliantly done,' Thomas admitted. 'No one will be expecting that. I guess that that's why this room is so busy.'

'Yep,' Mary agreed. 'People are just hanging around, waiting for the next fool to be pranked.'

'And the smell of food is the perfect bait,' Thomas added. 'It draws people to the witch because it's simply impossible to ignore it.'

'True,' Mary agreed. 'And to be honest, it really did make me feel a little hungry.'

'Really?' Thomas, once again, looked around for one of the waiters. 'They have canapés and a whole bunch of finger food going around. Do you want to go get some?'

Mary shook her head. 'Nah, I'll be OK.'

Thomas hesitated for a split second, debating his next move. He chose to roll the dice. 'Do you know what? I could do with some real food. How about we go get some dinner somewhere?' He checked his watch. 'It's still early, everywhere will be open.'

It was Mary's turn to hesitate for a second. Back at her apartment, she had decided not to eat anything before getting to the museum. She didn't want to feel or look bloated, but the witch's caldron fake smell had totally woken up her stomach, and it was hungry, so why not? She was really enjoying Thomas' company.

Mary half nodded, half wiggled her head from left to right. 'I guess I could do with some food as well. Nothing heavy, though.'

'Yeah, that's perfectly fine. There are hundreds of healthy food places around town. Quite a few around this area. Any preference? Or any type of food that you're not into?'

Mary shook her head. 'Not really. I'm pretty muck OK with anything.'

'Cool.' The smile that half parted Thomas' lips was somewhat intriguing, as if he had just thought of a place that would truly surprise Mary. 'So, since you're not from San Francisco, shall I pick?'

'Yeah, that's fine by . . .' Mary paused as her expression went from smiling to dead serious in record time.

Hold on just a second here, the voice inside Mary's head interrupted her thought. *How the hell does he know that you're not from San Francisco? You never told him that. And you don't really have an accent that can place you somewhere else.*

Right then, Mary could feel her palms starting to clam up from pure anxiety.

This date just went from 'great' to 'suspicious' in a nanosecond. We've got to get out of here. And I mean right now.

'Umm . . .' Mary pulled her shawl tighter around her shoulders. 'Do you know what?' She took a step back. 'I just remembered something really important. I'm so sorry but I need to go.'

'Wait . . . what?' Thomas frowned at her, clearly trying to figure out if she was being serious or not.

'I . . .' She turned her head to look behind her. 'Very stupidly forgot that I had somewhere else that I had to be tonight. I'm sorry but I really need to go.'

The confusion quickly spread from Thomas' eyes to his entire demeanor. 'Are you serious? What happened?'

Thomas took a step forward, but Mary took another step backwards. 'I just really need to go.'

'But . . .' Thomas looked around to see if there was anyone looking at them . . . anyone who might've spooked Mary. He saw no one. 'I thought that we're just about to go get some food. Did I say something wrong?'

'No.' This time Mary completely avoided eye contact. 'I just really need to go. Thank you again for the invite.'

Thomas watched in total disbelief as Mary quickly turned on the balls of her feet and practically ran out of the museum.

Thirty-Seven

Outside the museum building, Mary quickly crossed the open courtyard, where the laser lightshow was still going on, and hurried past the improvised bar at the impressive arched entrance. On the red-carpet ramp, she had to zigzag her way through several arriving guests before finally making it down to the road.

'Mary.' She heard someone call from the ramp behind her, just as she reached the street. She didn't slow down or look back. Instead, with her cellphone in hand, she headed across the road to the circular fountain with the colored light show. She was about to order an Uber when a city yellow cab pulled up by the fountain to drop a couple of guests. Mary returned her cellphone to her handbag and rushed towards the cab.

'Mary, please, give me just a minute.' Thomas caught up with her just before she managed to reach the taxi.

'I can't right now,' Mary replied, barely glancing back at Thomas. 'I've really got to go.'

'Please!' Thomas pleaded, as he stopped running after her. 'One minute, that's all I ask.' Instead of reaching for her arm to try to stop her, as most men would've probably done, Thomas kept his distance and simply raised his hands in a surrender gesture. 'After that, if you want, you'll never hear from me again. I promise you.'

Maybe it was the fact that he never put his hands on her to try to stop her from getting away, or maybe it was the sincerity that Mary could hear in Thomas' tone, but something about the respectful way that he'd approached the moment made Mary hesitate and slow down.

'One minute,' Thomas tried again, a little out of breath. 'That's really all I ask.'

Mary finally turned to face Thomas.

He breathed in a lungful of oxygen before recomposing himself. 'What just happened in there?'

'Nothing,' Mary replied, she too had to take a second to catch her breath. 'I just remembered that I have somewhere else that I've got to be, that's all.'

Thomas' head angled slightly to his left, while his left eye narrowed a touch. 'Mary, we both know that that's not true. Something spooked you in there.' He threw his right thumb over his right shoulder. 'And it wasn't that witch with the caldron. Either you saw someone who you didn't want to see, or I said or did something that completely rattled you.'

'No,' Mary insisted, giving Thomas a firmer headshake. 'Nothing like that. I just really remembered someth—'

'Mary, please.' Though Thomas cut her short, his tone was non-challenging . . . almost apologetic. 'I promise you that I'm not as stupid as I look. We both know that you don't really have somewhere else that you need to be right now. That was just the first excuse that popped into your head because something happened in there . . . something that frightened you. I saw the shift, Mary. I saw it in your eyes . . . on your face . . . on your demeanor. I heard the change in your voice too. And that shift . . . that change . . . was fear.'

Mary moved her weight from one foot to the other.

'And I get it,' Thomas continued. 'If I were in an exhibition, or a party, or wherever, and something spooked me, I'd also come up with a quick excuse and just leave. That'd be the most natural reaction for us all. I just want to understand it because I really don't think that option one is the correct one here, which leaves me with one single option – I either said or did something that completely rattled you.' Thomas, once again, lifted a finger to pause Mary before she had a chance to say something back. 'Whatever that was, Mary, I'm truly sorry for it. Whatever that was, I did it without realizing that it would upset or scare you. I just really don't have the slightest clue of what that was.'

While he spoke, Mary had been observing Thomas – his posture, his facial expressions, his mannerism, and once again, she failed to pick up any signs that could lead her to believe that he was lying.

'Could you please just help me understand what was it that I did or said that got you so on edge? That's all I ask. After that, I promise you, I'll walk away and you'll never hear from me again.'

Through the corner of her eye, Mary saw the yellow cab take off, but she didn't panic. Instead, she held Thomas' stare one more time. The sparkle in his eyes had vanished once again, this time substituted by what Mary read as confusion and sadness, but even then, despite the tense moment, the silence that followed didn't feel at all awkward.

Thomas waited, hoping that Mary would say something, anything that could help him understand what he'd done wrong, but she said nothing back. He allowed the moment to fade before giving Mary a sad nod, signaling that he understood that he should just go.

'For what it's worth, Mary,' he said, as he finally gave up and turned to walk away, 'tonight was one of the best nights I've had in a very long time.' His smile was shy, but truthful. 'Once again, I'm sorry for whatever I did wrong. It was never my intention to upset you.' He waved her goodbye. 'Take care of yourself, OK?' And with those words, he turned and walked away.

Thirty-Eight

As if playing to some sort of secret soundtrack written exactly for that moment, just as Thomas turned to walk away, the music and the light show at the fountain by which Mary and Thomas were standing changed to something a lot more dramatic. Thomas had taken less than four steps back in the direction of the ramp when Mary acted on pure impulse, disregarding even the voice inside her head.

'How did you know that I'm not from San Francisco?' she called out, her tone firm . . . demanding.

Thomas turned to look back at her, confusion showing in every corner of his face. 'I'm sorry?'

'Just now, in the exhibition.' Mary pointed at the Legion of Honor. 'When we were talking about where to go for food . . . you said something like – "since you're not from San Francisco, shall I pick?" How did you know that I'm not from San Francisco? And don't tell me that I've got an accent because I know I don't.'

Thomas gave Mary a very subtle shake of the head, as if he was having trouble understanding her. 'What do you mean, Mary?'

'I mean exactly that, Thomas,' she replied, her voice firmer still. 'How did you know that I'm not from San Francisco?'

Thomas' eyes narrowed at her. 'You told me.'

Mary didn't even hesitate. 'No, I never.'

'Well . . .' Thomas agreed with a single nod. 'Not in so many words, no.'

'And what the hell does that mean?'

He's just trying to buy time while he thinks of some sort of answer, the voice inside her head warned her.

Thomas took a breath. 'It's something that I do without even thinking about it,' he tried to explain. 'It's . . . just how my brain works, really.'

'What is?' Mary asked. The confusion was now all over her face.

'Reading between the lines,' he clarified. 'Double analyzing words and sentences to find hidden meanings . . . listening for what's not actually being said but is still there for you to hear. It's a necessity for the job I do. Unfortunately . . .' Thomas gave Mary an apologetic shrug. 'After so many years, my brain does it automatically and all the time, not just when I'm working. I really don't even notice that I'm doing it anymore.'

Mary returned the shrug, but hers was full of doubt. 'What the hell are you talking about, Thomas?'

'You've never been here before,' Thomas explained. 'At the Legion of Honor. You told me that, remember?'

Mary's brow furrowed, as if she was searching her memory.

Thomas read her expression and decided to help. '"Wow, this place is simply amazing." That's what you said once we stepped into the museum, remember? You were really surprised by how beautiful its interior was, which in turn surprised me, so I asked you if this was your first time at the Legion, and you said that in fact it was. Do you remember that?'

'Yes,' Mary nodded, her tone a lot less firm than a moment ago.

'OK, so from that fact alone, you told me two things that weren't actually spoken, but extracted from your context.' He used the fingers on his right hand, enumerating each reason as he spoke. 'One – you couldn't be from San Francisco. Every San Franciscan knows about the Legion, and they know how beautiful this building is – inside and out – because this place is like a heritage to the city. And two – you haven't lived in San Francisco for more than just months . . . probably not even a year. If you had and you enjoy art, which my educated guess is that you do, you would've been here before, for sure. In San Francisco, this place is right at the top of the list for any art enthusiast.'

Mary's look went one hundred percent pensive, as she pondered over everything that Thomas had just said.

'That was how I knew . . .' Thomas paused and pressed his lips together before correcting himself. 'Actually, a better word would be "deducted" that you weren't from San Francisco. Like I've said, my brain does things like that automatically and in a blink of an eye, without me even realizing that I'm doing it. I do apologize. I didn't mean to overstep a line, or upset you, Mary. I really didn't.'

That's actually not a bad explanation, the voice inside Mary's head accepted it. *It sort of makes sense . . . in a weird way.*

'So, what is it that you do?' Mary asked, her tone skeptical, but not nearly as much as minutes earlier. 'You said that it was a necessity for the job you do. So, what are you? A psychologist or something?'

Thomas' chuckle was subtle. 'No, I'm not a psychologist, but I do use a lot of applied psychology in what I do.'

'Which is?'

'I'm a . . .' It looked like Thomas was trying to figure out how to better phrase what he was about to tell Mary. 'Investor, of sorts . . . a venture capitalist, if you like. I get a lot of people coming to me with a new business idea . . . or an already established business with a lot of potential but lacking the funds and the direction to grow. Sometimes it's just a vision for a new business or start-up. They all come to me for one reason only – capital.' He shrugged. 'In that line of work, you need to learn how to read between the lines . . . how to break down their sentences and thoughts so that you can see the real bottom line – not the one that they are trying to sell you. You need to be able to spot the slightest inconsistency with what they're actually telling you so you don't fall victim to their plot. You have no idea how often people will try to sell you a bag of lemons, but make you believe that you are buying a suitcase full of gold. There are a lot of con artists out there, Mary, all of them looking for a quick and easy buck . . . and when I say "buck", I'm talking millions.'

Yet again, Mary got the feeling that Thomas was being as truthful as he could.

'I really wasn't trying to double analyze you, or anything like that, Mary. I'm sorry that it sounded like I was.' Thomas tucked his hands inside his trouser pockets and nodded a sad goodbye. 'Take care of yourself, OK?' For the second time, he turned to walk away.

And for the second time, Mary halted him before he had a chance to cross the road.

'Are you still hungry?'

Thirty-Nine

Thomas took Mary to a relatively low-key restaurant in Vista Del Mar, not that far from the Legion of Honor. The owners were a very sweet couple from west Malaysia who, already in their mid-fifties, had brought their expertise in cooking Malay and Pan-Asian street dishes to north San Francisco. The food was simple but incredibly tasty and just like Mary had wanted, quite light when it came to calories. Their selection of world wines was also very accomplished.

'Would you like to choose the wine,' Thomas said, undoing the top two buttons on his dress shirt, as he handed Mary the wine menu, which in truth was more like a wine booklet.

Mary took it and quickly scanned through it. The wines were grouped by countries, and the list was seriously extensive. She chuckled. 'I think that this goes a little beyond my understanding of wines.' She flipped through a couple more pages. 'Umm … I'm open to suggestions here.' Her eyebrows arched at Thomas. 'Anything you can recommend?'

'I'm sure we can find something. Let me see.' He once again reached for the wine list. 'OK, give me something to work with – red or white?'

'Red.'

'Alright, and would you prefer something a little lighter like a

Pinot Noir, or something a little more full-bodied, like a Malbec or Zinfandel?'

'I actually love Zinfandels,' Mary replied.

'OK.' Thomas smiled and flipped a couple of pages on the menu before pausing and angling his head slightly right. 'Oh!' There was no hiding the surprise in his voice.

'Found something?' Mary asked.

'Yeah, I think so. Have you ever tried any Zinfandels from Russian River Valley?'

'I don't think so.'

'Oh, then you're in for a great surprise.'

They ordered their meals and a bottle of Williams Selyem Fanucchi Zinfandel.

'Wow,' Mary said, as she had her first sip of her wine, after allowing it to breathe for a couple of minutes. 'This is very nice.'

Thomas breathed out relief before giving Mary a cheeky smile. 'One of my favorite Californian wineries.'

'Yeah, I can see why. Cheers.'

They touched glasses.

Mary and Thomas ate their meals, drank their wine, and chatted as if nothing had ever happened. Not once did Thomas mention the incident back at the Legion of Honor, which pleased Mary, but what had really surprised her was that throughout their entire evening, Thomas never asked her any of the typical questions that most men on a first date would ask. He never asked her about her past life, never asked her where she was from, or how come she'd ended up in San Francisco. He never even asked her what she did for a living, as if none of it really mattered to him. All they did was talk about art, wine, films and music, and laugh a great deal. Thomas turned out to be a great storyteller, always adding a touch of humor to just about everything.

'Would you like to have a look at our dessert menu?' the waiter asked, once Mary and Thomas had finished their meals. 'We have some great Asian sweets.'

Thomas simply lifted his eyebrows at Mary.

'Oh no, thank you.' Mary shook her head, lifting her hand at the waiter. 'I couldn't eat another bite of anything.' She nodded at her completely empty plate. 'That prawn salad was absolutely delicious, but also incredibly filling.'

'Same here,' Thomas agreed, also lifting a hand at the waiter before indicating his plate. There wasn't a scrap left on it. 'I couldn't eat another bite, but please send my compliments to the chef. Everything was simply delicious.'

'Thank you, sir. My parents will be really pleased to hear that.' The waiter put his hands together and gently bowed his head at Thomas before repeating the gesture at Mary. 'Ma'am.'

As the waiter walked away with the empty dishes, Thomas divided the little that was left of the wine between Mary's glass and his own.

'We could order another bottle, if you like.'

'Oh no!' She gave him a subtle shake of the head as she checked her watch. 'It's Wednesday evening. I've got things that I've got to do tomorrow morning,' she lied. 'And another bottle would mean that at the end of the night, counting what we already had back at the Legion, we would've drunk more than a bottle of wine each … that rarely ends up well. I'm actually already feeling a little tipsy.'

Thomas agreed with a head gesture. 'Yeah, you're right. A second bottle would probably be too much alcohol for a Wednesday evening, and when that happens – mistakes usually follow.'

'Um-hum.' Mary nodded before finishing her wine and once again locking eyes with Thomas. This time, they both held each other's stare for several seconds longer than any of the previous times. Mary was trying hard to read Thomas' intentions. She'd read an article in a women's magazine a few months back about body language and facial micro-expressions – what they could actually mean (from a romantic standpoint), and how to read and interpret them. It was a long article. Mary couldn't remember everything, but something that had stuck with her was when the article mentioned the eyes. It revealed that a lot could be gathered just from observing a person's eyes and eye movements, and Mary remembered that the article explained that as two people gazed at each other, if one of them had a strong romantic interest in the other, that person's eyes would often keep on redirecting their focus to the lower part of the other person's face – mainly tip of the nose and lips – considered to be the sensual glance area by body language experts.

Mary was trying to figure out if Thomas was focusing his attention on her lips or not. The problem was – instead of looking at his eyes, she kept on diverting her attention to his lips.

'Shall I order the bill then?' he asked, finally breaking the silent gaze competition.

Mary blinked out of her daze before nodding. 'Sure.'

Thomas lifted a hand to signal the waiter for the bill.

'But I'm getting this,' Mary added, already reaching for her handbag.

'What do you mean – you're getting this?'

'C'mon,' Mary countered. 'You took me to the opening night of a great exhibition and sent me an amazing gift.'

This time, it looked like it was Thomas who was observing Mary's expressions and micro-expressions.

'Plus,' she continued. 'It's the least I can do after the way I acted earlier.'

Thomas sat back on his chair and crossed one leg over the other before resting his hands on his thighs. 'I hear what you're saying, and it's appreciated.' He bit his bottom lip. 'But hear me out here, OK?'

Mary's eyes widened at Thomas, but the look in them wasn't a surprised one. In fact, she looked back at him in the same way that a mother would look back at her child when she already knew that the kid was about to hit her with some bullshit.

'I try to be as . . . modern as I can be, but when it comes to certain things, I'll admit that I am one hundred percent old school. And this is certainly one of them.'

Mary looked around, as if confused. 'This what? Dinner?'

'*First date* dinner,' Thomas corrected her, and the way in which he clearly held back his smile told Mary that he knew that he was getting ahead of himself right then. 'I invited you out, Mary,' he explained. 'I was the one who suggested, *and convinced you*, to come to a restaurant with me.' This time, he looked back at her with puppy eyes. 'Please, for the sake of my silly male pride . . . and I know it's silly – let me get this one and you can get the next one, if you like.'

Mary pursed her lips and twisted them to one side – a smile hidden somewhere between them.

Once again, Thomas read her like an open book. 'You noticed that I said "next one", didn't you?'

Mary nodded. 'I did. Very smooth. Subliminally putting forward the suggestion that there will be a second time.'

Thomas replied with a shy smile. 'Honestly, I'm really hoping that there will be . . . dinner, drinks, cinema, coffee, whatever, really. For me, it's been a great night. I really enjoyed your company.'

The waiter came back to them and placed the bill on their table, directly in front of Thomas.

'Plastic OK?' Thomas asked.

'Of course, sir. Let me just go get the machine.'

As the waiter turned and walked away, Thomas reached for his wallet and selected a credit card from the many he had before placing it inside the bill booklet.

'I haven't agreed that it's OK for you to pay this bill yet,' Mary said, nodding at the booklet.

'Seriously, Mary, it's my pleasure. Please, let me get it.'

Mary poked the inside of her left cheek with her tongue. 'How about we split it then? That's fair, isn't it?'

Thomas, once again, sat back on his chair. He looked one hundred percent relaxed. 'You really want to go Dutch? On the very first night out?'

'Why not?'

Thomas scratched the underside of his chin. 'Well, one of the reasons, like I explained, would be that by allowing me to pay for our *first-ever* dinner, you'd be doing my silly male pride a huge favor, which would be much appreciated, but a second reason, which is even more important, is that . . .' He took a moment, his eyes darting away from Mary before darting back to her. 'I come from a very superstitious family . . . just something I grew up with – I can tell you some crazy stories later, if you like – anyway, I don't really believe most of it, to be honest, but a few selected superstitions, so far, for me, have proven to be true.'

'Is that right?' Mary sounded like she was buying none of it.

'I'm being serious,' Thomas carried on. 'And one of those few is – never go Dutch on a first date. That's one hundred percent bad luck.'

'So, we're fine then,' Mary replied, matter-of-factly. 'Because this isn't really a date.'

Thomas' eyes widened at Mary. 'Ouch! Talk about being shut down. No mercy, huh?'

Mary smiled. 'That's what you deserve for such a bullshit story. Superstition? Bad luck for going Dutch? Really? I promise you that *I'm* not as stupid as I look.'

Thomas laughed. 'Touché.'

Hey, the voice inside Mary's head came back. *If he wants to pay, let him pay. It's one less time that you'll be using your credit card, and for us, that's a good thing, remember?*

Mary nodded at the voice, but Thomas thought that she was nodding at him.

'OK . . . fine,' she finally agreed. 'But with the condition that the next time, it's on me. Deal?'

'Absolutely.' Thomas' smile was a happy and sincere one because he knew that he'd just bagged a second date. 'You have my word.'

The waiter got back to their table with the credit card machine. He retrieved Thomas' card from the bill booklet, inserted it into the machine and handed it to Thomas, who punched in his pin number before returning the machine to the waiter.

'Is it OK if *I* leave the tip?' Mary addressed Thomas, reaching for her handbag for the second time. 'Or is that bad luck as well?'

'It's already included, ma'am,' the waiter said, as he pulled Thomas' card out of the machine, ready to return it to him.

'It's included,' Thomas confirmed.

'Well, I think he deserves extra,' Mary explained, grabbing two twenty-dollar bills from her wallet and handing them to the waiter. 'Plus, I don't like leaving electronic tips.' She fixed Thomas with a solid stare. 'Because when it comes to certain things, I'll admit that I am one hundred percent old school.'

Thomas began applauding, as he laughed. 'Touché, again.'

By sheer misfortune, the waiter tried to return Thomas' credit card just as he began clapping, which caused him to hit the card with the tips of his fingers and send it flying Mary's way.

'Oh, I'm so sorry, sir,' the waiter apologized, his eyes wide, as if he'd just done something terrible.

'It's alright,' Mary said, giving the waiter a sympathetic smile. 'Don't worry. I've got it.' She picked up the card, which had skidded over the table to land on her lap.

'So sorry again, sir,' the waited repeated himself, bowing at Thomas.

'It's OK. It was my fault. I wasn't looking.' Though the reply was addressed at the waiter, Thomas' concerned eyes were focused on Mary. Something had changed in his tone of voice. For some reason, right then, he sounded a little tense.

The waiter bowed one last time at them both before thanking Mary for the extra tip and finally walking away.

'Sorry about that,' Thomas said, trying to sound breezy and extending his hand at Mary, ready to get his card back, but Mary held on to it for a second longer. It wasn't only Thomas' tone of voice that had changed. His demeanor had changed as well. In just a few seconds, he went from being totally relaxed to looking quite anxious.

Mary peeked at the credit card in her hand and her heart stuttered.

'What the fuck?' she murmured. Her eyes stayed on the card for another second before jumping to Thomas, then back to the card, then back to Thomas again.

This time, he didn't hold her stare.

'Who the fuck are you? Really?' she asked, anger taking over her tone. She flipped the card around so it would face Thomas. 'Because your name, sure as shit, ain't Thomas is it?'

The happy smile that had graced Thomas' lips just seconds earlier had completely vanished. He looked like a school kid who had been caught out cheating on an exam. His attention finally went back to Mary. The look on his face was as serious as a heart attack.

Mary flicked the card back at him, almost hitting him on the face. 'Whoever the fuck you are,' she got to her feet, 'stay the fuck away from me, you hear?'

'I'll cut you a deal,' the man that Mary knew as Thomas said, as she got up to leave.

'Fuck you and your deal. How about that?' Mary reached for her shawl.

'I'll tell you who the fuck I really am,' he said, his tone almost as hard as hers. 'If you tell me who the fuck *you* really are . . . because all this . . .' he gestured at her, '. . . is nothing but a front, isn't it? You're not really who you're pretending to be – are you? And your name isn't really Mary, is it?'

Forty

To Mary, it felt like one of those movie scenes where everything and everyone stood completely still, while the main character kept on moving.

The man, who until then she knew only as Thomas, had kept his tone of voice as quiet as he possibly could, but it was a small restaurant, and the couple two tables to their right, despite not being able to hear what was actually being said, had clearly picked up that they were having some sort of argument.

Mary hooked her handbag over her right shoulder before looking back at the man. Though he'd tried to sound as angry as her, there was something awkward . . . a soft edge, perhaps, in the way that he'd delivered the sentence – 'I'll tell you who the fuck I really am, if you tell me who the fuck *you* really are . . .' The cursing sounded off when coming from him. As if he wasn't at all used to it. As if he'd just used it then to try to sound tough.

He seemed to sense her hesitation, and continued before she had a chance to walk away.

'Maybe I'm wrong . . . maybe your name really is Mary, or maybe it isn't. I don't really care to be honest. I'll call you whatever you want me to call you. A name is just a name, but whoever you are, you're certainly running away from something . . . or someone – a boyfriend, a husband, a partner, a lover, family – I don't know. Or maybe it's something a lot more serious. Maybe you're running away from the police or even the FBI.' He pressed his lips together, as his head angled slightly to one side, signaling doubt. 'But you don't really look like a hardened criminal to me. So, I'd say that option two – running away from the law – is out. That's not who you're hiding from, is it?'

Mary glared at him.

He leaned forward and placed his elbows on the table. 'There *is* a reason why I kept my real name from you, Mary, but it has absolutely nothing to do with who you really are . . . who you're running away from . . . or even why you're on the run.'

Mary was trying hard to leave, but that disarming magnetism that she had sensed about Thomas – or whatever his name really was – was still there, stronger than ever, and it was somehow holding her in place.

'This . . .' His index finger went back and forth between them a few times. 'What's happening right now is pretty much a repetition of what happened earlier at The Legion. It's just a sad misunderstanding. One that you, once again, jumped to conclusions before you've allowed me to explain.'

Mary stood where she was.

'And before you ask,' he continued, 'or jump to some more hasty conclusions, the reason why I know that you're running from something or someone, is exactly the same as the first time – reading between the lines, listening to what's not actually being said, but is still there for people to hear.' He lifted a hand at Mary. 'Your reaction back at the Legion,' he explained. 'Like I told you – I could see real fear all over you – and all that fear was instigated by the simple fact that I deducted that you weren't from San Francisco. That was it. Nothing else.' He paused for a second, as if to allow time for what he'd just said to sink in. 'The most logical conclusion from your evasive reaction would be that that fear was based on you assuming that I was someone who had been tracking you down and had finally found you. Why else would you run away, in a panic, like that?'

The man saw Mary's left hand close into a fist, but not a tight, anger fist. The movement was more like a pacifier than an anger gesture – she was pondering over what he'd just said.

'And just seconds ago,' he carried on. 'Once you read my real name on my credit card, that same fear came flying back to you, but this time with an added feature – anger – but not just at me for using a false name . . . anger at yourself.' He paused to observe Mary's reaction.

She stood completely still, except for her jaw, which had tensed – a strong indication that she was getting upset, angry, fearful, or any combination of those three emotions. She clearly didn't like being read like that. And he wasn't done yet.

'You're blaming yourself for not walking away earlier, back at the Legion, right? You're probably also blaming yourself for not realizing that I wasn't being truthful about who I really am, but like I've said before, Mary – the reason for that has absolutely nothing to do with you. That I can promise you.'

The anger that showed at Mary's tense jaw seeped considerably into her tone of voice. 'And like I've said before – fuck you, and stay the fuck away from me, you hear?' She finally turned to walk away.

'I give you my word that I will,' the man said, his tone controlled. 'But before you go, wouldn't you at least like to know who I really am?'

Forty-One

Despite having clearly heard Mary say – 'fuck you, and stay the fuck away from me . . .' – the couple sitting on the table to her right were trying hard not to look. Instead, they stared at each other in complete silence, their eyes wide, their lips pressed into thin lines, their bodies awkwardly stiff.

Mary had already turned her back on the man sitting at the table and taken two steps towards the exit, when he threw his trump question at her.

Still facing away from him, Mary paused mid-step. This time, her jaw didn't tense, but the tip of her tongue lightly touched her top lip, as she closed her eyes for an instant.

Fuck! Mary thought. What she really wanted to do was to keep on walking, but she knew that curiosity would practically kill her later because what if he was telling the truth? What if the reason he lied about his name had nothing to do with Nelson or who she was? He did have a very good explanation the first time around.

Mary reopened her eyes. There was no harm in listening . . . was there?

She turned to face him once again. They held each other's stare for a couple of silent seconds before Mary finally spoke.

'You've got one minute, not a second more.' Her eyebrows arched at him.

The man slid his credit card, which was still on the table after

Mary had flicked it back at him, towards where she'd been sitting. 'Would you please take a seat,' he said, indicating the chair across the table from him. His eyes moved slightly right then left, signaling that the tables around them had picked up on their argument.

Mary didn't seem to care. She didn't sit down either. 'Fifty seconds.' Her voice was crisp with annoyance.

'OK,' the man nodded before once again reaching for his wallet. From it, he retrieved a couple more credit cards and placed them all in a row – all three of them facing Mary. 'This is so that you can see that I'm not keeping the truth from you anymore.'

Mary noticed that since she'd read his real name on his credit card moments earlier, this was the third time that the man that she knew only as Thomas had mentioned lying about his name, but he never actually used the word 'lying'. He always referred to his action as 'keeping the truth from her' – another very powerful, psychological, subliminal trick.

Her eyes moved down to the credit cards.

'My real name is Quaddra Buckner,' he revealed, tapping his index finger on each of the three credit cards that he had placed on the table. He then returned to his wallet, this time retrieving his driver's license and placing it just above the row of credit cards.

Mary angled her torso slightly forward to read the information on the credit cards and on the driving license. The name matched – Quaddra Buckner – and so did the photo on the license.

'For this next part,' Quaddra said, 'I think you'll be more comfortable if you sit down, Mary.'

Mary poked the inside of her left cheek with her tongue once again. 'What do you mean – this next part?'

'Please, have a seat,' Quaddra urged her. His voice was back to its calm, almost serene tone. 'And I'll explain. You'll see how all this was, once again, just a big misunderstanding. I'm not who you're clearly imagining I am.'

Mary hesitated for a quick moment. While she did, she noticed that several pairs of eyes, not only the ones belonging to the couples sitting on the tables to their left and right, had settled on her . . . and that was definitely unwanted attention.

We either sit the fuck down or we leave, the voice inside her head warned her. *Because any second now people will start reaching for their cellphones and filming everything for their social media . . . and we really don't want that, do we?*

Mary finally sat back down, but as she returned to her seat, she was careful to slide her chair a couple of feet away from the table, so that her legs wouldn't sit completely under it, in case she needed to get up and run . . . or kick the table into Quaddra.

Forty-Two

The restaurant that Mary and Quaddra were in wasn't exactly full to capacity, but it was busy enough for a Wednesday evening, and their argument had already attracted plenty of attention. But as Mary returned to their table, she noticed that all the extra pairs of eyes that were on her just seconds earlier, had slowly begun moving their attention back to their own businesses. Nothing to see here, really – just a couple having a quick disagreement. Thankfully, no one seemed to have been filming any of it.

'Thank you,' Quaddra said, as Mary took her seat, placing both of her feet flat against the ground and keeping her back straight, not quite touching the chair's backrest, in case she needed to quickly get up and go.

'You can check my driver's license for signs of forgery, if you want.' He nodded at it.

Mary had no idea of how to check for a forged driver's license, but still, she picked it up and ran the tips of her fingers against it, maybe looking for some sort of roughness or anything that felt odd. She got nothing – no dents ... no boldness ... no unevenness ... nothing but a perfectly smooth document. She checked the photo – everything looked one hundred percent legit. She returned the driver's license to the table before fixing Quaddra with a solid stare.

'So? Your real name is Quaddra, not Thomas, but I still have no fucking idea of who the hell you really are, or why you lied about your name.'

'That was going to be my next step.'

'Was?'

'I mean . . . is.'

'OK, so let's hear it then.'

Quaddra nodded at Mary's handbag, which was still slung over her right shoulder. 'You're going to need your phone for this.'

'What?' Mary's brow creased. 'My phone?'

Quaddra nodded.

'Why?'

'You'll see.'

Mary made no motion for her handbag.

'This isn't a trick, Mary,' Quaddra said, nodding at his breast pocket. 'I could lend you my phone, but you might think that it's somehow rigged. By you using your phone, it lends credibility to what you're about to see.'

Mary studied the man sitting across the table from her. He seemed relaxed, his tone confident. She, too, acted as calm as she possibly could, finally reaching into her handbag to retrieve her cellphone.

'OK, now what?' she asked. 'Take a selfie?'

'No,' Quaddra replied. 'All you need to do is google my name.'

'Excuse me?'

'Just google, or use whichever search engine you prefer, and search for Quaddra Buckner . . . see what you get.'

Mary's gaze stayed on Quaddra for a few more seconds before her eyes moved to her cellphone screen. It stayed there for a second, before going back to Quaddra.

'Please, Mary, just do it.' He nodded at her firmly.

'Fine,' she said before unlocking her phone, calling up her browser app, and typing his name into the search box.

'Make sure you spell Quaddra with a double "D",' he reminded her.

'I have,' Mary confirmed, as she tapped the 'go' button on her screen.

The reception inside the restaurant was pretty good, and a result page loaded almost instantaneously.

Quaddra sat back on his chair, crossed one leg over the other, and allowed his stare to settle on Mary's face.

Right at the top of the result page, next to the words 'showing results for Quaddra Buckner', Mary could see a portrait photo of the man sitting across the table from her. In the photo, he looked to be a few years younger, but not many. His hair was a couple of inches longer, with the ends curling out in all different directions, just like on the first night she met him.

Mary's eyes moved down to the first result showing on the page. She didn't even need to click on it to understand why Quaddra had lied about his real name.

Forty-Three

While Mary typed his name into the search box on her cellphone's browser, Quaddra assumed a more relaxed position, but his full attention was on her. As she hit the 'go' button on her browser, he saw her eyes widening at the screen, followed by her lips being tightly pressed together before she rolled them into her mouth for an instant. He was sure that she was starting to understand.

Mary read the title link of the topmost entry on the returned results' page . . .

> Young billionaire entrepreneur, Quaddra Buckner,
> acquires two new businesses, including a second
> film production company in Los Angeles.

Her eyes moved to the second topmost result . . . then the third . . . then the fourth, which would redirect her to a Wikipedia page. Every time Quaddra's name was mentioned, it was accompanied by the word 'billionaire'.

'Back at the Legion,' Quaddra explained, finally collecting back his credit cards and his driver's license, 'when I told you that there are a lot of con artists out there, Mary, I wasn't referring only to the sort of con artists that come to me with a business pitch.'

Mary kept on scrolling down on the results page.

'Searching for someone's name on the wide web,' Quaddra

continued, 'right after meeting them for the first time, has become common practice nowadays. Everybody does it, including me. I've even seen people do it in the bathroom, just minutes after meeting someone at a bar, a club, a restaurant, or anywhere really.'

Mary's gaze finally returned to Quaddra. She'd seen it happen too . . . plenty of times actually.

'Which is completely understandable,' Quaddra said. 'You can find a lot about someone online and by doing so, save yourself a world of hassle.'

Mary wasn't about to argue with that logic.

'With such an odd name like "Quaddra", you don't even need to know my last name to come across dozens of online articles about me.'

Mary finally stopped scrolling. 'So, you thought that if I knew who you really were, I'd maybe try to scam you?' She sounded more hurt than offended, but her tone wasn't aggressive. 'You approached me, remember?' She paused and thought better of her words. 'Actually no,' her eyebrows lifted at him. 'You *chased* me – you didn't have my number or my address, so you tracked down Betsy, turning up at her place of work so that you could drop off that painting, together with an invitation for tonight.'

'I know,' Quaddra agreed. 'But still . . .'

'Still?' The hurt lingered in Mary's tone.

Quaddra pulled a face at her. 'C'mon, Mary. I know that I barely know you, but I can tell that you're an intelligent woman. I'm sure that you can easily imagine the kind of extra attention that the word "billionaire" would generate . . . even on those who aren't con artists.'

He's got a point there, the voice inside Mary's head commented.

Quaddra's eyes moved to his empty wine glass and Mary could tell that right then he really wished he had ordered another bottle.

'The truth?' he asked.

Mary's head tilted slightly to one side. 'Nah, the truth is so overrated. Can I please have the bullshit instead? That always works out much better, don't you think?'

Quaddra lifted both hands in a surrender gesture.

Mary allowed her body posture to relax a little, finally leaning back against the chair's backrest.

Quaddra took a second to organize his thoughts. 'OK,' he began. 'I think it's pretty clear that I'm attracted to you. I wouldn't have gone through everything you just described – tracking Betsy down . . . dropping off a gift . . . inviting you out tonight . . . plus . . . chasing after you when you stormed out of the Legion in the way you did . . . if I wasn't interested in you.'

'Yeah . . . I know that.' Mary sounded confident, but not arrogant.

'And would it be a fair assumption to say that the reason why you have accepted the invite to come out with me tonight is maybe because you're a little attracted to me too?'

Mary didn't break eye contact. 'Well, you invited me to the opening night of a very prestigious exhibition. According to Betsy – the hottest ticket in town tonight. It's hard to say no to something like that.'

'An exhibition you didn't even know was happening,' Quaddra countered. 'In a place you didn't even know existed. Is that really why you accepted coming out with me tonight?'

Busted.

Mary tried hard to hold back the smile that bubbled up to her lips. She did a great job, but not a perfect one.

Quaddra smiled back. 'So, it *would* be fair to say that you are *a little* attracted to me too . . . or at least were before all this crazy misunderstanding.'

'That would be a fair assumption, yes,' Mary finally caved in, her tone calm.

'Alright.' Quaddra's smile reached his eyes. 'So now let me ask you to please be as truthful as you can, OK?' He didn't wait for a confirmation. 'When Betsy handed you the painting, with the little note I wrote you, if I had added a last name to the name Thomas, would you have googled the name?'

Mary blinked at Quaddra before her eyes bounced down to her cellphone for a split second.

'Be truthful,' he urged her. 'At least to check that I wasn't some sort of serial killer or something.'

'Yes,' she admitted. 'I'd probably have googled it.'

'OK,' Quaddra nodded. 'So, I'm not going to throw you into a moral dilemma here, but please allow me to suggest a variation of that scenario.'

Mary could already guess what Quaddra was about to suggest, but she played along anyway. 'Go on.'

'Let's say that the woman who I was attracted to . . . the one who I had invited out tonight, had absolutely no interest in me whatsoever. Now let's say that on the little note that I left her, just like the one that I left you, I had used my real name, instead of a fake one.'

'And she googled it,' Mary said, guessing where that boat was heading. 'And she discovered that you're a billionaire.'

Quaddra nodded. 'What do you think are the odds, despite her having no interest in me at all, of her declining the invitation?'

'That's a horrible assumption,' Mary came back. 'Despite what you might think, Thom . . .' She paused and cringed before correcting herself. '. . . Quaddra, the whole world isn't really out to get you just because you're rich. Not everyone is a con artist, you know?'

Mary thought about telling him that she was also a millionaire . . . that she had more money than she knew what to do with . . . but that didn't make her doubt everyone she met . . . or think that everyone was a con artist.

No. The voice inside her head commented. *You doubt everyone for a completely different reason.*

Quaddra chuckled. 'I don't think that the world is out to get me, Mary, and I know that not everyone is a con artist, but that's not the only reason why people would go to great lengths to befriend me, or get close to me. A person in my position has a lot of friends . . . *everywhere*. A person in my position has the ability to open the kind of doors that most people can't even get close to.'

Mary shifted on her chair.

'With a simple phone call,' Quaddra explained, 'I can arrange for job interviews or meetings with the CEOs of pretty much any company you like. With a single email I can speed up documents and paperwork being processed by any branch of our judicial or administrative system. With a text message I can get you a film audition with Hollywood's top producers and film makers.' He paused to take in Mary's reaction. 'You're right – not everybody is a con artist, Mary, but everybody needs a favor here or there, and a man in my position can facilitate most favors.'

'So, you're like the genie in a bottle.'

'In a weird way,' Quaddra said back. 'To many people, I am exactly that.'

'Money is power, right?'

Quaddra nodded. 'A silly saying, but in an ultra-capitalistic society like America, a very true one. Another very sad truth in our society is that no matter what you look like, money – especially big money – has the power to make you devastatingly attractive in most people's eyes.'

Mary wanted to say that Quaddra didn't need any money to make him attractive, but she decided that that was a comment for another night.

Quaddra leaned forward and rested his elbows on the table. 'I really wanted you to come out with me tonight, Mary, but I wanted you to do that because you were interested in me, not because of who I am, or what kind of favor I could grant you.' He immediately lifted a hand to pause Mary before she could refute. 'That's not me judging you before getting to know you, Mary. That's just me taking one step at a time. I really didn't want my position in life being a factor in you accepting my invitation. I just really wanted you to like me for being me.'

The sincerity in Quaddra's tone didn't go unnoticed.

'I'm not a liar, Mary, and I didn't do what I did with the intention of disrespecting you in any way. I really hope you can understand that.'

They sat in silence for several long seconds, just staring at each other. Mary tried to imagine how many people, especially women, had tried getting closer to Quaddra just because of his fortune, or how influential he could be. She didn't even get close to the real number.

Quaddra was the first to break the silence.

'I guess that the fact you're still sitting here after all I've said, means that you're not so angry with me anymore and that you, at least in part, understand why I did what I did.'

'I do,' Mary nodded. 'And I'm also not a liar, so I'll admit that if I were in your position, I would've probably done the same.'

Quaddra's smile was truthful . . . thankful . . . happy.

'By the way,' he said. 'I didn't really mean what I said earlier.'

Mary looked back at him with concern. 'Which part?'

'The part about me telling you who I really am, if you tell me who you really are.' He shook his head. 'You don't have to. I'm usually a very good judge of character and like I mentioned before, you don't come across like a hardened criminal, so I'm pretty confident that you're not running away from the law.'

He watched as Mary took a deep breath, but stayed silent.

'Whoever you're hiding from,' Quaddra continued, 'that's your business and I'm sure that there's a very good reason for it. If one day you want to tell me about it, I'll be all ears, but I'd like you to only do so if and when you're good and ready to let me know. Trust is earned and it takes time. I know that very well. I'm not a hypocrite, Mary. I'm well aware that a universal truth about all of us is that we all have a past, and in that past, there will undoubtedly be moments that we aren't exactly proud of . . . moments that we'd rather forget . . . moments that terrified us down to our core . . . and moments that we'd certainly erase from our lives if we ever could. For some, those undesirable moments are much more than just moments in a timeline – they make up that person's entire past . . . a past full of pain and scars that they are trying hard to leave behind and start anew . . . all they need is a chance.'

Mary also wasn't a hypocrite. She knew that sooner or later that day would come – the day that she would have to tell someone about her past life. She just didn't think that it would be this soon. She took another deep breath and began with the words – 'my ex-husband'.

Forty-Four

Quaddra's full attention reverted back to Mary as soon as he heard the words – *my ex-husband*. He clearly wasn't expecting Mary to open up about her past right there and then.

Mary did open up, but she gave Quaddra a much more watered-down version of what had really happened, being very careful to never mention Nelson's name, always referring to him as 'my ex-husband'. She never told Quaddra about the beatings or the false imprisonment. She also never mentioned the trial, Nelson's incarceration, or the fact that she had legally changed her name. All she said was that after their divorce, for her own safety, she had reverted back to her maiden name of Mary Smith.

Anyone sitting before Mary right then would've had a million questions that they would've liked to ask her. Maybe Quaddra did too, but like a true gentleman, he simply sat quietly, listening in almost total silence, allowing Mary to tell her story at her own pace and in her own words. When she was finally done he only asked one question.

'If you don't mind me asking?' he said, his tone tender and sympathetic. 'Where's your ex-husband now?'

'I don't know,' Mary lied. 'East Coast, I presume.' She never mentioned that they used to live in Massachusetts either. 'That's why I've been moving around like a nomad for over a year now.'

Quaddra nodded his understanding, clearly picking up on Mary being deliberately evasive. 'Are you done moving?'

Mary's eyes darted away from Quaddra for an instant before she could answer him. 'I don't know. My lease contract is coming up, and I'll have to decide on it very soon.' She shrugged. 'I guess I was waiting and hoping that I'd feel safe somewhere before I tried settling down, but I don't think that that will ever happen. I mean . . . none of us are ever one hundred percent safe, are we? No matter where we are.' She paused, as if reflecting over her own words. 'But I like San Francisco, so . . . I don't know.'

Quaddra seemed to be sizing Mary up . . . taking in the pain in her words . . . the discomfort in her demeanor . . . the fear inside her eyes. He was about to say something, when she beat him to the punch.

'Do you want to get out of here?' There was a certain intensity in the way that she looked at him, as if she simply couldn't deny the chemistry between them anymore. 'Get some fresh air or something?'

'Sure. I'd like that.'

Quaddra and Mary stepped out into a starry night that wasn't exactly cold, but the wind-factor was starting to make it so.

'Ocean Beach is just a couple of blocks that way,' Quaddra said, pointing west. 'If you prefer to walk by the beach and catch some of the sea breeze.'

Mary nodded, but said nothing in return.

They'd taken less than ten steps in the direction of the beach when Mary simply turned to face Quaddra, pushed him against the brick wall just past the restaurant that they were in, and kissed him like she'd never kissed anyone before.

Forty-Five

Without saying a word, as soon as Quaddra closed the door to his two-story mansion in Pacific Heights, Mary threw herself into his arms – her body pressing tightly up against his. Quaddra's reply was to wrap his strong arms around her waist, in a grip that Mary not only welcomed, but clearly longed for. Their lips quickly found each other's and they kissed, but the kiss was more like an explosion of desire – two sinners fighting for a piece of the forbidden fruit, and they both seemed to be starving.

Quaddra took a step back, falling flat against the door behind him. Mary stepped into him, pressing her body even tighter against his, so tight that she could feel him hard against her thigh.

Oh my god! the voice inside Mary's head piped up. *Jackpot!*

Mary's breathing became quicker, more deliberate, as Quaddra moved his kiss down to the curve of her neck . . . his lips and tongue traveling slowly onto her right shoulder.

Mary moved her arms up, running her fingers through his hair and pulling his head down, deeper into her neck.

Quaddra responded by kissing the soft skin there before holding a tiny portion of it between his teeth for a second. It wasn't exactly a bite. He didn't apply enough pressure to leave a mark, but there was more than enough pressure to make

Mary moan – a moan that seemed to come in stages, alternating between moans and heavier breathing until her entire body was shivering.

Quaddra understood the signal and allowed his right hand to deliberately crawl over her breasts, feeling how hard her nipples were. His lips stayed on her right shoulder, but this time his teeth didn't bite skin – they bit the thin strap of her dress before dragging it sideways until it had slid off her shoulder. Before doing the same to the strap on her left shoulder, his lips paused at the center of her neck so that he could softly kiss her neck dimple.

Another deep moan.

Quaddra grabbed the strap on Mary's left shoulder between his teeth, but this time he slid it off slowly, allowing her to feel the tiny bristle hairs on his chin softly scrapping against her skin.

'Ahhhhh!' Mary's breathing became heavier still.

As the strap slid off Mary's left shoulder, so did the top half of her dress, dropping down to her waist to expose her naked torso.

Right then, Quaddra stopped kissing her for two reasons: one – he needed to catch his breath because he too could feel his skin turning into gooseflesh. And two – he just couldn't wait any longer. He wanted ... needed ... to look at Mary. His eyes furtively peeked at her naked upper body, and he held his breath. Mary had the sort of body that people only tended to see in sports magazines, or in the heydays of *Playboy* – her natural breasts were round and firm, and her midriff seemed to have been sculpted by an artist. She truly was a breathtakingly stunning woman.

Mary lost no time in grabbing Quaddra's hands and cupping his palms over her breasts, inviting him to softly squeeze her nipples before hungrily kissing him again, which he gladly obliged. As they kissed, she reached for the buttons on his dress shirt and hurriedly began unbuttoning them from the top, but with her eyes closed and desire making her hands shake, the job proved to be a little too cumbersome. She managed to undo only two buttons before she gave up.

'Fuck this,' she murmured, grabbing his shirt with both hands and simply ripping it open. Buttons rained down against the black and white marble floor like a spilt bag of Skittles.

Quaddra couldn't care less. He wanted her as much as she wanted him. He let go of her breasts and wiggled his body left and right to free his arms from the shirt, which, with Mary's help, was off his body and onto the floor in two seconds flat.

She didn't have to look to know that Quaddra's torso was lean and ripped. As she arched into him, she could feel his tight muscles against her skin . . . her stomach . . . her breasts.

Double jackpot! The voice inside Mary's head seemed to be dancing a jig.

As naked skin came into contact with naked skin, their kissing . . . their touching . . . their breathing . . . became more urgent . . . desperate even.

Quaddra kicked off his shoes at the same time that Mary reached down for his belt.

He placed his hands on her waist, and with a simple flip of the wrist, pulled her dress from her hips, allowing it to slide down to the floor.

Mary wasn't wearing any underwear.

Belt undone.

Trouser button undone.

Zipper down.

Mary rolled Quaddra away from the door, swapping places with him as she stepped out of her dress.

Quaddra's hungry eyes devoured her body and he was forced to catch his breath once again. As he did, Mary slid her hands down to his waist, and in one smooth move, brought his trousers and underwear down to his feet.

Now it was a party . . . and a *biiiig* party at that.

Neither of them could take much more of that foreplay.

Quaddra stepped out of his trousers, grabbed Mary by the waist and lifted her onto him.

Fireworks.

Forty-Six

Mary and Quaddra made love in the house's entrance hall before moving it to the living room table. By the time they finally made it to the bedroom, upstairs, they were both sore, a little bruised, and completely out of breath, but that didn't stop them from going at it for a third time ... and this time, Mary took the lead ... at least for a little while. Not because she wasn't satisfied with how Quaddra had fucked her. On the contrary, she'd never been so satisfied in all her life. She took the lead because from a cowgirl position, she could look at Quaddra and how he reacted to her touches, her kisses, her scratches and her hip thrusts.

And Mary could look at him all day long. His body was like an athlete's – fit and trimmed but not overly muscular, and the intense chemistry that exploded between them every time their bodies touched was something that Mary had only ever read about in romantasy books. It just couldn't be real ... could it?

'Oh my god,' Mary whispered, finally rolling off Quaddra before collapsing onto the bed sheets by his side. They were both glistening in sweat. Mary was trying hard to catch her breath, but failing miserably. She didn't even know if she was done climaxing yet or not. Her legs were still shaking and what she could feel flying around inside her stomach certainly weren't butterflies ... more like a fleet of supersonic jets.

'That was just . . . spectacular,' Quaddra whispered, just as out of breath as Mary. 'And also incredibly loud.'

Mary's gaze reverted back to him. 'What was?'

He locked eyes with her. 'The screams.'

Mary frowned. 'What screams?'

Quaddra frowned back, trying to read Mary's expression. 'Are you joking?' It didn't look like she was. 'The one just now was one.'

Mary's body was still shaking. 'Who screamed?'

'You did.' Quaddra's breathing was starting to normalize. 'Very loudly . . . a few times.'

'No, I didn't. Did I?'

Mary wasn't joking. She really couldn't remember screaming.

Quaddra nodded again as he smiled. 'Loudly. I thought you'd pulled a muscle or something.'

Mary smiled back. 'I pulled a muscle all right . . . just not one of mine.'

Their smiles turned into laughter.

'So,' Mary sounded intrigued. 'Quaddra . . . is that like a European name?'

'Nope.' He made that 'pe' really pop. 'Just as weird as it sounds, really.'

'I wouldn't call it weird.' Mary chuckled, trying to sound breezy. 'But certainly different . . . quite cool actually.'

'Thank you,' Quaddra said back. 'I got it for my birthday – present from my parents.'

Mary laughed. 'Wow! So how many times have you used that line before?'

Quaddra shrugged. 'When your parents decide to give you such an odd name, you've got to think of something. Everyone I meet, if they don't actually frown when I say my name, they usually go – "that's a different name". I simply figured out that a funnier response tends to break the awkwardness a little.'

Mary nodded. 'Yeah, I guess you're right.' She looked left then right. 'What time is it?'

'Late, I think,' Quaddra replied, turning to check the alarm clock on the bedside table. 'Yep, it's coming up to three-thirty in the morning.'

'Really?' Mary flexed her torso up to check. 'Jesus! How long have we been . . .'

'For a while.' The new smile on Quaddra's lips was a proud one.

'Hours?' Mary asked.

Quaddra simply raised his eyebrows at her.

'Oh God.' Mary pushed herself into a sitting position. Her legs were still a little unsteady. 'I've got to go.'

'What, now?'

'Yeah.' She swung her legs off the bed, the tips of her toes lightly touching the varnished wood flooring.

Quaddra's eyes darted to the window for a moment. Raindrops were running down it in fast and crazy patterns.

'It's raining,' he told her, his tone soft. 'Why don't you stay?'

Mary shook her head and tried to get to her feet, but her legs weren't quite there yet – not enough strength to hold her up. She sat back down onto the edge of the bed.

'Mary, please . . .' Quaddra also pulled himself into a sitting position. He extended his hand, allowing his fingertips to softly touch Mary's left shoulder. 'Stay. I can get you a cab in the morning, if you like. It's late and it's raining.'

'I can't,' Mary lied again. 'I really have to go.'

'Please,' Quaddra tried again. 'I'm a very quiet sleeper. I don't snore . . . I don't toss and turn . . . and I don't steal the covers . . . you won't even notice that you're sleeping by my side.'

'I doubt that very much,' Mary said, her eyes quickly peeking at the good stuff again.

Quaddra laughed before continuing. 'If you prefer, you don't even need to sleep next to me. I have a guest room.' He paused and bit his bottom lip while his right eyebrow arched. 'I have three, actually. You can take your pick.'

'You have three guest rooms in this house?'

Quaddra nodded.

'How many bedrooms do you have in here?'

'Umm . . .' He took a moment. 'Nine.' He still didn't sound too sure. 'I think.'

'Wow, that's impressive,' Mary said, finally getting to her feet. She immediately began searching the bedroom floor.

'What are you looking for?'

'My clothes.'

'They're in the entry hall,' Quaddra informed her, a cheeky smile playing on his lips. 'Right by the front door.'

Mary paused for a second before she nodded back. 'I guess we just couldn't wait, could we.'

'Hey, I was ready to offer you a drink . . . have a seat in the living room . . . maybe shoot the breeze for a while . . . show you the house.' The smile didn't leave his lips.

'Um-huh. I bet you were.'

Quaddra's eyes took in Mary's whole figure as she turned to face him again. Her skin was still glistening with sweat. 'God, you really are breathtaking.'

'Don't you start that again.' She moved towards the door.

'Where are you going?'

'To get my clothes.'

'You're really not staying?'

Mary shook her head. 'I can't.'

As she got to the bedroom door, her balance wavered just a touch and she slammed her right shoulder against the doorframe.

'Whoa, are you OK there?' Quaddra asked, quickly getting to her.

'I'm fine,' Mary said back, before explaining. 'When I get nervous, I get clumsy. I drop things . . . I bump into things . . .

it's just the way I am. In fact, I'm clumsy even when I'm not nervous.'

Quaddra smiled mischievously. 'Are you saying that I make you nervous?'

Mary gave him a look that could suture an open wound.

'Alright.' Quaddra took a step back, but that didn't stop him from trying one more time. 'Hear me out here, OK? Why don't we have a drink and wait for an hour or so? Maybe the rain will have stopped by then. I didn't get a chance to show you my bar . . . or my wine collection. I'm sure we'll be able to find something to your liking.'

'No.' Mary firmly shook her head. 'No more drinks tonight . . . but I'll take a glass of water before I go, if that's OK?'

Mary was clearly determined not to stay. Pushing any harder, Quaddra knew, wouldn't be a good move. 'Of course.' He nodded. 'I'll get it for you.'

Quaddra took Mary downstairs and into the kitchen. As he pulled the fridge door open, the light from inside illuminated part of his naked figure.

Mary paused, her eyes taking in every inch of his body. 'I'm going to go get my clothes,' she quickly said before desire took over again.

In the entry hall, Mary scooped her dress from the floor and slipped it back on before reaching for her shoes.

Quaddra brought her the glass of water and while Mary drank it down in large gulps, he collected his underwear and trousers from the floor and quickly put them back on.

'Thank you,' she said, returning the glass to Quaddra.

They locked eyes one final time.

'Me asking again,' Quaddra said, 'won't make you change your mind, will it?'

'No.'

Quaddra nodded. 'OK.' He reached for his tuxedo jacket and

retrieved his phone from the inside pocket. 'At least let me call you a cab.'

'No, it's OK. I can call one myself.' She slipped into her heels and threw her shawl around her shoulders.

'OK, hold on,' Quaddra lifted both hands at her. 'Give me just five seconds, OK?' He pointed upstairs. 'Please don't leave before I'm back. I promise that I'm not going to try to keep you here. Five seconds . . . please?'

Quaddra standing shirtless in front of Mary, with his arms, pecs and abs still gleaming with perspiration was a sight to behold. Mary could feel her nipples starting to harden under her dress once again.

'OK.'

Quaddra dashed away.

'What have I just done?' Mary asked herself.

Seconds later, Quaddra reappeared carrying a long overcoat.

'Please take this,' he offered it to Mary.

'Oh no, it's fine,' Mary replied. She didn't reach for the coat. 'The rain isn't that heavy.'

As if on cue, right then, lightning lit up the sky outside, quickly followed by a crack of thunder.

They both turned to look at the window.

'I think the rain disagrees with you,' Quaddra said, still holding out the coat. 'Just take it, Mary, please. It's raining . . . it's cold outside . . . and all you have is that shawl.'

Another lightning bolt. Another crack of thunder.

Once again, Quaddra seemed to have read between the lines, picking up on Mary's hesitation. 'If you're worried about you having to return the coat back to me,' he shook his head, 'you don't really have to. Keep it . . . throw it away . . . or better yet, drop it at a homeless shelter. It's a good coat . . . warm. Let someone who needs it more than us have it.'

Mary thought about it for an extra second before finally giving in and reaching for the coat. It was certainly too big for her, but it was warm and it would no doubt keep her dry. As she put it on and buttoned it up, she saw the label on the inside and her eyes widened. It was a Tom Ford coat, which was probably worth at least five thousand dollars.

'Can I say something else before you leave?' Quaddra asked. There was a sliver of sadness in his tone.

Mary held his stare.

'I'm not going to pretend that I know what you're thinking,' Quaddra began. 'I wish I did. I thought that after everything that happened tonight, we had at least gotten over that initial "awkward" hurdle, you know?' He smiled, clearly thinking back to the events of that evening. 'Because you have to agree that this was one crazy night.'

Mary smiled back. 'It was.'

'But you're still acting like you don't trust me.' He immediately lifted a hand at her. 'Which I can totally understand. Like I said before, trust is earned and it takes time – and if I had been through everything you'd been through . . . everything you told me . . . I wouldn't trust anyone so easily either. I have no problem with earning your trust, if you give me that chance. But you rushing out in the middle of the night, during a thunderstorm, after all this . . .' Quaddra gestured at the entrance hall. '. . .it tells me that maybe, all this, was just a huge mistake for you. It tells me that maybe you regret being here with me.'

The pause was deliberate, to assess Mary's reaction. She gave him an almost imperceptible shake of the head, but said nothing in return.

'For what it's worth, Mary,' Quaddra continued, his voice unwavering, 'to me, this wasn't a mistake at all. Far from it. Tonight was the best night I've had in . . .' He shook his head. 'I can't even remember the last time that I felt the way I felt tonight . . . the way I'm feeling right now. That's why I want you to stay. I don't want this to be just this.'

Silence.

Quaddra seemed to get the hint. He nodded at the impasse between them. 'If this is really what you want, then I promise you that I won't chase you . . . I won't drop by Betsy's workplace again with another gift, or an invitation. If that's really how you feel about tonight, you don't have to worry. You won't hear from me again, but please, before you throw that coat away, or hand it in to a homeless shelter, check the outside pocket.'

Mary frowned at him before placing her hands inside both pockets. There was a folded piece of paper inside the right one.

'That's my cellphone number,' Quaddra said, as Mary unfolded the note to look at it. 'If you change your mind . . .' He shrugged. 'Text me . . . call me . . . send me a nude . . . whatever.'

Mary half smiled, half laughed at the joke. She really did like his sense of humor.

'Seriously,' he continued, taking a tentative step closer to Mary, his magnetism still strong enough to hold her in place, 'I'd love to see you again . . . anytime. To me, this could be a lot more than just this.'

Just as Quaddra moved in to kiss her one last time, another crack of thunder exploded outside, loud enough to make Mary finally snap out of his spell before he was able to kiss her.

'I've really got to go,' she said, taking a step back, turning around and exiting his house.

And just like that, their crazy night was over.

Forty-Seven

For the next full week, Mary could think of nothing else but the night that she'd spent with Quaddra, replaying that entire evening inside her head on an endless loop – from the moment that he came up behind her at the Legion of Honor, until the second that she turned her back on him and ran out of his house in the middle of a stormy night. And Mary could remember every detail ... every touch they'd shared.

Mary took a seat on her sofa, placed her feet on the coffee table, and allowed her eyes to settle on the painting that Quaddra had given her. She had finally unwrapped it and hung it on her wall, and she absolutely loved it. The more she looked at it, the more details she uncovered – little subtleties that Betsy had expertly added to the painting here and there, like Easter eggs to be discovered – and the more details she uncovered, the more that the piece reminded Mary of her own childhood. It reminded her of her mother's endless stream of live-in boyfriends – most of them for no more than a year, maybe two, maximum. It also reminded her of the tears that she'd cried almost every night, and of the incessant bullying that she was subjected to from a very young age, but most of all, the painting reminded Mary of the night that she'd finally had enough – enough of the constant beatings ... enough of the pain ... and certainly enough of her mother's boyfriend's stench not just all over her skin and hair, but inside her as well. That one night, as her mother and her boyfriend had another drunken argument in the living room, Mary, knowing exactly what would happen once her mother had fallen asleep, had packed a small bag with just a few items of clothing, and as they screamed and cursed at each other in the living room, Mary jumped out of her bedroom window, and disappeared into the night.

She was only fifteen years old.

She never went back.

They never came looking.

But that wasn't the real reason why Mary liked that painting so much. It wasn't because of what the mirror revealed about the girl's past – all the pain, the anguish, the suffering. No, what Mary loved most about that piece was the other side – the woman staring at the mirror and how, from a scared, broken and bruised little girl, she had blossomed into a beautiful and strong woman – a woman who would never again take abuse from anyone. The mirror in that painting was simply the past. The woman starring at it was the present ... she was the future ... and Mary was trying hard to be that woman.

On paper, she was only twenty-seven years old. Samantha Stewart would've been thirty-five, but Mary Smith was still only twenty-seven. Regardless of how she looked at it, she was still so very young, and Nelson Stewart wasn't going to be the last guy she'd ever dated ... she knew that. It had been over a year since her divorce and if Mary was honest with herself, Quaddra would at least make it into the 'boyfriend material' category. He was hot, he was kind, he was courteous, and he'd treated Mary with a lot of respect, despite all her mad outbursts. Even though it was pretty clear that he was completely into her, after Mary had run away from his house, in the middle of the night, like a gunslinger outlaw, he kept his promise ... he didn't try to contact her again ... and that showed character.

Right then, Mary wondered if for the past week, Quaddra had thought of her at all, because no matter how hard she tried, she simply couldn't stop thinking about him.

Oh, for fuck's sake, give him a call already. The voice inside Mary's head sounded sick and tired of all those thoughts. *You know you're going to. And not to worry you or anything, but a guy like Quaddra, how many women do you think are in line to go out, date, jump in bed with him . . . whatever they can get, really? He's certainly sweet on you, but that won't last forever, do you understand what I'm saying here?'*

Mary did . . . and the voice had a point.

She checked her watch – 8:15 p.m. – Thursday evening.

'OK, fuck it.'

Mary reached for her cellphone. She didn't have to look at the piece of paper that Quaddra had left inside his coat pocket to know his number. She already had it memorized.

Forty-Eight

They arranged to meet the next day, Friday, in the Theater District – not that far from Quaddra's house, actually – but this time, Mary picked the place. She decided on a small Spanish tapas bar and restaurant called The Pawn Shop, on Mission Street, considered a hidden gem in San Francisco by those who appreciate authentic Spanish food.

Quaddra arrived at the restaurant at exactly 7:30 p.m. – the time that they'd agreed on – while Mary was fashionably late, but only by ten minutes. The restaurant itself was indeed a 'hidden' gem, easily missed by anyone who didn't know about it because, from the outside, it did truly look just like a regular pawnshop, with guitars, stereos and old typewriters displayed on the front window, together with a large neon sign that read 'Cash for Gold'.

Mary wore the outfit that she'd bought that afternoon – a very elegant/casual black dress with silver details adorning both shoulder straps.

Quaddra, too, wore a much less formal outfit than he had the previous week.

The chemistry between Mary and Quaddra was, once again, off the charts from the get-go. As they took a table, towards the back of the restaurant, Mary wasn't really sure of Quaddra's intentions, but all that she could think of was 'how fast can we order and eat so that I can rip those clothes off your body?'

Quaddra was thinking exactly the same, but they both did their best to act as civilized as they possibly could. They ordered eight different tapas dishes between them and a very nice bottle of Rioja Reserva. The conversation was, just like last Wednesday, very light – books, music, theater, films . . . and all of it was punctuated by a lot of laughter – until Quaddra decided to touch on a much more delicate subject.

'Mary,' he said, as he refilled her wine glass, then his. 'I've got something that I wanted to talk to you about.'

'OK,' Mary said, noticing that Quaddra's expression had gained a more serious quality.

'You told me that in the past year,' he began, 'you've been moving around from place to place like a nomad, right?'

'A little . . . yeah,' Mary replied, her tone skeptical.

'And I assume that the reason for that,' Quaddra continued, 'is because it makes it a lot harder for anyone to be able to track you down when you're moving from city to city, and state to state . . . and by "anyone", I mean – your ex-husband.'

Mary sipped her wine slowly, her eyes studying Quaddra.

'Are you doing your thing again?' she asked. 'The read-between-the-lines party trick?'

'I am,' Quaddra admitted. 'And I'm sorry, but this time there's a good reason for it.' He paused and checked himself. 'At least I think it's a good reason.'

'Is that right?'

Are we getting ready to do another 'get up and go' job here? the voice inside Mary's head asked.

'Well,' Quaddra came back. 'Just hear me out for one minute, OK? If you think that it's a crap reason, I'll drop the subject and I'll never come back to it again. How does that sound?'

Mary had another sip of her wine and her left eyebrow lifted slightly at Quaddra.

He understood that as 'OK'.

'Since you've been moving around a lot, I'm assuming that you're renting short-term rental accommodations – maybe three months at a time, maybe more ... I don't know ... but probably nothing longer than a year, am I right?'

Mary stayed silent.

Quaddra took that as a 'yes'.

'And the way I see it,' he continued, 'the reason why you keep on moving around, is because one of the ways in which you could be tracked down would be by someone finding your name tied up to a lease agreement somewhere in the country.'

Mary still said nothing back.

Quaddra nodded at her. 'Let me warn you that I'm taking all your silences as a positive response.' He waited. Got nothing back. Proceeded. 'OK, so here's the reason why I brought all this up.'

Mary braced herself.

Quaddra took a sip of his wine before continuing. 'Take one of my apartments,' he said, his tone casual.

'Excuse me?' Mary cocked her head back just a little.

'I'm an investor, remember?' Quaddra explained. 'And one of the fields that I invest in is property. I have several properties scattered all around California ... quite a few right here in San Francisco.' He paused, giving Mary a chance to better grasp what he was saying. 'Take one of my apartments ... or a house if you prefer.'

Mary sat back on her chair before letting out a deflated breath. 'I don't need charity, Quaddra.' She sounded offended and a little angry. 'I'm quite capable of taking care of myself. I'm also capable of paying for my own place.'

'Oh no.' Quaddra immediately sat forward on his chair, raising both hands at Mary in a 'just a second' gesture. 'You got me all wrong – probably because I explained this to you like a second grader trying to explain algebra.' He clarified, knowing that he could've done a better job. 'I'm sure you're more than capable of taking care of yourself and paying for your own place. I wasn't offering you charity, Mary. Not at all.' The new pause was a much more thoughtful one. 'Let me try this again, OK? Last time you told me that the contract on the place that you're living at the moment is coming to an end, and that you'd have to make a decision on where to go from here, right?' He didn't wait for a reply. 'So, what I'm suggesting here is – instead of going back to a realtor to find your next apartment, or house, or whatever . . . rent it from me.'

Mary angled her head at Quaddra.

'I'm not suggesting any shady deals here either. I really don't do those. Everything would be done above board and by the book, the only difference is – you can put whatever name you like on the contract.' He threw his hands up in a hands and shoulders shrug. 'Sign it Luke Skywalker for all I care.'

Mary's eyes narrowed at Quaddra.

'What I'm really offering you here, Mary, isn't charity. It's just a chance for you to make it even harder for anyone to track you down because your name will not appear on a lease contract anymore, that's all.' He raised a hand at Mary again before explaining. 'Every lease applicant in the country gets screened for approval. I'm sure you know that, right? Credit check . . . background check . . . references . . . all that stuff. When they do, their names go into a Rental Applicant Screening Service database, which can be used as a way of finding someone.' Quaddra allowed Mary a couple of extra seconds. 'It's one less thing for you to worry about, and maybe you won't have to carry on moving around like a nomad all the time.'

Mary stayed silent, but her brain was working at speed.

She still had about two weeks left on her contract, and she had already decided that she'd like to stay in San Francisco, but for now, that was a detail that she was keeping to herself.

'Full disclosure here?' Quaddra asked, taking advantage of Mary's hesitation.

Mary's eyebrows shot up to her forehead to indicate that that was a silly question.

Quaddra looked down at their table and his lips moved ever so slightly, but no sound came out. To Mary, it looked like he was trying to put the sentence together inside his head first, so not to phrase it in the wrong way.

'In all honesty,' he said, his eyes, once again, meeting Mary's. 'This is also me being a little selfish.'

Mary's eyebrows stayed up her forehead. 'You being selfish?'

Quaddra nodded. 'A little . . . yeah.'

Mary simply waited.

'Your plan is great, Mary,' Quaddra told her. 'The more you move around, the thinner and more complicated the trail to you gets, until, one day, it becomes practically invisible. Any intelligent person would easily figure out that the more cities, or better yet, the more states you move in and out of, the quicker that process becomes. And you are a very intelligent person.' He paused to observe Mary's reaction.

She gave nothing away, except for a ghost of a smile that for a split second hovered over her lips.

'So, I'm guessing that,' Quaddra continued, 'once your rental contract is up, the intention is maybe to leave San Francisco, probably even California.'

This time, Mary's poker face was unreadable.

'And this is where my plan becomes a little selfish.' Quaddra had a large sip of his wine. 'I'd really love if you stayed in San Francisco.'

Mary stayed silent, while Quaddra finished the rest of his wine.

'Like I promised,' he finally said, 'I won't mention this again, but . . . just think about it, OK?'

Mary, too, finished her wine, and silence settled between them, but even then, it didn't feel at all awkward. In fact, to Mary, it felt comforting.

They gazed into each other's eyes, but the gaze didn't stay there for long, quickly dropping down an inch or so to each other's lips.

'Do you want to get out of here?' Quaddra was the one who broke the silence.

'I thought you'd never ask.'

Forty-Nine

From the restaurant, Mary and Quaddra went straight back to Quaddra's house in Pacific Heights, less than fifteen minutes away, and just like in the previous week, as soon as they stepped through the front door, they were all over each other – kissing, touching, biting – all of it eager . . . desperate . . . as if they were each other's last supply of oxygen. It took only a few seconds for both of their clothes to be, once again, scattered all over the floor in the entrance hallway, but this time, at least, they made it into the living room and onto the luxurious high-pile rug.

'Wait,' Quaddra whispered, already half out of breath. Mary was lying on top of him, her nipples so hard they were practically pocking dimples onto his skin. Her willing lips had just moved from his neck down to his chest, and judging by how quickly they were moving, they couldn't wait to reach the full prize.

'What?' she whispered back, lifting her head off his chest, but only slightly.

'Before we get covered in carpet burns, do you want to move this to the sofa . . . or to the bedroom?'

'Why?' Mary asked, before allowing her lips to continue their journey for a couple more seconds. They moved down to his belly button. 'I like the burns.' This time she fully lifted her head to look Quaddra in the eye. As their gaze met, she bit her bottom lip. 'I like a little pain.' She added a disarming wink to the end of that sentence. 'And don't worry, we will move it to the sofa ... and to the bedroom.'

Her lips returned to the job at hand.

Quaddra closed his eyes and took a deep, quivering breath.

After they satisfied each other on the rug, they did move it to the sofa, but after that, they didn't make it to the bedroom.

'Oh my god,' Mary said, as they were trying to go from the living room to the bedroom upstairs. 'Is that a pool table?'

Quaddra nodded. 'Yeah, that's the games room.'

Mary smiled, her head angling sideways. 'I always wanted to get fu ...'

Before Mary could even finish her sentence, Quaddra was already bending her over the table. Mary let out a moan so inviting that even she was surprised. She stretched her arms wide and held onto the two center pockets as firmly as she could – the anticipation almost making her hyperventilate.

From what she'd seen so far, in bed, Quaddra could read Mary like a lit billboard, knowing exactly when to turn down the tenderness and up the roughness ... and vice-versa.

Mary took a quick look over her right shoulder. As her gaze found Quaddra's, she gave him an inviting smile before spreading her legs. 'Take me whichever way you want.'

Quaddra reached for her hair and pulled it. 'Oh, don't worry, I will.'

'Oh God!' Mary moaned in a whisper. She was, once again, trying hard to catch her breath, as Quaddra rolled off her to lie by her side on the pool table. They had changed positions a few times, with the last one having both of them on the table. 'Did I ...' Mary's voice was just as unsteady as the rest of her body. 'Did I scream again?'

'Uh-huh.' Quaddra nodded before they both broke down laughing.

'Argh,' Mary winced, reaching for her knees, which were red-raw and completely scuffed, just like her elbows, the palm of her hands, her lower back and the rear of her shoulders.

'Are you OK?' Quaddra lifted his head to look at Mary, propping himself up on his elbows. That was when he saw the scuffs all over Mary's body. 'Oh, damn!' He brought a hand to his mouth. 'Those gotta hurt. I'm so sorry.'

Mary turned her head to look at him. He had quite a few scuffs himself. 'Remember I told you? I don't mind a little pain. Nothing to be sorry about.' She looked left then right. 'But on that subject, I am the one who's sorry.'

'What for?'

She indicated the pool table. There was a small tear on the table's green bed cloth, just by the bottom right-hand pocket, and a pretty large one running parallel to the left rail. 'I seem to have ruined your pool table.'

Quaddra shrugged. 'It's just a table … and this …' His eyebrows arched, as he nodded at the space between the two of them. '… is worth way more than that.' He craned his neck to kiss her shoulder.

There were distinct tones of tenderness in Quaddra's voice that Mary had never heard before … not in anyone's voice. She smiled at him and they stared into each other's eyes for several silent seconds.

'God, you are beautiful,' Quaddra said, running the back of his index finger against the contour of her chin.

'Thank you,' she said back, allowing her eyes to run the length of his body. 'You are … OK … I guess.'

Quaddra laughed.

'I need a shower,' Mary said, hopping off the pool table.

'Sure,' Quaddra said, also getting back on his feet, before nodding at Mary's scuffs. 'But those are going to sting.'

Mary moved closer and kissed his lips. 'Do I have to remind you again?'

'Yeah, I know.' Quaddra nodded. 'You don't mind a little pain.'

'That's right,' Mary confirmed. 'Plus, you're coming to the shower with me to sooth the pain.' She reached for his left hand and dragged him out of the games room.

Back in the bedroom, after a long shower, they were both dressed in white fluffy bathrobes. Quaddra had just come back from the kitchen with two large glasses of water.

'Thank you,' Mary said, taking one.

'You're not going to run off in the middle of the night again, are you?' Quaddra asked.

Mary stretched her lips into a humorless smile as she looked back at him.

'I'm not criticizing,' he said in his defense. 'I'm just checking.'

Mary didn't need to be an expert to be able to read what was written all over Quaddra's demeanor. It showed in the way that he was looking at her. He really wanted to ask her, once again, to think about his suggestion ... to consider taking one of his properties and staying in San Francisco. But he didn't have to.

'The properties you mentioned earlier,' Mary asked. 'Are they furnished?'

Quaddra held back on a smile that would've made him look like a kid on Christmas morning. 'Yeah, all of them. But if you don't like the décor, you can change it in any way you like. It's not a problem.'

'Do you have anything in or around the Dogpatch?'

'The Dogpatch?' Quaddra took a minute. 'No, I don't think so ... but I do have a warehouse conversion apartment in Bayview.' His head angled at Mary. 'Not that far, to be honest. But it's not a big apartment – two bedrooms, if I'm not mistaken. Immense living room, though.'

'A two-bedroom apartment sounds ideal. I don't need much.' Mary thought about it for a few more seconds. 'When could I have a look at it?'

'Umm ... any time you like. I can arrange it for tomorrow morning, if you want.'

'There's no big rush,' Mary replied, sounding breezy. 'How about sometime next week?'

'Sure,' Quaddra agreed. 'But I'll have to send someone else to show you the apartment,' he explained. 'I'm scheduled to fly to New York on Sunday. I've got a series of meetings arranged for next week.'

'Oh, OK.' Mary did her best to keep the disappointment from invading her tone. 'When are you back?'

'Hard to say with these kinds of meetings,' Quaddra replied. 'It all depends on the outcome, but hopefully by next weekend.'

Mary nodded her understanding. 'Do you have time tomorrow?'

'Yes, of course. Do you really want to see the apartment?'

'Why not?' Mary nodded. 'How about tomorrow afternoon or early evening?'

'Sounds perfect.' This time, the Christmas morning smile exploded on Quaddra's lips.

Fifty

Bayview was the next neighborhood along from the Dogpatch, just south of it, in fact. Quaddra's warehouse-converted apartment was located at the far north end of Bayview – less than a twenty-minute-walk away from Mary's present address. The flat sat on the top floor of a beautiful old, redbrick, ex-storage facility, positioned just across Islay Creek Channel. To Mary, the apartment was a dream.

'I thought you said that this was a small apartment,' Mary said, as she walked back into the living room from the outside balcony. The apartment was almost twice as large as the one that she lived in at the moment.

'It is,' Quaddra said back, with a frown. 'It's only a two-bed.'

Mary chuckled. 'Two, quite large bedrooms ... plus a pretty impressive kitchen, and a living room we could play basketball in. Look at this.' She broadly gestured at the living room.

'What about the furniture ... the décor ... what do you think? Like I've said, you can change it if you want.'

'No, I like it,' Mary said, having a seat on the large, L-shaped, leather sofa that faced the floor-to-ceiling windows with views of the Channel and the San Francisco Bay. 'Did you decorate it yourself?'

'Me? No,' Quaddra replied with a chuckle and a shake of the head. 'This is an investment property. Every time I acquire one, I hire a decorator to kit them out. I just wouldn't have the time . . .' His head angled left. 'Or the knowledge.'

Mary stayed silent, her eyes roaming the living room space one more time before settling back on the incredible window view.

'So, what do you think?' Quaddra had a seat next to Mary and reached for her hand. 'I can give you a very good deal.'

'No.' Mary pulled her hand away before lifting a finger at Quaddra. 'I told you – I don't need any charity. If I take it, I'll pay the regular market price.'

'Fine,' Quaddra came back, hands lifted in surrender. 'Market price it is.' There was a long pause. 'So . . . will you take it?'

Mary got back on her feet and walked over to the open-plan kitchen. She looked up at the ceiling, then down at the floor before leaning back against the kitchen counter.

'Yeah,' she finally said. 'I really like it. I can see myself living here for a while.'

'Yes!' Quaddra cheered, leaping to his feet. He did nothing to hide his happiness. 'Here.' He handed Mary the apartment keys. 'It's yours.'

Mary looked at him sideways. 'I haven't signed the contract yet. And there's no rush, remember?'

'Sure, I understand that, but like I told you – I'm flying to New York tomorrow and I'm not exactly sure when I'll be back. The apartment is unoccupied anyway. If you take the keys now, then you can move your stuff in whenever you like and at your own pace. No rush.'

Mary still looked unsure.

'Seriously,' Quaddra pushed, reaching for her hand and placing the keys in it. 'Just take the keys. It's easier this way . . . and since you mentioned the contract, have you thought about which name you'd like me to put on it?'

Mary paused for a second.

'Anything will do,' Quaddra pushed. 'For example – give me a name that starts with the letter . . .'

"W".'

'"W"?'

'Um-hum.'

'I don't know . . . umm . . . Wendy?'

'Wendy is a great name. She's even got her own burger place.'

Mary smiled.

'Now pick a last name . . . anything will do.'

'I don't know,' Mary looked flustered.

'Give me a teacher's name from when you were a child . . . quick . . . don't think . . . just say it.'

Mary shrugged. 'I don't know . . . Mr. Crowley?'

'Wendy Crowley,' Quaddra looked pensive for a moment. 'It works. What do you think?'

'Wendy Crowley.' Mary said the name to herself. 'Yeah . . . it does work.'

'Wendy Crowley it is,' Quaddra confirmed before stepping closer to Mary to kiss her. 'And just like that . . .' He snapped his thumb and forefinger. '. . . your name is off any property leasing agreement. Good luck to anyone trying to find you from now on.'

They kissed again.

'Thank you,' Mary said. 'I really mean it.'

'One hundred percent my pleasure,' Quaddra replied. 'I'm just so glad you're staying in San Francisco.'

'Yeah, me too,' Mary admitted before turning to look at the view from the window one more time. 'I like this city . . . a lot.'

'Well, this calls for a celebration, don't you think?' Quaddra asked. 'Are you hungry? How about we go get some early dinner somewhere around here? I don't know this area too well, but I know that Bayview is famous for its diversity in restaurants – especially smaller, street-food kind of places.'

Mary smiled. ‘Yeah, I could eat. But I have a better idea.’ She reached for Quaddra’s hand. ‘How about we christen this place first?’ She gestured towards the hallway that led deeper into the flat and into the bedrooms. ‘Those beds look really comfortable.’

Quaddra smiled, as he followed Mary into the hallway. ‘I really like the way your mind works.’

Fifty-One

It took Mary just a single cab trip to move all of her stuff from her old apartment in the Dogpatch, to the new one, in Bayview. Despite still having about a week left on her contract, she chose to make the move on Thursday morning, just five days after Quaddra had shown her the converted warehouse flat.

Quaddra, himself, ended up having to stay in New York City for eight days, but while he was away, he and Mary exchanged text messages, or phone calls, at least once a day. As soon as he was done with his last engagement, he flew straight back to San Francisco International. That was one of the many advantages of having his own private jet. Quaddra never had to wait for a scheduled flight.

He landed at San Francisco International at around 10:15 p.m. on Monday evening, and from the airport, he went straight to Mary's apartment. Sure, he was tired, but he couldn't wait to see her, and she couldn't wait to see him.

In the weeks that followed, their romance blossomed like tulips in April. When Quaddra wasn't away, which was something that happened constantly, due to the many businesses and investments that he had scattered all over the country, he and Mary just couldn't get enough of each other, doing practically everything together – from early morning runs by the Bay and chilled-out film nights at home, to movie premieres and gala dinners with celebrities in completely extravagant surroundings.

Despite Quaddra now knowing exactly where Mary lived, she would stay over at his place a lot more often than he would stay at hers, and within five weeks of what by then had to be considered 'dating', the voice inside Mary's head started to notice a familiar pattern.

Oh, great. Here we go again.

The comment had come a few days ago, just as Mary had used her own set of keys to enter Quaddra's house before typing an eight-digit alphanumeric code onto the keypad to disarm the alarm.

This is exactly how it all starts. That was exactly how it started with Nelson, remember? Your own set of keys . . . knowing the alarm code . . . coming over to his place while he's still at work . . . you know exactly what I'm talking about, don't you?

'So? Quaddra is nothing like Nelson?'

The voice inside Mary's head couldn't really argue with that statement . . . at least not yet. In hindsight, even in the very earlier stages of the dating game, Nelson had already started to show signs that hinted at a narcissistic personality, like the fact that he was always very authoritative, having to have the last word in just about anything – from what they would be having for dinner that night to what outfit would best suit Mary for the evening. From the very start of their relationship, it was always his way or no way.

Quaddra, on the other hand, was completely different . . . at least so far. He'd always listen to Mary's opinion on everything, having taken her advice on numerous occasions. He was also always considerate and kind, and way more than once Mary heard him say – 'You know what? That's a good point. I never thought of that. You're right' – something that Nelson would never have said, even when he knew that he was wrong.

All I'm saying here is – take it easy, OK? Things seem to be moving just a little bit too fast.

This time, it was Mary who couldn't argue with the voice inside her head, but she felt happy, something she hadn't felt in quite some time.

Back at her place, Mary stripped off her running clothes and stepped into the lukewarm shower. She only had ninety minutes to get ready.

She knew that if she went for a run so late in the afternoon, she'd be cutting it really close, but running relaxed her, and she really needed her nerves to settle for the evening because tonight was the night that she had always dreaded, but knew it would be coming sooner or later. She called it 'the ceremonial approval' night. That was when she would be formally introduced to Quaddra's close circle of friends as his official girlfriend, and their approval was practically a prerequisite for their relationship to sail on smoothly.

Mary had always hated those nights. She could delay them, but there was no escaping them. Every relationship had one, and tonight Quaddra had arranged for an 'informal' cheese and wine night at his house.

'Just a few close friends, that's all.' Those had been his exact words. 'It will be a nice, relaxed evening.'

But Mary knew that the evening would be anything but relaxing. She'd been there before, and the format to such 'approval nights' was always the same, regardless of them being a small cheese and wine get-together, or a large ballroom party. Sometime during the course of the evening, everyone in that cheese and wine party would somehow find themselves alone with Mary – in a corner, in a room, in the kitchen, by the pool outside, in the hallway . . . it didn't matter – they would all get their five minutes with the 'new girl', in which they would interrogate her as if she were a criminal.

Mary was sure that she'd have no problems with any of Quaddra's male friends – she was undeniably attractive, intelligent and very charming . . . when she wanted to be. Guys tended to always gravitate towards her, and she knew that she could win them over without even trying. But women? That was a completely different ball game. Most women she'd ever met actually hated the fact that she was beautiful, intelligent and charming. And from the conversations that she'd had with Quaddra since they'd started properly dating, she got the impression that most of his female friends had, at some point, tried their luck with him, and Mary knew from experience that the kind of jealousy that derived from – 'what the fuck does she have that I don't?' – was rarely beatable. The fact that Mary seemed to have come out of nowhere to win Quaddra's heart, with nobody having ever met or heard of her before, would not sit well with any of his female friends. But other women's jealousy, bitching and bickering were nothing new to Mary.

She got out of the shower, blow-dried her hair and chose a simple but very effective outfit – black skater dress that effortlessly added emphasis to her hourglass silhouette, and beige, ankle-strap, stilettos. That was it. She needed nothing else to look stunning. The makeup, she kept modest, allowing her natural beauty to shine through. All she did was accentuate her lips and her eyes, which were, once again, back to their original bright blue color – no more contact lenses.

Are you ready for this? the voice asked, as Mary adjusted her dress, checking herself in the full-length mirror by her apartment door.

'As ready as I'll ever be.' She reached for her handbag.

Good. Let's go do this.

Fifty-Two

'So, Mary, tell us – how did you and Quaddra meet . . . business trip somewhere?'

It took less than five minutes from the formal introductions as Quaddra's guests arrived for the evening, for the first question to be thrown at Mary, and it came from Carol, who was standing next to Rachel. They had both met Quaddra years ago, at university, and there was zero doubt in Mary's mind that he had slept with both of them – probably even together – but jealousy, especially of things that had happened in the past, had never been Mary's style. She truly couldn't care less. Everyone had a past.

Carol and Rachel were both holding half-empty glasses of white wine and staring Mary down as if they were about to go into a boxing ring with her. All three of them were by the cheese table, though only Mary was holding a plate.

Mary licked a blob of plum chutney from the tip of her index finger before turning to look at them. They were both unnatural blondes, and their hair and makeup seemed to have been professionally done for the evening.

From the get-go, Mary could tell by the way that they were looking at her that those two couldn't wait to get her away from Quaddra so that they could launch their first assault. And they seized the very first opportunity they got.

Mary was about to reply to Carol when Quaddra, who was

standing with two of his buddies by the drinks table, came to Mary's rescue. He knew exactly how intimidating Rachel and Carol could be, especially when they ganged up on someone.

'How are we doing, babe?' he asked, approaching the three women.

As soon as Quaddra said the word 'babe', Mary saw the glance that Carol gave Rachel, silently communicating that that would definitely be a topic for discussion once they were by themselves, but they weren't alone in their communicating glance. Quaddra also sent one Mary's way and his came accompanied by a very subtle bottom-lip biting that clearly said – 'I'm so sorry about this'.

Mary gave him an almost invisible smile that replied – 'Don't worry, honey . . . I've got this'.

'We were just asking Mary how the two of you met,' Rachel said, smiling at Mary, who easily understood the importance of the question. That, right there, was a tight group of friends. Some of them had probably known each other since kindergarten, with that circle remaining pretty small throughout their whole lives. Joining that 'elite' group was a task that, most who had tried, had failed, Mary was sure of it. But Mary also understood where they were coming from. They were simply trying to look out for their friend.

'We met at an indie art exhibition, in the Dogpatch,' Mary replied, as she dropped a small dollop of plum chutney onto her plate.

'What actually happened was . . .' Quaddra quickly took over, before the onslaught of questions began. 'We were both swinging from left to right and angling our heads in front of a black canvas.'

'What?' Brian, Rachel's partner, asked, though everyone frowned at Quaddra at the same time.

Quaddra told them the story.

'After that,' he added, 'I sort of acted like some creepy little stalker, I'm afraid to say.' He lifted his hands at the group, as their questioning stares settled on him. 'At the exhibition,' he explained. 'I missed the chance to ask Mary for her phone number, so I . . .' He glanced at Mary and smiled.

She smiled back.

'Had to pull a few strings to find out how I could get in touch with her,' Quaddra continued. 'Luckily, Mary was friends with one of the artists who were exhibiting that evening. I managed to get a message to that artist, who kindly passed the message to Mary.'

Mary knew exactly why Quaddra had added those details. He wanted all of his friends to know that he was the one who had chased Mary, and not the other way around. That would certainly give them all food for thought.

Just seconds after Quaddra finished telling his story, the doorbell rang.

'That'll probably be Megan,' Carol said, nodding at Quaddra. 'She's always fashionably late – French style.'

'That's for sure,' Quaddra agreed.

There was something in the way that Quaddra said those words that made Mary frown at him, but the mystery didn't last long because Carol wasn't about to miss such a great opportunity for a quick dig.

'Quaddra and Megan used to date,' she said.

Next to her, Rachel nodded before adding, 'For quite a while.'

'It wasn't that long,' Quaddra was quick to counter.

'You guys dated for about a year,' Carol said before looking at Mary. 'For Quaddra, that's a hell of a long time.' Those words were followed by another silent communicating glace between her and Rachel, but this time everyone in the room could read it. It clearly said – 'Let's see how long this one will last'.

Fifty-Three

Quaddra didn't have 'live-in' staff. He never thought it necessary. He lived alone and traveled so often that the house would be empty on average at least two to four days every week, but it was a very large house, with ample outside space, a swimming pool, a beautiful garden and a pool guesthouse. He certainly needed help to keep all that clean and organized, and the help consisted mainly of three people, four times a week – Antonia and Gabriela (mother and daughter), who attended to the main house, and Jonas, who took care of the pool, the garden, and was pretty accomplished when it came to anything DIY.

For the cheese and wine party, Antonia and Gabriela were helping with everything kitchen wise, the cleaning and welcoming the guests as they arrived. Gabriela was the one who opened the door for the new and final batch of guests, and Carol was right, it was Megan, a woman who Quaddra had dated a while back, together with her best friend, Kristie, and Kristie's husband, Tyler, who also happened to be Quaddra's best friend. They'd known each other since lower school.

From the second that Mary was introduced to Megan, Mary could already tell that Megan didn't like her.

'Wow!' Megan had said, taking a step back to look at Mary from head to toe. 'Just look at you. You're gorgeous.' Her eyes bounced over to Quaddra for a split second. As they did, Mary could practically see a drop of venom start to blob up right on the corner of Megan's lips.

'Thank you,' Mary said, returning the fake smile. 'So are you.'

That was no lie. Megan really was a stunning-looking woman. She also held herself with the self-confidence of a CEO. Mary wasn't at all surprised to see that all the other women in that room, in one way or another, seemed to look up to Megan. To that group, she was, without a doubt, the Queen Bee.

The evening preceded just as Mary had predicted it would. Every time she was far enough away from Quaddra, one of the guests would, all of a sudden, magically appear by her side, and it would, almost always, be one of the girls.

More than once, during the course of the evening, Mary caught Megan staring at her from a distance, and those were the sole definition of the "what-the-fuck-does-she-have-that-I-don't?" looks. Mary didn't have to be an expert in body language to see that Megan still had feelings for Quaddra.

At the drinks table, Mary poured herself another glass of red wine, but as she was about to walk over to Quaddra, an arm looped through hers, steering her in a different direction.

'So c'mon, Mary,' Megan said, making a beeline to the French doors that led outside, and dragging Mary with her. 'Tell me a little about yourself. I'm so curious. I hear that you're from New York, so how come you ended up in San Francisco?'

They walked out to the pool area and Megan made sure to drag Mary all the way to the other side, where Kristie and Rachel were already waiting. No sign of Carol, but they were well away from all the other guests.

Brilliant, Mary's mental voice commented. *We're being ambushed by the Pink Ladies.*

'Mary was just telling me what brought her to San Francisco,' Megan announced, as she and Mary joined the other two women.

Mary's eyes circled the group. 'You girls aren't planning on pushing me into the pool, are you?' She calmly sipped her wine.

Kristie and Rachel chuckled at the same time.

'Why would we do that?' Megan replied, her gaze quickly pinging to her two friends. 'We're not ten years old, Mary.'

Could've fooled me, Mary thought.

'So,' Megan insisted, 'why move all the way across the country like this? New York to San Francisco . . . east coast to west coast.'

'I didn't,' Mary lied, taking two steps back from the pool, just in case.

All three of them looked back at her with question marks in their eyes.

'Earlier I was asked where I was from "originally",' Mary explained. 'And the answer to that question is New York City, but I haven't lived in New York for years. Y'all just assumed that I'd been living in New York before I came to San Francisco.'

There was an odd, hesitant moment between Megan, Rachel and Kristie.

'So, where were you living before San Fran?' Megan again.

Mary had another sip of her wine. 'OK, let's do this.'

'Do what?' Megan countered.

Mary knew that she had to tread carefully. She really didn't want to make enemies of these women.

'I completely understand where y'all are coming from,' Mary began. 'You've all known Quaddra for years, maybe even decades. You guys are a very tight group of friends. You hang out together all the time . . . and you probably know everyone Quaddra knows.' There was a quick, breathing pause. 'Then, all of a sudden, here I am, seemingly out of nowhere, the new girl . . . a complete outsider, and I'm dating your friend.'

'Dating?' Megan chuckled. 'It looks like you've practically moved in already.'

The comment got sneaky smiles from Rachel and Kristie.

'Just a second ago,' Mary continued, looking directly at Megan, 'you told me that y'all weren't ten years old, right? So how about we all act that way as well? Just ask me what you want to ask me. There's no need to beat around the bush with these silly, tiptoeing questions.'

Megan straightened up, never shying away from Mary's stare. 'And what is it that you think we want to ask you?'

'If I'm after Quaddra's money. That's what you're all worried about, isn't it? That I'm just an opportunist?'

All three women glanced at each other. It took only three seconds for Megan to give Mary a 'fuck it' shrug.

'So . . . are you?' she finally asked. 'After his money?'

Mary could feel the wine starting to take effect, so she decided to hold back on another sip because she really didn't want to mess things up.

'I never knew who Quaddra was,' she told them. 'I'd never seen or heard of him before until I met him in that arts exhibition, months ago, and when we met, he gave me a false name. He told me his name was Thomas. That's the man I was attracted to – Thomas, not Quaddra. Just a very interesting guy who happened to be at the same art exhibition that a friend of mine had invited me to.'

The three women standing before Mary exchanged another quick glance – one that Mary could easily read. They all knew that Mary was telling the truth because somehow, they all seemed to know that the false name tactic was something that Quaddra sometimes used. Mary wasn't sure if that was something to worry about or not.

'Look,' she continued, 'I understand that none of you have any reason to trust me. You have no reason to believe in anything I say either, but I'm sure that all of you trust Quaddra. And I'm also sure that all of you can understand that no one gets to where he is in life without being pretty savvy and a damn good judge of character. And if you don't know this already, believe me, he has a gift when it comes to reading people. Somehow, he can see right through you.'

The three women shuffled on their feet before Megan side-nodded at Mary. 'He did the read between the lines thing with you too?'

Mary bit down on the smile that bubbled up to her lips. 'Right on the first night out.'

'Yeah, he does that,' Megan agreed. 'He just can't help it.'

'And he does it well,' Mary added. 'It's fucking scary the way he can read you.'

Megan chuckled. 'Get ready,' she warned Mary. 'Because it will get quite annoying sometimes.'

This time, Mary smiled. 'I can imagine it will. Any tips?'

Megan laughed first, quickly followed by Rachel and Kristie.

'Easiest thing is don't try to hide anything from him. He will read you like a lit billboard if you do,' Megan said.

Right at that moment, Quaddra and Tyler appeared by the French doors that led back into the house. They were looking around, clearly searching the garden and the pool area when they both seemed to clock the four women by the pool at the same time. And they both went rigid as soon as they saw the group.

'Oh fuck!' Quaddra said, looking at Tyler. 'They've ambushed Mary.'

'Oh, that's not good,' Tyler said back. 'Megan can be a real bitch sometimes.'

'You're telling me? We've got to go rescue her.'

But as both of them took their first hurried steps in the direction of the group, they saw and heard all four women laugh . . . together.

'What the fuck?' Tyler said, as he and Quaddra slowed down a touch. 'Are they . . . bonding?'

Quaddra did look rather puzzled. 'It . . . looks like it.'

'What? That quickly? And with Megan in "bitch boss mode"?'

'I'm as confused as you are, Tyler.'

'Damn,' Tyler commented. 'Mary has got to have some amazing people skills to defeat that firing squad that fast. Most women would be crying by now, not laughing.'

'Yeah,' Quaddra smiled, a glint of admiration in his eyes. 'She's a keeper.'

Fifty-Four

'I love you!' Quaddra said it first – four months into their relationship.

The words had come out in a papery whisper, and just as they were done having sex, but not immediately afterwards ... not in the heat of the moment. Quaddra had lain by Mary's side for several minutes, regaining his breath, and getting his thoughts and the courage together.

He would've said it earlier ... much earlier, in fact. Probably just a month after he and Mary started dating, but he truly didn't want to scare her away. They had talked about her marriage and her divorce ... not in great depth, but enough for him to understand that to Mary 'love' had become more than just a scary word. It had become a scary feeling – something that could so easily mutate from a glittery fairytale into a devastating nightmare in the blink of an eye.

But Quaddra had fallen head over heels for Mary. He knew that she already knew it, but he wanted her to know that he wasn't afraid to say it – not to her, or anyone else.

'I love you!' he said it again, this time gazing deeply into Mary's eyes, and as he did, he saw something change in them. Was it fear? Happiness? Sadness? Indifference? Despite all his people skills, Quaddra couldn't tell.

Silence took over the room for a long moment.

'Honey,' Mary finally cut through it, her tone seemingly firm, but Quaddra picked up a slight quiver in her voice. 'That's just pillow talk.' She gave him a peck on the lips before trying to joke it all away. 'I'm good in bed, what can I say?'

As Mary tried to turn away, Quaddra placed a soft hand on her shoulder. 'Mary.'

She paused, doing her best to fight the tears that were about to well in her eyes. It took a second before she was able to look at him again.

'You don't have to say it back ... though I hope that one day you might, but I want you to know that I do love you with every atom of my being, and that I'm not afraid.'

Mary laid silent by Quaddra's side for a long while before getting out of bed and taking a couple of steps in the direction of the bathroom.

Quaddra pulled himself up onto a sitting position, as a knot began tying itself around his heart before choking at his throat because he had lied. He'd just told Mary that he wasn't afraid, but the truth was that he was petrified, but not of saying that he loved her. He could scream that from the rooftops. He was terrified of losing Mary ... and right then, he believed that his love for her had done just that.

The silence between them stretched, making time feel like it was standing still. And that was the first ever time that the silence between them felt awkward.

Quaddra really wanted to say something ... anything that could make that moment untie itself, but what could he say? That he was sorry for having fallen in love with her?

Mary took a third step in the direction of the bathroom, but then suddenly stopped. It'd been a year and a half since Nelson's trial, and since then she'd been careful ... very careful, actually. With the exception of gangster-suit man back in Nashville, she had no indications that her ex-husband was catching up to her, so maybe . . . just maybe . . . it was time to stop living in fear and finally start rebuilding her life.

All of a sudden, Mary turned around, jumped back into bed and into Quaddra's arms.

'Damn you,' she said, holding his face in between her hands, her eyes glassy with tears.

'Why?' he asked.

'Because I love you too.'

Fifty-Five

There was no doubt that that first 'I love you' night, just over a couple of months ago, had been a somewhat terrifying experience for both Mary and Quaddra, but since then, their relationship had flourished to the point that Mary barely spent any time in her own apartment anymore, though she had insisted in carrying on paying her rent. The few items of clothing that had once shared a small corner of Quaddra's wardrobe had now moved into her own walk-in closet, as Mary finally began shopping again – dresses, shoes, jackets, handbags ... and she bought it all with her own money, not Quaddra's, though he'd often surprise her with a gift or ten.

Despite it being a whole new experience for Quaddra, he loved the 'living together' lifestyle, and his romance 'kung-fu' was strong, with tender words and sweet gestures here and there, hidden notes in shoes and jacket pockets, surprise candlelight dinners ... anything to make sure that she knew that she was always at the forefront of his mind. Whenever he wasn't working, which wasn't often, he and Mary would be together, which at first seemed to displease some of his friends. The argument was that Mary was maybe monopolizing his time, but nothing could've been further from the truth. Mary was the one who'd always insist that Quaddra would see his friends whenever he could ... go for a 'boys' night out' ... and not lose touch with those who he'd always been closest to. It had been his choice to spend most of his free time with her. But if Quaddra's romance game was strong, then so was Mary's charm, and slowly but surely, her charisma began winning over all of Quaddra's friends, including Megan.

'Come in,' Quaddra called from inside his home office, after Mary had knocked twice. That was the only door in the entire house that was always kept closed. When Quaddra was in there, he needed total concentration to deal with all the phone calls, the business transactions and the ridiculous number of stocks that several of his companies traded daily. Blink and he could miss out on, or even lose, millions in one wrong move. When he was traveling, or in his office in downtown San Francisco, his home office door was always locked.

Quaddra had once tried to show Mary how to trade, but the numbers on the screens changed so quickly, it gave Mary a headache in less than five minutes. The stock market certainly wasn't for her.

Mary opened the door and stepped into the large and overly chilled office. The entire house was air-conditioned, but Quaddra kept the temperature inside his office a couple of degrees below what most people would consider comfortable.

'Hey baby,' Quaddra said, peeling his eyes from his computer screen. 'Do you need me for something?'

'No, not at all,' Mary said, walking over to kiss him on the lips. 'I just came in to tell you that I'll see you later. I'm off for dinner and drinks with the girls and you know how that usually turns out, right? So, I might be a little late. But there's plenty of food in the fridge.'

Quaddra knew that 'the girls' meant Megan, Carol, Kristie, Rachel and a couple more of their friends. He smiled at Mary, proudly. He still couldn't believe how fast she had won them over. He kissed her again. 'Have fun.'

As Mary got to the office door, Quaddra halted her. 'Oh, baby, hold on.' He did his best to sound breezy. 'I forgot to ask you . . . you know that I have to be in LA for a few days next week, right?'

'Um-hum!' Mary nodded. This was something that she knew had to do with Quaddra's film production companies.

'I was thinking,' he continued. 'How about you come with me? After I'm done with business, we could hang out down there for a few days . . . maybe do some shopping? Beverly Hills . . . Rodeo Drive . . . Hollywood . . . you'll love it. You could also meet up with your friend if you want.'

Mary gave Quaddra a subtle shake of the head, as if confused. 'Friend? Which friend?'

'The one who painted that piece you love so much,' Quaddra clarified. 'Betsy – didn't she move to LA?'

Mary nodded. 'Yeah, she did.'

Just a couple of months after Mary met Quaddra, Betsy had decided that as an artist, Los Angeles would be a better option for her, so she simply upped and moved.

'You could meet up with her, go shopping . . . she might even have a new piece that you might like. She's still painting, right?'

'I think so. That's why she moved to LA.'

'We could also go check out Culver City and all the movie studios.' He shrugged. 'If you want, I can even ask someone to introduce you to a few A-list celebrities. Owning two film production studios has its perks, you know?'

Mary chuckled as she pulled a face at Quaddra. 'As if meeting any kind of celebrities is something I care for.'

'OK, fuck the celebrities then, let's just have fun in LA.'

'Honey, I can't,' Mary said back. 'Not on such short notice. There are two separate exhibitions happening next week. I've told you about them, remember?'

Since Mary had decided to stay in San Francisco, she'd also decided that she needed to find something to do – not necessarily a job, she didn't really need the money – or the 'clock-punching' hassle – but she needed something to occupy her days and her mind with. Back in Massachusetts, before she married Nelson and moved to Woburn, Mary used to manage one of the largest independent bookshops in Boston, and that would've been her first choice – anything to do with books – until Quaddra suggested that maybe she should try art galleries, as it so happened that Steiner & Patch – the same art gallery that they had met in during the indie art exhibition – was hiring.

Mary didn't know much about art galleries, but she was a very quick learner, and the fact that she had practically volunteered to work for almost no pay was enough to swing the two gallery owners to give her a shot . . . part-time . . . three times a week.

The work was mostly office and admin stuff, which she could easily do from home – but Mary enjoyed spending her afternoons at the gallery. There was something very calming about being surrounded by art, and the two gallery owners were absolutely hilarious.

'There are two separate exhibitions happening next week,' she reminded Quaddra.

Quaddra grimaced as he nodded. 'Yeah, I'd forgotten about that.'

'I have to be there, honey. I'm sorry.'

'Nothing to be sorry about,' Quaddra said, before quickly coming up with an alternative. 'So, how about we take a holiday when I get back then? Once you're done with the exhibitions? We could go somewhere different.'

'A holiday?' Mary frowned.

'Yeah, just the two of us . . . no work . . . no deals . . . no stocks . . . no exhibitions . . . just us.'

Mary looked back at Quaddra a little sideways. 'Honey, I think that the cold air in here is really affecting your brain. You told me that you haven't had a holiday in over five years, not because you don't want to, but because you can't. You told me that you can't leave your businesses unattended, not even for a day.'

'Well, I'm sure that Ricky can keep the boat afloat for a week or so.'

Richard Ortiz, or Ricky, as his closest friends called him, was Quaddra's right-hand man. He was as streetwise as a drug dealer and as clued up as Quaddra was when it came to reading people. Mary had met him several times in the past months. His wife, Nancy, was as sweet as pumpkin pie.

Mary tried studying Quaddra's expression. She got nothing. 'This is all very sudden, honey. Is something wrong?'

'Wrong?' Quaddra shook his head. 'No, not at all. I just really wanted to spend some quality time with you. Away from everything and everyone.'

Mary carried on studying him.

'Is there anywhere that you've always wanted to visit, but never did?' Quaddra was trying hard to sound nonchalant. 'Anywhere? Somewhere romantic perhaps?' He winked at her. 'I've got a private jet. We can go anywhere you like . . . anytime.'

Mary didn't give the idea too much thought. 'No, not really.'

'How about Europe then?' Quaddra sounded like he was getting excited.

'Europe?'

'Yeah, but not your regular tourist destinations like London, Paris, Rome, Athens . . . nothing like that. I was thinking of something a little more exotic like Prague, Krakow, or Lake Como . . . have you been to any of those places?'

Mary took another moment. 'You want to go to Europe?'

'With you . . . yes.'

Mary bit her bottom lip.

Quaddra read the moment and seized it like a pro. 'C'mon, we could both use some time away . . . from everything and everyone, don't you think? I know I could.'

He wasn't wrong. Mary could really do with some time away . . . far away from everything and everyone.

'I guess you're right,' she finally agreed. 'It would be nice to go somewhere. And Europe sounds like fun. I'll talk to Mr. Steiner at the gallery and get a week or so off. How does that sound?'

'It sounds amazing.' Quaddra jumped to his feet and walked over to Mary to kiss her again.

His secret plan was beginning to work.

Fifty-Six

Before flying to LA, Quaddra and Mary had agreed that once he was back and she was done with the two gallery exhibitions, they would fly to Vienna, in Austria, and then simply play it by ear – eleven days and as many, or as few, cities and countries as they wished. No pressure . . . no schedule . . . just the two of them doing whatever they felt like on the day. Mary really liked that idea. It reminded her of her days traveling the Deep South, and the more she thought about it, the more excited she got.

The first of the two exhibitions that Mary had talked about happened the night after Quaddra had flown to Los Angeles, and it had been practically a repetition of the one in which they'd first met – twenty-two brand-new artists, exhibiting their works for the very first time, and for one night only. Mary loved the idea of giving 'new blood' a chance to showcase their talent. Her biggest involvement had been with the artists' selection – and the evening had been a complete success. The attendance had been the largest that the gallery owners had seen since they started their 'Indie Art Exhibition' project just over three years ago. On top of that, ninety-eight percent of the works exhibited that night were sold, which was the gallery's largest sale number for a single exhibition night – across the board – not only for the 'Indie' night.

Mary couldn't have been any prouder, or happier, and she couldn't wait to share the 'success' news with Quaddra, but the exhibition night had been an exhausting one, to say the least, and by the time that she was finally done for the evening, it was coming up to 1:30 a.m. on a Thursday morning. So, she decided that she would call Quaddra when she woke up – whatever time that might be – and meanwhile Mary and the two gallery owners, Harvey and Cory, celebrated the evening's success with a chilled bottle of Louis Roederer Cristal Champagne.

'Shall I call you a cab?' Harvey asked Mary, as all three of them finished the last of the Champagne.

'Nah,' Mary replied, putting down her glass before checking the sky outside. 'It's a nice evening. I'll walk.'

'Nice morning, you mean,' Cory corrected her. 'And what do you mean, "you'll walk"?' His eyes pinged to his partner before moving back to Mary. 'It will take you at least two hours to walk to Pacific Heights from here, not to mention that at this time of night, with so many deserted streets, it's way too fucking dangerous, Mary.'

'At this time of the morning, you mean,' Mary corrected him, doing nothing to curb her smile.

Cory accepted the dig-back gracefully, giving Mary a salute. 'I can see that the Champagne hasn't affected your quick thinking, but seriously – way too far and too dangerous for you to walk back. Just jump in the cab with us and we'll drop you off.'

'You're right,' Mary finally accepted it. 'It would've been a long and probably a little dangerous walk back to Pacific Heights, but tonight I'm staying at my apartment in Bayview.' She pointed south. 'It'll take me less than fifteen minutes to walk there from here.'

Harvey and Cory's art gallery was located at the southernmost corner of the Dogpatch neighborhood, barely a stone's throw away from Bayview.

'Oh yeah!' Harvey said, giving Mary a nod. 'I forgot that you have a place in Bayview.'

'I don't stay there much nowadays, but it's a beautiful apartment, and much easier to get to from here than Pacific Heights.'

'Everything OK between you and hubby?' Harvey asked.

'Yeah, yeah,' Mary chuckled. 'He's just away . . . again. He flew to LA last night.' She paused before revealing a tiny secret. 'I also don't really like staying in the house when he's out of town. It's too big . . . it feels too empty . . . and a little eerie to be honest.'

Cory laughed. 'Yeah, that's a horrible problem to have – my mansion is way too big.'

Mary and Harvey laughed with him.

Cory checked his watch. 'Still, it's almost two in the morning and this is San Francisco – at least two hobos per block at any time – and some of them become a little feral at night, you know what I'm saying?' He mimed snorting a line of cocaine.

'I'll be fine,' Mary reassured them. 'I've got my pepper spray in my bag.'

Harvey and Cory were still a little reluctant, but by now they both knew Mary well enough to know that no matter what they said, they'd never win the argument.

They all got up and put their glasses away.

'Do you need help rearranging the gallery tomorrow?' Mary asked.

'Today, you mean?' Cory hit her again.

'Touché.' Mary returned the earlier salute.

Cory and Harvey both knew that it was Mary's day off.

'Nah, we'll be OK,' Harvey said, looking around. 'We'll get it all sorted out, easy. You go rest, girl. You've definitely earned it.'

They all said their goodbyes, locked the shop and went their separate ways. Mary swapped her heels for some comfortable pumps and headed south in the direction of the Islay Creek Channel and the 3rd Street Bridge. At a brisk walk, it took her only about three minutes to reach the bridge.

It was a nice morning for a walk – not particularly warm, but not exactly cold either – nothing that a simple cardigan couldn't handle. At the bridge, the wind did pick up a little, but so did Mary's pace, and in less than a minute she had made it to the other side. From there, it was a quick ten-minute walk to her apartment.

She got to Hudson Avenue and turned left, and a few minutes later Mary was entering a six-digit code into the numeric keypad at the front door of her apartment building. As soon as she entered the last digit, the door emitted a muffled hiss before its lock mechanism disengaged. Mary pushed it open and stepped into the building, a movement that automatically activated the lights inside the long entrance hallway.

The entire warehouse had been converted into luxury flats, and Mary's one was located on the top floor. The lift was just to her right, a couple of steps past the entrance door, but Mary had always preferred the stairs, which were right at the far end of the hallway. She got to them, but paused just as she took the first step up.

Something wasn't right.

The door, the voice inside her head warned her.

That was when Mary realized that she never heard the door click closed behind her.

Sixth-sense, women's intuition, premonition, divination, gut feeling . . . it didn't matter what people called it – since she was a little girl, Mary had always trusted hers. They varied in type and intensity. Sometimes it was just a shiver at the base of neck, sometimes an odd, suffocating knot at the back of her throat, and sometimes, and these were the rarest ones, she would feel every inch of her body turn into gooseflesh.

Right then, at the bottom of that stairwell, Mary got all three of them at the exact same time, practically paralyzing her in place. She didn't have to look to know that the reason why she hadn't heard the door click closed behind her was because there was someone else there.

Fear spread through her body faster than blood, but what really made her heart freeze in place was the voice that echoed through the corridor – sharp and cold like a killer's blade.

'So, you call yourself Mary Smith these days, do you?'

Fifty-Seven

Earlier that evening, when Mary arrived at the gallery, a few hours before the exhibition was due to start, she never noticed the person standing quietly across the road, slurping on an ice-cream cone, while calmly observing her. In fact, Mary had never noticed that same person tracking her for the past two weeks, shadowing her every move. Wherever Mary went, her tracker followed – always sporting a different look . . . something simple . . . unnoticeable . . . something that would never get Mary to look twice, even if they passed each other on the streets.

For those in the know, the rule was simple – the more that you looked like your mark, the less your mark was bound to notice you – and that had been the biggest difference between the person tracking Mary this time and gangster-suit man back in Nashville. This time, Mary's tracker was a woman.

Thanks to so many biased TV-shows and a still very male-dominated world, when a mark was on the lookout for anyone following them, they tended to pay a lot more attention to men than to women – and Mary's tracker had no doubt that Mary would've been on the lookout.

During the past two weeks, while following Mary around, the woman had taken hundreds of notes, documenting everything she could about Mary, but Mary seemed to be a very clued-up mark, staying as far away from a routine as she possibly could.

Her jogs differed in day, time, location and route. She had no gym membership, no library card and no social media presence. Mary also didn't own a car, even though she could clearly afford one. As far as her job was concerned, Mary didn't seem to stick to any specific days or times either, probably doing most of her work from home, but tonight, Mary was at the gallery, greeting every arriving guest with a wide and warm smile.

For a brief moment, the woman standing across the road pondered the idea of sneaking into the gallery and maybe even mingling with the guests – it was a public and very busy exhibition after all – but she couldn't really risk Mary noticing her, regardless of how much the thrill of the challenge excited her. True, the woman knew that sooner rather than later she'd have to be face-to-face with her mark, but she also knew that the Indie Art Exhibition wouldn't be the right place – too public, which in turn made it too dangerous. No, the woman needed a much more private setting . . . something much more personal.

It was with that in mind that that morning, when she saw Mary exit the gallery, say goodbye to the two owners, and *walk* southward, instead of jumping into a cab like she usually did, she knew that Mary was heading to her apartment in Bayview, not the mansion that she seemed to share with her partner. All that the woman needed to do was get there first, which wasn't a problem because while Mary didn't drive, the woman did.

Less than fifteen minutes later, the woman watched as Mary rounded the corner, approached the old warehouse building, and entered her access code into the keypad by the door.

The woman had been to the building before. She'd studied its layout and taken several notes, including the fact that it took the front door exactly seven seconds to click back shut after it'd been pushed fully opened, which Mary had done.

So, as Mary stepped into the building, the woman stepped out of the shadows, her rubber-sole shoes making barely any noise, as she picked up the pace to reach the door with a full second to spare.

No one outside on the streets . . . no one inside in the hallway . . . except for Mary.

It wouldn't get much more private and personal than this. The woman knew that.

She smiled to herself as she quietly held the front door open while she slipped into the hallway . . . just behind Mary.

It was showdown time.

Fifty-Eight

'So, you call yourself Mary Smith these days, do you?' Mary heard the woman's voice come from behind her, sending goosebumps flying all over her body and tying a knot at the back of her throat.

But Mary didn't panic.

In a synchronized movement that seemed rehearsed, she swiveled her body around, while her hand reached into her handbag for her pepper spray. Her fingers wrapped themselves around the small canister just as she and the woman standing across the hallway from her finally locked eyes.

The knot at the back of Mary's throat reached the size of a golf ball.

The woman took off her baseball cap and allowed her dark hair to tumble down past her shoulders. She was wearing a gray NYU sweatshirt, faded blue jeans and white running sneakers.

Mary's eyes widened, as adrenaline flooded her body fast and hard, making all of her senses spark like fireworks. Her fingers tightened their grip around the canister inside her handbag and right then, Mary was sure that she could hear her heart echoing inside that hallway.

Maybe the woman could hear it too because she immediately raised a hand at Mary.

'Easy now. You're not going to have a heart attack, are you?'

Her gaze darted to Mary's handbag before coming back to Mary. 'Or spray me with pepper spray?'

Something pirouetted inside Mary's stomach and threatened to erupt up her throat and out of her mouth, but instead of vomit, what dribbled out of Mary's lips were words.

'What the fuck?'

Mary knew that woman.

She'd seen her in court, over a year and a half earlier, during Nelson's trial, but the woman hadn't been sitting at the back like gangster-suit man had. She hadn't been part of the audience either. The woman standing across the hallway from Mary had been a witness. In fact, she'd been 'the' witness – the Prosecution's Secret Weapon, brought in right at the last minute to completely collapse Nelson's defense.

Mary took a deep breath, trying desperately to keep her heart from exploding. She knew that she wasn't drunk enough to be seeing things, so this had to be true.

The woman looked a little different – a few pounds lighter . . . her hair longer and wavier, perhaps – but there was no doubt in Mary's mind that right there, inside the entrance hallway of her apartment building in Bayview, San Francisco, Mary was staring at Candice Logan – Nelson's lover – the woman who had testified that she had ended her eleven-month affair with Nelson because she couldn't take the beatings anymore.

'How . . . ? Why . . . ?' The sentence choked in Mary's throat and in a millisecond, fear swapped sides with anger. She decided to go with 'what'. 'What the fuck are you doing here?'

Candice finally allowed the door to shut behind her before walking over to where Mary was.

Mary didn't move, as she seemed to be paralyzed to the spot at the bottom of that stairwell. Her hand stayed inside her handbag, but her fingers loosened their grip around the pepper spray canister.

Candice stopped right in front of her, both women gazing deeply into each other's eyes.

'You really want to know what the fuck I'm doing here?' she finally asked, her tone firm and angry in equal measures.

Mary held Candice's stare for two seconds too long before she finally smiled.

Candice smiled back, her arms wide. 'It's nice to see you again, sis. I missed you.'

Mary simply walked into the hug. 'I missed you too.'

Fifty-Nine

'I really love what you did with your hair,' the woman said, using the tips of her fingers to tuck a loose strand of hair behind Mary's right ear. 'It really suits you.'

They were sitting in Mary's living room, sharing a bottle of Château Haut-Brion.

'I like yours too,' Mary said back. 'I've always loved you with long hair.'

'I prefer it long as well,' the woman agreed, hooking her hair with her hand and throwing it over her left shoulder, mermaid style. 'But it desperately needs a trim. Can you see the split ends?'

Mary leaned closer to have a better look. 'Barely, but I can easily do that for you. I'm great with hair – you know that.'

'I do.' The woman smiled. 'That's why I mentioned it.'

Mary's stare stayed on the woman for several unblinking seconds before refocusing on a neutral spot on the ceiling.

The woman was quick to notice the change.

'OK, sis, what's wrong?' she asked.

Mary's eyes went back to her, the look in them dead serious. 'What's wrong?' She broadly gestured at the two of them sitting side-by-side in her living room. 'This, Julia . . . what the fuck are you doing here?'

Julia, which was the woman's real name, not Candice, looked back at Mary with the same serious expression. 'First of all, you know I hate it when you call me Julia. My mother called me Julia, and I hate that bitch.'

'OK, so what name are you using now, Jules?' Mary asked.

Mary used to call her 'Jules'... when they were kids ... back in England.

'Denise,' Julia replied. 'Denise Johnson.'

Mary pursed her lips as she nodded. 'Denise Johnson ... I like it.'

'So do I.'

'OK,' Mary continued. 'So let me repeat the question, Denise – what the fuck are you doing here?'

'What do you mean ... *Grace*?' Denise gave it back as good as she got.

Grace was Mary's real name – Grace Mitchell – not Mary Smith, not Samantha Stewart, not even Samantha Chambers. In fact, her full name was Grace-Kelly Mitchell – named after the actress – as Grace's mother had been a huge fan. But as far as she knew, Denise was the only person who knew her real name and where she had really come from. Her mother had died years ago. She'd never known her real father and Mary had never told a soul who she really was.

'Don't call me that,' Mary said, her tone flipping from tender to firm. 'You know I don't like it. No one calls me that. *No one*.'

Since Mary and Denise had left England, they both decided that their real names, Grace-Kelly and Julia, were dead to them. They would never use them again and they would never tell anyone about them.

'Well, you called me Julia first.'

'And I'm sorry. OK? I was just caught completely by surprise here.'

Denise had another sip of her wine. 'Apology accepted.' She bit down on a sarcastic smile. 'So, you decided to go with Mary Smith ... really? A little common, is it not?'

'That's the idea, Denise. Now would you please stop dodging my question?'

'What question is that?'

'What are you doing here?' Mary repeated the question for the third time.

Denise frowned at her. 'What do you mean – "what am I doing here?" – you called me, sis, remember? Asked me to come?'

For the second time that morning, Mary felt her heart falter inside her chest. 'I did what?'

Sixty

Mary and Denise weren't really sisters, but they had known each other since they were both young teenagers, back in the UK. To escape being beaten up and sexually abused by her mother's drunken boyfriend, Mary, or Grace-Kelly, as she was then, had run away from home in the middle of the night at the age of fifteen. The abuse had started when she was only twelve years old.

Denise's childhood story, or Julia Cunningham, as she was known back then, hadn't been that much dissimilar. She, too, had run away from a terribly abusive household in her early teens. Her stepfather, a greasy-haired, big-bellied slob of a man, who consistently smelled of fried onions and kebab meat, had started forcing himself onto her on the night of her thirteenth birthday. The abuse repeated itself at least once a week for exactly two years, until her fifteenth birthday, when Julia sneaked up on her drunken stepfather, who had fallen asleep on the living room couch, after forcing himself into her once again. The sight disgusted Julia, and she decided that she'd had enough. If her mother wouldn't do anything about the abuse that she knew was happening, then Julia would. In the kitchen, she boiled a full kettle of salty water before pouring the scalding liquid onto her stepfather's testicles and smashing the kettle against his head. She didn't stick around to find out what happened next.

A few weeks later, Grace and Julia met by chance on the streets of Liverpool, northwest England. Grace had come from one of the poorest suburbs in Birmingham and Julia from Blackpool, in Lancashire. They were both fifteen, homeless, hungry and hurting – but most of all, they both hated their families, especially their 'stepfathers' – and a sad truth about humanity was that 'hate' could bring people together and create a much stronger bond than 'love' ever could.

The two girls immediately became more than friends. To each other, they became the cool sister that neither girl ever had, and very quickly discovered that they had something else in common other than their deep hate for their families. Even at such a young age, they were both breathtakingly pretty . . . and theirs was the kind of pretty that would make intelligent men do the dumbest of things, make tough men cry, sturdy men go weak at the knees and important men crawl at their feet. Theirs was the kind of pretty that would make husbands divorce their wives and leave their children behind . . . it was the kind of pretty that men and women would die – and kill – for.

'If you have it, flaunt it.' That was what Dylan, a boy who they'd also met on the streets of Liverpool, used to tell them.

He was a couple of years older than Grace and Julia, and worked at a small traveling funfair called ZigDust, where he was in charge of one of the 'rigged' games of chance. The three of them quickly struck up a tight friendship, and Dylan managed to convince Mr. McKeelan, the funfair owner, to take the girls in and give them a job. It wasn't much, or even a good job – mainly cleaning and helping out with the children's rides – but it kept them fed and a roof over their heads.

It was then, as they traveled around with the funfair, that the two girls discovered that they both had a natural talent when it came to picking up different accents. Whichever city they landed in – Liverpool, Newcastle, Birmingham, Manchester . . . it didn't matter – they could pick up the local accent in a matter of minutes . . . and they would both sound pitch perfect.

Recognizing how useful the girls' beauty and their incredible ability to easily blend in with the locals would be to him, Dylan decided to teach Grace and Julia how to con and pickpocket people on the streets. It was Dylan who taught them their first-ever con, a different spin on the classic 'cup and ball' game – three cups, one ball – find the ball.

One night, while their funfair was in Leeds, Yorkshire, after scoring the most amount of money that they'd ever scored on a single evening, pickpocketing shoppers during Christmas season, the three of them decided to celebrate with a couple of bottles of Champagne. Dylan had tried it once, but neither of the girls had ever had Champagne before.

At the time, Dylan was eighteen years old and both Grace and Julia just sixteen.

The three of them danced, and laughed, and drank, but what the girls didn't know was that while they were getting drunker and drunker on bubbles, Dylan was getting high on crystal meth and dropping small rocks of MDMA into the girls' glasses. Two bottles quickly became four, and the girls began feeling light-headed and unsteady in a way that they'd never done before. It didn't take long for the world around them to start spinning, turning the room into a kaleidoscope of dizzying shapes and colors until they both passed out.

What exactly happened next, and for how long, they had never really found out, but Grace, who had crashed out face-first on top of some cushions in a corner of the room, opened her eyes for just an instant. Not long enough for her to be able to see anything, but definitely long enough for the entire room to spin around her once again. Grace felt something come alive inside her stomach before it fast-tracked its way up to her throat. No time to look for a bucket or a bathroom. Instead, Grace stuck her face between the cushions and vomited . . . twice . . . that helped wake her up a little, but she still didn't really know what was going on. What Grace did know for sure was that she needed a large glass of water and some fresh air . . . pronto. She wiped her mouth with the back of her hand before slowly shifting her position on the cushions and that was when she saw Dylan across the room from her.

'What the fuck?' Those words came out tasting of puke.

Dylan was dressed in just his underwear, and he was lying on top of Julia, who was still passed out, but completely naked – her blouse, bra, jeans and panties, all discarded to one side.

'What the fuck?' Grace called again, bile-spit flying out of her lips, as she tried to push herself into a sitting position. Her head was still all over the place, but the shock of what she'd just seen was sobering her up faster than black coffee and a cold shower. 'What the fuck are you doing, Dylan?' She managed to find the strength and crawl a couple of feet towards him.

Caught red-handed, Dylan had paused for a split second, but he was way too high, drunk and invested in what he was doing to be able to stop. Instead, he twisted his body around and slapped Grace across the face . . . hard.

'Get off me, you fucking slag. She likes it. You gonna have to wait your turn.' His face was awkwardly contorted, with a maniac look inside his eyes.

Grace fell backwards, as a blob of blood formed at the corner of her lips.

Dylan turned his attention back to Julia.

'Jules,' Grace tried yelling, knowing pretty well what was just about to happen, but the alcohol and the tears had weakened her vocal cords considerably. 'Wake up, Jules . . . please . . . wake the fuck up.'

'You better shut the fuck up before I shu—' Dylan never finished his sentence. As he began turning his head to look back at Grace . . . BAM . . . his face was met by the thick end of one of the empty Champagne bottles ... the one that Grace had swung at his head.

Blood flew up in the air from the cut just above his right eyebrow and Dylan dropped like a dead weight. He wasn't dead though, and it took Grace the will of gods not to slice his penis off and shove it inside his mouth.

'What the fuck is wrong with men?' Grace kept on asking herself, as she finally managed to wake Julia up before helping her get dressed.

Julia was still too out of it to understand what had just happened.

After stripping Dylan of all the cash he had – enough to see them through at least a couple of weeks – Grace tied him to the bed and simply left him there, bleeding from a head wound, on the floor of that dirty caravan.

And that was how, at only sixteen years of age, Grace and Julia found themselves having to run away from abusive men for the second time in their lives ... and Grace had a feeling that it wouldn't be the last time either.

Sixty-One

Denise's answer made Mary's blood run cold inside her veins.

'What do you mean I called you and asked you to come?' The nervous edge to her tone was punctuated by fear.

'The secret phone,' Denise said, her eyes narrowing at Mary. 'The one that only *you* know the number to? You left a message, didn't you? Almost a month ago?'

Mary could feel her entire body tensing. 'What message did you get, Denise?'

'The one with no "Hi, sis", no "Hey, I hope you're well", no greeting of any kind. Just you being you and going straight into business. It had to be you, Mary, because it was your voice and you used both code words – the opening and the closing one – like you always do.'

'And what did I say on the message?'

'Simple … quick … like always,' Denise explained. 'You told me that Mary Smith was now living in San Francisco.' She nodded at Mary. 'I'm assuming that after the Nelson job, you managed to get that government-endorsed identity change that you were talking about, right? No phony documents here.' Denise didn't wait for a reply. 'And then you said that you were dating again, which we both know means that the wheels were already in motion with a brand-new target. That was you, wasn't it?'

'Yeah, that was me,' Mary agreed. 'But you said that I asked you to come to San Francisco.'

'Didn't you?'

'No.' Mary shook her head. 'Didn't you hear the whole message? The ending? You must have if you heard me say the closing code word.'

'What ending?'

Mary threw her hands up in the air. 'The one that I said, "give me three to four months to solidify things and I'll get back to you".'

'Oh, that ending?' Denise sounded nonchalant. 'Yeah, I heard that.'

More hands in the air, this time with a headshake. 'And what part of "give me three to four months to solidify things and I'll get back to you" didn't you understand, Denise?'

Denise shrugged carelessly. 'Well, I haven't heard from you in a year and a half and then, all of a sudden, "ping" – voice message ... "*I'm in San Francisco ... bla, bla, bla ... new target ...*" – and you know me ... I get curious ... I get restless. I wanted to see what this was all about. Plus, I really missed you, sis.' She shrugged. 'So here I am.'

Mary took a moment, her brain trying hard to slot pieces into places. 'OK, first of all – how the hell did you find me? I mean ... I did say that I was in San Francisco, but I never gave you an address. You know that I would've never done that. What I would've done, like always, would've been to set a meeting location ... somewhere where no one would see us together.' She paused, her expression worried. 'There are over six hundred and fifty Mary Smiths in the San Francisco area. I know that you didn't check them all.'

'No, just you,' Denise replied, a proud smile on her lips. 'Been following you around for two weeks now.'

'Two weeks?' Mary's eyes almost exploded out of their sockets.

'You're losing your touch, sis,' Denise joked.

'Fuck you!'

'I was just *kiddiiiing*.' Denise lifted her hands in surrender, giving Mary her best 'puppy eye' look. 'I've been tracking you from a very safe distance. You wouldn't have noticed me because you can't notice what you can't see. You taught me that, remember?'

'Of course I do.'

'And you're still laser sharp,' Denise continued. 'No routine, even with your runs ... no car, so I assume no driver's license ... no social media accounts ... even the name registered to this apartment isn't yours – Wendy something – how did you manage that?'

'Not important right now,' Mary said back. 'What's important is you telling me how the hell you found me. If I'm still laser sharp, how did you get to me?'

'C'mon, think about it,' Denise urged Mary, giving her a few seconds before helping her. 'The code? Your new phone number?'

Mary's eyes widened at the same time as her jaw dropped. 'You tracked it?'

Denise nodded.

Mary and Denise had developed their own messaging code system years ago – after they ran their second wedding con. The code was simple, but very effective. Every time a message was left, it had to start and finish with two different code words, which changed with every month of the year. Once the message had been delivered, the person who had left the message would destroy the SIM card and the phone that she had used, but a new phone, with a new number, would already be in place. That new number would be coded into the message – a code that was practically unbreakable without knowing the key, which only the two of them knew – so that at any one time, they knew how to get in contact with each other.

'How?' Mary asked. 'How did you track my burner phone?'

'It's not that hard,' Denise explained. 'If the phone that you want to track is live and "pinging", all you need is the right equipment.' She immediately lifted a hand at Mary. 'Relax. For it to work, you need to know the target's phone number, which no one else other than me would know because no one else can crack our code.' She paused for a moment. 'You haven't given the new number to anyone else, have you?'

'Of course not.' Mary got up and started pacing the room. 'And did you do the tracking yourself, or did you have help? Does anyone else know that you're here, Denise? Anyone else have my burner phone number?'

'No,' Denise replied. 'No one knows. I did the phone tracking myself and then destroyed the equipment. The phone was "pinging" from this building. From there, all I needed to do was watch and wait.' She pulled a funny face at Mary. 'And it took me three days to finally find you. You don't come back here that often, do you?'

Mary stopped pacing. 'You're sure that no one else knows, Denise?'

'*Yes*, I'm sure. Jeez, relax. We're good. I promise you – there's no trail.'

Denise could be a lot of things, but she was never careless . . . Mary knew that very well.

'So,' Denise asked, changing the subject. 'Is this new guy at least good in bed?'

Mary's eyebrows arched as she nodded, while biting her bottom lip.

Denise chuckled. 'That face . . . really?'

Mary just carried on nodding.

'Well, I guess I'm going to find out soon enough, aren't I?' The pause was deliberate, accompanied by a cheesy smile. 'So, when do you want me to start fucking your future husband?'

Sixty-Two

Even at the crack of dawn and with the early morning breeze blowing in from the west, the temperatures outside were already getting close to 65°F. Before answering Denise's question, Mary reached for the aircon remote control and switched it on to 'low'.

'That's why the message said – "give me three to four months to solidify things and I'll get back to you", Denise. Everything is in motion, but it's still very early days. It will be months until you're able to meet him and start working your magic.'

Denise sat back on the sofa and crossed one leg over the other. 'Before we go into any details about the wheels in motion and all that, I just need to know – what changed?'

'What do you mean?'

'What I mean is that you said . . .' Denise paused and corrected herself. 'No, you swore that Nelson would be our last job, remember? No more "wedding" cons after Massachusetts because the more we do them, the more dangerous it gets for us afterwards. We're not stealing lunch money here, sis. We're taking almost everything they've got and sending them to prison for something that they didn't really do, and to be honest, I'm getting really tired of running and hiding away like a fugitive.'

Mary nodded. 'Me too, and that's why we need to do this one last job – because this is *THE* job . . . this is life-changing. We do this and we'll never have to do another con again ... ever. I promise you.'

'Umm ... funny!' Denise couldn't sound any more sarcastic if she tried. 'Where have I heard that before?'

'OK.' Mary tried a different approach. 'Let me ask you this – how much do you still have left?'

'What?' Denise frowned at Mary.

'We've done three jobs in fourteen years, Denise,' Mary reminded her. 'I married Phillip back in the UK.' She lifted her hands at Denise. 'Fine, that was our first job. We were both very green and didn't really pick the best target. He got us what? About four hundred and fifty grand each?'

'Something like that.'

'Then we moved to the US and you married Erick,' Mary continued. 'Another mistake because although he looked like the real deal, he was hiding a lot of debts, remember? We barely managed to clear two hundred grand between us.'

'Yeah, he was a real asshole,' Denise commented. 'He actually deserved what he got.'

'No shit,' Mary agreed before continuing. 'And then I married Nelson. Finally, we got it right. After I liquidated everything back in Massachusetts, we came out with just a little over nine mil – about four point five million each, right?'

Denise nodded.

'And how much of all that do you still have left?'

Denise lips stretched into a thin line before she gave Mary an unsteady nod. 'A little.'

Mary's eyes widened at her. 'You've spent most of it already? Really?'

'We've been running this "wedding con" for fourteen years now, sis,' Denise said back, matter-of-factly, moving back onto a sitting position. 'You said so yourself – Nelson was the first time that it really paid off big. I had quite a lot of ground to make back.

And what's the point in doing these long-ass cons, if we're not going to spend the money once the con is over?'

Mary couldn't really argue with Denise's logic, but it also gave her a chance to restate her own. 'Exactly, and this is where this job comes in, Denise. If we get this one right, and I know we will, this *will* be the last job . . . ever. And I'm not only talking about cons . . . we'll never have to work another day in our lives because Quaddra is a billionaire. No dodgy deals with shady individuals . . . no money tied up in businesses . . . nothing like that. I'm talking about his bank accounts and his investments – untangled money that the judge can easily order to be moved from his accounts to mine.'

'Yeah, I've checked him out a little,' Denise said in reply. 'What sort of name is Quaddra, anyway?'

'You've checked him out?'

'I've been following you around for two weeks, remember? I saw you with him . . . found out who he was . . . and read a few articles on the net. That's all.'

'Please tell me that there was no contact,' Mary's tone was serious, almost angry, because she knew how Denise liked to operate. 'You didn't bump into him on the streets, or sit next to him in a restaurant or a bar, or anything like that, did you? Did you talk to him?'

'No. Nothing like that. I'm not stupid. Absolutely no contact. I just checked him out – Quaddra Buckner, right? He was easy to find because who the hell is called Quaddra? Does it actually mean anything?'

In silence, Mary studied Denise for a few more seconds until she decided that she wasn't lying. 'Yeah, it means that he has a billion dollars attached to his name.'

Denise didn't look too impressed.

'You don't really understand what that means, do you?'

'Yeah,' Denise nodded. 'It means that he's rich.' She followed the nod with a shrug. 'So were all the previous ones.'

'He's not rich, Denise. He's a fucking *billionaire.*' Mary placed a hand on Denise's thigh, her voice calm ... calculated. 'Most people don't really grasp the real difference between one billion and one million, so let me break this down to you in easy, more understandable terms, OK?' She lifted her left index finger. 'One million seconds is equivalent to about eleven days.' She paused, giving Denise a chance to wrap her head around that figure. She then lifted her right index finger in opposition to her left one. 'One *billion* seconds is equivalent to about thirty-one point five *years*. Not days, Denise ... *years*.' Mary paused again.

Denise's frown was a pensive one.

Mary knew she'd got her. She wiggled her left index finger. 'Eleven days.' Right index finger wiggle. 'Thirty-one point five *years*. Do you see the difference now? We do this right and we'll be set forever – no more cons ... no more jobs ... no more anything. We could buy our own island and spend the rest of our lives sipping cocktails on the beach.'

Sixty-Three

Mary didn't have a lot in her apartment in terms of food, so she ordered a breakfast delivery from Jolt N Bolt in the Dogpatch.

'So,' Denise said. They had both moved from the sofa to the dinner table in Mary's living room. 'How did you meet this Quaddra guy?' She reached for a mozzarella, tomato and basil croissant that had come with their order. 'When did you decide that he would become a mark?'

'Well,' Mary began. 'I met him here in San Francisco, but I learnt about him almost a year ago. About six months after the Nelson job.'

'What?' Denise almost choked on her croissant. 'You started looking for a new mark six months after Nelson? Are you nuts?' Mary's lips parted, as she was about to utter a reply, but Denise didn't give her the chance. 'And what the fuck, Mary? If we were to do this, this was supposed to be my turn to wed . . . your turn to be the mistress, remember? Too risky otherwise. What the hell were you thinking?'

'That's the thing, Denise, I wasn't looking for a mark at all.'

'Is that so?'

Mary paused her with a hand gesture. 'After I got my identity change, I relocated to Nashville for six months.' She saw no point in revealing anything about her encounter with gangster-suit man just outside The Whiskey Bent Saloon. She didn't want

Denise to worry about something that Mary was sure posed no threat anymore.

'From Nashville,' Mary continued, 'I traveled around, bouncing from city to city and state to state for almost two months. It was during that time, while in the Deep South, that I came across an article in a newspaper about this young billionaire, who had just acquired a couple of companies on the West Coast. There was a picture of him on the article – not a bad-looking guy – so I decided to dig a little deeper. The idea was just to start doing some groundwork and if he looked and sounded like a viable mark, I would then get in touch with you and pass on all the info because as you've said – it was your turn to wed, my turn to be the lover.'

'So, what happened?' Denise asked, reaching for her orange juice. 'You forgot to get in touch? Or was he just too cute and you decided that you wanted "first dip"?'

Mary lifted a finger at Denise. 'I'll get to that. Just give me some rope here and you'll understand, OK?'

Denise didn't look too pleased, but she played along. 'OK, I'm listening.'

'So,' Mary continued. 'Like I said, I dug around a little and it turned out that this young and filthy rich guy started out as some computer genius or something, who, years ago, when mobile apps were still in their infancy, created a couple of apps that became the industry standard. A few years after that, he sold his company to Google for an absolute fortune, but unlike what most would expect, this guy, despite being young and with over half a billion to his name, wasn't the splashy kind. He didn't seem to be into showing off his fortune by sailing up and down the Pacific in luxurious yachts, or dating supermodels, or anything like that. This guy was a "keep yourself to yourself" filthy rich-type.'

'Living by the rule then,' Denise said.

'Exactly.'

This was something that Mary and Denise had come across a

long time ago – a list of rules for success – and the very first one was: if you're doing well in life, if you are successful in whatever you do, shut the fuck up. The more you brag about it, the more jealousy you will attract, and jealousy is never good.

'So, you relocated to San Francisco,' Denise said.

'I did,' Mary confirmed, as her lips stretched into an apologetic smile. 'And yes, I could've . . . should've contacted you back then . . . passed on what I had on him . . . and asked you to relocate to San Francisco and get the ball rolling.'

'So why didn't you?'

'Honestly? Because I knew that you would've fought it with the same arguments you gave me just a moment ago – it's too soon after the last job . . . I'm tired of running and hiding . . . and all of that jazz.'

'Which is true,' Denise countered, her tone annoyed.

'And I agree,' Mary accepted it. 'But like I said – I really wasn't looking for a new mark, Denise, but this was too great an opportunity *at least* not to investigate further. So instead of having an argument with you about the pros and cons of this job nine months ago, I decided to relocate and do that further investigation myself.'

'I see.' Denise still looked doubtful.

'There's also the fact that it takes a lot more commitment and time to play the wife role than it does to play the lover,' Mary told Denise. 'And you hated having to play the wife with Erick.'

'Yeah,' Denise agreed. 'That I'll give you.' Mary was slowly winning her over. 'So how did the two of you actually meet then? Same as before? Bump into him at a party, or a bar, or something?'

'Actually no,' Mary replied, after having a sip of her coffee. 'That was the original plan, but things played out quite differently this time.'

'What do you mean? Like how differently?'

'Well, as soon as I got to San Francisco, I got the ball rolling. I had already found out where he lived, so I began the usual recon work . . . followed him everywhere, trying to establish some sort of routine, you know? Usual stuff – find a place where he tended to go with a little more frequency – gym, nightclub . . . whatever – but in Quaddra's case, there was no place that could really offer me the chance to casually bump into him. He's got a gym at home . . . he has all his shopping delivered to his house . . . he only goes out for lunches and dinners with his close friends, or if it's work-related . . . no nightclubs . . . no golf clubs . . . no tennis clubs . . .' Mary shrugged. 'There was nothing, Denise, with *maybe* one small exception.'

'Which was?'

'Quaddra loves wine,' Mary revealed. 'And there was this one little wine shop that he tended to go to often enough to almost create a pattern. So, my plan was to wait until he visited the shop and follow him inside. I would then, very clearly, pretend to be totally undecided on what to purchase – not knowing which wine pairs well with which dish and all that crap, you know?'

'The old damsel-in-need-of-a-little-help trick,' Denise chuckled. 'Works like a charm every time.'

'That's why I was going with it, but I didn't get the chance to.'

Denise finished her croissant and sat back on her chair. 'Why? What happened?'

'Because we truly met by chance,' Mary explained. 'At least a couple of months before I was ready for it.'

'Stop . . . really? How? Where? At the wine shop?'

'No.' Mary shook her head. 'At the gallery I'm working at at the moment. The place I was last night.'

She proceeded to tell Denise the cappuccino story and how she'd met Betsy at Jolt N Bolt. She then told her about the invite to the indie art exhibition and the black canvas, with the older couple in front of her, rocking their bodies from side to side.

'So,' Mary continued, 'as the couple moved over to look at the next piece along, the person who was standing next to me asked . . .' She put on a deeper voice. '. . ."Did you actually see any of the things that they were talking about"?'

'And it was him?' Denise asked, her expression clearly indicating that she was now enjoying the story.

'Yep,' Mary confirmed.

'Stop . . . so what did you do?'

'I fucking froze, that's what I did.' Mary chuckled. 'Inside my head I was going – *Oh my god. It's him. It's fucking Quaddra. What the fuck is happening right now? Why is he here? And why is he talking to me when I look like a goddamn hobo?*'

'What do you mean? Why would you look like a hobo?'

'Because I was dressed like shit, Denise,' Mary clarified. 'And wearing barely any makeup. Not only had I completely forgotten about the exhibition, so I left home in a hurry, but my wardrobe at the time was a joke – five, maybe six pieces – and none of them exactly glamorous.'

'So, what happened next?'

'Well, I tried my best not to panic . . . to keep it cool . . . trying to be charming and all.'

'You're always charming,' Denise said, nodding at Mary.

'Well, that night, I didn't think that my powers of seduction were really up to scratch,' Mary told her. 'In fact, I thought I blew it because he walked away from me within a minute.'

'What? For real?'

'Yeah. No smile . . . no flirting . . . no nothing. He just walked away. I was already thinking that I would have to go back to my original wine-shopping plan, you know? Bump into him again there – like in a week or so – but this time, dressed to kill.'

'But that wasn't how it happened, right?'

'No. I bumped into him again at the exhibition, like ten . . . fifteen minutes later. We got talking, and this time . . .' Mary gave Denise a shy smile, '. . . there was definitely flirting . . . from his side.' The smile turned into a serious face. 'Until I fucked it all up.'

Sixty-Four

'Thomas?' Denise asked, as she and Mary moved their conversation to the L-shaped sofa in front of the panoramic windows that faced the San Francisco Bay.

'That's the name he gave me at first,' Mary confirmed. 'And that was when I fucked up.'

'How do you mean?'

Mary half grimaced. 'I knew his real name was Quaddra, and I was not expecting him to give me a false one, so when he introduced himself to me as Thomas, I frowned at him, as if Thomas was the weirdest name I'd ever heard in my life.'

'And he noticed it.' Denise phrased it as a statement, not a question.

'Of course he noticed it. Wouldn't you?' Mary exaggerated a frown that made her eyebrows almost touch above her nose.

Denise laughed. 'What did he say?'

'He asked me if there was something wrong with his face.'

Denise laughed again, harder this time. 'What did *you* say?'

'The first crap that came into my head,' Mary explained. 'Which was that he didn't look like a Thomas. I then tried to patch that bullshit up by telling him that I used to have a teacher called Thomas when I was a young girl, so I always associated that name with his image, which Quaddra looked nothing like.'

'That doesn't sound so bad,' Denise tried to reassure Mary. 'It's believable.'

'Maybe, but I still thought I'd blown it because he never asked me for my number, though I really thought he would. The flirting was definitely there . . . the chances were definitely there, but nope – he just walked away . . . again.'

'You didn't ask him for his number, did you?' Denise, once again, dipped her chin to look at Mary.

In their game, asking a mark for his number was a very big 'no-no'. For it all to seem legit, the mark is the one who has to do the chasing . . . not them.

'Of course I didn't.'

'So, what happened?' Denise asked. 'You bumped into him for the third time?'

'Not even close.' Mary quickly explained what happened in the days following the exhibition – the gift, the note, the invitation, and their first date at the Legion of Honor. 'And that was when I excelled, Denise.'

'What do you mean?'

'My performance,' Mary explained. 'I honestly deserved to be nominated for an award that night.'

'Why?' Denise got even more comfortable on the sofa. 'What did you do?'

Mary told her about the first hissy fit she threw when Quaddra had suggested that she wasn't from San Francisco.

'You actually legged it?' Denise's eyes became two large marbles. 'Just left him there, right in the middle of the exhibition?'

Mary nodded, a proud smile on her lips. 'Ran all the way down to the road, like Cinderella leaving the ball at midnight.'

'That was risky,' Denise commented. 'What if he hadn't come after you?'

'No chance of that,' Mary said back, her tone full of confidence.

'I knew he would. He was already firmly on the hook. All I was doing was reeling him in . . . tight.'

'Had you two kissed yet?'

'Nope, but I knew I had him.' She paused just to heighten the suspense. 'But my second hissy fit was really the one that was worth the Oscar.'

'What do you mean "second"?' Denise appeared confused. 'On the same evening?'

Mary took her time explaining what happened after she'd run out of the Legion of Honor – how Quaddra had apologized to her, the restaurant in Vista Del Mar, the dinner, the conversation, and what happened when the bill came.

'That was my chance to play the role of a scorned woman,' Mary said. 'Who had just been lied to.'

'You did not.'

'I did . . . and it was an Oscar-winning performance.'

'This bitch.' Denise's lips stretched into a wide smile before she high-fived Mary.

'To keep me from running off on him again,' Mary carried on, 'he came clean and explained why he'd given me a false name when we first met. As a small "quid pro quo", I told him my story.'

'Which story are you talking about?' A hint of worry crept into Denise's tone.

'Abusive husband, who I had divorced,' Mary clarified. 'I told him that I was trying to start a new life for myself – that's why I'd been traveling for a while. I also told him that the reason why I had been so skittish about him knowing that I wasn't from San Francisco and giving me a false name was because my ex-husband wasn't the type who'd let go easily.'

Denise's face almost dropped, but Mary was quick to calm her down.

'It's alright, Denise. Abusive ex-husband is a very, very

common story in the USA. You know that. I never mentioned Nelson's name, or my married name, or Massachusetts, or the fact that Nelson is in prison.'

'And he never asked about any of it?' Concern was still cloaking Denise's words.

'No,' Mary confirmed. 'He's actually a very understanding kind of guy. He knows that everyone has a past. He also told me that when I was good and ready to tell him about mine, he'd be ready to listen.' She shrugged. 'After that . . . I mean, after dinner, we ended up at his place, and we fucked for the first time. Since then, it's been pretty much smooth sailing.'

Denise's eyes avoided Mary altogether.

'What's wrong?' Mary asked.

'Nothing. He just sounds like he's a nice guy, and I've seen you together. You do look like a very happy couple. Are you sure that you want to destroy his life?'

'Don't do that, Denise,' Mary said, her tone serious.

'Do what?'

'Start getting soppy on me.' Mary repositioned herself on the sofa, moving closer to Denise. 'He's a mark, Denise . . . and he's a man. They are all the same. You know that. Might not look like it just yet, but in time, he'll come round. They all do. The story always repeats itself – kind, understanding, caring and loving at first, but the façade never lasts. Very soon, the lying and the cheating starts . . . why? Because no matter what we do, Denise . . . no matter how much we sacrifice . . . no matter how much in love we might be with them . . . no matter how beautiful, sexy, loving, understanding, supportive, or whatever we are . . . we are *never* enough.'

Denise looked down at the floor, but Mary softly touched her chin and brought her gaze back to her.

'Have you forgotten it already?' Mary asked, her tone firm, but not aggressive. 'Your mother gave her life to your stepdad, and her *life* wasn't enough for him. He wanted yours too . . . and he took it, with absolutely no regards for how much pain and devastation he was bringing into your life. He took it simply because he wanted it. Our childhood . . . our innocence . . . our trust . . . our possible future . . . we were both robbed of all that. And that's something that we'll never get back. And why did they do it? Simply because they couldn't keep it in their pants. One minute of pleasure for them, and a whole life of hurt and psychological destruction for us. They wear the crown, and we wear the pain . . . forever. Does that seem like a fair trade to you?'

Denise was clearly fighting back tears.

'Quaddra might seem like the perfect man at this point in time, but trust me, that just won't last. It never does. Very soon the hurt will start – emotionally, psychologically, maybe even physically . . .' She smiled at Denise. 'And that's why we take them for everything they've got.' She paused to make sure that Denise had locked eyes with her. 'One last time, sis . . . I promise you . . . and then we're done. We'll live in luxury for the rest of our lives. No more cons . . . no more stupid men. They can all go fist themselves. So, what do you say?'

Denise wiped her eyes clean of tears before nodding. 'Let's go get this motherfucker.'

Sixty-Five

'Why did we have to drive this far for lunch?' Denise asked Mary, as they were shown to their table at the small taqueria in Westlake, on the northernmost edge of San Mateo County.

'Because I can't risk the two of us being seen together, Denise,' Mary whispered, as they took their seats. 'You coming to my place was already risky enough.'

'Maybe I should've knocked at the door at Quaddra's house instead,' Denise said, pulling a defiant face at Mary. 'You're practically living there already.'

'That would've been a terrible mistake.'

'I know, sis. God, I was just joking. Would you relax a little.'

'I'm serious, Denise,' Mary volleyed back. 'You know the rules. You turning up at my apartment in the early hours of the morning was crazy irresponsible. What if someone had seen us together?'

'Like who?'

'I don't know . . . maybe a neighbor, or someone.'

'Do you know any of your neighbors?' Denise challenged.

'That's not the point.'

'Of course it is,' Denise cut Mary short. 'And even if somebody had seen us together, what could they say – that they saw you talking to another woman in the hallway?'

Mary glared at her.

'No one could identify me.' She pointed to her baseball cap.

'My hair was tied up and tucked under my hat, like so . . . my top is twice my size.' She pinched her sweatshirt, just above her breasts, and stretched it out to demonstrate how large it really was before indicating her face. 'And I'm wearing no makeup. You mentioned looking like a hobo earlier . . .' She used both index fingers to point back at herself. 'Well, I'm the bag lady . . . the sole definition of a "forgettable" person.'

'Still a risk, Denise, and you know it. Let's just stick to the rules from now on, OK?'

A waitress came to their table, and they ordered two mezcalitas and a selection of assorted tacos.

'Talking about rules,' Denise said, once the waitress was out of earshot. 'How about the psychologist side of the plan? Have you got that ball rolling yet?'

'Of course,' Mary replied. 'Those have always been our trump cards – the psychologist and the lover. No jury on this planet can argue with those two witnesses. The psychologist testifies to the domestic abuse and the violence and the lover confirms it. They are our game-set-match cards. Especially with the evidence package.'

Another key element in Mary and Denise's wedding con was the 'evidence package' that got mailed to whichever therapist they were using at the time, just as the trial had started. The package contained all the Polaroid photos that either Mary or Denise had taken of their 'bruises' since they had met their mark, in this case Quaddra. Also included in the package were several Dictaphone tapes, where either Mary or Denise – whoever was playing the wife – would describe the 'abuse' in detail, including dates. Those dates would perfectly match the therapist's notes, because Mary and Denise both knew that therapists would *always* make a note every time they noticed a new bruise on their client. In a court of law, that kind of information, when given by a well-respected psychologist, would weigh very heavily in their favor.

'So, you've started the package already?' Denise asked.

'Of course.'

'And when did you start seeing the therapist?'

'Ten months ago,' Mary replied. 'The same week that I moved to San Francisco.'

'That's what? Five, six months before you met Quaddra?'

'A little over five months,' Mary confirmed.

'And who is she? How did you find her?'

'Her name is Dr. Lillian Fox,' Mary explained. 'And I found her through an internet advert I saw almost a year ago, before I even moved to San Francisco. I checked her out and she was perfect – well known, with a great reputation and very well respected. In court, her testimony will be worth its weight in gold. Trust me.'

'And how's it going with her?' Denise asked.

'Smooth as silk,' Mary's tone was full of pride. 'During those five initial months, before I met Quaddra, we've talked about all the normal therapy subjects – childhood, family, love life . . . you know the drill. Then, five months into therapy, there's a mention of me having possibly met a new love interest. A couple of weeks later, the love interest has become a full-blown romance and boom, every now and then, a few expertly placed bruises start showing up – arm, shoulder, legs – same as always. Never something too exposed or too visible like on my face, neck or hands. She gets to see them every now and then because sometime during the session, I accidently hitch up my sleeve a little too much, or my blouse, or my skirt, or whatever.'

'Has she asked about them yet?' Denise questioned.

'She mentioned them, yes.'

The waitress came back with their drinks. 'The food will be right along.'

'Oh, there's no rush,' Denise said, giving the waitress a sympathetic smile. Once the waitress was far enough away, Denise's attention returned to Mary, but this time, it was full of concern. 'Hold on a second here. Doesn't California law require a therapist to tell the police if they suspect that a patient of theirs is being a victim of domestic abuse, domestic violence, or both?'

'That's exactly right, yeah,' Mary replied, as she sipped her drink. She didn't seem concerned.

Denise frowned. 'And how isn't that a problem, sis? You said that she's already noticed the bruises, right? If she reports it – which, by law, she must do – the cops will come knocking ... Quaddra will probably be arrested ... and that's that. End of. We'll walk away with nothing.'

'Yeah, but she won't report it.' There was real confidence in Mary's tone.

'How can you know that, Mary?'

'Because of one tiny detail ... but a very important one.'

'Which is?'

'Doubt.'

Denise's head recoiled back half an inch. 'Meaning?'

'Meaning that Dr. Fox is a very well-known therapist,' Mary began. 'With a solid reputation. A reputation that she won't want to tarnish. For her to go to the authorities with a "suspicion" about one of her clients, that "suspicion" has to be pretty undeniable, because if she makes a mistake ... if it turns out that there was no abuse happening at all ... if it turns out that I was just clumsy, like I told her I was ... her "solid" reputation will take a huge hit – and that's the last thing that a therapist of Dr. Fox's caliber would want.' Mary lifted a finger at Denise, for emphasis. 'Plus, I never told her who my partner was. She doesn't know his name, his profession, or anything, but I made damn sure that she understood that he was a very, very influential figure. The kind of influential that could end careers, if he got rubbed the wrong way. Do you know what I'm saying?'

Denise took a second.

Mary smiled. 'She knows very well that, like you've said – if she reports it, the cops will probably come knocking ... Quaddra will be, at least, taken away for questioning . . . and that would certainly rub him the wrong. That means that she knows that if she gets this wrong, it's the end of her career. I never, not once, complained about Quaddra to her. I never said anything bad about him either . . . meaning that I never "explicitly" voiced any sort of concerns about him. So, sure, she might have suspicions, but she will also have doubts . . . the kind of doubts that will make her second guess her decision every time. Why? Because her career is on the line.' Mary shook her head. 'Without concrete proof, she won't risk it because the consequences can be too damaging, and concrete proof will only come with the "evidence package".'

Denise chewed on all that for a moment. 'You really got good at this, didn't you?'

Mary took a bow. 'I'll take that as a compliment.'

'So, you stuck with the "being clumsy" story?' Denise asked.

'Of course – and of course I made sure that Dr. Fox noticed that said clumsiness seemed to have magically appeared just after I started dating Quaddra. Small bruises at first, but soon they'll start getting just a little larger, which will coincide with my mood changing to sadder and sadder, and me becoming more and more withdrawn. I'll start showing a little fear just weeks before the grand finale.'

'So how often do you see her?' Denise asked.

'For now, once a week,' Mary replied. 'I have a session tomorrow afternoon actually, but just like always, I'll increase the sessions to two a week, once the wedding is out of the way.'

'How about Quaddra?' Denise pushed. 'He must've noticed the bruises too because the two of you are practically living together.'

'Of course he has,' Mary confirmed. 'But I laid the groundwork right on our first night together.'

'What are you talking about?'

'How clumsy I can be.' The smile on Mary's lips was a smug one. 'We had just finished having sex for the first time,' she recounted. 'I was exiting the room and bumped my shoulder on the doorframe ... hard. When he asked if I was alright, I told him that I'm usually clumsy, but I get even more clumsy when I get nervous.'

Denise chuckled. 'You're a bad bitch.'

'Since then, he's seen me bump into tables, chairs, desks, the kitchen sink, the fridge, the bed ... you name it.' She nodded firmly. 'He's getting used to it.'

Denise sat back and had a sip of her mezcalita, just as the waitress came back with their selection of tacos.

'So, the stage is all set then,' Denise said, as she rolled herself a Tinga de Pollo Taco.

'Pretty much so,' Mary replied, making herself a Taco Alambre.

'How about the romance?' Denise asked, in between bites. 'How's that going?'

Mary paused and allowed her eyes to slowly move to Denise. She bit her bottom lip to try to curb the smile that was already more than apparent. 'He's going to propose ... when we go to Europe.'

Denise almost spat out half of her taco. 'You guys are going to Europe? What the fuck? Have you lost your mind?'

Mary was already expecting that exact reaction. 'Don't worry, Denise, we're not going anywhere near the UK. We'll fly to Austria, and we'll take it from there. But Quaddra will go wherever I suggest. Plus, the reason for the trip isn't because we need a vacation or anything like that. He's going to propose, and he wants to do it in a unique location ... somewhere "romantic".' She used her fingers to draw quotes in the air.

'How do you know he's going to propose?' Denise finished her Tinga de Pollo and began preparing another one. 'He didn't tell you that, did he?'

'Because I saw the receipt for the ring,' Mary replied. 'Bought at Tiffany, about a week ago.'

'Wow,' Denise commented. 'That's fast, isn't it? How long have you guys been dating?'

'Five months. Yeah, it's fast, but not as fast as Nelson. He proposed in three and a half months, remember? And Phillip in five.'

'Either men are too fucking easy,' Denise chuckled, 'or you're too fucking hot.'

'Both.' Mary laughed.

Denise laughed with her. 'So, when are you guys going? To Europe, I mean.'

'When he's back from LA,' Mary replied.

'And when will that be?'

'Whenever he's done with whatever business he's dealing with this time. It could be a couple of days . . . it could be a week . . . or it could be this afternoon.' Mary's tone went back to being stern. 'That's why you turning up at my place the way you did was so goddamn risky, Denise.'

Denise used a napkin on her mouth before replying. 'I knew that he was away, Mary. I saw him leave the day before yesterday. I also saw you leave the gallery this morning, after the exhibition, on your own and heading towards your apartment, not his house . . . which clearly meant that you weren't expecting him back yet. Give me some credit, please.' She, once again, pointed at herself. 'Not just a pretty face, you know? It's not only you who's good at this.'

'I know. I just want to get this completely right so that we can finally stop doing it for good.'

'I'll definitely drink to that,' Denise said, as she reached for her cocktail. 'Cheers!'

'Cheers!' They touched glasses. 'Where are you staying at the moment? Not in San Francisco, right?'

'For the time being, yeah,' Denise replied, after downing her mezcalita. 'A nice little hotel downtown.'

'No, you're not.' Mary's tone left no room for discussion. 'Not until I give you the green light that it's time for you to casually bump into Quaddra somewhere.'

'Mary, this is San Francisco,' Denise tried arguing. 'Not Woburn, Massachusetts.'

'It doesn't matter,' Mary fired straight back. 'Shit happens, Denise, you know that, and I'm not taking any unnecessary risks here. This . . .' she gestured at the table that they were sitting at, '. . . will be the last you'll hear from me until I give you that green light . . . and the last time we'll see each other until you walk into that courtroom, as a last-minute witness for the prosecution.'

Denise filled her cheeks with air before blowing it out slowly. 'Do I get any kind of ballpark timeframe here, or what?'

'Hard to say,' Mary replied. 'Like I've explained, the engagement is just around the corner. From there, I'll push for a quick wedding, and I don't think that we'll have any problems in making it a very small gathering. Quaddra was an only child and his parents are gone – father died of cancer a few years back and his mother passed away during the Covid pandemic. Friends-wise, he's got no more than just a handful and like I've said, he likes to keep himself to himself, so I'm sure that he won't want any sort of extravagant party or anything.'

'So, what are we talking about here?' Denise insisted. 'Six months? More? Less? I really just need a ballpark figure.'

'I don't think that it will be less than six months.'

As if on cue, Mary's cellphone rang inside her handbag.

'Talking about the devil.' She winked at Denise before taking Quaddra's call, and just like that, her voice went soft and seductive.

'*Honeyyyyy* . . . I was wondering why you hadn't called me yet.' Even though he couldn't see it, Mary made a sad puppy face. 'I miss you.'

'This bitch,' Denise whispered to herself, while shaking her head at Mary.

Sixty-Six

On the phone that afternoon, Quaddra had told Mary that unfortunately, he would have to stay in LA for at least another day. He'd explained that the meetings were going well, but he expected it all to take another day or so before a deal was finalized. But none of that was actually true. There had been no business meetings ... no deal to finalize ... no new company to acquire. That was not the reason why Quaddra had flown to Los Angeles.

Days ago, when he'd asked Mary if she would like to come on this trip with him, he knew that she would say no. The truth was, he hadn't forgotten about the exhibitions that Mary had worked so hard to organize, like he'd pretended he had, but inviting her and having Mary say that she couldn't come made the whole trip seem a lot more legit.

Quaddra *was* due to meet someone that evening, but this was no business meeting. On the contrary, tonight, it was all about pleasure ... at least for him.

In his room, he checked the contents of his briefcase, yet again. He had everything he needed, including the brand-new Polaroid camera, bought and paid in cash that afternoon at a small pawnshop in South LA.

Quaddra didn't really like to use digital images. They were way too easy to alter – filters, retouching apps, deep fake programs – the market was completely saturated with them. Polaroids, on the other hand, were old school. One click and boom, seconds later he had a hard copy of a photo right in his hands – no filters, no alterations, no photoshopping and no second copies. Every photo was real and unique – developed and printed right there and then, giving him a tangible and very personal piece of history – a moment frozen in time. But better still, Polaroids left no trail behind ... no digital signature of any kind. The images didn't get stored on a hard drive where others could find them, or sat on the cloud where they could be accessed over the Internet. You either physically had them, or you didn't. To Quaddra, that was their biggest appeal.

He locked his briefcase before retrieving his cellphone from his coat pocket and placing it on the table. Rule number one was if you were planning on doing something in secrecy – leave your phone behind. Quaddra had always said that, in reality, a cellphone wasn't actually a phone – it was a tracking and listening device, with a phone capability. He knew that only too well because one of his companies was amongst the market leaders in GPS and satellite tracking systems.

In the bathroom, Quaddra checked his reflection in the mirror one last time. The fake beard, the long hair and the light color contact lenses didn't actually look too bad and, right then, he wondered what Mary would think of that look.

'She would probably like it,' he decided, glancing at his watch. It was time to get going.

'Everyone has a past ... a history'. He remembered saying those words to Mary at the restaurant, on their first-ever night out. What he didn't say, but it was just as true, was that 'Everyone also has secrets, and for some, those secrets are as dark as they come'. Quaddra was sure that Mary had hers; whatever they might be ... and he no doubt had his own.

Sixty-Seven

Mary hugged herself, as her gaze settled on a neutral spot on the white rug under her feet. They were coming to the end of their session, and, to Dr. Lillian Fox, the psychologist that Mary had been seeing for a little over ten months now, Mary's facial expression seemed intriguing.

'Is everything OK?' Dr. Fox asked, her voice calm and composed, as always. She was sitting in her usual wingback Chesterfield armchair, just across the room from Mary. Her right leg was crossed over her left one in a relaxed position. She held a pen in her right hand, with a notepad resting on her lap. Yes, the session was being recorded, that was standard common practice, but Dr. Fox liked to take notes of visible details . . . things that the digital voice recorder could never capture.

Mary nodded shyly, but voiced no reply.

'Anything bothering you?' Dr. Fox asked. 'Anything at all?' She found Mary's posture to be a little tense, with her facial expression showing an odd combination of happiness and concern.

Dr. Fox was maybe a couple of inches taller than Mary and several pounds heavier, with intelligent dark eyes that sat behind round spectacles. Her hair, which was a shade darker than her eyes, was long and shiny, and she always had it either up in a ballet bun or loose, slung behind her head from her right shoulder to her left one, mermaid style. That afternoon, Dr. Fox had chosen the ballerina look. The sleeves of her pleated satin top were rolled up to her elbows, half exposing her arms.

'I love that tattoo, you know?' Mary said, nodding at Dr. Fox's right forearm.

Dr. Fox did know that. Mary had told her so on their very first session and several times during their subsequent ones. The tattoo covered most of the outside of Dr. Fox's right forearm and it showed the two main characters from the classic Christmas animation movie, *The Nightmare Before Christmas* – Jack Skellington and his girlfriend, Sally. In the tattoo, Jack and Sally were facing each other. In their hands, they held each other's bleeding hearts.

'I hate Christmas,' Mary told Dr. Fox . . . again. 'But I love that film. It's a great love story.'

Dr. Fox said nothing back. She knew that mentioning the tattoo was one of Mary's most used evading tactics. It had happened several times before.

The doctor waited in silence.

Mary pressed her lips together, before allowing them to stretch into a half smile, but her eyes didn't seem to smile with them.

Dr. Fox pushed. 'Is there anything that you'd like to talk about, Mary?'

Mary's acting was so on point that if this were an audition for the main role in some major Hollywood production film, she'd get it, hands down.

'You seem just a little . . . on edge today,' Dr. Fox said, her eyes carefully studying Mary.

This time, Mary allowed a full smile to take over her lips. 'I think . . .' The pause was deliberate . . . calculated. 'I think that my partner is going to propose.'

During her therapy sessions, Dr. Fox had always been at the very high end of professionalism. Always calm, collected and analytical, with almost no emotional display whatsoever, but Mary's revelation caught the doctor completely by surprise and her eyes widened behind her glasses.

'Really?' This time, it was the smile in Dr. Fox's eyes that didn't reach her lips.

Mary bit her bottom lip and nodded.

'You *think* he's going to propose?' the doctor asked, quickly scribbling something down on her notepad. 'Or you know for sure that he's going to propose?'

'He's going to propose,' Mary confirmed, no doubt in her tone. She had stopped hugging herself, allowing her arms to rest by her sides – her hands clasped together on her lap. 'I wasn't supposed to have seen it.'

'The ring?'

Mary's eyebrows arched. 'The receipt for the ring. And a few days ago, just before he flew down to LA on business, he mentioned the idea of the two of us going on a holiday to somewhere romantic.' Her head angled to one side. 'The writing is on the wall.'

Dr. Fox observed Mary's eye movement together with her demeanor. She was still getting mixed signals. 'When?'

'When he's back, tomorrow or the day after,' Mary replied. 'So, we might be going as soon as next week . . . maybe.'

Dr. Fox allowed the silence to spread across the room for a few seconds before she spoke. 'And how do you feel about that?'

Mary took in a breath, as her gaze moved to the psychologist in the armchair. Dr. Fox had always captivated Mary in a way that Mary couldn't quite explain. It wasn't just her attractiveness. It was a combination of everything – her elegance . . . the cadence in which she spoke . . . her unflinching composure . . . how intelligent and independent she was . . . even the small mole that she had just above her right eyebrow seemed like the perfect imperfection. In different circumstances, Mary would've loved to have Dr. Fox as a friend.

'I feel great,' Mary finally replied, renewing her smile – this one, excited.

Another analytical appraisal from Dr. Fox. 'You feel great as in – you're happy that your partner is going to propose?'

Mary looked away for a fraction of a second, as if she had to think about the answer for an instant. Once again, she gave her psychologist an answer that didn't exactly fit the question.

'I love him so much.'

Dr. Fox noted something down on her pad. 'And you're convinced that you would like to spend the rest of your life with him?'

Mary's acting was boarding on spectacular – the way that she avoided Dr. Fox's eyes before bringing her arms up to hug herself again, this time a little tighter, being careful to allow the hug to hitch up her right sleeve just enough so that the new bruise on her wrist would peek out.

Mary saw that Dr. Fox saw it. Her eyes stayed on it until Mary unhugged herself, pulled her sleeves down a touch and returned her hands to her lap.

'I am, yes,' Mary replied, at last. 'What can be better than spending the rest of your life with the person you love?' She indicated the tattoo on the doctor's arm. 'Jack and Sally. That's how I see us.'

Dr. Fox allowed a sympathetic smile to blossom between her lips. 'Why don't you tell me a little about him?' she asked, her concerned eyes finally moving from Mary's right wrist back to her face. 'About your relationship.'

Mary paused, frowning at the psychologist. 'I've told you about him a thousand times.'

That much was true. Mary had told Dr. Fox about Quaddra several times since they'd started dating. In fact, Mary had mentioned her partner in every session she'd had with Dr. Fox since, but Mary had always been very careful never to mention his name. She didn't want Dr. Fox to google it and find out that Quaddra was a billionaire. The trick was to make Dr. Fox believe that Mary was head over heels in love with her partner, and that she would've said yes to marriage regardless of how wealthy he was. That was the sort of testimony that won trials.

'He's loving and caring,' Mary finally replied, her smile bright, but not so much. 'Very attentive, funny, intelligent . . . he's the kind of man that you dream of, you know? And he loves me . . . he really does.'

Mary was very careful as to her intonation and her posture, as she delivered her last sentence. She really made it sound like – 'And he loves me . . . he really does' – was said more to convince herself than anyone else. As if she had deliberately left a tag ending out of her sentence – 'And he loves me . . . he really does . . . *despite everything*'.

As she delivered the sentence, her left hand cupped over her right wrist, as if trying to erase the bruise under her sleeve. Psychologists called it a tell-tale reflex. In essence, it was a subconscious giveaway. It happened when a subject would unconsciously somehow drive attention to a part of the body associated with a memory, distressing or not.

Dr. Fox noticed the movement.

As Mary cupped her left hand over her right wrist, her eyes settled on her watch. 'I think our time is up, Doc.' She got to her feet.

Dr. Fox also checked her timepiece. Mary was right. Their time *was* up. She calmly closed her notepad and got up from the armchair.

'Mary, wait,' she called, halting Mary as she was just getting to the door.

Mary paused and turned to look back at the doctor.

Dr. Fox reached for one of her cards on her desk, scribbled something on the back of it and handed it to Mary.

'If you ever feel the need to talk . . . about anything . . . anything at all . . . feel free to give me a call anytime, OK?'

Mary took the card and looked at the private cell number.

'And I don't mean it as doctor/patient,' Dr. Fox added. 'We can chat as friends in a much more relaxed atmosphere, if you like.'

Mary's gaze met Dr. Fox's and she gave her a shy smile. Internally, she was already thinking of something sad. Not sad enough to make her cry, but enough to glass her eyes over.

It took her only one second.

'Thank you, Doc. I really appreciate it.'

Sixty-Eight

Quaddra flew back to San Francisco on Sunday morning, and he and Mary spent the rest of the day together … in bed. On Monday, he left the house early, as he had a full day of meetings in his office downtown, but these were all for real.

Mary had just come back home from her daily morning run by the Bay when Antonia, the senior housemaid, walked into the kitchen carrying a full basket of laundry.

'Miss Smith,' she called, grabbing Mary's attention.

Mary had asked her countless times to call her 'Mary', but Antonia never did. To her, it would be disrespectful to address her employers by their first names.

Mary lifted her eyes from the magazine that she was reading. 'Hi Antonia.'

'Did Mr. Buckner cut himself while he was away?' Antonia asked.

Mary frowned at her. 'Cut himself? What do you mean?'

Antonia reached into the laundry basket to retrieve a gray, long-sleeved sports shirt that belonged to Quaddra.

'Maybe I'm wrong,' she said, walking over to where Mary was sitting. 'But this looks like a little blood, doesn't it?' She showed Mary the tip of the shirt's right sleeve, where a few small dark-red specks could be seen. 'Or is it wine?'

Mary recognized the shirt as one of Quaddra's moisture-wicking running shirts. Its materials reduced perspiration and kept body moisture locked in. She had a couple of similar tops herself.

Mary took the shirt and looked at the dark dots on the sleeve from several different angles before stretching the fabric and bringing it to her nose. All she got was a faint scent of Quaddra's usual cologne. She then rubbed her thumb and forefinger against the stains for a couple of seconds. The fabric under them had hardened a touch. Like it would've had with dried blood.

'He didn't mention anything to me,' Mary finally replied, her tone a little concerned. 'But you're right. This does look like blood, not wine. That's strange.'

'Oh, don't worry,' Antonia said, reaching for the shirt. 'I can use Tide Oxi on it. That thing is like magic. It gets rid of all sorts of stains.'

'Actually, no,' Mary said, holding on to the shirt. 'Leave it with me, Antonia, and I'll ask Quaddra when he gets in this evening.'

That evening, Quaddra got home just a few minutes past eight o'clock. Mary was sitting in the study/library room, reading a book on psychology.

'Hey babe,' Quaddra said, poking his head through the door. 'How was your day?'

'Hey honey.' Mary put down the book and walked over to Quaddra to kiss him. 'All good . . . easy. Dropped by the gallery this afternoon to sort a few things out and that was about it, really. How was yours?'

He put his arms around her. 'One meeting after another.' He kissed her again. 'Same old, same old, but I do have some great news.'

'Really?' Mary smiled. 'Do tell.'

'As discussed.' Quaddra kissed her again. 'Vienna – tickets bought and hotel booked. Europe baby.'

They had talked about their trip last night, with Quaddra insisting that they flew in his private jet. It was way more practical and convenient than a commercial airliner, but Mary told him that she'd heard too many stories about things going wrong with private jets, especially during long-haul flights. Quaddra did try to explain how safe private jets really were and that his pilot, Bill Stoneheart, was ex-military, with over twenty years of flying experience, but Mary really wasn't having any of it. In the end, Quaddra simply gave in.

'When?' Mary asked.

'Friday,' Quaddra told her. 'Just like we agreed. Flight departs at 7:45 p.m. We'll make a quick stop in Frankfurt because we're flying Lufthansa, but from there to Vienna is a quick one-and-a-half-hour hop.'

Mary's fake smile was flawless. 'I guess I better start packing then.'

'Start packing?' Quaddra frowned and chuckled at the same time. 'It's Monday, babe. We're going on Friday . . . and we're only going for eleven days.'

'I don't like leaving things until the last minute,' Mary replied, reaching for Quaddra's hand and pulling him away from the study. 'Are you hungry?' They started walking in the direction of the kitchen.

'Starving.'

'Great. Antonia made her famous roast chicken with Mediterranean vegetables. It's in the oven.'

'Oh my god, it's like she read my mind. I love her roast chicken. I'll go get the wine.' He pointed in the direction of the cellar. 'Any preference?'

'Not really. Surprise me.'

Quaddra did, choosing a South African Pinotage Reserva – it paired perfectly with roast chicken.

They sat at the kitchen table.

'Honey,' Mary said, as Quaddra poured some hot gravy over his chicken. 'Did you hurt yourself while in LA?'

Quaddra's forehead creased. 'Hurt myself? What do you mean?'

'Antonia was doing the laundry today,' Mary explained. 'And on one of your running shirts – gray, long sleeve, sweatproof – there appears to be a few speckles of blood on the right sleeve.'

'Blood?' Quaddra put down his fork. 'Are you sure?'

Mary nodded. 'Yeah, let me show you.' She got up from the table and went into the laundry room.

'Fucking stupid, Quaddra!' Quaddra whispered through clenched teeth, his hands clenching into fists. 'Fucking stupid!'

Seconds later, Mary walked back into the kitchen with Quaddra's shirt.

He took it and just like Mary had done earlier, looked at the stains from different angles before stretching the fabric and smelling it. 'That's odd,' he said, his gaze still on the shirt, his expression intrigued. 'I don't remember . . . ohhhhhh!' His eyebrows arched as he looked back at Mary. 'James, the bleeder.'

Mary looked somewhat confused. 'James, the bleeder?'

'Yes,' Quaddra explained. 'At the Marina.'

Mary gave Quaddra a subtle shake of the head, followed by a half shrug.

'Yesterday morning, I was up by 5:00 a.m.,' Quaddra clarified. 'Just couldn't sleep anymore. I thought about giving you a call, but it was way too early, so I decided to go for a run at the Marina. Like I said, it was early, not that many people out and about, but there were a few, mainly on the Ocean Front Walk. Anyway, I was right at the end of my run when an older gentleman, who was just a few feet ahead of me, got a pretty intense nosebleed.'

'Oh god!' Mary grimaced.

'It was weird too because he didn't fall or bump into anyone, or anything like that. He just started bleeding, mid-run.'

'How old was he?'

'Not young . . . late sixties, I think, but in pretty good shape.' Quaddra put the shirt down on the table. 'Anyway, I did what I could to help – tipped his head back and told him to breathe through his mouth. Someone else saw it as well and came over to assist, so we both got the guy to the nearest bench and sat him down. By then, it was almost six in the morning and the beach lifeguards were getting to their posts. The other guy stayed with the bleeder, while I ran up to a lifeguard post and got someone with a first-aid kit to come and help.'

Mary picked up the shirt again. 'You never told me any of this.'

'I had actually forgotten about it,' Quaddra said back, matter-of-factly. 'But the funny thing is, I had my sleeves pulled up.' He mimicked the gesture.

'So was the guy OK?'

'Yeah, he was fine,' Quaddra replied, reaching for his fork. 'I hung around until the lifeguard had stopped the bleeding, just to check if he needed any more help, you know? Maybe I could get him a cab home or something, but he didn't live too far, so, to be on the safe side, I walked back with him. His name was James, and he told me that he used to box in his younger years. That's why he gets those nosebleeds every once in a while. His nose has taken its fair share of punches during his boxing days.'

'Aww, that was so very kind of you, honey.'

'We all need a little help every now and then, babe, no matter who we are. Anybody would've done the same.'

'No, they wouldn't,' Mary said, with a shake of the head. 'They would've taken out their phones and recorded everything for their social media, but not everyone would've helped . . . and even fewer would've stuck around like you did just to see if you could be of any more help. You're amazing, do you know that?' She stepped closer to kiss him again.

Even though he was lying, Quaddra did feel somewhat proud

because he knew that if the bleeder scenario had really happened, he would've helped, just like he told Mary.

'I don't think I am,' he replied. 'But I think that we're living in a pretty shitty world when being kind is considered to be an exception.'

Sixty-Nine

The flight from San Francisco to Vienna had been a lot more pleasant than Quaddra had expected. True, he hadn't flown commercial long haul in quite some time, so he wasn't exactly sure of what to expect, but he was positively impressed by the airliner's service and their individual, and quite luxurious, first-class cabins – and so was Mary. During their eleven-hour flight to their layover in Frankfurt, Mary and Quaddra had managed to join the mile-high club – inside their private cabin, of course – and still get a clean seven hours plus of decent sleep each, something that Quaddra had to admit it would've never happened if they had taken his private jet.

On their way from the airport to their hotel in central Vienna, Mary and Quaddra agreed that for the next eleven days they would forget about everything and simply have a blast – eat whatever they wanted . . . drink whatever they wanted . . . and do whatever they felt like . . . no holdbacks. This was vacation time – no talking about dieting, or business, or the gallery, or anything else other than enjoying themselves.

'So, babe,' Quaddra asked, as they exited the famous Vienna State Opera after watching an impressive ballet production of *The Sleeping Beauty* that had brought tears to Mary's eyes. 'Tomorrow will be our third day here in Vienna. Seven more days left before we have to fly back. Have you thought of anywhere else you'd like to go?'

'Umm . . .' Mary reached for Quaddra's hand, as they walked past the world-renowned Moulin Rouge on Walfischgasse. 'I did . . . yes.'

'OK, tell me.' Quaddra sounded truly excited. 'Where would you like to go next?'

'I was thinking,' she began. 'Since we have no agenda, why don't we just go mad?' Right then, Mary looked like a school student about to suggest that they skipped class.

'O. . .kay.' Quaddra's eyes narrowed to slits. 'I'm listening. What kind of mad? What do you have in mind?'

'Well,' Mary replied, her head bouncing from left to right. 'This is Europe, where you can get just about everywhere by train, right?'

'Uh-huh.'

'So how about we just turn up at the train station in the morning, check which trains are going where, pick one from the board . . .' Mary shrugged. 'And just go?'

Quaddra paused and turned to look at Mary, searching her face for any hints of a joke. He found none.

'You're serious? Like backpackers do?'

'Exactly,' Mary agreed.

Quaddra chuckled. 'Except that instead of a backpack, you've got three huge suitcases.'

'Are you telling me that you're not up for a challenge?' Mary winked at Quaddra, with a mischievous smile on her lips. 'You're going to chicken out?'

Quaddra's face lit up. 'Oh no, if you're serious, it's definitely on. I love that idea.'

'Oh yeah, I'm dead serious.' She kissed him again. 'But before we do that, I was thinking of something else.'

'Yeah?'

'Since we're already in Austria, why don't we visit Salzburg? It's only about three hours away on the train.'

'Salzburg?' Quaddra's intrigued eyes met Mary's. 'What's in Salz—' He paused before snapping his thumb and forefinger. 'Of course,' he said, his head tilting back slightly. 'Your favorite film.'

On their first-ever night out, at the Malaysian restaurant, after the exhibition at the Legion of Honor, when they chatted about art, wine, music and films, Mary had told Quaddra that her favorite TV show was *Vamp Blood*, but her favorite film was something completely different – a musical, released in 1965, staring Julie Andrews and Christopher Plummer.

'*The Sound of Music*, right?' Quaddra said.

Mary looked back at him a little surprised. 'You remember?' She actually knew every song in that film by heart.

'Of course I remember,' Quaddra said back. 'And yes, a lot of it was shot in Salzburg.' His eyes glinted with enthusiasm. 'That's a fantastic idea, babe.'

'It's supposed to be a beautiful town,' Mary added.

'And the birthplace of Mozart.'

'So will you go?' Mary gave Quaddra another dose of her puppy eyes.

'Of course I'll go, my love.' Quaddra kissed her again. 'That's why we're here, remember? To do whatever the hell we feel like doing and go whatever the hell we feel like going . . . and Salzburg sounds like a brilliant choice before we go mad on the departures board.' His turn to wink at her. 'I say we go tomorrow morning, what do you think?'

Mary's smile almost lit up the entire street. 'Sounds like a plan.'

'We're so doing this.' Quaddra lifted his right hand and they high-fived each other. 'Salzburg here we come.'

'You know,' Mary said, lacing her fingers behind Quaddra's neck. 'I didn't think I could love you any more, but you just proved me wrong.' They kissed again. 'And I think that before we go, we should make good use of that enormous Jacuzzi in our hotel room one last time, what do you say?'

Quaddra looked down at Mary's shoes. 'I say that if you weren't wearing high heels, I'd race you back to the hotel.'

'I'll get the water going in the Jacuzzi,' Mary said, as soon as they walked back into their penthouse suite.

'OK,' Quaddra said back, getting rid of his suit jacket as he walked over to the bar. 'I'll get us a drink. Wine or Champagne?'

'Champagne, bitte,' Mary replied, making use of one third of all the German she knew before disappearing into the bedroom.

This was Quaddra's chance. He reached for his cell phone and quickly typed a text message.

QUADDRA: We'll be in Salzburg tomorrow by lunchtime. I'll make sure that we're at the bridge sometime between 7:00 and 7:30 p.m. Be there.

He put down his phone and popped open the bottle of Dom Perignon that they had left chilling in the fridge. Before Quaddra was able to pour the Champagne into two glasses, his phone vibrated once on the bar counter.

UNKNOWN: We'll be there.

Seventy

With a little help from the concierge at the Ritz-Carlton, the hotel where they were staying in Vienna, even at such short notice, Mary and Quaddra managed to book two first-class tickets on an early train from Wien Westbahnhof to Salzburg Hbf. The concierge also helped them secure the presidential suite at the Bristol Hotel – one of the most luxurious hotels in Salzburg Old Town. The hotel was also less than three minutes' walk from where Quaddra needed to make sure that Mary would be that evening.

They arrived in Salzburg just a few minutes past eleven, had lunch at the award-winning Polo Lounge restaurant in their hotel, and by 1:00 p.m., Mary and Quaddra were being picked up from the Marktplatz for a very private 'The Sound of Music' tour.

Nineteen locations and four-and-a-half hours later, they were finally back at their hotel room, with Mary still buzzing from the tour.

'That was absolutely amazing,' she said, wrapping her arms around Quaddra's waist. 'Thank you so much for making it all possible, and for arranging everything so quickly.'

'One hundred percent my pleasure, babe,' Quaddra said back, giving her a peck on the lips. 'And I'm the one who should be saying thank you. Truth be told – I hadn't been expecting the tour to be so much fun. I fully enjoyed it.'

'And I'm so glad you did,' Mary kissed him back before

allowing her eyes to move to the complimentary cheeseboard that the hotel had just delivered to their room, together with a bottle of pink Champagne on ice. 'Are you hungry?'

'I'm getting there fast,' Quaddra replied. 'You?'

'Yeah, I could certainly do with some food.' Mary walked over to the cheeseboard and reached for a couple of grapes.

Quaddra checked his watch. 'It's twenty past five now. We could have a light snack here . . .' He nodded at the board. 'Take a shower, get ready, and go for dinner sometime around . . . seven?' He made the suggestion sound as breezy as he could. 'According to the tour guide, there are plenty of great restaurants around this area.'

'Seven sounds good,' Mary agreed.

They showered and got ready, Quaddra being at least twenty minutes ahead of Mary.

While she put the final touches to her makeup, he stared out of their top floor window, with views of the Salzach River. Salzburg really was an astonishing-looking town, with incredibly well-preserved, medieval and baroque architecture, but Quaddra's thoughts were on something else entirely. His plan, as crazy as it had sounded when he first came up with it, was working. All he needed to do now was get her there.

Quaddra's cellphone vibrated inside his jacket pocket, snatching him away from his thoughts. He reached for it and quickly checked the screen.

UNKNOWN: We're ready. Waiting for your signal.

Seventy-One

Quaddra had just deleted the message and returned the phone to his pocket, when Mary walked back into their presidential suite living room.

'OK, honey, I'm ready!'

Quaddra turned to face her and paused, his breath catching as his lips stretched into a half smile, half jaw drop. 'Wow!'

'Do you like it?' Mary asked, doing a spin – catwalk style. She wore a very elegant red, sleeveless, V-neck, high slit evening dress, with black Christian Louboutin stiletto heel sandals and a matching clutch bag. Her makeup was, as always, perfect, with her hair loose, falling down to her shoulders.

For a moment, Quaddra seemed completely lost for words. 'I . . .'

Mary stepped closer.

'You look . . .' He blinked and shook his head, as if trying to wake up from a dream. 'Absolutely stunning.'

'You're very kind,' Mary said, reaching for his hand. 'You look incredible yourself.'

Quaddra was wearing a brand-new tailored suit from Gieves and Hawkes, dark blue in color, with Josh Driver black shoes.

'Danke schön, Fräulein,' Quaddra replied, also doing his version of a catwalk spin, but definitely not as good as Mary's. 'Shall we?'

Down in the hotel lobby, as they exited the elevator, heads began turning, and Quaddra was pretty sure that none of them was doing so to look at him.

'You two look like . . . perfection,' the hotel concierge said, as they walked past his station. The name on his tag read 'Conrad'. He was as tall as Quaddra, but not as physically fit. His smile seemed almost permanent.

'Danke schön,' Mary said back, nodding at Conrad.

Quaddra simply smiled his thanks.

Conrad reached behind his station for something that neither Mary nor Quaddra could quite see what it was.

'You are going to ze bridge, right?' Conrad spoke with a typical Austrian/German accent, where every 'th' took on a 'z' sound.

Mary frowned at him before looking at Quaddra. 'The bridge?'

Quaddra's eyebrows arched at Conrad. 'What bridge?'

'Markartsteg Bridge,' Conrad replied, pointing east. 'It's just about two minutes' walk from here.'

Quaddra bit his bottom lip as he gave the concierge a slight sideways look. 'What's on Markartsteg Bridge?'

It was Conrad's turn to frown at the stunning-looking couple. 'Ze love lock bridge.'

'Love lock bridge?' Mary's gaze ping-ponged between Quaddra and Conrad.

'Yes,' Conrad explained. 'Where couples write zeir names on a padlock and lock it onto ze bridge railing as a sign of zeir ever-lasting love. It's for good luck.'

'Oh!' Mary exclaimed. 'Like in the movies?'

'Yes,' Conrad confirmed. 'And Markartsteg Bridge is beautiful. More beautiful zan ze one in Paris. Zere are so many different color padlocks all over ze railings, and zei are all zer for one reason . . . love. You can feel it in the air when you walk across ze bridge. It makes ze hairs . . .' He rubbed his left forearm, '. . . go puff.' He lifted his hands with his fingers wide apart and pointing up. 'You'll see.' He finally offered Quaddra what he had retrieved from behind his station. 'Zis is a gift from ze hotel.'

Quaddra took it and Mary craned her neck to have a look. Conrad had handed Quaddra a red, heart-shaped padlock, with the keyhole right at the center of it. The padlock came with two keys and a marker pen.

'You must do it,' Conrad urged them. 'You are such a beautiful couple, and Markartsteg Bridge will bring you good luck and happiness . . . I promise you. It's a magical bridge in a magical city.' He nodded at the padlock in Quaddra's hands. 'Write your names onto ze padlock and lock it onto ze bridge. You'll be forever happy.'

'A magical bridge, huh?' Quaddra's eyes moved from Mary to Conrad.

'In a magical city.' Conrad gave them a firm head nod.

'Do you want to do it?' Quaddra asked, as he and Mary stepped out onto the streets. It was just past 7:00 p.m. on a beautiful, perfect night, where a full moon shared the sky with a thousand stars.

Mary bit down on a smile. 'Do you?'

'Why not?' He looked down at the padlock and pen. 'We're here, anyway. We've got a padlock. We might as well.'

'Yeah, but I didn't think that you would be into something superstitious like that.'

'I'm not,' Quaddra agreed. 'Superstitious, I mean, but I do love what it's supposed to mean . . . the everlasting love part.' His head angled to one side. 'I really want that to be true for us.'

Mary gave Quaddra another dose of her puppy eyes. 'Me too, honey.'

'So, let's do it,' Quaddra said, his eyes sparkling with excitement. 'Maybe it *is* a magical bridge.'

'In a magical city,' Mary said back, with a smile.

Quaddra turned to face south. 'According to the concierge, the bridge is just over there.' He pointed straight ahead. 'How about we do it now, before we go for dinner?'

'Sure.' Mary held on to Quaddra's arm.

It really did take them just two minutes to get to the bridge, and the bridge really was just as beautiful as Conrad had described it. Padlocks of all different sizes and all different colors covered one hundred and twenty yards of railings . . . on both sides. And Conrad wasn't lying when he told them that they would feel something in the air when they crossed the bridge.

'This is amazing,' Quaddra said, reaching for his phone to snap a couple of pictures.

Mary nodded and did the same. 'There must be tens of thousands of padlocks here.'

'At least,' Quaddra agreed. 'And like the concierge said, they're all here for one reason – hope of everlasting love.'

Mary hugged herself and rubbed her arms. 'And yeah, the hairs on my arms have gone "puff".' She mimicked the concierge's hand gesture from earlier.

They walked past two other couples locking their padlocks onto the railings and found a spot towards the center of the bridge.

'How about right here?' Quaddra suggested, indicating a large enough gap at the bottom of the railing.

'Looks good.' Mary nodded.

Quaddra unwrapped the padlock and handed it to Mary, together with the marker pen. 'How about we do it like this – you write my name and I'll write yours, like we're wishing for each other.'

Mary laughed. 'For someone who isn't superstitious, you sure caught on quick.' She took the pen and the padlock. 'Do I write it anywhere?'

'I guess,' Quaddra replied, with a single shoulder shrug.

'OK,' Mary said before narrowing her eyes at Quaddra and pointing at him. 'It's Quaddra, right?'

Quaddra dipped his chin to look back at her. 'Oh, you've got jokes tonight, have you?'

Mary blew him a kiss, as she wrote Quaddra's name onto the padlock, just above the keyhole. 'Here you go.' She handed the padlock and the pen to him.

Quaddra took it and wrote Mary's name directly under his. 'OK, here it goes.' He unlocked the padlock and handed one of the keys to Mary, keeping the second one for himself. He then got down on his knees to lock the padlock to the bottom of the railing.

'You know, Mary?' he said, his gaze still on her. 'Every time I look at you – when I'm waking up in the morning, when you're stepping out of a shower, when I'm coming home from work or a trip . . . it doesn't matter when . . . it doesn't matter where . . . you always take my breath away . . . every time. And tonight, when I saw you walking into the living room back at our hotel, my heart almost stopped.'

'Aww, baby!' Mary reached down and placed her right hand on his left cheek.

Quaddra kissed her palm before locking the padlock onto the bridge, but he didn't stand up . . . he stayed down on his knees. 'I know that in modern society, everlasting love is becoming something of a unicorn. Couples don't really stay together like they did in the old days. But just look at this bridge and all these padlocks – every single one of them wishing for that everlasting love . . . hoping that this bridge really is magical, but if you allow me, Mary Smith, I'll show you that the magic of my love for you comes from here.' Quaddra brought his right hand to his chest and tapped it twice. 'From deep inside my heart.' He threw his key into the river. 'Not from a magic bridge.'

'What . . . ?' Mary shook her head ever so slightly. 'What are you saying, honey?'

'Look up,' Quaddra told her.

'What?'

'Look up,' he said again. 'Right over there.' He lifted his right arm and pointed at the sky to the east side of the bridge.

Mary's gaze moved from Quaddra to the star-filled sky. 'What am I look—' She paused midsentence, her eyes narrowing at what she was seeing. All of a sudden, it looked like the stars were moving. Either that, or a whole bunch of UFOs had just come calling. 'What's going on right now?' Her eyes went back to Quaddra.

'Don't look at me. Look at the sky.'

Mary did . . . again. The stars . . . the UFOs . . . whatever those were, they were still moving, and there were more coming . . . from both sides.

Passersby were now stopping to look as well, all pointing at the moving lights, which were now starting to form a pattern.

Mary finally realized that the lights weren't stars, or UFOs . . . they were drones, flying at high speed.

In the blink of an eye, they all bunched together to form an enormous red heart, just like their padlock, before exploding in all different directions to spell the words:

MARY SMITH, WILL YOU MARRY ME?

An unsynchronized chorus of gasps and 'Aww's' came at them from all corners of the bridge.

Mary's jaw dropped, as her gaze returned to Quaddra, who was still on his knees, but now holding the most beautiful diamond ring, displayed inside an open Tiffany's ring box. Her hands immediately cupped over her mouth, as her eyes welled up with tears.

Mary knew that Quaddra would propose during their trip to Europe, but not in a million years was she expecting it to be something as magical as this.

'And if you give me the chance, Mary Smith . . .' Quaddra said, as if he could read her thoughts, '. . . I'd love to show you how this magic will never end.'

The tenderness in his voice was like nothing Mary had ever heard before – from anyone.

Over the years, Mary had become an expert in pretending. She could cry on demand and at the blink of an eye . . . she could appear to be madly in love, when inside she was burning with hatred . . . and she knew how to lie and deceive better than any lawyer north or south of the Mississippi . . . but right then, the tears in her eyes were one hundred percent real, and so was the rapid beating of her heart. She chuckled nervously, as she nodded.

'Yes!' She smiled and the tears that had welled up in her eyes began streaming down her face.

'Yes?' Quaddra asked, just to be sure.

'Yes,' Mary repeated it, much louder this time, offering Quaddra her left hand.

Quaddra retrieved the ring from the box and slid it onto Mary's ring finger.

Over in the distance, the drones dissolved into another crazy dance in the air, reshaping and reforming . . . first into a new, pulsating heart . . . and then to spell out a new sentence.

SHE SAID YES . . . CONGRATULATIONS!

The entire bridge erupted in cheers and applause.

Seventy-Two

From Mary and Quaddra's engagement back in Salzburg, things moved fast – very fast, actually – and it was Quaddra who pushed for a speedy wedding.

His argument was simple – since Mary had said yes, why wait? What would they be waiting for, anyway? Neither of them wanted a big party, so there was no need to hire a wedding planner or go through months of preparation. Neither of them was religious, so a church wedding, where they'd have to wait months for a slot at the right church and have to go through countless hours of rehearsals, was also out of the equation. All they really needed to do was invite the few friends that they wanted to invite, book a date with a justice of the peace, and get married … no muss, no fuss.

Mary didn't argue with Quaddra's logic. In truth, the faster that they got married, the faster she could put the rest of her plan into action. There was only one thing that she needed to do first – sign a prenuptial agreement – and Mary had been the one who had suggested it, on the same night that they got engaged.

'I love you, honey,' Mary said, once they got back to their hotel after they got engaged on Markartsteg Bridge. 'So, so much … and I would marry you tomorrow, if that's what you wanted … but I'll only do so if I sign a pre-nuptial agreement.'

Quaddra truly never saw that coming. 'What? Why?'

'Exactly because of the reason I just told you,' Mary explained. 'I love you, and that's the reason why I'm going to marry you.'

'Baby, I know that.'

'I know *you* do, but every single one of your friends think that I'm with you because you're rich.'

'And since when do I ever care for what others might think, honey,' Quaddra came back.

'It's not about you caring or not for what others might think, honey. I know that you don't. This is about the future,' Mary explained, her performance impeccable. 'It's about me not having to forever endure the looks that I know I'll be getting from everyone, whenever I enter a room, with or without you, simply because I'm your wife. It's about the onslaught of criticism that's about to come my way, as soon as they know we're engaged. It's about all the jokes that people will make . . . the behind-the-back comments . . .the digs.' She lifted both hands at him. 'I know that that's not something personal. People won't be doing it just because it's me, Mary Smith. Whoever married you would get it. I know that you know that. It comes with being too successful.'

Quaddra did know that. Unless he married someone who was publicly known to be at least as wealthy as he was, there would always be talk of 'gold digging'.

He gave Mary a sideways nod, accepting her argument. 'You're right. People are dicks.'

'I am marrying you because I'm in love with you,' Mary said again. 'But we live in a paranoid society – one where couples actually require a court of law document to prove that they are in love and that they aren't marrying each other for money.' She paused for effect. 'Please, honey, it will make me feel so much more comfortable knowing that we have it.'

It took Quaddra a couple of seconds before he nodded back

at Mary. 'Sure, my love, if that's what you want . . . I'll get my lawyers to draft a prenup as soon as we're back.'

'That's what I want.' Mary smiled and kissed his lips again.

'Then that's what you'll have.'

No, Mary wasn't crazy. On the contrary, she knew exactly what she was doing.

She couldn't give a flying fuck for what Quaddra's friends thought of her. That was just what she told him as an excuse. In truth, the prenuptial agreement was to put *his* mind at ease.

Quaddra was a billionaire, and Mary was just someone who he'd met at an art exhibition. Not matter what he told her, no matter how much in love he truly was with her, the worry of her being a 'gold digger', however small, would always be there, lurking in the background. That, after all, had been the reason why Quaddra had developed the habit of giving strangers a false name in the first place – to try to avoid the opportunists. He was a very intelligent man, he wouldn't be so successful if he weren't, and if there was one thing that success had taught him it was that no matter how well he thought he knew someone, he never really knew someone well enough – everyone had secrets. And that had been why Mary had played the prenuptial agreement card. A prenuptial agreement, especially one suggested by her, would go a long way towards easing Quaddra's doubts about her real intentions. This was Mary proving to Quaddra that she wasn't after his money.

Yes, she knew that a prenuptial agreement would completely overrule the traditional 50/50 split that had become the base for negotiations in most divorce settlements in the USA. In their particular case, she would make sure that their prenuptial agreement stipulated that should Mary and Quaddra ever get divorced, Mary would have no rights to any of Quaddra's already existing fortune and none of his properties. Whatever wealth he'd accumulated before their marriage would be completely out of her reach and there would be nothing that her lawyers would be able to do to overturn that . . . but Mary wouldn't just be divorcing Quaddra. She would be suing him for criminal domestic violence, physical abuse, battering, and false imprisonment and captivity – and that was a criminal lawsuit, not a divorce settlement – in which case, a prenuptial agreement meant absolutely nothing.

Her lawyers would be requesting compensation for physical injuries and for all the psychological torment and trauma that he had caused her . . . and with that, they would be able to take everything – prenup or no prenup.

Seventy-Three

Quaddra proved to be a true romantic at heart, suggesting that they hire out the Legion of Honor as the venue for their wedding. That was where he and Mary had gone on their first-ever date, even though Mary had always insisted that it hadn't been a date 'per se'. He'd also suggested that they got the Malay couple, who ran the restaurant that they'd gone for dinner afterwards, to prepare the wedding buffet and dinner. In short, Quaddra wanted to give his wedding guests a quick snippet of his and Mary's first-ever night out.

Mary had found the idea adorable, and if that really was what Quaddra wanted, she'd be fine with it, but she did argue that hiring out such a public venue, like the Legion of Honor, would, no doubt, attract its fair share of unwanted attention, like tabloids and paparazzi, something that neither of them were very keen on. In the end, Quaddra agreed with Mary, and they decided to use the grounds of Quaddra's mansion for their wedding.

It had been a simple but very classy ceremony, four months after they got back from Europe, and with only a handful of guests. Mary had invited Harvey and Cory, the owners of the gallery that she worked at, but unfortunately, they couldn't attend, as they were holidaying in Europe at the time. Mary also invited Betsy, who had flown over from LA specially.

Unsurprisingly, Quaddra had asked his childhood friend, Tyler, to be the best man at their wedding, and to keep things simple, Mary had asked Kristie, Tyler's wife, to be her bridesmaid.

Since Kristie and Mary met, all those months ago, at Quaddra's cheese and wine party, they had become quite good friends, but that hadn't been the real reason why Mary had asked Kristie to be her bridesmaid. Kristie was Megan's best friend, who was Quaddra's ex-girlfriend. True, since that same cheese and wine party, Mary had also managed to win Megan over, somewhat, but Megan clearly still had feelings for Quaddra, and she could still be a real bitch when she wanted to. Having Kristie as her bridesmaid had been a tactical move by Mary, not a friendly gesture.

With the wedding finally out of the way, Mary was free to properly begin implementing the rest of her plan . . . and since Quaddra had pushed for a speedy wedding, she also decided to move things forward a bit.

Mary and Denise had run this same con three times before. It was a long-game con that if done properly would pay very well – in the past fourteen years, they had both made several millions each – but sending people to prison for something they hadn't really done had a special way of pissing them off. For that reason alone, once the con was over, both Mary and Denise would always move cities – states, preferably. They'd also undergo a full looks and identity change – something that didn't really pose that much of a problem when you were a millionaire – documents could be bought, and so could privacy – but what really set their con apart from most regular cons was that theirs had a legal side to it. They weren't simply stealing the money and running, like regular criminals. The money was awarded to them by a judge – it was all completely above board and legal – and it was that legal side of the con that Mary and Denise both knew had a very short shelf life.

In the US, people could easily get divorced twice, with a very hefty settlement, and no one would bat an eyelid, even if both divorces came in a relatively short amount of time. The statistic was that over 55 percent of marriages in the USA, within three to five years, would end up in divorce. A third divorce was still doable, but was much riskier, and that had been why Denise had said that if they were to run their con again, especially inside the USA, it was her turn to play the wife, but Mary wasn't exactly worried. Yes, this would be her third wedding, but only her second inside the USA. The first time that Mary had gotten married, she was over five thousand miles away, in London, England.

Seventy-Four

Nineteen Years Ago

London

Grace and Julia both knew how vindictive Dylan and his traveling funfair mates could be, so after they left him bleeding on the floor of his dirty caravan back in Leeds, they didn't stick around for the consequences. They made their way straight to the railway station and jumped on the very first train they could. They didn't really care where it was heading. They just wanted out of Leeds ... fast ... any direction would do.

At that time in the morning, they weren't exactly overwhelmed with choices, but the second train on the departures board – leaving in just fifteen minutes – was heading to London, a city so big and so populated that they could both easily become the proverbial 'needle in the haystack' – and right then, there was nothing that Grace and Julia wanted more.

Two hours and fifteen minutes later, they were stepping out of the train and onto Platform One at King's Cross Station, Central London.

That was the very first time that either of them had been to London, and as they walked through the station and out onto the streets, they were immediately mesmerized by everything they saw – the Christmas lights ... the over-the-top decorations ... the noise . . . the sheer size of the station itself . . . and the number of people roaming the streets. They'd never seen anything quite like it before. Everything seemed different . . . livelier . . . louder . . . and overflowing with energy . . . but more importantly – everything seemed so full of potential. If Grace and Julia were to start a new chapter in their lives, just the two of them, they couldn't have dreamt of a better place to do so than London.

By the very next day, they discovered the West End and the streets of Soho, where the influx of tourists was simply never-ending, and if there was one thing that Dylan had taught them well, it was that tourists were easy pickings.

The next three years seemed to fly by in a hurry, with Grace and Julia becoming better and better at their cons. Their most profitable one was still the 'attention diversion and pickpocketing' scam, and Julia could pick a pocket as if she were a ghost, but Dylan had also taught them that cons were like magic tricks, and a good con artist, just like a good magician, should always diversify and come up with new tricks to surprise the audience . . . and that was exactly what Grace and Julia did.

By then they were both nineteen years of age and the two girls who had once been early bloomers had fully reached their first blooming stage – from puberty to adulthood – and they'd bloomed into two devastatingly attractive women. No matter where they went – makeup or no makeup – heads would turn, and they soon found out that women desired them just as much as men did, if not more.

That was the trigger for Julia to suggest that they stepped up their game, and her plan was simple. Since both of them were always being hit on and chatted up by men and women, why not exploit that side to their advantage?

Julia was the one who put forward the idea that they simply allowed themselves to be chatted up *and* picked up. What Julia suggested was that instead of pickpocketing tourists in the streets for their wallets, or whatever they had inside their handbags (small pickings), why not go back to their hotel rooms with them? What Julia was suggesting wasn't prostitution. They wouldn't be offering sexual services for money. The idea was simply to get into their hotel rooms. Once there, the choice of what to take would, in theory, increase exponentially . . . but they were well aware that so would the risk.

The most important lesson that they'd learn from pickpocketing tourists in the streets of London over the past three years had been to always be observant . . . to take their time scouting the crowds for the right mark . . . and to drop everything and simply walk away if they ever sensed trouble or had a bad feeling about something. Trusting their guts was a big part of being a con artist and a pickpocket. While observing the crowds, searching for the right targets, Grace and Julia had, many times, spotted other pickpockets and con artists at work. They'd also seen many of them get caught, and when that happened, there was something else that they'd noticed. If a male target caught somebody picking their pockets, they would, more often than not, become physically aggressive. Women targets, on the other hand, were much more docile. They would get angry, no doubt about that, and usually, verbally aggressive, but very rarely would they resort to physical violence.

With that in mind, they decided to do a trial run of the 'hotel room' con, mainly to check how comfortable they would feel with being alone with a mark behind closed doors. And just like any of their cons, this one had a specific set of rules.

Rule number one: women only – never go back to a hotel room with a male target . . . or a couple.

Rule number two: once inside their room, spike their drink – not with any horrible drug – just a simple sedative . . . something that would make them go to sleep fast. Once that happened, the room was theirs.

Rule number three: never physically hurt a target.

Rule number four: keep the takings small. Once the mark woke up again, she would realize that she'd been conned – the hotel security and the police would then usually get involved. If the takings were small, a report would be filed in, but chances were that the police wouldn't put that much effort into finding the perpetrators because the con would be considered 'petty theft', and the Metropolitan Police had much larger fish to fry than petty criminals.

And rule number five: to be on the safe side, once the con was done, whoever had run it – Grace or Julia – wouldn't run another con at that same hotel for at least six months. The good news was they were in London, where there was no shortage of tourists or hotels.

The trial run went a lot better than either of them had expected, and Julia had been right – inside their hotel room, the choice of what to take, once the mark was down and out, did increase exponentially – cash, jewelry, cellphones, laptops, expensive handbags . . . the choice varied from mark to mark – but it was all there, just asking to be taken.

Their new con proved to be very profitable indeed, just as long as they stuck to their rules and picked the right targets – and Grace seemed to have some sort of sixth sense when it came to choosing a mark.

For the next two years, Grace and Julia did less and less of the street pickpocketing and more and more of the 'hotel room' con. The marks were mainly picked at bars, restaurants and nightclubs around the most affluent neighborhoods in London – never at their hotels. One thing that Grace and Julia had realized quiet early on was that scammers and pro sex workers could easily be spotted at hotel bars, lobbies and restaurants. They were always the ones there by themselves – drinking alone, eating alone and sitting alone – always well dressed, but never spending much . . .

and they were always looking around, as if searching for someone. Once they were spotted by the hotel security, one of two things would happen. Either they would be asked to leave, and if that happened, they would never be able to show their faces in that hotel again. Or, in the case of a sex worker, they'd be allowed to hang around at the hotel bar if they were classy enough, but for a percentage of their profits.

It was at the beginning of one of those nights – dubbed 'pick-up nights' – that Grace met Phillip Evans, the first man she ever married.

Seventy-Five

Fourteen Years Ago

London

That night, Grace had chosen to go out in one of her favorite neighborhoods in Central London – Knightsbridge – very classy and very touristic, with a high number of upper-class restaurants, bars, pubs and nightclubs scattered all over the place. Her first stop had been a very elegant cocktail lounge on Brompton Road, not that far away from Harrods, the world-renowned department store.

Grace looked stunning, like she did every night, but on that particular evening there seemed to be something else about her, a different sparkle, perhaps, as if she could sense that something special was about to happen. For that Friday evening, she had chosen a blue sleeveless dress that went down to about mid-thigh. Her auburn hair, or better yet, her auburn wig, fell down past her shoulders in perfect mermaid waves. Her shoes were the kind of shoes that women with a lot of money would recognize and appreciate.

The cocktail lounge wasn't exactly busy, but it was still early – just past eight o'clock in the evening – and spotting the right mark was always a waiting game. Grace knew that well … and she could play that game better than most. She'd been sitting at the bar for less than ten minutes, nursing a barely touched cocktail that had been served in a smoking goblet, when she heard a male voice come from her right.

'Hi there . . . I couldn't help but notice you sitting here, all by yourself. Do you mind if I join you?'

Grace glanced at the guy trying to chat her up. He looked like a typical young executive, with his neat suit, designer shoes and pristine appearance. His cologne was very masculine, with a hint of leather to it, and he held himself with the sort of confidence that most women would find attractive.

'Sorry,' she replied. Her tone was friendly, but not overly so, and the smile on her lips was polite, but not inviting. 'I'm actually waiting for someone.'

'Well,' the man countered. 'I'm someone.' His smile, on the other hand, was a smirk.

'You certainly are,' Grace agreed, as she had a micro-sip of her cocktail. 'Just not the someone I'm waiting for.'

'But I could be . . . if you give me a chance.' He moved closer, taking the stool next to hers. 'Trust me, you won't regret it.'

Grace turned to finally face the man who, in less than ten seconds, had already burnt all his bridges.

'I'm Steven.' He offered Grace his hand. 'And it's a real pleasure to meet you.'

Grace didn't take it, her eyes narrowing at him just a fraction, as if she was trying to place him. 'Oh, hold on . . . I think I know you.'

Steven hesitated for a moment. 'Do you?' His head tilted right. 'Where from?'

'I do,' Grace nodded, her tone calm. 'You're one of those blokes who never takes the hint, aren't you? One of those for whom "no" never means "no".'

Steven's eyebrows arched, carelessly. 'C'mon! You must know that "no" is nothing more than a pit stop on the road to "yes".

Most of the time "no" doesn't actually mean "no" . . . it just means "try harder".'

'No, it isn't, and no, it doesn't,' Grace replied. There was no play in her voice. 'It never did . . . and it never will. "No" will always mean "no". But you really don't seem to understand that, do you?'

'Ooh, feisty. I like that.'

Grace shook her head in an 'I give up' gesture. 'I rest my case.'

'Hey, mate.' This was a new voice. Not Steven's. 'You heard what the lady said. She's not interested.'

Grace looked right. Standing a few feet behind Steven was a second man. This one was a couple of inches shorter than Steven and quite a few pounds lighter too. His face, though, seemed fuller and more chiseled. His black hair was tousled in uneven and imperfect waves, which made him look like an Emo kid who had grown up but was still a little reluctant to lose the hairstyle. He was handsome in his own quirky way, which made him uniquely handsome, and Grace really liked that.

Steven turned to look at the man. 'Sorry, mate, what was that?' He sarcastically angled his head in the direction of the new arrival.

'The lady said she isn't interested,' the man repeated himself, without backing an inch. His tone was non-aggressive . . . diplomatic even. 'So please, just grab a drink and leave her be.'

Steven chuckled before getting to his feet and squaring up to the shorter man. 'I have a better idea, mate – why don't you go mind your own business . . . and leave *us* be?' His right index finger went back and forth between him and Grace a couple of times.

'I *am* minding my business,' the man replied, meeting Steven's stare.

'Oh!' Steven seemed taken aback by the man's reply. He turned to face Grace. 'Is he the bloke you've been waiting for?'

'No, she's not waiting for me,' the man beat Grace to the answer.

Steven looked back at him, intrigued. 'So how is this your business, mate?'

'Because this is my bar,' the man replied, with a single nod. 'And you seem to be harassing one of my customers, which makes it my business. So please, before I ask security to escort you out, just grab a drink . . . on the house . . . and leave the lady alone.'

Steven paused for a fraction of a second before addressing Grace. 'I'm not harassing anyone, am I?'

'Mate,' the man's voice was a lot firmer this time. 'I'm really trying to make this easy for you. Take the hint.'

'Oh, he's not so good with hints,' Grace tried to explain, her expression relaxed.

'It appears so,' the man agreed.

Steven took another moment before shrugging. 'Fine, nothing interesting happening here anyway. I'll take that drink on the house, though.'

'Not a problem.' The man gestured at the bartender. 'Sergio, please serve the gentleman . . . whatever he wants.' His stare returned to Steven, and it stayed on him until he finally walked away to the other end of the bar.

'I'm so terribly sorry about that,' the man said, turning to face Grace. 'Some people are just clueless.' Only his eyes moved right to indicate Steven.

'Nothing to be sorry about,' Grace said back, meeting the man's stare. Other than how attractive he was, she'd also noticed that on his left wrist, he was wearing an F.P.Journe watch.

Over the past two years, Grace and Julia had become a lot more knowledgeable in the lifestyle of the wealthy. To better identify what to take once they were inside the mark's hotel room, they read about brands, special editions and collectors' items in jewelry, fashion, watches, handbags, shoes, perfumes, pens . . . even hats . . . and they both had a pretty good eye when it came to spotting expensive items.

'Could I offer you a drink on the house,' the man continued. 'As an apology.'

'No apology needed,' Grace said back. 'There was no harm done.'

The man bowed his thanks, placing both hands over his heart. 'Still, whenever you're ready, your next drink is on the house. I insist.' He gave Grace a polite nod. 'Enjoy the rest of your evening.'

The man turned to walk away, but Grace halted him.

'So, this really is your bar?'

The man faced her again, his lips hiding a smile, while his forehead creased just a touch.

'I thought that that was just . . .' She shrugged. 'I don't know.'

'Bollocks?' the man said, the smile finally breaking through.

Grace smiled back. 'Yeah ... you know ... just to get him to go away.'

'Trust me . . . I do talk a lot of bollocks, but not this time. This really is one of my bars.' He extended his hand. 'I'm Phillip . . . Phillip Evans.'

'Grace Mitchell,' she replied, shaking Phillip's hand.

That night, Grace didn't go back to a hotel room with a mark. She didn't go back to Phillip's place either, but she did spend most of her evening chatting to him. He was funny and a great conversationalist, but that wasn't all. Underneath all the jokes and the undeniable charm, there seemed to be a deeper substance to him. He was articulate, intelligent and kind . . . but best of all, he was rich . . . richer than any mark that Grace or Julia had ever targeted.

Seventy-Six

Fourteen Years Ago

London

Grace's chance meeting with Phillip that night got her thinking. The 'hotel room' con was a good con, bringing her and Julia a steady income, but they both knew that running the same con for two years straight, especially such a risky con, was pushing their luck. They'd never been caught, but they'd run into trouble plenty of times during those two years. Even before Grace had met Phillip, she and Julia had already begun discussing a few new ideas, but they were all small, street-type cons – the kind that would keep them going from one day to the next, nothing more – and Grace was growing really tired of that grinding.

'Please tell me that you're fucking kidding,' Julia said, once Grace told her about her new idea for a scam.

'I'm dead serious, Jules.'

'No, you can't be,' Julia said back, her eyes wide at Grace. 'Unless you've lost your mind because what you're talking about here is real marriage, with a wedding dress, guests, a priest, a church, a ring . . . the fucking lot . . . including a *legal* document saying that you're married.'

'Followed by a divorce with a settlement for millions,' Grace added, her voice calm.

'Fuck! And how long will that take?'

'Two years,' Grace replied. 'Maybe less.'

'Two fucking years?' Julia's jaw dropped. 'For a single con? Are you fucking high?'

'The "hotel room" con has been our most profitable con to date, isn't that right?' Grace said.

'Yeah, but—'

'We've been running it for two years, Jules,' Grace cut her short. 'And how much have we made in that time? The two of us together?'

'I don't know.'

'I do. Just under one hundred grand. And the two of us combined have run the con seventy-four times in two years.'

'OK.' Julia was sure that Grace was right. She had everything written down and catalogued in a file.

'That's seventy-four times that we've put ourselves at risk. Seventy-four times that we could've gotten caught. Think about it.' She gave Julia a moment. 'This is *one* con, Jules.' She lifted her right index finger at Julia. 'One. And at the end of two years, we'll both be in the millions . . . *millions*.'

That word alone made Julia pause. 'I need a drink.' She got up and poured herself a large glass of white wine. 'Do you want one?'

'I'm OK for now, ta.'

Julia sat back down before having a healthy sip of her wine. 'So, who is this bloke? Where did you meet him?'

Grace told Julia everything she knew about Phillip Evans.

'Grace,' Julia countered at the end. 'Do you really think that a millionaire – someone who owns bars and restaurants in London – will simply up and marry someone he just met on a random night, without asking for a pre-registration agreement? Because if you do, you're living in a fantasy.'

'Pre-registration agreements aren't legally binding in this country,' Grace informed Julia. 'Did you know that?'

Julia frowned. 'No, I didn't. Are you sure about that?'

'I'm positive,' Grace explained. 'They do exist, and in case of a divorce, they're taken into consideration by the judge, but legally, they don't mean anything.' She allowed Julia a moment so that the information could sink in. 'And who cares if I sign a pre-registration agreement, anyway. The real money won't come from the divorce settlement.'

'What? What do you mean? Where's the money going to come from then?'

Grace tilted her head to one side, her eyebrows angling up curiously.

Julia knew that look well enough. 'You already have a plan, don't you?'

'I have an outline,' Grace admitted. 'But you and I . . . I just know that we can come up with something great.'

Julia took a breath before refilling her wine glass. 'OK, walk me through this plan of yours, step-by-step.'

Seventy-Seven

Usually, Mary would wait at least a year before sending Denise a message so that they could start implementing the 'mistress' phase of their 'wedding con'.

After her marriage to Phillip Evans, Mary quickly discovered that what was commonly known as the 'honeymoon period' of a marriage would either be on its last legs, or well and truly over by the first-year anniversary. By then, the petty arguments would've already started ... the sex life would've lost at least half of its sparkle, if not all of it ... and the husband would be much more welcoming to flirts from other women than he would've been just a few months earlier – but this time, Mary decided to move things up from the one-year mark to eight months ... and she did so for two main reasons.

Reason number one was simple – Quaddra would, no doubt, be Mary and Denise's last-ever con. Denise wasn't the only one who had grown bitterly tired of running and hiding like a fugitive every time they finished a con. Mary didn't want to do it anymore either. She was tired of running, tired of the lies, tired of pretending, and she sure as hell was tired of not knowing who she really was anymore. Yes, it was a good con, one that in the past fourteen years had earned them millions, but it was also very risky, and Mary just couldn't wait to be done with all of it – forever.

Mary had truly never intended to run the 'wedding con' more

than just once. Her divorce settlement from Phillip Evans back in the UK was supposed to have set her and Denise up for life, but things turned out a little differently from what she and Denise had expected.

They were just two young women in their early twenties and neither of them understood anything about business. They had no idea that despite how wealthy Phillip seemed to be, almost all of his capital was tied up into his business – his restaurants and cocktail bars – and neither of them was going to take over Phillip's businesses and run them, so after the divorce, Mary liquidated everything for an absolute bargain price.

At the time, Mary and Denise didn't really care for what could've been. They'd just made more money with that one con than they'd ever made before – almost one million pounds between the two of them – and for two very young women who, just a few years before were pickpocketing people on the streets of London, one million pounds was crazy money.

The decision to travel to America came not because they were thinking about running the con again. They just wanted to get the hell out of the UK before someone figured out what they'd done. The choice had been between the US and Australia, and the US won on a coin toss. Another coin toss decided their first stop in America – Vegas – and that proved to be a huge mistake.

Las Vegas was an incredible city, considered by many to be the biggest circus on the planet – a show town that never slept and never disappointed. It was a city full of lights, people, shows, games, laughter, and of course . . . money. Grace and Julia didn't gamble their million pounds away, but two young women, splashing cash around like millionaires would always grab the attention of the wrong people, especially in a city like Vegas, and the two young con artists fell victim to a much more experienced and seasoned gang of con artists – electronic hackers – who managed to upload a remote access program to Grace and Julias' cellphones.

The program allowed the hackers to observe, in real time, Grace and Julia using any of their smartphone applications . . . including their internet banking one.

It took the con/hacker gang just a few days of listening in and tracking Grace and Julia's internet banking activity to be able to pretty much clean them out. If not for the fact that Grace and Julia kept a significant amount of cash locked in their hotel room safe, they would've lost everything they'd made within ten days of landing in Vegas – a true 'welcome to America' block party.

It had been Julia who had suggested that they run the con again. By then, they were both living in Chicago and she had just met someone called Erick Middleton, an entrepreneur who, on paper, looked like the real deal – easily worth close to ten million dollars – but the truth was that he owed money to some really nasty people.

For their second run, the roles were reversed – Julia played the bride and Grace became the lover. Their natural talent in being able to pick up an accent with tremendous ease, once again proved invaluable for the success of their con, as neither woman wanted to reveal that they were British. But Erick wasn't just involved with some dangerous people. He was a pretty nasty piece of work himself. Julia didn't have to fake the bruises, the beatings, or the abuse . . . and neither did Grace. When the divorce settlement came, just a year and a half after Julia and Erick's wedding, the extent of Erick's debts and dodgy dealings was finally revealed. Out of his ten million plus fortune, all that he really had left to his name was about one hundred thousand dollars in investments, which the judge awarded to Julia, but in all honesty, neither Grace nor Julia cared for how much money they'd be making anymore. They just wanted Erick out of their lives forever, and for that they tightened their 'in court' game somewhat, faking even knife wounds. Erick was tried for attempted murder and received a total of twenty-seven years in prison.

But Erick had friends . . . a lot of very dangerous friends . . . and it was after their con on Erick Middleton that Grace and Julia had to rethink their tactics. That was when they decided that they would have to split up, at least for six months to a year – tracking two separate people was much harder than tracking two people together.

They also came up with the idea of the burner phones and the code words that had to be used at the beginning and the end of every message. But the events from Vegas, together with the fact that they knew that some of Erick's friends would be looking for them, had truly rattled both women, so they created one extra level of security – a single code word, which if used anytime throughout the message, signaled trouble, as if one of them was being forced to leave a message. If either of them heard that specific word in the message it meant ABORT – pack the fuck up and leave . . . now.

Julia had hated the idea. The last thing that she wanted to do was to be away from Grace, and she really didn't want to run the 'wedding con' anymore. Grace didn't want to run it anymore either, but she wasn't going back to pickpocketing.

From Chicago, Julia moved to Miami, in Florida, and changed her name to Candice Logan. Grace moved to Boston, in Massachusetts, and changed her name to Samantha Chambers. That was where she met Nelson Stewart.

Call it third time lucky, but finally, after eleven years, Grace and Julia's 'wedding con' did pay off. They both walked away from Nelson with a little over 2.5 million dollars each.

Back then, before the scam, Grace had told Julia that Nelson would be their last con, even if it didn't pay off . . . and she one hundred percent meant it, until she saw an article in the newspaper about a young billionaire entrepreneur called Quaddra Buckner, and Quaddra wasn't just rich . . . he was dirty, rotten, filthy, stinky rich.

But there was a second reason for Mary wanting to move the 'mistress' phase of their 'wedding con' forward by four months. And it was that second reason that was keeping her up at night and making her question just about everything because Mary truly never saw this coming. She never thought it possible either, because if there was one thing that she knew for sure about herself was that she hated men. They were arrogant, conceited, opinionated, controlling, irresponsible, self-centered, and in most cases, avoidant of criticism. In her experience, they were also always abusive in one way or another – physically, verbally, emotionally, psychologically, or a combination of those. No matter which way Mary tried to look at it – as a daughter, stepdaughter, lover, friend, fiancée or wife – men had always used her . . . they'd taken what they wanted and discarded her as if she was trash – that was why she hated men so much.

So why the hell was she falling desperately in love with Quaddra?

Seventy-Eight

That week, just like it happened almost every month, Quaddra was back in Los Angeles, but this time he really did have several work meetings to attend. His film production company had been approached by one of the largest TV studios in America to run the entire production and marketing for two brand-new TV series, both of them with budgets in the millions. The first was to air in just three months, and the second in five, so time wasn't something that they had in abundance. Quaddra was spending most of the week in LA to personally oversee the negotiation of several different contracts and to sit in on auditions for roles in both productions.

It had been a very long Friday, after an even longer week, but they were finally done with the auditions for the first production. In the past three days, Quaddra and his team had seen well over nine hundred actors and actresses, who were auditioning for just eight roles. It had been a shattering process, but the team was positively confident that they had managed to select the best candidates for the roles. The news would be communicated to the selected eight over the weekend and filming would commence on Monday morning in Malibu. That was when the real exhausting work would start, they all knew that. But for now, or at least for what was left of that Friday evening, it was time to celebrate a little because, truth be told, they had somehow managed to pull a gigantic rabbit out of a tiny hat.

To celebrate their massive achievement, Quaddra had booked a table at the famous Umbrella Social Club at the SIXTY Hotel, where he was staying in Beverley Hills. The Umbrella Social Club was an exclusive rooftop bar and lounge that offered stunning views of Beverly Hills, Century City and downtown Los Angeles.

'When do we start auditions for the second production?' Quaddra asked, just as a young and very pretty waitress, with eyes that seemed to have been carved out of emeralds, brought two bottles of Champagne to their booth.

'That'll start on Wednesd—' Bill Steeler tried replying, but paused mid-word as he clocked how attractive the waitress was. Bill was the cast director for both series and just like Quaddra, he'd sat through all nine hundred plus role auditions in the past three days. 'Damn, you're incredibly pretty,' he addressed the waitress, who politely smiled back, as she poured Champagne into six flutes.

'Thank you, sir,' she replied in a sweet voice. 'I appreciate the compliment.'

'Are you an actress, by any chance?' Bill pushed.

'No, sir, I'm not.'

'Would you like to be?'

Bill's question got back a wide-eye look from everyone at the table, including Quaddra.

'No, sir, I don't think I would,' the waitress finally replied.

It was Bill's turn to look back at her with wide eyes. 'What . . . you like being a waitress?'

'No, sir, I like being a medical student.' And with that, the waitress walked away.

'Very fucking subtle, Bill,' Quaddra said, once the waitress was out of earshot. 'Would you like a bib to help you with the drooling?'

'Did you all not see her?' Bill asked, his stare bouncing from person to person on their table. 'Her eyes? She's absolutely beautiful.'

'So is your wife,' Emily, the company's art director, reminded Bill.

'I was just making an observation. That's all,' Bill came back, his hands up in surrender.

'And salivating at the mouth while doing so,' Emily added. 'Like a ravenous wolf.'

'Anyway, a toast,' Quaddra said, lifting his glass at everyone. 'It's been a very challenging week, but I think that we've managed to select a killer cast. To a job well done. Cheers!'

'Cheers!' the reply came in a chorus of voices.

'Yeah, but don't get too comfortable, people,' Emily reminded everyone. 'Because we'll have to start the process all over again on Wednesday for the second production.'

'Yeah, but we have a little bit more time for that,' Austin, Emily's assistant, offered. 'We won't have to cram nine hundred plus auditions into three days.'

'You're right,' Emily agreed. 'We have five days for that, but we also have fifteen roles to fill, not eight.' She nodded at Austin. 'Expect another marathon.' She turned to address Quaddra. 'Will you be back in LA for the auditions again?'

'I will,' Quaddra confirmed. 'I'm flying back to San Francisco tomorrow, but I'll be back here on Wednesday. What time do we start?'

'Nine a.m. sharp.'

'I'll be here.'

Despite it being a celebratory evening, none of them was really willing to make it a long night. They were all exhausted, and they all had only two days to recoup before filming started on Monday, and filming was always a lot more demanding than auditions. They finished both bottles of Champagne, had a single cocktail each, except for Quaddra, who had ordered a single malt, and called it a night.

Quaddra hadn't finished his Scotch, but since everyone was already gone and it was still quite early – not even 11:00 p.m. yet – he decided to take his drink down to his penthouse suite and give Mary a call. He exited his booth, walked around the lit rooftop swimming pool, past the bar, and into the elevator. He had a sip of his whisky and was about to use his room key on the lift floor-button pad, when a very well-manicured hand stopped the doors from closing. Quaddra's eyes moved from his whiskey tumbler to the doors, which slowly slid open again.

The woman who entered the lift was simply stunning. Her long brown hair was French braided, which made her look like some sort of goddess out of Asgard or something. She wore an elegant, sleeveless black dress that screamed 'first date' – not too conservative, but not too revealing either. She was slender, but with perfect muscular toning, and her eyes, which were as dark as her dress, had a hypnotic quality to them. But it was the expression across the woman's face and her demeanor that really caught Quaddra's attention. She looked completely flustered.

Quaddra took a step back to make room for her, despite the lift being large enough to accommodate six people. The woman looked up and their eyes met for a fraction of a second. There was something in them that Quaddra couldn't exactly place – some odd mix of anger, disappointment and sadness all rolled up into one. She extended her arm to press one of the buttons, but her shaky hand hesitated for a beat, as if she was unsure of which floor she was going to.

'Which floor would you like?' Quaddra asked, nodding at the button pad. His tone was comforting.

Her hand recoiled. 'Umm . . .' She breathed out heavily enough for Quaddra to hear it. 'Ground, please.'

Quaddra pressed it and the doors, once again, slid closed. As they did, the woman did a mini jerk, as if the sound of the doors closing unnerved her.

'Miss, are you alright?' Quaddra asked, keeping his distance. He didn't press the button to his penthouse floor.

The woman kept her eyes on the door. 'I will be, as soon as I get out of here.'

'Do you need any help? Can I call someone for you? Maybe get you a cab to take you somewhere?'

The woman finally turned and looked at Quaddra. Her eyes stayed on his face for just a moment before they moved down to his whiskey tumbler. 'Are you going to finish that?'

Quaddra's eyes blinked at the question. 'Ahh . . .' He half extended his arm. 'Would you . . .'

Before he had even finished the sentence, the woman took the tumbler from his hand and drank it down in one large gulp.

Quaddra's eyes widened at her. 'Salud!'

The woman cringed, as if she'd just drunk gasoline from the hose. 'What the hell was that?'

Quaddra blinked again. 'Macallan, twenty-five-year-old sherry oak release.'

She gave the glass back to Quaddra. 'Sounds expensive.'

'Hum!' Quaddra pressed his lips tightly together.

She nodded at him. 'Thank you. It . . . helped a little.'

Quaddra looked down at the empty tumbler. 'You sound like you could do with another drink.'

The woman breathed out, but didn't reply.

They reached the ground floor and the doors slid open again.

'Would you like another drink?' Quaddra asked, just as the woman was about to step out of the lift.

She paused and turned to look at him. Her beauty was mesmerizing.

Quaddra half lifted his empty tumbler at her. 'I could do with another drink. This one seems to be all done.'

The woman looked like she wanted to laugh at Quaddra's joke, but something was stopping her.

'I'm not going back up to that bar . . . sorry.'

There it was again – the odd mix of anger, disappointment and sadness all rolled up into one, but this time it was on her tone of voice as well.

Quaddra nodded. 'I'm fine with that. This is Beverly Hills. There's no shortage of bars and cocktail lounges around here. Do you want to go find somewhere else?'

The woman took a moment to study Quaddra.

'I'm not sleeping with you,' she said, as she looked Quaddra straight in the eye. 'If that's what you're after.'

He lifted his left hand and thumbed his wedding ring. 'Good, because that was never on the cards.'

The woman took another few seconds, sizing Quaddra up. 'So . . . you're offering to buy a complete stranger a drink out of the goodness of your heart?' A thin layer of sarcasm coated her words.

'We are a breed in extinction,' Quaddra said back. 'I know that. Very, very rare, but there are still a few of us around.'

A ghost of a smile finally shadowed on the women's lips.

Quaddra extended his hand. 'I'm Thomas.'

Somehow, the woman was already expecting to hear that name. She gently shook his hand. 'I'm Denise. Nice to meet you.'

Seventy-Nine

The message from Mary, when it came, just twelve days earlier, caught Denise completely by surprise. Its format was the same as always – a voice message left on her burner phone – a code word started the message, and a different code word ended it. The code words matched the month that they were in, and the 'abort'word was never used, indicating that the message was legit. The reason why it surprised Denise so much was because it seemed too soon.

The previous message that Denise had received from Mary had come nine months earlier, and all it said was that Mary Smith was now Mary Buckner. Knowing the month that Mary had gotten married, this second message, giving Denise the green light to move on with the 'mistress' phase of their con, was at least three months premature. That was why Denise had listened to the message twice before deleting it – to make sure that the code words were correct and that she hadn't missed the 'abort' one.

She hadn't. This was for real. It was time to play her part.

To avoid the off chance of Denise bumping into Quaddra somewhere by accident, Denise had decided not to stay in San Francisco, and she figured that her best plan of action would be to move to Los Angeles.

Mary had told Denise about Quaddra's businesses in LA. She explained that he would make the trip from SF to the City of Angels at least twice a month. Yes, he had businesses scattered all over the US – Silicon Valley, Dallas, Detroit, Columbus, New York, Washington DC and Seattle – but due to how demanding the movie industry was in Hollywood, his film production companies in Los Angeles required more of his time and attention than all of his other companies combined, and to Denise, that information was key.

One thing that playing the 'mistress' role had taught Denise over the years was that being in the same city as your lover was a *bad* move – at least for Denise, who wasn't really in love with the mark, all that she was doing was playing a part.

A cheating husband and his lover living in the same city would open the door to quick, 'last-minute', opportunistic encounters, like an evening when the wife was supposed to be home but decided, 'last minute', to go out with the girls. In cases like that, it was almost a guarantee that the cheating husband would contact the lover for a quick 'pop around' job . . . and that was something that Denise simply hated. If the lover lived in a different city, all meetings, in theory, had to be prearranged. That had also been the reason why back in Massachusetts, Mary and Nelson lived in Woburn and Denise lived in Boston.

Yes, there was a downside to living in a different city from the cheating husband, but after playing the role of the mistress twice, Denise had enough experience to be able to navigate that minefield pretty well.

So, after considering all the pros and cons of staying in San Francisco or not, Denise decided to 'not'. She would still have to meet Quaddra 'by chance' somewhere once Mary had given her the green light, and since she'd learned from Mary that Quaddra would be in LA at least twice a month, Los Angeles became the clear choice.

Twelve days ago, after Denise had listened to Mary's message, she called Mary's new burner phone and left a message of her own. The message was simple and brief. It told Mary that Denise was now based in LA before asking Mary to let her know the next time that Quaddra would be making the trip from San Francisco to Los Angeles. The next day, Denise got a new message from Mary with Quaddra's upcoming travel schedule.

Since Quaddra's arrival in the City of Angels just a few days ago, Denise had been tracking him like a stalker – but the man seemed to do nothing else other than work. For days on end, Denise had been on him from the crack of dawn all the way until bedtime, just waiting for an opportunity to get him by himself – breakfast, lunch, dinner, drinks . . . any chance would do – but Quaddra was like a machine, going from meeting to meeting, or spending countless hours locked inside studios – no lunch or dinner breaks.

Denise was starting to think that maybe her 'moving to Los Angeles' plan hadn't been a good idea after all, but when she saw him and his team leave the production company's building together earlier that day, she sensed that maybe an opportunity was just about to show itself. They were all laughing and congratulating themselves, and Denise had had enough experience observing crowds to know that that group was celebrating something.

In the boot of her car, Denise had at least three different outfits – one for a casual daytime encounter, one that would suit a more upmarket location, and an evening dress that would suit most types of night out, so when she realized that Quaddra and his team were going for drinks at the rooftop bar at the same hotel that he was staying at, she quickly changed into her evening dress and retouched her makeup. Her hair had been professionally French braided just a couple of days ago – a hairstyle that would suit pretty much any occasion.

Denise arrived at The Umbrella Social Club rooftop bar about fifteen minutes after Quaddra and his party. She immediately clocked them at a booth by the pool and took a seat at the bar – far enough away for her not to be noticed by anyone at the booth. She ordered a cocktail and quickly began hatching a plan in her head.

Since they were at the rooftop bar at the SIXTY, Denise was hoping that one of two things would happen. Either Quaddra would retire to his room early, leaving his party to continue the celebrations by themselves, or he would be the last to go. Those two options were ideal because in both cases she would get a small window of opportunity to get Quaddra by himself.

There was a third option as well, which was Quaddra and his party leaving together. They would then all get into the lift together and Quaddra would jump out on the penthouse floor. That was the only option that would mess things up for Denise, so when she saw the entire group getting up and leaving Quaddra behind, she knew that this was her chance.

The bullshit story that she had come up with was simple, short, but very believable – another take on the 'damsel in distress' tale. Denise was an actress who had gone to The Umbrella Social Club for a 'business' meeting and a possible script reading with the producer for a brand-new TV series, but it turned out that there was nothing 'business' about the meeting. All the producer really wanted to do was take her down to his room and have sex with her. A very distraught Denise had then told the producer to go fuck himself and left the rooftop bar almost in tears . . . and that was when she, 'by chance', bumped into a very attractive man inside the lift at the SIXTY Hotel, just as the doors were about to close.

Eighty

It had been three and a half months since Mary had called Denise with the green light for her to start implementing the 'mistress' side of their con.

To keep things as real as possible, Mary and Denise would always keep their communications down to a minimum. Messages were only exchanged if truly necessary, so the last message between them had been the one that Mary had left Denise with: Quaddra's LA travelling schedule for that particular month.

In real life, a mistress wouldn't message her lover's wife to update her on how the affair was going, so why would they do it?

Keep it simple . . . keep it real.

That tactic also played a huge part in the surprise effect at the end of their con. In several months' time, when Denise had to walk into that court of law, as a last-minute witness for the prosecution, Mary wouldn't have seen her for well over a year. Denise would certainly look different . . . very different in fact, and that would reflexively trigger a realistic surprise reaction from Mary – the kind of reaction that is very hard to fake.

But the fact that there had been no more exchanges between Mary and Denise was a message in itself. No news was good news. It meant that Denise had encountered no problems in moving ahead with her role in the con, which, in turn, would mean that her affair with Quaddra was well under way. Their plan was working, just like it always did . . . so why did Mary feel so low and betrayed? Why did she have to fight a panic attack every time that Quaddra mentioned that he was flying back to LA again? Why did she feel like crying, and fighting, and screaming blue murder until he held her tight in his arms to calm her down like he always did when she felt anxious about anything? Why did she miss him so much every time he was away?

Mary hated the way that she was feeling inside because she had never experienced anything like that before. Love, or at least 'real love', had never been part of her vocabulary. She hated the anxiety that woke her up in the middle of the night every time Quaddra was away . . . because she knew that instead of sleeping by her side, he was probably inside Denise.

Jealousy, it seemed, was a monster that Mary had no idea how to tame, so she did the next best thing, which was to stick to the plan.

Since her wedding, Mary's visits to her therapist, Dr. Lillian Fox, had increased to two a week, but every few weeks, she would cancel a session or two, only to turn up at the next session with a larger, perhaps more severe bruise. The bruises didn't go unnoticed by Dr. Fox, and neither did the fact that Mary seemed to have become a little 'clumsier' after the wedding.

Quaddra, on the other hand, barely noticed any of them, but that was because the majority of Mary's bruises weren't real. They were applied using professional stage makeup.

Over the years, Mary had become somewhat of an expert in creating fake bruises. She'd watched countless videos on YouTube and spent hours upon hours practicing, copying the exact tones from real battery bruises from photos that were easily found on the Internet. Even from just a short distance, it was almost impossible to tell that the bruises were fake. But for the Polaroid photos that Mary would take every now and then as a record, and for the final act – the night that she would finally call 911 – Mary would give herself real bruises, real cuts, and real hematomas … the kind that would cause outrage in a court of law. But she wasn't quite there yet.

Mary and Quaddra were actually just about to celebrate their first wedding anniversary, and Quaddra had suggested that they went back to Salzburg … to the bridge where he'd proposed … to the padlock that they had left there as a symbol of their everlasting love.

When Quaddra first mentioned his idea, Mary felt something knot somewhere between her heart and her throat. What she really felt like doing was slapping him across the face and asking – 'what everlasting love, you cheating sonofabitch? Why don't you ask your lover to go with you?' – but that would've been gold coming from a woman whose only reason for being in that relationship was to run a con that would end up destroying Quaddra's life. Mary couldn't lose sight of that, so instead of screaming and fighting, she hooked her arms around his neck, kissed him with the same passion that she'd always had, and told him that she just couldn't wait to be in Salzburg with him again.

Eighty-One

Due to Quaddra's extremely busy work and traveling schedule, his and Mary's trip back to Salzburg wouldn't exactly coincide with their wedding anniversary. The options were to either fly to Austria ten days before their wedding date – staying for a maximum of four days – or seven days after it – staying for a whole week. Mary chose option two, but that didn't mean that they wouldn't celebrate on the actual date. On the contrary, for their special day, Quaddra had booked a table at Sons & Daughters – a two Michelin-starred restaurant, located in Nob Hill, just north of Union Square.

Mary wasn't working that Monday. Quaddra knew that, so he made arrangements for a very colorful surprise.

At exactly midday, a flower-delivery man rang the front-gate doorbell at Mary and Quaddra's mansion to deliver a mesmerizing bouquet – pink flowers only – containing lisianthus, roses, germini, oriental lilies and soft gypsophila.

'Wow, that's absolutely beautiful,' Gabriela, the younger of the two housemaids said, as she entered the kitchen, where Mary was just transferring the bouquet from its delivery package into a very glamorous dark glass vase.

'I know,' Mary said back, her smile brightening the room. 'Isn't it just? But I think that they might've made a mistake with the card.'

'Oh really?' Gabriela asked, taking a step closer. 'Why?'

Mary pulled the card from its envelope and showed it to her. There were only two letters printed on it. The first showed right at the center of the card – the letter 'I'. The second was down by the right-hand corner – 'Q'.

Mary and Gabriela both knew that 'Q' stood for Quaddra, but what was the 'I' right at the center of the card?

'That's odd,' Gabriela commented. 'It's such a gorgeous bouquet for the flower shop to have made such a silly mistake. Do you think that the printer ran out of ink and they didn't notice it?'

'I'm not sure,' Mary said before shrugging. 'But it doesn't really matter. The flowers are beautiful, and Quaddra can tell me what the card was supposed to say when he gets home tonight.'

At exactly 1:00 p.m., when the front-gate doorbell went off again, Gabriela was the one who received the second bouquet at the front door.

'Mrs. Buckner?' she called, carrying the new bouquet out onto the pool area, where Mary was stretched out on a sun lounger, working on her tan. 'Either the flower shop has really made a big mistake.' The smile on Gabriela's lips already telling Mary that she didn't believe that that was the case. 'Or Mr. Buckner has decided to shower you with flowers.'

Mary moved her sunglasses up to her head, as her eyes widened at the new, exquisitely arranged bouquet – this one a striking combination of purple, blue and white flowers.

'Or maybe the flower shop realized their mistake with the card in the first bouquet,' Gabriela suggested. 'And this is how they decided to apologize.'

'What ... with a brand-new bunch of flowers?' Mary asked. 'Some apology that is.'

'I wouldn't be surprised,' Gabriela said, confidently nodding at Mary. 'Nobody wants to lose a customer like Mr. Buckner.'

Mary got to her feet and reached for the card.

'Oh, you've got to be kidding me,' she said, her head shaking at Gabriela, as she bit down on a smile.

'What?' the girl asked, the expression on her face was total disbelief. 'They made a mistake again?'

'It's not a mistake.' Mary showed Gabriela the card. This one had a single word printed at the center of it – 'love'. The letter 'Q' was, once again, printed at the bottom right-hand corner of the card.

Gabriela looked confused. 'What?'

Mary returned the card to the envelope. 'How many flower vases do we have in the house, do you know?'

'I'm not sure of the exact number, but we've got a few.'

'Well,' Mary's head angled in the direction of the house, 'get them all out, because if I'm right, we're going to be getting a few more of these today.'

Gabriela still looked a little unsure of what was happening.

'Quaddra is forming a sentence,' Mary explained. 'Word by word . . . card by card . . . bunch of flowers by bunch of flowers.' Her head jerked back in the direction of the house. 'I.' She lifted the second card. '"Love" . . . we're going to have to wait to see what comes next. Typical Quaddra.'

Gabriela laughed. 'That really is typical Mr. Buckner,' the girl agreed. 'And so cute at the same time.'

Mary nodded. 'I know. He really is a hopeless romantic. C'mon.' She turned towards the house. 'Let's go get some vases out.'

Throughout the rest of the day, every hour, on the hour, a new impressive bouquet of flowers was delivered to Mary – from midday, until four o'clock. Each one with a card containing a single word – I . . . love . . . you . . . so . . . much.

The last bouquet was delivered at 5:00 p.m. sharp – an incredible arrangement of large red roses. The card that came with it was a little different from the previous five. It contained six words, instead of a single one – 'Happy One Year Anniversary, My Love'.

When Quaddra got home, an hour after the final flower delivery, Mary was sitting in the living room – three flower vases to her left, three flower vases to her right.

'Oh!' Quaddra paused, as if he was surprised by what he was seeing. 'You bought some flowers?'

Mary got to her feet, trying hard not to smile. 'You're one silly, silly man, do you know that?'

Quaddra put down his briefcase. 'I couldn't choose,' he said, matter-of-factly.

'So, you decided to buy the whole shop?' Mary got to him and put her arms around his neck.

'You deserve all the flowers in the world.' Quaddra put his arms around her waist and they kissed.

'Well,' Mary said, looking left then right. 'It looks like I've got all the flowers in the world . . . and they're all gorgeous, my love, thank you so much.'

'Happy one year anniversary, babe.' They kissed again. 'The first of many to come.'

Mary's fake smile was the most truthful she could find. 'I really hope so.'

Quaddra checked his watch. 'OK, our reservation at Sons & Daughters is at seven thirty.' He grabbed his briefcase. 'Let me drop this in my office and go take a quick shower, OK? I won't be long.'

'Go,' Mary urged him, turning to face the flowers. 'I'll distribute these around the house and then I'll get changed.'

As Quaddra made his way to his office, Mary tried to decide which bunch of flowers would look best in which room. They were all exquisite in their own right. The irony was that one of those magnificent bouquets was just about to flip her entire life upside down.

Eighty-Two

Mary decided to start with the living room, or at least its east quarter, and since the curtains that covered the French doors that led out to the fire patio carried a few different shades of pink, matching some of the cushions on the large sofa closest to that door, she placed the pink bouquet – the one that had been delivered at midday – on the low coffee table that sat between the sofa and the armchairs.

Perfect.

Five bouquets left.

Mary took a step back and tried to decide which one to go for next. It didn't take her long before she pointed at the gorgeous yellow and white bouquet that was delivered at 3:00 p.m.

'Definitely the entry room,' she said, as she scooped up the vase with both hands.

The front doors to Quaddra and Mary's mansion opened straight into an ample and brightly lit entry room, where the floor was tiled in black and white Italian marble. At the center of that room, a round chrome and glass table greeted every arrival. The vase already on it contained a very nice selection of dried pampas grass, but the yellow and white flowers would work much better in brightening the room a little more, giving it an even better welcome feel.

A minute later, Mary was back in the living room, studying the four bouquets that were still left.

'Of course,' she said, nodding at the blue and purple one.

Purple was Quaddra's favorite color, so why not place that vase in their bedroom? And she knew exactly where it would go.

Mary picked up the vase and headed upstairs. But before she reached the double stairwell that led to the house's second floor, she noticed that the door to Quaddra's office, which was just a little further along, to the right of the double stairwell, was open – something that rarely happened. Quaddra must've forgotten to lock it after he dropped his briefcase in there. That gave Mary an idea – since purple was Quaddra's favorite color, why not brighten his office with some flowers, because truth be told, that room could really do with some color.

'Why not?' She shrugged. 'It will be a nice surprise. He will love it.'

Instead of taking the stairs going up, Mary veered right and quickly stepped into Quaddra's office. In there, she looked around for a spot where she could place the large vase. This was definitely a man's den work office, full of sharp edges and dark colors everywhere, but to the right of the door, pushed tightly against the wall, was a Victorian-style chest of drawers, where Quaddra kept a small selection of Hors d'Age cognacs.

'This is perfect,' she said, turning around to look back at Quaddra's desk, which was set directly across the room from the chest of drawers. 'Yep, it will look great right here,' Mary agreed with her own assessment. All she had to do was reposition some of the cognac bottles to create a little space right at the center.

She placed the vase on the floor, ready to rearrange the bottles, when she noticed something odd about the bottom drawer – the one by her right foot. Its pull handle looked slanted. It didn't look like it was broken . . . it was just out of line.

'Weird!' she whispered to herself, as she studied it. The handle didn't seem to have come undone from the drawer. It looked to be properly screwed in place, just like the handles in all the other drawers, but it was lop-sided – its right edge about an inch higher than its left one.

Mary grabbed the handle and tried pulling the drawer open, hoping to check the screw on the inside, but the drawer didn't budge.

She held on to the chest and pulled the drawer harder still.

Nothing. The drawer seemed stuck.

She got down on her knees and bent over to have a better look at it. The handle definitely wasn't broken. It wasn't coming apart from the drawer either.

This time, instead of trying to pull the drawer open, Mary tried twisting the handle in place to see if it would move back into a straight line – left edge leveled with its right one. There was a slight resistance, but to her surprise, the handle twisted in the same manner that a door handle would. As it did, she heard a clicking sound come from the wall to her right.

'What the fuck was that?' She frowned, letting go of the drawer handle, her eyes searching right. It took her a moment before she finally noticed that the large filing cabinet that was pushed up against that wall now seemed skewed, as if its right side had been pushed forward a little.

'What the hell?'

Mary stood up straight before approaching the cabinet. She was right – its right edge wasn't pushed up tight against the wall anymore – it had moved forward about three inches or so, creating a gap between the cabinet and the wall behind it. The only problem was that behind the cabinet, there was no wall. What Mary was looking at was a secret door – spy-movie style.

'Are you fucking kidding me?' she whispered, angling her body a little to the right to try to see through the gap.

It was too dark. She couldn't see anything.

Curiosity was screaming at Mary to pull the cabinet forward so that she could open the secret door and look inside.

Why did Quaddra have a secret door in his office?

What did he need to hide so badly?

But two of the first lessons that Mary had learnt as a con artist were to be patient, and to be careful. No one could survive for very long in the con world without both components. So instead of opening the door, Mary turned around to look behind her. She was still alone in Quaddra's office, but she wasn't risking it ... not until she was certain that she wouldn't get caught, so what she did was quickly run out of the office before taking the stairs up to the landing on the second floor, where a long corridor led deeper into the house. Hers and Quaddra's bedroom was right at the end of that corridor.

'Baby, are you out of the shower yet?' she called, loud enough so that if Quaddra was done with his shower, he would've heard her.

No reply.

Mary still needed to be certain, so she ran halfway down the corridor and listened for a moment, but she couldn't hear if the shower was still on or not.

'Baby?' She called again, even louder this time.

'Just getting out of the shower, honey,' Quaddra replied from their bedroom. 'Do you need me?'

'No, no,' Mary called back. 'Just checking.'

'I'll be ready soon.'

'Take your time. There's no rush.'

But there *was* a rush ... at least for Mary.

She ran back downstairs as if the house was on fire.

Back inside Quaddra's office, she approached the cabinet and carefully pushed it back towards the wall. Despite how heavy the module was, it surprised her how easily it moved back before clicking into place again, as if the whole thing was on well-oiled wheels, which it probably was. She took a step back and looked down at the floor – there were no marks, no scratches ... nothing.

This was a state-of-the-art Murphy door, but what the fuck was behind it?

Whatever it was, it was clearly something that Quaddra wanted to keep a secret, so Mary wasn't about to go snooping around with her husband in the house. Instead, she grabbed the flower vase that she had left on the floor by the chest of drawers and quickly exited Quaddra's office.

Eighty-Three

'Are you OK, honey?' Quaddra asked Mary, once the waiter had poured them both a glass of Henri Giraud Argonne Rose Vintage. 'You've been quiet all the way on the ride here … and you've barely looked at me.' He angled his body a little left then a little right, to try to catch Mary's eye. 'Have I done something to upset you?' He paused for effect. 'While I was in the shower?'

Take a breath and play it cool, the voice inside Mary's head warned her.

'No, honey, of course not.' Mary forced herself to look back at her husband, before reaching for his hand over the table.

'Are you upset because I should've invited you into the shower with me?' Quaddra tried again.

Mary chuckled.

'If I had, baby,' Quaddra added, 'we would've never made dinner. You know that.'

'That's true,' Mary replied, finally sending a smile Quaddra's way.

'Or maybe you're a little disappointed in me?'

'Why would I be disappointed in you? I'm the happiest I've ever been in my entire life.' Mary felt as if something was tightening its grip around her heart because that statement was one hundred percent true.

'I don't know,' Quaddra sipped his Champagne. 'Maybe

because our celebrations seem a little rushed today due to me having to travel tomorrow morning . . . again.'

Quaddra had to fly to Seattle early in the morning to attend a very important board meeting for one of his companies. Mary knew that. She had it in her diary.

'I've never once complained about your traveling schedule, my love,' Mary was quick to counter. 'And I never will. I understand how committed you are to your work, and how demanding it is. I told you that when we started dating. Nothing has changed.'

'Or maybe it's because the only present I've given you for our anniversary was just a bunch of flowers.' Quaddra immediately lifted a hand to stop Mary's comeback because he knew it would come. 'But please let me rectify that.' He reached into his pocket for a pink square box, with a pink ribbon and placed it on the table, in front of his wife. The box was a little larger than a CD box and about two-and-a-half times thicker.

Mary cupped a hand over her mouth. 'Are you serious right now?'

Quaddra nodded at the pink box. 'Go ahead. Open it. I hope you like it.'

Mary pulled the pink ribbon from the box before lifting its lid.

'Oh my god!' Her face almost melted. 'This is . . . too much.'

Mary was looking down at a diamond necklace – an eighteen-carat, white gold necklace, with fifty-seven round, brilliant cut diamonds in a row.

'There's no such thing as a "too much" when it comes to my love for you, baby. So, do you like it?'

The tears in Mary's eyes weren't pretend.

'Who, in their right mind, wouldn't like a necklace this stunning, honey? This is insane.'

'That's because I'm insane about you.'

Mary's stare was still on the necklace.

'Put it on,' Quaddra urged her. 'Let me see how it looks.'

'The way these diamonds are shining,' Mary said, their eyes meeting again, 'if I put this on right here, it will probably blind half of the restaurant.'

Quaddra smiled.

'How about I put it on when we get home,' Mary suggested, giving Quaddra a sexy wink. 'I can wear just this . . . nothing else.' She squeezed his hand. 'Would you like that?'

'So . . . so much.'

'OK . . . my turn.' Mary reached into her handbag.

There was no doubt that Mary's mind was racing at a thousand miles per hour after she had discovered the secret door in Quaddra's office, but she was still able to remember to grab the correct handbag before leaving their house – the one with Quaddra's present in it.

Mary placed the professionally wrapped box on the table, in front of her husband. This one was also square and about three to four inches high. 'Happy anniversary, honey.'

'Oh, baby.' Quaddra's smile reached his eyes. 'You didn't have to get me anything. You already gave me everything when you married me.'

'You deserve extra.' Mary smiled back. 'Open it. I hope you like it.'

Like a kid opening his first present on Christmas morning, Quaddra ripped the paper from around the box. 'No way,' he said, as soon as he read the name on the lid of the box. He lifted it to find an F.P.Journe Quantième Perpétuel watch inside. This was a very similar watch to the one that Mary had seen on Phillip Evans' wrist, fourteen years ago, in London.

'You've got to be kidding me.' Quaddra's gaze moved to her.

'So, you like it?'

'Who, in their right mind, wouldn't like a watch like this, honey? This is insane.'

Mary laughed. 'That's because I'm insane about you. Go ahead. Put it on. Let me see how it looks.'

Quaddra reached for it, but paused just as his fingers brushed against the watch. 'How about I put it on when I get home? I can wear just this.' He winked at Mary.

She laughed again . . . harder this time. 'Deal.'

Both of their meals were absolutely exquisite. No wonder customers had to wait months to get a booking for that restaurant.

'So,' Quaddra asked, 'would you like to have a look at the dessert menu?'

Mary shook her head. 'I don't think I could eat another bite.'

'Yeah, me neither.' The smile he gave Mary was suggestive. 'So how about we go back home so that we can both try on our presents?'

Mary mirrored her husband's smile. 'I'd like that.' But what she really wanted to say was – 'Sure, why don't we do that inside your fucking secret room behind the filing cabinet?'

Eighty-Four

Mary and Quaddra had sex wearing just their anniversary gifts, and this was the first ever time that Mary had had to fake an orgasm with Quaddra. Not because he didn't feel good inside her, like he always did, but because she just couldn't stop thinking about that secret door.

Once Mary was done faking it, Quaddra fell asleep with his arm around her, like he'd done countless times before. Mary loved when he did that, but not tonight. Tonight, once they came back from their anniversary dinner, Mary noticed that Quaddra's office door was still unlocked. He'd never locked it before they left. After sex, Quaddra never left the room. He went into the en suite bathroom, but he never actually left their bedroom, which meant that his office was still unlocked.

Once Quaddra placed his arm around Mary, it was like he had locked her in place, so instead of moving, she simply laid there, listening to his breathing, as it slowed down to a steady rhythm, until he'd fallen asleep.

Mary tried to push the image of the door behind the cabinet away from her thoughts . . . tried falling asleep feeling Quaddra's warmth surrounding her – something that she had always loved – but tonight it was no good.

What Mary really wanted to do was slowly slither her way out of her husband's grip, get out of bed, and go check what the hell was behind that secret door, but she'd seen that film before . . . plenty of times, actually. This was when fiction imitated real life, or real-life imitated fiction. Mary wasn't really sure which, but it always happened . . . like Murphy's Law. As soon as she got out of bed and went into his office again, Quaddra would wake up and catch her there, red-handed. If Mary got out of bed and went into the kitchen, or to read a book in the study, or even for a run, Quaddra would carry on sleeping like a baby. He would never even notice that she was gone, but the second that she stepped into his office and activated that secret door mechanism, just like in a movie thriller, he would wake up. That was just the way the world turned – if something could go wrong, it would.

As Quaddra slept, Mary tried reasoning with herself, arguing that billionaires were eccentric people and that they liked doing things and buying things that they had no real need for, just because they could. The voice of reason tried to argue that a secret room in the house of the super-rich, more often than not, was nothing special, tending to be something rather silly, like some kind of novelty room. It pondered that for all she knew, Quaddra could simply have a fridge full of cold beer hidden behind that cabinet. That was something that the super-rich would do just for the fun of it – just because he saw it in a film and thought it would be a cool thing to have. Or it could be a collectors' room, where he kept his hidden collection of baseball cards, or Matchbox cars, or something. Quaddra was also an investor, so it stood to reason that he would probably have a secret vault in the house somewhere. What if he invested in gold, and the vault was full of gold bars? Or diamonds? Or cash? Or anything of extreme value that he didn't trust the banks with?

Fighting the voice of reason was Mary's paranoid self, arguing that she had also seen this film before, and Quaddra's secret room could be an armory, in which case he could be an arms dealer, or a gun for hire . . . a paid assassin. He certainly traveled more than enough to warrant that possibility. That was what paid assassins did, wasn't it? Traveled a lot and had a secret weapons room in the house. At least that was what they did in the films.

The secret room could also be full of drugs, Mary's paranoid self told her, in which case Quaddra would be a drug lord.

All of those paranoid options terrified Mary, because if any of them were true, her plan was dead in the water.

It wasn't that hard to con a rich guy out of millions with a wedding sting, or to send him to prison with an 'abusive husband' tag, if the plan was well-thought-out and executed, but she couldn't do that to a drug lord, or a paid assassin. Those people wouldn't go quietly. In fact, they wouldn't go at all. She was the one who'd be gone . . . way before she managed to finalize her divorce or take Quaddra to court.

That night, Mary never fell asleep. Her brain just wouldn't disconnect.

Quaddra did roll over, taking his arm with him, sometime around 1:30 a.m. Mary's curiosity was killing her. She needed to know what was behind that secret door, but she didn't want to get out of bed and risk it. Murphy's Law was real. Her life was flooded with examples, and this was one that she didn't want to add to her long list.

At 5:30 a.m., Quaddra's alarm went off, half an hour before his regular time, but that was because he needed to be on the tarmac at San Francisco International early. When he rolled over to kiss Mary, she pretended to be asleep.

'Stay in bed, baby,' he whispered into her ear. 'It's too early. I'm going to shower and shave and get ready. I have to be in Seattle by ten.'

Mary moaned a reply and turned to face the other way.

Quaddra got out of bed, entered the bathroom and closed the door behind him.

Mary opened her eyes and turned to look at Quaddra's side of the bed.

'What the fuck do I do?' she whispered the question to herself. She knew that this would probably be the only chance that she would get. She also knew that she didn't need long. All Mary wanted to do was to have a look behind that filing cabinet to know what it hid. For that she only needed a few seconds.

From the bathroom, she heard the shower being turned on.

Quaddra liked to shave in the shower, and his showers always took around ten minutes . . . never less.

Mary only really needed one.

If you're going to go, you've got to go now, the voice inside her head told her.

Mary quickly swung her legs from under the covers and off the bed. She was still naked, wearing just her new diamond necklace. She took a tentative step towards the bedroom door . . . then a second one before she paused.

'What the fuck are you doing?' she asked herself. 'If you want to go, then you better go quick. Stop wasting time by tiptoeing.'

Antonia and Gabriela, the two housemaids, would arrive at 6:00 a.m., so for now, there was only Mary and Quaddra in the house.

Without wasting another second, Mary rushed downstairs to Quaddra's office. She'd been right – he'd never locked it once they came home from the restaurant. The door was still ajar.

She stole a peak at the stairwell behind her to make sure that it was clear before stepping into the office and quickly reaching for the handle on the drawer at the bottom right of the Victorian chest.

Mary grabbed the handle as firmly as she could and twisted it clockwise.

Click. The sound came from her right, disengaging the filing cabinet from the wall. Mary moved to it in a hurry.

'Please be a vault,' she whispered, with her eyes closed, practically making a wish. 'Please be a vault full of gold bars or something.'

She took hold of the cabinet with both hands and pulled it open, this time, all the way. The movement triggered a row of ceiling lights to come on inside the concealed room. The only problem was – it wasn't a door . . . it was a stairwell – and this wasn't a hidden room . . . it was a hidden basement.

'What the fuck?' Mary gasped, feeling her heart playing catch up with her rapid breathing.

'Maybe the vault is downstairs,' she told herself, trying to stay positive.

From the gap behind the cabinet, the stairs, which were solid concrete, moved down about five steps before snaking around and back on itself, which meant that the basement would be directly under Quaddra's office.

Pure instinct made Mary turn around and look behind her.

Nothing. She was still alone, as she knew she would be. It hadn't even been a minute since Quaddra had gone into the shower.

Mary drew in a deep breath and took the steps going down into hell knows what. As the stairwell snaked back on itself, she had to go down another twelve steps before reaching the basement at the bottom, and as she did, her body went rigid.

This definitely wasn't a hidden vault.

It wasn't an armory or a drugs room either.

This was something much, much worse.

Eighty-Five

The room that Mary was looking at was larger than Quaddra's office – about one and a half times larger. Two rows of fluorescent ceiling lights bathed the entire space in a glow that was more comforting than bright. At the center of the room, there was a rectangular workstation that was almost the same size as their eight-seater dining table upstairs. There was a computer at the center of the workstation and not much else, but Mary's attention was solely on the wall directly in front of her . . . on the other side of the workstation.

'What the actual fuck?' Mary whispered, feeling her legs weaken under her.

The wall across the room from her was partially covered by newspaper clippings, printouts and photographs – Polaroid photographs – and there must've been well over a hundred photos on that wall.

Mary stepped around the workstation to get a better look, her eyes moving up and down and left and right, jumping from Polaroid to Polaroid . . . printout to printout. The more she saw, the faster her heart hammered the inside of her ribcage.

The Polaroid photos were all of different women – close-ups of their faces . . . their hands . . . their bare feet . . . and their naked bodies. But these weren't glamour photos. These women weren't smiling or posing for the camera.

Mary stepped closer still.

The photos were arranged in columns: from top to bottom – face, hand, body, bare feet and, finally, face again – each column seemed to represent a different woman. Under the final facial photo, the one at the bottom of the column, came printouts – sometimes a couple, sometimes more, and sometimes just a single page. A few of the columns also displayed a few newspaper clippings. Mary's stare jumped between some of them for a quick moment before she allowed her eyes to take in the entire wall at once. The women's hands were always bound together by zip ties – in every hand photo – either above their heads or behind their backs. Their nails seemed brutally broken, with some ripped from their beds, which were caked in dry blood. The skin on their palms and fingers was scuffed and torn in places.

Their naked bodies – and once again, there were several different photos per woman – looked savagely beaten, cut and bruised, with various-sized hematomas showing around their breasts, ribs, hips, groin, back, buttocks and upper thighs.

At the top of each column, there were three different facial photos for each woman, and they all followed the same pattern – eyes open . . . eyes shut . . . and inconclusive – because their faces were so swollen from battery that Mary couldn't tell if their eyes were open or not.

In every open-eye photo, there was more than just tears in their eyes . . . there was terror – the kind of terror that Mary imagined a person would experience if they knew that they were about to die in a very hideous and painful way – and Mary had a horrible feeling that that had been exactly what had happened to all of these women. The reason why she thought so was because on the last facial photo – the one at the bottom of every column – their eyes were fully shut, the skin on their faces was lifeless and dull, with a rubbery quality to it, and their lips all showed an odd shade of purple. Mary had seen that same shade of purple on lips before.

She saw them on internet photos, when she was analyzing physical battery bruises so that she could copy them using makeup. That shade of purple only showed on the lips of cadavers.

And then there were the marks around their necks – sometimes ligatures, sometimes round hematomas the size of thumbs and fingers, and sometimes lacerations that looked so deep, they had almost been decapitated.

'What the fuck is this?' she whispered in a faulty voice, her own eyes glassing over, her heart practically relocating to the back of her throat. Whatever she was looking at, it was something that Quaddra clearly didn't want anyone else to know about. Whatever that wall was, it was disturbing, sickening, grotesque, and so frightening that Mary had started to feel sick.

You need to get the fuck out of here, Mary, the voice inside her head screamed at her. *You need to get the fuck out of this fucking room . . . NOW.*

Disoriented from an overwhelming mixture of fear, cold and confusion, Mary took a couple of steps back to butt-lean against the edge of the workstation and re-steady herself, but as she did, her left hand hit the computer keyboard on the station, waking up its monitor.

'What the fuck?' Mary whispered, as her eyes moved from the wall to the PC screen.

The image that had materialized on it was that of a naked woman, who had been tied up to a heavy wooden chair, reminiscent of the old-style electric chairs that she had seen in so many movies before.

The woman had clearly been tortured, with her entire body severely battered, bruised and cut. Blood had trailed down from her nose, lips and ears, creating a crazy labyrinth of red lines across her face before dripping down onto her exposed breasts. Her right eye was practically swollen shut and it looked like someone had taken a large bite out of her bottom lip.

'What the fuck is this?' Mary asked herself.

Nothing good, the voice inside her head replied. *Let's go. We really need to get the fuck out of here.*

On the top right-hand corner of the screen, Mary could see a timecode – 02:22 – indicating that that was a video, not a photograph like the ones on the wall just behind her.

Mary, don't you fucking dare. We need to GO!

But Mary's curiosity was stronger than her fear, and almost without realizing it, she reached for the spacebar on the keyboard.

The video started playing.

Eighty-Six

As the footage started playing on the screen, there was nothing else that Mary could do but hold her breath and hug her naked body to keep her from shivering even more.

Do you really want to watch this? the voice inside her head sounded like it was losing its grip. *Because I sure as hell don't. We need to go.*

But Mary didn't . . . couldn't move. She had to watch.

On the screen, the woman, who was shaking and sobbing, coughed, spitting a red mist of blood onto the air.

Too fucking loud, the voice warned Mary, who immediately reached for the volume key on the keyboard and turned it almost all the way down.

'Please . . . please don't do this.' Mary heard the woman plead in a barely audible voice that was strangled by fear and tears. Her pronunciation was completely erratic due to the huge chunk missing from her bottom lip. 'Please don't. I'll do whatever you want.'

'Shisss.' A second voice came through the tiny speakers. 'It will all be over soon. I promise you.'

That was when Mary's heart stopped beating and her body went cement-rigid, because she knew that voice. She could recognize it in her sleep. That was Quaddra's voice. She was absolutely certain of it.

Mary, please, the voice inside her head begged her. *Let's get the fuck out of here before it's too late.*

Right then, a second person appeared on the screen – male, tall, well built and dressed in a dark jumpsuit. He walked around to the other side of the woman on the chair before pausing directly behind her.

Mary could taste puke gathering at the back of her throat.

Despite the long-hair wig, the fake beard and the light color contact lenses, she had no doubt that the man in the video was her husband – Quaddra – and he was holding a hunting knife.

'What's happening right now?' Mary's voice was just as unsteady as the one belonging to the woman in the video.

This time, the voice inside her head didn't have to answer. On the screen, fake-beard Quaddra grabbed the woman by the hair, violently pulled her head back, exposing her neck, and in one swift movement, sliced her throat open from ear to ear.

'Oh my god!' Mary's hands shot up to her face to cover her nose and mouth, as her eyes filled up with tears. 'He just . . . killed her.'

On the video, the woman started convulsing, as blood and life slowly left her body, cascading from the large wound on her neck in uneven, foaming waves. The desperate, gargling sound that she emitted was like nothing Mary had ever heard before, but to Mary, the most shocking image . . . the one that she knew would stay with her forever wasn't the woman dying, or the blood sheet that was slowly covering her body. The image that she knew would never leave her was the smile on Quaddra's lips. It was a contorted, evil-looking but pleased smile that she had never seen before . . . until then.

That's it. We need to fucking go . . . NOW.

Mary wasn't arguing with the voice in her head anymore. She reached for the computer mouse, moved the pointer onto the video's playhead, and slid it back until the timecode on the right-hand corner of the screen read 02:22.

Good thinking, the voice agreed.

With her body shivering uncontrollably, Mary quickly ran back up the stairs and into Quaddra's office. She had no real idea of how long she'd been down in that basement of horrors, but the house still sounded quiet. She pushed the filing cabinet back against the wall until she heard it click in place. As she turned to exit the office, she caught a glimpse of the clock on the wall, above the Victorian chest of drawers – 5:37 a.m. Though it had seemed like an eternity, she'd only been gone from her room for a few minutes. Quaddra should still be in the shower.

Still shivering and with her breath as steady as a rope bridge, Mary ran up the stairs and back into her bedroom. The en suite bathroom door was still shut, and she could still hear the shower going.

'Fuck!' she breathed out, as tears flooded her eyes. She could feel vomit coming up from her stomach again, and again, she managed to swallow it back down.

'What do I do? What do I do?' Mary asked herself, completely out of breath, but not because she had run up the stairs. This was pure fear.

Get back into bed and pretend that you are sleeping, the voice inside her head told her. *If there's one thing you excel at, it's pretending. So, get back under those covers, close your eyes, ease down your breathing and that's it. Quaddra will be gone in minutes.*

Mary nodded to herself before she jumped back into bed, facing away from the en suite bathroom. She concentrated on her breathing, which right then, was shallow and loud.

'Get a grip, Mary,' she whispered, pulling the covers over her head. 'Get a fucking grip.'

She closed her eyes tight and forced herself to count down from ten, focusing on her lungs as they expanded and contracted to take in and expel oxygen . . . listening to her breath as it came in and out of her body. By the time she got to zero, Mary had finally gotten a grip on her nerves.

When Quaddra came out of the shower, just a few minutes later, Mary lay as still as she could . . . eyes shut . . . listening to her husband's movements. She heard him step into his walk-in closet and come out a few minutes later – probably fully dressed in a dark designer suit – but she didn't want to look. Mary really didn't want Quaddra to know that she was awake.

It took another couple of minutes before Mary heard Quaddra's footsteps getting closer, rounding the bed to her side.

Mary's body went stiff.

Quaddra kissed her on the cheek. 'I've got to run, my love,' he whispered into her ear.

'Ummm,' Mary moaned, just like she would've done on a normal day.

'Stay in bed and sleep tight.' He kissed her again. 'I'll call you when I land, but I'll be home tomorrow, anyway.' One final kiss. This time, on Mary's lips. 'I love you.'

Quaddra tasted of mint mouthwash and smelled of Tom Ford Black Lacquer, his favorite cologne.

Mary kept her eyes shut as she murmured back. 'I love you too.'

After Quaddra had left their bedroom, she waited in total stillness for several minutes before she couldn't take it anymore. That was when she exploded in sobs.

Eighty-Seven

Mary sat in her en-suite bathroom, with tears streaming down her face, and the door securely locked behind her. Quaddra had left the house just twenty-five minutes ago and since then, all that Mary could do was cry.

She knew that she needed to get a grip on herself, she needed to calm down and think of what to do next, but how the hell do you calm down and get a grip of yourself when you just found out that your husband, the man that you've been sharing a bed with – a life with – for over a year and a half, had a fucking chamber of horrors just under your house.

'Did he kill all those women?' she asked herself in thought.

The answer came from her internal voice, like a sucker punch to the gut.

Of course he did. Why the fuck else would he have their photos in his basement . . . photos showing different stages of their torture? Not to mention that fucking video. We didn't look, but do you really think that that was the only video he had saved in that computer? He probably has a video for each of them.

Mary closed her eyes for a moment then opened them again, but it didn't really matter. What she saw down in that basement kept on playing and replaying inside her head like a horror film on an endless loop, regardless of whether her eyes were open or not.

'This can't be fucking real,' she whispered to herself, as she slapped her face as hard as she could a couple of times. 'Wake up, Mary . . . fucking wake up. This has to be a nightmare. What else could this be?'

Reality, her internal voice replied.

The horror film kept on playing inside her head in its never-ending loop. Then, all of a sudden, it paused.

Mary's body stiffened to nearly spasms.

'Holy shit . . . the printouts . . . the newspaper clippings,' she said out loud.

Down in that crazy basement, Mary's eyes had settled on a couple of different printouts and newspaper clippings for just a few seconds. The printouts all seemed to be internet articles of some sort . . . the clippings, from different newspapers around the country.

She splashed her face with some cold water and tried to think. Her memory was usually very good with things like that. She could read something today, and still remember a lot of it in a few months' time. She had no idea of how she did it. It wasn't down to some technique or anything. It was just something that she was born with and it happened effortlessly – when she wasn't freaking out, that was.

'Calm down and you'll remember,' Mary told herself and immediately went back to her breathing exercise, counting back from ten. This time, she had to do it twice before she felt her heart slowing down to a steadier rhythm.

Mary hadn't stopped to properly read the printouts, but her eyes had scanned through what looked to be news headlines, right at the top of the printouts. All she needed was to . . .

Mary gasped, sucking in a lung full of oxygen.

She immediately exited the bathroom and rushed to her bedside table, where she retrieved pen and paper before writing down a name – Kelly Holder, City Terrace, California.

That had been one of the names that she had read on the

headline on one of the printouts – Kelly Holder, from City Terrace, in California. She was certain of it.

'C'mon,' she urged herself. 'Think . . . think.'

It took her almost a full minute, but there it was again – as if the horror film inside her head had re-engaged, only to slow down as her eyes moved from one printout to the next.

'Aileen Thompson,' Mary said the name out loud as she wrote it down, just under Kelly Holder. 'From Chicago, Illinois.' Those were the two names that she'd read on that wall.

In a flash, Mary reached for her cellphone, opened her internet browser, and typed the name 'Kelly Holder', then 'City Terrace', then 'California'.

It took her cellphone browser just a second to return a results page. The headline for the first link was – 'Kelly Holder, missing in Los Angeles'.

Mary tapped on the link and a new webpage loaded onto her cellphone screen.

> Kelly Holder, a twenty-three-year-old actress, who lived in City Terrace, an unincorporated area of East LA, was reported missing by her flatmate on 19 July 2024.

Mary's eyes widened at the screen. That was over a year ago. She and Quaddra weren't married yet, but they were certainly dating already.

She returned to the article, which went on to explain that Kelly was originally from Spokane in Washington, but she had moved to LA to pursue her dream of being an actress. She'd been living in Los Angeles for only a year when she went missing. The missing persons investigation was still ongoing. The article ended with a recent photo of Miss Holder.

'Oh fuck!' The word dribbled out of Mary's lips as her eyes settled on Kelly Holder's picture. In it, Kelly was wearing a white sweater and smiling at the camera. Her black hair was tied up into a messy bun on the top of her head.

Mary had only looked at the photo on the wall in the basement for maybe a couple of seconds, if that, but she was sure that it was the same girl.

'Fuck, fuck, fuck.'

Mary cleared the search box and typed in the second name she could remember: 'Aileen Thompson'. She then typed in the word 'Chicago'. A second later, she had another results page. The headline for the first link read – 'Aileen Thompson, twenty-six-year-old dancer, disappears without a trace'.

Mary tapped on the link and it was as if she was watching a nightmare come alive right before her eyes. The article was pretty similar to the one that she'd just read about Kelly Holder. Aileen Thompson, a twenty-six-year-old pole dancer from Chicago, was last seen on 15 May 2022. She worked at a gentlemen's club called PoleKatz in the downtown area of Chicago, and she had disappeared after finishing her Saturday shift, in the early hours of Sunday morning. The article also ended with a portrait photo of Aileen.

Right then, Mary remembered that she had all of Quaddra's traveling dates, right from when they'd started dating, marked down on the calendar in her cellphone. Knowing exactly when Quaddra would be away or not was important to her plan.

'Fuck, fuck, fuck.'

Mary called up her calendar app and swiped back until July 2024, and as she did, her heart stuttered. The day that Kelly Holder was reported missing – 19 July 2024 – had been a Friday. Quaddra had arrived in Los Angeles at the beginning of that same week, and he'd stayed until the weekend.

Mary was about to put her phone down, when she remembered something else . . . something that sent a cold shiver running down her spine.

'The blood,' she said, her eyes fixed on the calendar app on her screen. 'Oh fuck!'

July 2024 was when Denise had turned up at her old apartment in Bayview. That was the trip that Quaddra had made to LA and when he got back, Antonia had found specks of blood on the sleeve of one of his running shirts. Quaddra had told her that the blood belonged to an older gentleman, who'd had a nosebleed while running at the beach, but that had to be a lie. That was probably Kelly Holder's blood – the woman that Quaddra had murdered that week.

A drop of water fell on Mary's cellphone screen and she blinked. Only then did she realize that she was crying.

'No, no, no,' she tried telling herself. 'This isn't happening. This isn't for real. It can't be. This is just a sad coincidence.'

Well, that fucking basement under his office sure as shit is for real, the voice inside her head volleyed back. *And those photos on the wall are no fucking coincidence. They are all Polaroids – the same type of photos that you use to register the bruises on your body. The reason why you use them is because they can't be altered . . . they can't be photoshopped. Those are the real deal . . . you know that. And shall I remind you of that video? That gargling noise? That poor woman's face as he sliced her throat open? Those images seemed pretty fucking real to me.*

Right then, something else came back to Mary. In her cellphone's calendar, she only had Quaddra's traveling dates since they'd started dating, but Quaddra kept a paper calendar on the wall in the kitchen, so that Antonia and Gabriela knew when he'd be away. As the old year ended and the new year started, Mary had seen Antonia change the old calendar for a new one and just out of curiosity, she'd asked Antonia if she threw the calendars away. Antonia had replied that she never did. They were all in the attic storeroom, above the large three-car garage outside.

Instead of going into the kitchen and asking Antonia where

exactly in the storeroom the old calendars were, Mary decided to go look for herself. Being busy with something would calm her down and give her time to think. Plus, Mary asking about the old calendars would certainly make Antonia wonder.

In the storeroom, it didn't take Mary long to find the box labeled 'Calendars and Misc'. Antonia was an extremely organized person and the storeroom looked more like a file room than anything else. Every box in there was properly labeled and neatly stored in shelves and modules.

Mary pulled out the box from the shelf and sat on the floor with it before throwing its lid to one side and rummaging through the large wall calendars. The one from 2022 was the second from the top. She took it out and flipped the pages until she got to the month of May.

As her eyes found what she was looking for, bitter bile dripped from her throat into her mouth. Aileen Thompson was last seen on Sunday, 15 May 2022, in Chicago, as she finished her pole-dancing shift. Quaddra had arrived in Chicago on Friday, 13 May 2022, and he'd stayed until Tuesday, 17 May.

Another coincidence? the voice inside Mary's head asked.

Mary felt the room begin to spin around her.

How could any of this be real? How could someone like Quaddra, the most understanding and the kindest person she'd ever met ... someone who had never, not even once, shown an ounce of violence while around her, turn out to be this kind of monster?

Because evil doesn't always wear an ugly mask, the voice inside her head replied. *Its best disguise is hiding in plain sight.*

All of a sudden, things began making a lot more sense inside Mary's head. The reason why Quaddra hated publicity ... the reason why he stayed well away from social media ... the reason for his obsession with anonymity ... the reason why he had a very small group of friends ... had nothing to do with the fact that he was a billionaire. He was simply keeping the odds in his favor. The less recognizable he was, the easier it would be for him to approach strangers in places like strip clubs and seedy bars.

It was then that Mary remembered something else that practically froze the blood in her veins.

'Oh, hell no!' she said as she got to her feet. 'No, no, no, no.'

A second later, she was running out of the garage, fueled by pure terror.

Eighty-Eight

Mary's voice was still unsteady when she left Denise a new message.

'Denise,' she said, after using the correct opening code word. 'ZigDust, ZigDust, ZigDust.'

'ZigDust' was their abort code word. It was the name of the traveling funfair where they had met Dylan, all those years ago, back in Liverpool. Only Mary and Denise would know what it meant.

'Abort, Denise. Please abort. Just pack your bags and get the fuck out of LA. Do it now. Do not . . . I repeat – *do not* get in touch with Quaddra again. I'll explain later, but he is *not* who you think he is. He's not who I thought he was. Your life could be in serious danger. Please just get out of there, OK? Abort. ZigDust. Please call me when you're safe. Get out of LA first then call me. OK? I love you.'

Mary finished the call by giving Denise her new burner number before finalizing it with the closing code word.

The next call that Mary placed wasn't to the police. She called her therapist, Dr. Lillian Fox, asking for an emergency appointment. And that was why that morning, at exactly 11:00 a.m., Mary was being ushered into Dr. Fox's office.

Mary took a seat at the usual couch, but she didn't sit back, like she usually did. This time, she sat right at the edge of the seat ... only the tips of her shoes touching the floor ... her hands clasped together and stuck between her thighs – textbook defensive posture.

In over two years of therapy, Dr. Fox had never seen that look on Mary's face – an unsettling mixture of doubt and pure fear that was truly worrying.

'Would you like a glass of water?' Dr. Fox asked, already pouring Mary a glass from the jug on her desk.

Mary's jittery eyes met the doctor's. 'Thank you,' she took the glass, but didn't sip the water. She simply held it with both hands, resting it on her lap.

'Mary, what's going on?' Dr. Fox asked, taking a seat in her usual wingback Chesterfield armchair, but this time she did not have her notepad with her, and she did not activate the recording device either, which indicated that she wasn't treating this as a regular session. 'Does this have anything to do with the bruises?' Her tone was concerned, but not rushed.

'You mean the ones on me?' Mary asked.

'Yes,' Dr. Fox replied. 'The ones on your body, Mary. The ones that have nothing to do with you being clumsy.'

Mary used her thumb and forefinger to rub her eyes, as if she was fighting back tears. 'No,' Mary finally replied, with a nervous shake of the head. 'This has got nothing to do with that, but I'd like to give you this.' She reached for the package that she had brought with her and handed it to Dr. Fox. 'If you could please keep it for me.'

'What is this?' Dr. Fox asked, accepting the package.

Under normal circumstances ... if everything had gone to plan, the 'evidence package' was only posted to the therapist during the opening week of the trial, but these were far from normal circumstances, and Mary had learned a long time ago that it truly was much better to be safe than sorry.

'Just ... photographs and tapes documenting everything.'

Dr. Fox tried to read Mary's eyes. 'Everything as in . . . what?'

Mary didn't reply.

'Mary, if you're in danger, you have to let me know. I promise I'll do everything I can to help.'

'I don't know if I am yet,' Mary finally replied. 'But let's call that insurance.' She nodded at the package. 'You can look at the photos and listen to the tapes later, but I didn't ask for an emergency appointment to discuss what's in there.'

'OK.' The doctor's analyzing gaze stayed on Mary. 'So please tell me the reason for the emergency appointment.' She sat back down on her chair. 'Because from where I'm sitting, Mary, you look like you're one step away from a meltdown.'

Mary finally had a sip of her water.

'OK,' she began, with a deep breath. 'I'm not even going to waste your time or insult your intelligence by trying to convince you of a hypothetical situation, with "let's suppose", or defer the scenario to someone else with "asking for a friend" – kind of bullshit. If I did that, you'd know that I was talking about myself, anyway, and that the situation wasn't hypothetical at all, wouldn't you?'

Dr. Fox nodded. 'By creating a hypothetical situation, or deferring the scenario to someone else, the person believes that—'

'I really don't need an explanation, Doc,' Mary cut her short. 'What I need is some advice. And you're the best person for that right now.'

'OK.' Dr. Fox didn't seem offended by the interruption. 'So how can I help?'

'I need advice about . . . going to the police,' Mary said, her gaze moving down to the glass of water on her lap.

'And what do you think that you should contact the police about?'

'I, by chance, discovered something about a friend,' Mary lied. 'Something criminal.'

Mary knew that if she tried to hit Dr. Fox with 'my friend

found out that her husband has a secret room in their house', the doctor would immediately know that she was talking about her own husband, not a friend's. But she didn't want Dr. Fox to know that the person at the center of what she was just about to reveal was Quaddra. At least not yet.

'OK. How criminal are we talking about here?'

'The worst kind. The kind that can land the person on death row.'

'Murder.' Dr. Fox didn't phrase it as a question.

'That's the one,' Mary confirmed.

Dr. Fox took a moment. 'Was it self-defense?'

'No. Not even close. We're talking a heinous case of violence here.'

Dr. Fox's eyes widened at Mary. 'Well, in that case, then you should absolutely go to the police. Is there proof?'

'There is,' Mary replied. 'But I can't get to it at the moment.'

Dr. Fox lifted a hand to Mary. 'Mary, if you really want my advice, then please stop tiptoeing around the subject. You asked for this meeting, so tell me what happened . . . what did you discover . . . and what were the circumstances in which you discovered it. Any advice is only as good as the information that the person giving the advice has received. I can't form an opinion, or offer you any useful advice if I don't know all the facts.'

Mary had another sip of her water. She had already thought of a whole new story to feed Dr. Fox. It was simple, believable and to the point.

'While at a friend's house,' she began again. 'I, by chance, stumbled upon a secret door. I should've left it alone. It wasn't my house, but curiosity got the best of me, and I decided to snoop around.'

'Alright.' The expression on Dr. Fox's face was curious. 'And what did you find?'

'A chamber of horrors,' Mary replied, looking away from the doctor.

'Could you maybe be a little more specific?'

Mary drew in another deep breath. 'I walked into a room where the walls were plastered with photographs . . . Polaroid photographs.' From there, Mary went on to explain what she had actually found in the basement under Quaddra's office, including the video footage.

Dr. Fox listened to Mary's accounts in complete silence, until she was done.

'Are you sure about that?' Dr. Fox asked, her mouth semi-opened, her gaze distraught. 'Because if you are, Mary, then we're possibly talking about a serial killer here.'

'I am sure. Yes.'

Dr. Fox finally understood why Mary was so unraveled. 'Did you manage to snap a photo of those walls, or of the video you saw?'

'No.' Mary shook her head. 'I didn't have my phone with me at the time. But you can check it for yourself. Kelly Holder and Aileen Thompson. Those are the only two names I remember from that wall. Kelly Holder was from LA and Aileen Thompson from Chicago. I've already checked the Internet for information. They both went missing – Kelly Holder last year and Aileen Thompson in 2022. And I know for a fact that this friend of mine was traveling to those exact cities when both of those women went missing.'

Dr. Fox reached for the notepad on her desk and wrote both names down. 'Did you tell your husband about this? What did he say you should do?'

Mary did her best to control her facial expression. She didn't want to give anything away. 'No, not yet. He's away on business. But he's the type who will totally freak out and go straight to the cops. He's an "act first, think later" – kind of person. Not exactly helpful in these situations.'

Dr. Fox took a moment, tapping her pen against her notepad, trying to organize her thoughts. 'I'm not a lawyer, or a police officer, Mary, but as far as I'm aware, if you don't have a photo of the walls in this secret room you've found . . . a photo of these Polaroid pictures, or of the video images you saw on that computer, then you'll have a problem if you go to the police.'

Mary nodded. 'I've got no proof.'

'Exactly,' Dr. Fox agreed. 'Since this secret room is located inside a private property, the police would need a warrant to be able to enter the premises and check the room for themselves, and they won't be able to get one without evidence. In their view, all you have at the moment is hearsay.'

'I know.' Mary had spent the whole morning, from the time that she'd disconnected from her call to Dr. Fox, until her emergency appointment, surfing the Internet with those exact same questions.

'Do you think you can get back into your friend's house and obtain proof?' the doctor asked. 'Use your phone and snap a few pictures of these walls?'

Mary looked back at her as if Dr. Fox had gone mad. 'Are you kidding? I've seen this film before, Doc. The stupid woman who goes snooping around when she knows she shouldn't dies next. No thank you.'

Dr. Fox could easily understand Mary's concern. 'OK, let me ask you this – how close would you say you are to this friend of yours?'

'Pretty close – best friend kind of deal.'

'And does your friend have any indication that you've discovered this secret room?'

'No. None.'

'And you said that from what you've gathered, your friend has been doing this for quite some time.'

'By the looks of it,' Mary replied. 'Yes . . . years.'

'And how long have you known this friend of yours for?' the doctor asked.

Mary pursed her lips, still trying to not give anything away. 'For quite a while. Since I've moved to San Francisco, really.'

'OK.' Dr. Fox moved a hand up to her chin, as she pondered over something. 'And did you, at any moment during the time that you've known this person, ever feel threatened or in danger while in this person's presence?'

'Not at all.' Mary bit her bottom lip, as she shook her head. 'Not ever. To be honest, this is probably the kindest and most understanding person I've ever met, after my husband. It makes no sense.'

'It actually makes a lot of sense, Mary,' Dr. Fox explained. 'Contrary to popular belief, most serial murderers lead a very normal life. They have families . . . they have kids . . . they hold steady jobs . . . they are active in their communities . . . all the traits of an upstanding and common citizen. That's the reason why so many of them operate for years before they are actually caught, if they're ever caught. They look normal . . . they act normal . . . in fact, they are normal, except for this one thing that turns them into complete monsters. Some can flip that switch on and off whenever they want.'

Mary focused on her breathing. 'I think that that's the case here.'

'You said that you never felt in danger in the presence of this friend,' Dr. Fox continued. 'Do you know of any of your mutual friends who have gone missing since you've known this person?'

Mary shook her head. 'No. No one.'

Dr. Fox crossed one leg over the other. 'As a psychologist,' she finally explained, 'what that tells me, is that neither you nor any of your mutual friends are either under threat, or in this person's killing scope.'

Mary frowned. 'I'm not sure I'm following you, Doc.'

'Behind every serial killer's murder there's a "drive",' Dr. Fox clarified. 'A reason why they do it. Something that pushes them to kill. It could be for sexual pleasure, or an uncontrollable urge that they can't explain, or because the voices in their heads tell them to do it . . . it doesn't matter, but there's always something that drives them to kill . . . something more powerful than they are. But regardless of what that drive is, their victims are never picked at random, even when it seems that way.'

'So how are they picked?' Mary asked.

'Usually because they match certain criteria,' Dr. Fox explained. 'Those criteria are specific to each killer, and it can be just about anything – a physical trait, a personality characteristic, the way the person dresses, or walks, or speaks, or acts . . . it doesn't matter, but a victim is never really chosen at random. They are chosen because they trigger something in the killer.'

'OK?' Mary still sounded unsure.

'The point I'm trying to make here, Mary,' Dr. Fox continued, 'is that since you're close with your friend and you said that you never, not at any moment, felt threatened or in danger while in this person's presence, it means that you do not fit his "victim" criteria. You and your friends do not trigger his killing urges.' She paused Mary with a gesture. 'The reason I've used "he" as a pronoun is because you've said that the wall inside this secret room was plastered with photos of women, right?'

Mary nodded.

'Ninety-nine point nine percent of all serial offenders who target only women,' Dr. Fox explained, 'are male. So, it's safe to assume that this friend of yours is male.'

Mary nodded.

'And you really never felt threatened? Even a silly innuendo . . . an ill-timed joke that made you uncomfortable . . . something?'

'No.' Mary's resolve left no room for argument. 'Not ever.'

Dr. Fox went back into thinking mode. 'You said that you don't want to try to get back into this secret room to obtain photographic proof, right?'

'No fucking way.'

'Unfortunately,' Dr. Fox told Mary, 'I don't think that you have too much of a choice. You said that your friend gave you no indication that he knows that you know about this secret room, right?'

'He doesn't,' Mary confirmed.

'And if I had to guess why that is,' Dr. Fox carried on, 'I'd say that's because since you discovered this room, you haven't acted any differently while in his company. And that's exactly what you need to continue doing. If you start acting differently next time you and your friend get together, alarm bells will start ringing in his head.'

Mary brought a hand to her face and cupped it over her mouth.

'A common trait, not only in serial offenders,' the doctor said, 'but in any criminal, is that they're always in a high state of alert. They don't want to get caught. Any changes to routines, moods, behaviors, or even the way a person looks at them, will be picked up by their alert radar, which is always on. You said you two are close, so if you start distancing yourself from him out of the blue, he'll notice. If you act scared or apprehensive next time you see him, he'll notice. If you, all of a sudden, start avoiding contact, he'll notice. If you act *any* differently than you ever did when you two are together, he'll notice. Can you see where I'm going with this?'

Mary closed her eyes and sucked in a deep breath.

'I won't pretend to understand how difficult it will be for you to act normal next to someone who you now know is a monster, but if you behave any differently, Mary, assuming that you haven't got this wrong, then the danger flips to you, regardless of whether you're in his victim scope or not, because if he finds out you know, the "drive" becomes his survival ... not an uncontrollable urge.'

'Fuck, fuck, fuck. Why did I have to go in there?'

Dr. Fox took the empty glass from Mary's hand and refilled it with water before returning it to her.

Mary immediately took a large sip.

'So,' the doctor said, as she sat back down, 'going back to the reason why you asked to see me today, my advice would be, do your absolute best to act like you would if you had never discovered this secret room. Don't let him know that you know, but the most important thing is, keep your eyes open for an opportunity to get back into that room and snap just a few shots of these photographs on the wall, or even a video, if at all possible. All you'll need is a few seconds in there, that's all. Once you have that, the game changes. Then yes, get the police, the FBI, whoever you want to arrest this guy. I'll go to the police with you, if you want me to.'

'That's a lot easier said than done, Doc,' Mary came back, tears starting to well up in her eyes again.

Dr. Fox grabbed a tissue from the box on her desk and offered it to Mary. 'You're right. It really won't be easy, but I think that it's the only plan of action here. I've known you for about two years now, Mary. You're a good person with a strong moral compass. I think that even if you wanted to, you wouldn't be able to just walk away and do nothing to stop this guy from hurting anyone else in the future ... because he will. These people don't ever stop, Mary, unless somebody stops them ... and from everything you told me, at the moment, it seems like you're the *only* one who can do that.'

Mary finished the entire glass of water in three large gulps.

'If what you've found is real, Mary,' Dr. Fox added, 'then this isn't something that you'll be able to just brush under the carpet and move on with your life. If you try to do that, your subconscious will crush you with guilt.'

Mary cursed herself under her breath because she knew that Dr. Fox was right.

Eighty-Nine

Mary had always been a great planner. She wouldn't have survived this long in the con game if she weren't. But the quality that really set her apart from other con artists was her incredible ability to compartmentalize.

Dr. Fox was right. Mary had known Quaddra for almost two years, and in all that time she'd never, not even once, felt threatened or in danger while in his company. Quaddra had never even raised his voice at her, never mind showing any signs of being physically violent. Their sex life was varied – sometimes tender, sometimes rougher, sometimes kinky, sometimes a mix of all three, but always consensual . . . always within limits . . . never pushy . . . and never, ever aggressive. If Quaddra had a sick urge to torture and murder women, then, just like Dr. Fox had said, Mary didn't seem to meet his 'victim' criteria. If she did, she'd be another Polaroid on that wall by now. So, theoretically, as long as Mary carried on acting like Mary . . . like she never knew about that secret basement, she would stay out of danger, and the best way for her to do just that was to compartmentalize – something that she was brilliant at.

This wouldn't be easy. Mary knew that. Especially given the fact that she had less than a day to get her mind wrapped around the absolute insanity of what she'd discovered and into the right frameset.

The idea was very straightforward. Mary would have to bundle the new Quaddra – the one with a basement of horrors under his office, the one with a sick urge to torture and murder innocent women – into a tight package and store that package away in a hidden compartment inside her mind. That compartment wouldn't be touched until she was ready to go to the police with the proof she needed.

The other Quaddra – the one that she had married, the one that she was conning, the one that she was falling in love with – would stay exactly where he was, at the forefront of her mind. And that would be the Quaddra that she would see every time that she looked at him, every time that she kissed him. That was the compartmentalization part of the plan.

The 'obtain proof' part of the plan was just as straightforward. Quaddra kept the keys to his office on a keychain that he carried with him everywhere he went. But because access to his secret basement came via a state-of-the-art Murphy door hidden behind a filing cabinet, a door that he had no idea that Mary knew about, that keychain was just that – a regular keychain. He didn't keep it on a piece of string around his neck at all times, or locked inside a combination safe somewhere. When Quaddra was at home, he would empty his pockets onto his bedside table in their bedroom, and that was that. The office key, together with his wallet, and whatever else he had in his pockets, would be right there – on the table. Mary saw that key every day. All that she needed to do now was grab it, and she was planning on doing so as soon as possible for a very simple reason – the compartmentalization of the two Quaddras wouldn't be easy to execute, but Mary knew that she could do it, she just didn't know how long she'd be able to do it for before the enormity of the danger that she was putting herself under began to really creep in, and once that happened – game over.

Ninety

Quaddra returned home from Seattle the next day like he'd said he would, and Mary was surprised with how well she was able to isolate 'evil Quaddra' into some hidden part of her mind and keep him there, allowing her to concentrate only on 'good Quaddra'. And her performance was worthy of a standing ovation.

As Quaddra got back home, Mary kissed him like she always did, they had dinner and shared a bottle of wine like they'd done countless times before, and they had sex as if they hadn't seen each other in months . . . and this time, Mary didn't even have to fake it.

'Every time you come back from one of your trips,' Mary said, as Quaddra rolled off her to his side of the bad, his breathing labored, his smile so wide it practically reached his ears. 'You come back . . . hungry, if you know what I mean.'

Quaddra took a moment to catch his breath. 'That's because I miss you so much. But . . .' Their eyes met. 'You seemed pretty hungry yourself, baby.'

The smile on Mary's lips was just as wide as Quaddra's, her breathing just as labored. 'That's because I miss you more.'

'We've been married for a year,' Quaddra said, turning on his side to look at Mary. 'We dated for nine months before that, and you still take my breath away . . . every time.'

'And so do you,' Mary replied, her chest rising and falling hard with each breath. 'As you can clearly see.'

'I'm not talking about only when we're in bed, honey,' Quaddra countered. 'That's just a bonus. I'm talking about all the time.' He ran the back of his index and middle finger against her left cheek. 'Whenever I look at you . . . no matter where we are . . . my heart beats faster. It happened right on that first night that I saw you at that art exhibition and it has never changed in all the time that I've known you. You complete me in a way that it's hard to explain. It's like . . . if I'm a ship, you're the ocean that carries me forward, do you know what I mean?'

Mary held his gaze for several long seconds. 'Is this pillow talk, baby? How good was I tonight?'

Quaddra laughed. 'You were fantastic, as always, my love, but this isn't pillow talk. This is real talk. I love you so much.'

Mary slid a little closer to Quaddra to kiss him on the lips before whispering. 'And I love you so much back.'

'I really can't wait to be back in Salzburg with you next week,' Quaddra said, reaching for her hand and kissing it. 'That was so much fun.'

'That was absolutely crazy,' Mary corrected him, her memory clearly taking her back to the private drone show that Quaddra had organized when he asked her to marry him. She swung her legs off the bed and put her panties back on. 'I'm going to go get some water, would you like some?'

'Actually, yes. Can you get me a bottle of sparkling, please, baby?'

'Coming right up.'

Mary exited their bedroom, leaving the door open. At the bottom of the stairs, she turned around and looked right. Quaddra's office door was closed. She looked up, towards the second-floor landing.

No Quaddra.

The kitchen was ahead of Mary, past the stairs, and past the office. In her normal walking pace, she headed towards it, and as she reached the door to Quaddra's office, she, very casually, without losing a stride, tried the handle.

Locked.

'Of course it would be locked,' she whispered under her breath. 'Why wouldn't it be?'

In the kitchen, Mary grabbed two bottles of sparkling water from the fridge and headed back upstairs, and as she got to their bedroom door, she was surprised to find Quaddra already asleep – the bedside lamp on his side of the bed already switched off.

Mary didn't move. She simply stood there, at the door to their bedroom, watching as Quaddra breathed in and out in an even and steady pace – a pace that she recognized only too well. That was Quaddra's sleep-breathing pace.

A bead of cold sweat pearled on the back of Mary's neck before slipping down along her spine. The bedside lamp on her side was on. Its glow was strong enough to allow Mary to see that Quaddra's wallet, together with his keys were right there, where she knew they would be – on his bedside table.

Of course, she wanted to execute the 'obtain proof' part of her plan as soon as possible so that she could get the hell away from that house and from Quaddra. She just never imagined that an opportunity would present itself so soon.

At the door to their bedroom, Mary hesitated for a beat, pondering her options. She'd been a con artist for a very long time and as such, she fully understood how huge a part 'luck' played in her game – so if 'lady luck' ever smiled at her, even if only for a fraction of a second, she had to smile back, because she never knew when she'd get the chance again.

You're not doing anything wrong, the voice inside Mary's head tipped in. *All you're doing is placing a bottle of water on his bedside table, like he asked you to.*

Mary knew that, but she also knew that this was when compartmentalizing made no difference at all. Acting normal, as if she didn't know anything about Quaddra's secret, was one thing. Risking getting caught by stealing his office keys when he was less than two feet away from her was something completely different, and Mary was worried that the beating of her heart, which to her sounded like a twenty-one-gun salute going off every half a second inside her chest, would wake him up.

She paused, closed her eyes, and urged herself to get a grip.

The walk from their bedroom door to Quaddra's bedside table was done quickly and on tiptoes. Once there, Mary placed the water bottle on the table, and just like her old self – the professional pickpocket – allowed her pinky finger to smoothly hook itself through the ring on the keychain that held Quaddra's office key.

Once a pickpocket, always a pickpocket, because the movement was seamless and soundless, and just like that, she had Quaddra's office key palmed in her right hand.

Quaddra's breathing stayed steady, his body still, his eyes firmly shut. The twenty-one-gun salute going off inside Mary's chest didn't seem to bother him. Mary held her breath, stepped away from the bedside table and tiptoed back to the bedroom door. She was about to leave the room and run downstairs, when she remembered that she didn't have her cellphone with her.

The whole point of getting back into Quaddra's secret basement was so that she could obtain photographic or video proof of what was down there.

'Fucking stupid!' she silently mouthed the words, as she paused and turned around. Her cellphone was on her bedside table.

Mary breathed in through her nose and held it in her lungs while she tiptoed back to her side of the bed – a little faster this time than she did moments earlier.

Absolutely no movement from Quaddra.

Mary picked up her cellphone and right then, wished that she had grabbed her robe from the ensuite bathroom before going down to the kitchen. There was no way that she would risk crossing the room for it now.

By her bedside table, she stood still for several seconds, watching Quaddra, as his midriff expanded and contracted with each breath. It looked like he was reaching deep sleep.

That was her chance and she knew it.

More tiptoeing, even faster this time, and as Mary reached the outside of her room, the tiptoeing became more urgent, until she reached the landing at the top of the stairs, where it turned into a mad sprint.

Ninety-One

At the bottom of the stairs, Mary unlocked the door to Quaddra's office and quickly stepped inside. As she did, she knew that the incessant shiver that had just started running up and down her spine wasn't just because Quaddra kept the temperature inside his office a few degrees below comfortable. That did play its part, but the head-to-toe goosebumps, the unsteady hands, the shallow breathing . . . all of it was pure fear and anxiety, not cold.

Mary closed the door behind her and took a moment to try to calm herself down. Instinct told her not to turn on the lights. Instinct also told her not to touch anything that didn't need touching either.

The curtains on the large west wall window were drawn shut, but Quaddra never overlapped one side over the other, which meant that there was always a gap running the entire length of the curtains. That evening, it wasn't a large gap – less than two inches, actually – but it was large enough to allow the full moon, high on the sky outside, to project some light into the office. In seconds, as her eyes acclimatized, the darkness surrounding Mary began to disassemble itself into the shapes of the room – the desk, the computers, the filing cabinets, and the Victorian chest of drawers.

As soon as Mary was sure that she could get to the chest and then the filing cabinet without bumping into anything, she moved to it . . . fast. At the chest, she lost no time reaching down for the handle on the bottom right-hand drawer and twisting it clockwise.

Click. The filing cabinet to her right disengaged from the wall.

The twenty-one-gun salute inside Mary's chest became a rapid-fire cannon.

She stood up straight and rushed to the cabinet before pulling it all the way open.

Just as before, the movement triggered the lights on the stairwell to activate, followed by those downstairs. Against the darkness of the office, the light coming up from the basement burnt at Mary's eyes, but she didn't care. Barefoot and only in her panties, she, once again, took the stairs going down to what she knew was a horror show.

'Don't waste any time, Mary,' she told herself, already activating the camera on her smartphone even before reaching the basement under Quaddra's office. She needed to stay focused on the task of photographing those walls. She wasn't there to look at those Polaroids. If she did, she would get emotional, she knew she would, and that would make her lose valuable time.

The air down in the basement felt even colder than in Quaddra's office, and Mary's skin, which was already gooseflesh, seemed to enter frostbite mode. Her whole body began shivering, and she had to clench her teeth hard to stop them from clattering.

After circling the workstation at the center of the room to get closer to the wall, Mary held her cellphone at eye level and used her index finger to repeatedly tap the shutter button on her screen. As she did, she slowly moved the phone around, trying to capture the entire wall, but she was so scared and so cold that after just a few seconds, she didn't seem to be able to tap the screen anymore – her finger becoming stiff and unresponsive.

'Fuck this,' she whispered, and she was sure that she could see her breath in the air.

With shaky fingers, she switched her cellphone camera into 'video' mode, tapped the shutter button once, and began shooting a clip.

Mary started at the far left of the wall, being careful to capture an entire column, from top to bottom, before moving on to the next one along, but as she moved her phone down to the bottom of the first column, she noticed something that she hadn't noticed the first time – a small plastic container – about the same size as a shoebox.

Without pausing the recording, she peeled her eyes away from her cellphone screen to look at the container. Only then did she realize that there were similar containers, on the floor, at the bottom of every column, and they were all lidless.

'What the fuck?'

She took a step closer, angling her body slightly forward, to look inside the first shoebox – the one at the far left, at the bottom of the first column.

Mary's heart stuttered ... re-engaged ... then stuttered again.

Inside that first container, Mary could see a dainty silver bracelet, a hairbrush, a small compact powder case, and a pair of panties – black lace.

'Oh, fuck me!' The words came out strangled by tears, because Mary knew exactly what she was looking at.

Those were possessions – victims' possessions.

In films – and Mary had seen plenty of them – the FBI called them 'trophies' and 'momentos'. The reason why serial killers took them was because 'trophies' symbolized their power and victory over the victim, while 'momentos' were souvenirs that helped the killer relive his crimes as a fantasy – the killing ... the rape ... the torture ... the abuse ... everything – over and over again. The items in those boxes were used to preserve the memories of the victims and to fuel Quaddra's twisted sadistic desires. The once victims' belongings were now nothing more than Quaddra's personal 'fetish' toys.

'What in the actual fuck?'

Mary felt something somersault inside her stomach and she was forced to pause the recording and take a step back.

'Don't puke, don't puke, don't puke,' she told herself, crossing her arms over her stomach and angling her torso forward just a touch.

It took her a few seconds, but the trick seemed to work.

Mary swallowed down the acrid taste in her mouth, breathed out despair, and nodded at herself, as if saying – 'OK, let's finish this and get the hell out of here'.

She tapped the record button on her screen once again, but as she tried to pick up from where she'd left off, she heard a familiar voice come from behind her.

'You shouldn't be in here, Mary.'

Ninety-Two

'You look beautiful today, sweetheart.'

Those were the words that Mary's stepfather used to say to her, every time he entered her bedroom, reeking of alcohol, roll-up cigarettes and stale sweat.

And no words had ever scared her more . . . until now.

As she heard Quaddra's voice coming from behind her, Mary went rigid – every muscle in her body tightening almost to the point of cramping. She exhaled and it came out heavy, as if she'd just crossed the finish line at a marathon.

'This room . . . is not for you, Mary,' Quaddra said, and for the first time ever, Mary detected something in his voice that she had never heard before – anger.

She finally turned around, her eyes shifting from her cellphone to Quaddra.

He was standing at the bottom of the stairwell, wearing only his boxer shorts. His expression looked relaxed, but his eyes scared Mary. There was a fire burning in them that she had never seen before . . . not in anyone's eyes.

'Baby . . .' Mary tried, her voice so unsteady that it didn't sound like her own. 'What is this?' She brought her right hand down – the hand holding her cellphone – but she never tapped the stop button. The phone was still recording. 'What is this room?'

Quaddra kept his arms by his side. There was no tension in his posture.

'You know what this room is, Mary.' As if Quaddra had flipped a switch, the tone in his voice went back to being calm and relaxed. There was no rush . . . no recrimination . . . no anger.

'No.' Mary shook her head. Her tone, on the other hand, was still jittery, maybe even a little more so now given Quaddra's composure. 'I don't know what this room is.'

'So why were you filming it?'

'I . . .' Mary couldn't think of anything to say. Her eyes moved down to her cellphone before returning to Quaddra, and as they did, they filled up with tears. 'Why?' Some of the tears moved down to her throat. 'Why do you do this? Where does it come from? You're nothing like this.'

Quaddra stepped away from the stairwell, moving to the left of the workstation. That was the shortest distance between Mary and the stairwell. For her to get to it, she would either have to go through Quaddra, or round the workstation through the other side. Too far. She would never get to the stairwell before Quaddra got to her and she knew it. Still, she took a step back, trying to maintain a reasonable distance between Quaddra and herself.

'You think that this is a choice?' Quaddra asked, his eyes shifting to the wall for a heartbeat before coming back to Mary.

'Of course it is,' Mary replied. 'Everything we do is a choice.'

'That's not true,' Quaddra said, with a very subtle shrug. 'No one choses to have cancer, for example . . . or MS . . . or Parkinson's . . . or Alzheimer's . . . or any other terrible illness that will completely alter their lives.' He took another step forward.

Mary took another step backwards.

'This.' Quaddra indicated the wall again. 'Is exactly the same, Mary. This is my cancer. I didn't choose this. It was chosen for me.'

'Chosen for you?' Mary looked back at Quaddra in complete disbelief. 'Chosen by who?'

'By my genes, Mary . . . by the biology in me . . . by my DNA.' Quaddra peeked at the wall again. 'This isn't a consequence of a fractured mind. I was never abused as a kid. I was never bullied in school either, and I don't come from a broken home. I was a great student . . . a happy child . . . and adored by my parents. I also never had any problems with women and I don't hear voices in my head. None of the clichés fit me, Mary, except that for some reason I was *born* with this . . .' Quaddra clenched his teeth, as if what he was about to say angered him. 'This never-ending desire to do this.' He indicated the wall again.

'What the hell are you talking about?' Tears began rolling down Mary's cheeks.

'You think I didn't try *not* to be this person?' Quaddra chuckled. The fire inside his eyes seemed to be gathering momentum. 'I tried . . . God, I fucking tried, but it just kept on coming back . . . stronger . . . angrier . . . hungrier . . . and there's only one way to feed it.' He extended his left arm to indicate the women on those Polaroids. 'But as long as I feed it every now and then, it leaves me alone, Mary, so that I can have a normal life.'

'A normal life?' The words came out unclear. The cold and the fear were starting to sink down to Mary's bones. She could barely control the clattering of her teeth anymore.

'Well,' Quaddra shrugged again. 'My life with you is pretty normal, isn't it? My life with my friends is normal. My life at work is normal.' With his fingers spread apart, he moved his left hand in the direction of the wall a couple of times, in a pumping motion. 'I keep this completely separate. Never in San Francisco. Never anyone I know. Never close to those who are important to me.'

Mary's eyes pinged to the wall then back to Quaddra. 'These women were important, Quaddra. Maybe not to you, but they were important – to their partners, their mothers, their fathers, their siblings . . .' Mary didn't want to cry, but the tears just kept on coming. 'All of these women . . . however many there were, they were important.'

'Nineteen,' Quaddra said, matter-of-factly.

Mary's eyes narrowed at him.

'Nineteen women,' he repeated it, his head tipping towards the wall.

'Jesus Christ!' Mary breathed in through her nose, but the air came in in lumps, as if the air around her was barely breathable. 'You've tortured and murdered nineteen women?'

'So far,' Quaddra replied, his voice so calm it was chilling, but Mary noticed that his eyes moved to the workstation as he said those words.

Instinctively, she looked in the same direction, and what she saw made her go dizzy.

Just to the left of the computer monitor there was a new set of Polaroid photos . . . a new woman . . . but Mary could only see the top-most photo.

'Did . . . did you kill her?' Mary asked, pointing at the set on the workstation, her voice a lot thinner than seconds earlier . . . her heart tying itself into knots inside her chest . . . the room threatening to whirlwind around her. The Polaroids on the workstation were of Denise.

Quaddra seemed to detect a different tone to Mary's voice because his head angled slightly to one side, as if concerned. 'Why? Do you know her?'

'Did you kill her?' Mary asked again, tears streaming down her face, her voice beginning to falter.

Quaddra didn't reply. Instead, he took another step forward. 'I'm going to need that phone, Mary,' he said, nodding at the cellphone in Mary's hand.

Mary took another step backwards.

'This is the last thing I ever wanted, Mary. Why did you have to come in here?'

Mary moved back, feeling panic starting to set in. Her brain was clearly preparing her body for fight or flight.

'I so wish that you had never found this room, my love. We could've been so happy . . . we *were* so happy.'

Mary took one more step back and realized that she was reaching the end of the workstation, which meant that the advantage had swapped sides. She was now closer to the stairwell than Quaddra was. All she needed to do was round the workstation and shoot for the door. Quaddra would have to chase after her, because going back the way he came was now the longest way around.

'I would've never hurt you, Mary,' Quaddra continued. 'Ever, but you were never supposed to be in here.' His stare shifted to the phone in Mary's hand one more time. 'I'm really going to need that phone, Mary.' The fire in his eyes began seeping into his voice. He was getting ready to make a move. Mary could tell. 'But I promise you that I'll make this quick, OK? No pain.'

Terrifying fear took over Mary, sending her heart rate into the stratosphere, with blood flowing away from her heart and into her limbs, getting them ready to throw harder punches, or run faster. She had already checked the workstation for any objects that she could use as a weapon, or to defend herself, but other than the computer and the Polaroids, there was nothing else on it, and she was already too far away from the computer to be able to reach it.

'I really didn't want to have to do this, Mary.'

'So don't,' Mary said back, as adrenaline flooded her system, causing her pupils to dilate.

'Unfortunately, it's not that simple, my love,' Quaddra said, taking another step in Mary's direction. 'But I give you my word that I'll make this as quick and as painle—'

Mary knew that there was no way that she could fight Quaddra off when he launched for her, which he looked like he was just about to do. The way she saw it, her only chance was to try to catch him off guard and attack first ... and that was exactly what she did.

Ninety-Three

Before Quaddra could finish his sentence, Mary did the only thing that she could think of. Using the only weapon that she had at hand, she stepped into his path and as hard as she could, threw her phone straight at him, catching him completely by surprise. At such short distance, her aim was almost perfect, and the phone hit Quaddra across the bridge of his nose. It was a heavy phone, encased in a metal case for maximum shock protection. For Quaddra, it was as if he'd been struck across the face by a construction brick.

As the metal case connected with his nose, soft tissue and flesh were immediately torn open, sending blood flying into the air and into Quaddra's eyes.

'Arghhhh!' The scream he let out was guttural – full of pain and anger. He stumbled back several steps, while his hands shot to his face. Blood dripped through his fingers. 'You fucking bitch.' He used the heels of his hands to try to clear the blood from his eyes, without much success. 'Now I'm going to make you suffer.'

Right then, the only 'fight' that Mary had in her was the phone to the face, and she was fresh out of it. She knew that if she got physical with Quaddra, she didn't stand a chance. He was bigger, stronger and faster than her in every way. With the 'fight' part out of the way, all that was left for Mary to do was 'flight', so while Quaddra tried to blink the blood out of his eyes, Mary turned on the balls of her feet and ran, as fast as she could, rounding the workstation. By the time she reached the stairwell, Quaddra was still half blind and on the other side of the workstation. Mary didn't look back, taking the stairs up to the house two at a time.

The lights were still off in Quaddra's office, and since adrenaline had dilated Mary's pupils, the shock of coming from the light in the stairwell into an almost pitch-black room practically blinded her, but there was no way that she was slowing down. She blinked once and made a beeline for the door, but her legs were still unsteady from fear and cold, and the beeline was more like a zigzag. As she got closer to the door, she lost some of her orientation and slammed her right knee against the edge of the Victorian chest.

'Arghhhh, fuck!' Mary cursed through gritted teeth, as she felt a soaring pain start at her knee before spreading throughout the rest of her body with lightning speed. She paused for just a second before taking her next step, which almost brought her to the ground, as the pain was still too intense for her to put any weight onto her right foot.

Hopping on one leg it would have to be.

As Mary finally got to the door, she heard footsteps coming from the stairwell.

'Fuck, fuck, fuck.'

The pain . . . the fear . . . the cold . . . the total desperation to get away . . . all of it took its toll on Mary's thinking because at the door, instead of turning left and heading towards the living room and the house's front door, she turned right and headed towards the kitchen. Only when she busted through the door did her brain re-engage.

What the fuck are you doing in the kitchen? the voice inside Mary's head asked.

Too late to turn around now, as she could already hear Quaddra at the door to his office.

'Arghhh, arghhh, arghhh . . .' He sounded angry beyond belief.

Mary hopped onto the other side of the large kitchen island and immediately reached for the cordless phone on the counter, but she was so scared . . . her hands trembling so much . . . that she dropped it onto the work surface as soon as she took it out of its cradle.

'Fuck!'

Practically out of breath, Mary reached for it again, with both hands this time. Shaky fingers or not, Mary had just managed to dial 911 when Quaddra kicked the kitchen door open, and if she was scared of him before, the sight of what he looked like then petrified her soul.

Quaddra's face was completely covered in blood, which was still oozing from his facial wound – running down his cheeks, over his lips, and dripping down from his chin onto his chest and the floor. His hands were also covered in crimson red. The fire inside his eyes was still there, but it had joined forces with rage and specks of blood to create some kind of hell furnace, and since his face, hands and torso were bathed in plasma, Quaddra looked like some blood-thirsty psychopathic killer straight out of a horror movie.

Mary dropped the phone again, this time, onto the floor.

'That was a cheap shot, Mary.' Even his voice sounded different – deeper . . . darker . . . but at the same time, controlled.

'Stay the fuck away from me,' Mary yelled, as she hopped back a couple more steps.

'Oh, what's the matter, honey?' Quaddra asked, blood spitting from his lips and dripping from his chin as he spoke. 'Did you hurt yourself?'

'Stay the fuck away from me,' Mary told him again, but there was no conviction in her voice . . . just fear.

'I'm afraid I won't be able to do that, my love.'

What was really terrifying Mary right then, was that Quaddra seemed to be in no rush. He knew that he could get to her whenever he wanted. This was now a game to him. One that he knew he couldn't lose.

For just a split second, Mary's mind wondered if this was what Quaddra did to all his victims – play some crazy cat-and-mouse game . . . chasing them around . . . making them believe that they had a chance of escaping, when the truth was they were already dead – they just didn't know it yet. Mary pictured Denise fighting Quaddra with every molecule of strength she had in her body, because she knew that Denise *would* fight him.

You better concentrate on the here and now, the voice inside Mary's head said, bringing her back to the kitchen.

Quaddra wasn't blinking so much anymore. Blood was still cascading from the wound on his nose, but it wasn't spilling into his eyes.

'You don't have to kill me,' Mary said, her head shaking at him, her heart beating in her throat. She had no idea if her 911-call had connected or not. She had no idea if an operator was on the line or not, or even if the phone was still working after it hit the floor, but she wasn't really talking to Quaddra right then. She was talking to the phone . . . she was talking to hope. 'In the same way that you didn't have to kill any of those women.'

'But I did,' Quaddra said back. 'In the same way that I now have to kill you.' He took a couple of unrushed steps in Mary's direction, rounding the kitchen island through the right side.

Mary hopped back once again, but this time she tentatively placed her right foot on the floor. The pain was still there, on her knee and shooting up her leg, but the 'fight or flight' adrenaline that was still flooding her system had anesthetized enough of it for her to be able to stop hopping on one leg. She took another step back, and as she did, her eyes made contact with the knife-block that Antonia always kept on the kitchen counter – six laser-sharp Japanese knives that could slice through almost anything with tremendous ease.

Without missing a beat, Mary reached for one of the knives, grabbing a six-inch blade with a thick wood handle.

'Stay the fuck away from me, Quaddra,' she yelled again, extending her right arm at him.

Quaddra chuckled. 'What do you think that you're going to do with that, Mary?'

'Come closer and you'll find out.' The blade did not look steady in Mary's hand.

Quaddra allowed his lips to break into a smile that scared Mary because it didn't look like a smile. It was just a meaningless gesture – muscles pulling skin over his skull – which made the smile look creepy and lifeless, as if his whole face was being operated by a puppet master. Add the fact that most of his body was, by then, a crazy mess of smeared blood, and Quaddra looked like a creature who had been summoned from the depths of hell.

'Oh, c'mon, Mary,' Quaddra said, lifting his left hand to his face again, as if he was going to wipe some of the blood away, but that was just a distraction tactic.

As Mary's attention moved to his hand, Quaddra launched himself at her, right arm extended, aiming for her throat.

This time, Mary was the one who was caught completely off guard, especially by how fast Quaddra had moved. Somehow, he had managed to bridge a six-foot gap in a fraction of a heartbeat, as if he really was some creature from beyond.

Instead of stabbing the knife at him, all that a terrified and desperate Mary was able to do was to reflexively angle the knife up, trying to protect her face. Out of pure luck, she managed to place the knife just between her throat and Quaddra's hand, and as he closed his fingers around it, the laser sharp blade sliced through his palm, almost down to the bone.

'Arghhhh!' Quaddra's hand immediately recoiled back, the sudden jerking movement sending more blood flying up into the air before splashing down over Mary's face and naked torso.

'Fucking bitch!' Quaddra yelled, taking two steps back. His left hand shot to his right one to try to contain the bleeding.

Mary also wobbled back a couple more steps, her eyes blurred by tears, her whole body shivering from fear and adrenaline, her face, hair and torso splashed with Quaddra's blood.

'I told you to stay back.' Her voice came out one octave higher than normal.

If adrenaline had anesthetized some of Mary's knee, it seemed to have done the same to Quaddra's hand, because despite how deep the cut to his right palm was, he launched himself at her again, with even more power this time, but this time, Mary was a little more prepared for it and she managed to swing the blade from left to right and top to bottom.

Quaddra, once again, covered the distance between him and Mary in a flash, which completely shortened Mary's defensive movement, taking most of the power away from the stabbing. The knife entered Quaddra's front a few inches below his left shoulder. The wound was deep enough to cause a lot of pain and bleeding, but far from enough to be able to stop him from smashing into Mary, sending both of them crashing to the ground – Mary falling backwards and Quaddra falling on his stomach.

As they hit the floor, the knife scattered from Mary's hand and she panicked. It was now the two of them in a floor-wrestling match, with no weapons. If Quaddra managed to grab hold of Mary, wounded or not, it was over.

As Quaddra lifted his head to look at her, she began crab-crawling backwards – on her hands, butt and feet – as fast as she could to, once again, try to put some distance between the two of them.

It didn't work.

Before Mary could get away, Quaddra extended his right arm, sending more blood flying Mary's way and somehow, he managed to grab hold of her left ankle.

'Where the fuck do you think you're going?'

Fueled only by panic, Mary kicked out her legs in utter desperation – once, twice, three times – that was when her left foot connected with Quaddra's nose. The wound already on its bridge sliced open even more, and Quaddra, with another guttural scream of pain, let go of Mary's leg, bringing both hands to his face. Blood dripped from his hand, nose and shoulder, creating a small red and viscous pool on the kitchen floor. Mary desperately back-crawled some more, her legs still kicking wildly, until she was out of reach from Quaddra's arms.

The knife that had scattered from her hand had ended up by the fridge, which was where Mary had managed to back crawl to. She grabbed it again, and with her back pressed tightly against the fridge, extended her right arm out to defend herself one more time, but Quaddra was still where she'd left him – by the kitchen island – holding both hands to his face.

That was Mary's chance.

Using mostly her left leg, and with a little help from the fridge handle, she managed to pull herself up and back to her feet, but as she did, she saw that Quaddra was also getting back up. The veins in his arms looked pumped, as if he'd just finished a heavy workout. Blood covered his face like a mask, but it was the pure rage and anger that burned in his eyes that truly terrified Mary. She needed to get out of there, and she needed to get out of there now.

'I'm going to bleed you dry,' Quaddra said, as he tried to launch himself at Mary one more time, but as he did, he stepped straight into the small pool of blood that he had created on the kitchen floor. His foot slipped awkwardly and he crashed down again . . . hard.

Now this really was Mary's chance.

Fucked up knee or not, Mary turned around and ran out of that kitchen as fast as her legs would carry her.

Out of breath and in pain, she ran past the stairwell that led upstairs and crossed the living room in a hobbling sprint, but it was only when she reached the entry lobby that hope seemed to come back to her. Through the glass panels that flanked their mansion's front door, Mary could see red and blue flashing lights approaching the house. The 911 call had connected. An operator had been on the line and heard everything that was going on in that kitchen.

In tears, half naked and covered in blood, Mary opened the front door and ran outside, straight into freedom … or so she thought.

Ninety-Four

As soon as Mary opened the door and stepped outside the house, spotlights from several police cars homed in on her.

'SFPD . . . freeze,' the first police officer yelled.

'He's in there,' Mary yelled back, throwing her left thumb over her shoulder. The lights were too bright for her to be able to properly see. 'He's in the kitchen.'

'Put down the knife,' a second police officer called. 'And get on the ground . . . NOW.'

'He's in there,' Mary yelled again, as tears overcame her, her voice breaking. 'He's in the kitchen.'

'Lady,' the first officer yelled again. 'I need you to put down the knife and lay down on the ground. I need you to do that now.'

It finally dawned on Mary what that scene would've looked like from their point of view – some hysterical woman, running out of the house, semi-naked, with her face, torso and legs covered in blood, and carrying a bloody knife in her hand – 'psycho killer alert'.

It was actually surprising that she hadn't been gunned down yet.

'OK . . .OK.' Mary threw the knife on the ground and lifted her hands, partially shielding her eyes from the bright spotlights. Only then could she see that there were three police cruisers in front of her house, and six handguns pointed straight at her.

'OK. Now slowly get down on your knees then lay flat on the ground . . . belly first.'

Mary hopped down onto her left knee. Her right one was still too tender for her to be able to bend it properly.

'Now lay flat on the ground, keep your chin pressed against it, and place your hands behind your back. Do it now.'

Mary did as she was told.

In seconds, a police officer was kneeling on her back before placing a pair of handcuffs around her wrists.

'Who else is in the house?' the officer asked.

'My husband,' Mary replied, her voice rushed and drowning in tears. 'Who was trying to kill me. He's a serial killer.'

'Your husband is a . . . serial killer?' the officer asked, a lilt of sarcasm in his voice.

'Yes,' Mary said, as the officer grabbed her by the arms and helped her to her feet. 'Check the basement in his office. The evidence is all there. He's murdered nineteen women.'

The officer locked eyes with Mary, and he must've seen the fear in them because he frowned at her.

'Go check,' Mary urged him. 'Please, go check.'

'First, I need to place you inside a cruiser while we check the house for any more occupants, perpetrators or victims, OK? You said that your husband is in the kitchen?'

'That was where he was . . . yes.'

'Anyone else?'

'No.'

'No more attackers . . . only you?'

'I'm not an attacker.' Mary's voice was desperate. 'I was defending myself.'

'OK.' The officer nodded. 'And your husband, what's his name?'

'Quaddra . . . Quaddra Buckner . . . but you have to check the basement . . . you have to.'

'Trust me,' the officer said, as he walked Mary to one of the police cars before helping her onto the backseat. 'We'll check everything. Don't worry, OK?' He paused and nodded at her. 'Give me a second.' He closed the door, without slamming it, and retrieved something from the cruiser's boot before opening the back door again. 'Here. Let me put this over you.' He was holding a police high-visibility coat.

Mary had been so terrified and confused that she'd forgotten that she was almost naked. She leaned forward on the seat and the officer placed the coat over her shoulders before zipping it up at the front.

'Are you hurt?' he asked. 'Do you need medical assistance?'

'No.' Mary shook her head. 'It's not my blood.' As soon as she said those words, she realized what they would sound like to a police officer.

The officer looked back at her with concern. 'So, I'm guessing that the blood on the knife that you were holding isn't yours either, right?'

'I was defending myself.' Mary began shivering again, but this time it wasn't fear, or cold. The shock of everything that had just happened to her was beginning to settle in.

'OK, you just sit tight,' the officer said, with a half nod. 'I'll be back.'

Mary had no idea of how long she sat on the backseat of that police cruiser, but it felt like an eternity. She saw one of the police cars leave and an ambulance arrive, closely followed by a new police car. This one wasn't a black and white unit. Its red and blue lights flashed from its front grill and from inside its windshield. Mary had seen enough movies to know that that was a detective's car, and she breathed out relief. The officer had probably found the basement and radioed it in. The two men who stepped out of the unmarked police car would be homicide detectives. Mary was sure of it. This nightmare was finally coming to an end.

Mary sat back on the seat and began concentrating on her breathing when she saw Quaddra, seemingly passed out, being wheeled out of the house and into the ambulance on a patient transport stretcher.

'What the fuck!' Mary's eyes followed the stretcher all the way from the house until the ambulance. 'Did Quaddra hit his head when he slipped on his own blood, or what?'

All of a sudden, the back door to the cruiser was pulled open again, startling Mary. It was the same police officer who had placed her on the backseat and covered her with the high-visibility coat.

'Did you find the basement?'

'Nope,' he replied, his eyes widening at her while he nodded. 'But I found a pretty battered and bloody victim in the kitchen. Stab wounds, funnily enough.'

'But it's there,' Mary practically yelled at the officer. 'The basement is there. Take me back inside and I can show you how to get . . .'

'I'm arresting you on suspicion of attempted murder,' the officer cut her short.

'What?' Mary's eyes ballooned up in their sockets. 'Attempted murder? I wasn't trying to kill him. He was trying to kill me. Didn't you hear the 911 call?'

'No,' the officer shot back. 'We don't listen to emergency calls. We respond to them.'

'So go listen to it. You'll see that . . .'

'Listen,' the officer interrupted Mary again. 'You have the right to remain silent. Anything you say can and will be used against you in a court of law . . .'

'Look,' Mary said back, her voice, once again, going up a pitch. 'You need to go back in there and check the basement. This is all wrong.'

'All I need to do is take you in to the station, lady,' the officer said, once he was done reading Mary her rights. 'Which I'm going to do right now.' He closed the door on her.

Seconds later, the officer and his partner got into the driver and passenger's seats.

'If I were you,' the driver said, addressing Mary again, as he started the cruiser, 'I'd start thinking about a lawyer ... and a very good one.'

Ninety-Five

Mary didn't have a lawyer, at least not one who she kept on a retainer. She'd never had any need for one. If her wedding con had gone to plan, the case itself would've sequestered the services of the District Attorney's office, and she would have the top prosecutors in the state fighting for her.

This was different.

But the police officer was right. If she didn't manage to clear this up quickly, she would need a defense lawyer, and a very good one at that.

At the police station, before putting Mary into a holding cell, they took her mugshot and collected her fingerprints, her DNA and samples of the blood on her skin for further analysis. Throughout the entire process, Mary didn't say a word. She didn't ask for her phone call either ... not yet. What she did do was try her best to organize her thoughts and come up with a plan of action.

As it stood, Mary was staring into an abyss.

Circumstantial evidence put her at the wrong end of events ... and that evidence had been witnessed by police officers. All they saw was a hysterical, semi-naked woman come running out of a house, half covered in blood, and holding a knife ... a knife that she *had* used to stab Quaddra with. As the officers entered the house, they would've found Quaddra on the floor inside the kitchen, swimming in a pool of his own blood.

Yes, there was the 911 call, which would score a few points for Mary, but Quaddra was a very intelligent man. He had probably shut the door to the secret basement once he came up from there, before following Mary into the kitchen – that was why the officers hadn't found the basement yet. Once the officers found Quaddra in the kitchen, he certainly flipped the story around because in all honesty, he was the one injured, not Mary. It would've been very easy for him to spin a tale saying that she had gone mental on him and tried to stab him to death out of jealousy . . . greed . . . revenge . . . whatever . . . and that was why Mary was in that holding cell, instead of Quaddra.

'Fuck!' she cursed under her breath, as she buried her head in her hands. The way Mary saw it, it didn't matter if she had a top defense lawyer or not, her only chance of getting out of this crazy mess was if she managed to convince a police officer, a detective, a CSI agent, whoever she could, to go back to the house and check the basement before Quaddra was discharged from the hospital. If Quaddra got back to the house first, he would need just minutes to take down that entire wall and make that computer with all that footage disappear. Once that was done, there would be no evidence of his crimes . . . and Mary wouldn't be staring into an abyss anymore – she'd be falling into it, headfirst.

She needed to act *now.*

'Hey, I need to talk to someone,' Mary called at the top of her voice, as she got to her feet, ready to slam her fists against the heavy cell door when she heard it being unlocked.

'Let's go,' a young police officer said, with a jerk of the head, as he pulled open the door.

'Go where?'

'Interrogation room,' the officer replied, signaling her to put her hands together so that he could cuff her again. 'A detective wants to talk to you.'

Mary breathed in hope. 'About fucking time.'

Ninety-Six

The interrogation room looked exactly like the ones that Mary had seen in so many movies before – rectangular, small, claustrophobic, with a metal table at the center of it, a large two-way mirror along one of its walls and, in the corner of the room, a video camera mounted high on the wall. The fluorescent light beaming down from the ceiling was at least fifty watts brighter than usual – designed to make the person being interrogated uncomfortable.

The officer sat Mary down at the table, but didn't uncuff her hands. 'A detective will be with you shortly.'

As soon as the officer left the room, closing the door behind him, Mary got to her feet and approached the two-way mirror.

'Look,' she addressed the mirror. 'There's no need for anyone behind this mirror to leave me simmering here for God-knows-how-long before coming in to talk to me. I've seen too many movies to know that that is standard practice. I know that first you're supposed to observe my movements for signs of guilt before coming in here, but let me tell you right now – we're losing valuable time. I have extremely important information that needs to be acted on now. And I mean *now*. If you guys miss this, a serial killer will walk free.' She paused, trying to steady her voice. 'Yes, you've heard it right – a *serial killer*. This isn't a desperation play . . . this is fucking real. I promise you.'

Mary stayed facing the mirror for half a minute before sitting back down. Five seconds after that, the door to the interrogation room was pulled open again and a tall African-American man entered the room. He was dressed in a dark-gray suit that seemed too small for his frame. Mary had seen him before. He was one of the two men from the unmarked police car at her house, earlier that evening.

'Mary Buckner?' he asked, and Mary felt a sting in her heart at the sound of that name. 'I'm Detective William Kendall with the San Francisco Police Department.'

'Nice to meet you,' Mary said back, her voice anxious. 'We really need to talk.'

'So, it seems,' Kendall said back, as he took a seat across the table from her.

'What time is it?' Mary asked.

'Why, do you have somewhere you need to be?'

'Please,' Mary said, her head shaking and dropping down half an inch, in a disapproving gesture. 'We can play whichever silly power game you want to play later, but right now, all that we'll be doing is wasting time. I just asked for the time. It's not a tricky question.'

Kendall held Mary's stare for a little longer before finally checking his watch. 'It's 2:33 a.m.'

'And where's Quaddra?' Mary asked with more than enough urgency in her voice. 'Is he still at the hospital?'

'Are you referring to the person who we found stabbed in the kitchen . . . back in the house that you came running out of with a bloody knife?' Kendall asked back.

'Yes.' Mary's eyebrows angled up as she nodded once. 'Quaddra . . . my husband . . . the man you found in the kitchen. I saw him being carried out on a medical stretcher. I assume that he was taken to the hospital.'

'That's correct,' Kendall confirmed. 'It looks like you did a pretty good number on him. There was a lot of blood in that kitchen – all of it his.'

Mary leaned forward and placed her elbows on the table. 'Is he still in the hospital, or has he gone back to the house?'

'Why do you care? Is it because you failed to kill him? Want to try again?'

'I was defending myself.'

Kendall angled his body to one side to look at Mary. 'It doesn't really look that way, does it?' His voice was calm, his tone condescending. 'The person you stabbed is pretty physically fit . . . quite muscly too. Are you telling me that you got into a physical altercation with him and he's all banged up and cut, being all stitched up in the emergency ward while you . . .' He pursed his lips while he looked at Mary again. 'Don't seem to have a scratch on you? That's pretty hard to believe. Unless you're a secret ninja.' He moved his hands about, mimicking karate chops. 'Is that who you are, Mary Buckner . . . a ninja?'

'I know how this looks, OK? And I can explain everything to you in a moment, but right now I really need to know if he's still at the hospital or if he's gone back to the house . . . please, this really is important.'

The desperation in Mary's eyes was real.

Kendall stared straight into them. 'Why?' he asked, sitting back on his chair. 'Why is it so important? What difference does it make?'

'It makes *all* the difference,' Mary replied in an urgent voice before proceeding to tell him about the secret basement, the Polaroids . . . the trophies . . . the computer . . . the video . . . everything. 'If he gets back to the house before you guys get to that basement,' Mary said in conclusion, 'he'll get rid of all the evidence down there.' Her eyes filled up with tears again. 'I'm telling you . . . please . . . if he's still in the hospital . . . please go back to the house and check it for yourself – bottom right-hand drawer on the Victorian chest inside his office, which is to the right of the main stairwell. You've got to do it before he gets back.'

Kendall had listened to Mary's story in complete silence, his eyes carefully studying her expressions, her movements, her breathing . . . all of it. When she was done, he kept his eyes on her for several extra seconds before they moved to the two-way mirror, as if he could see through it.

'I'm not going anywhere,' Mary added. 'You already have me. I'm cuffed and in a holding cell. All I'm asking is for you to go check. The house is just about a mile from here. It will take you five minutes to drive there at this time.'

Mary was right, they had taken her to the San Francisco Northern District Police Station, which was just about a mile from Pacific Heights.

'If you don't go check,' she continued, 'trust me . . . a crazy psychopath will walk away free . . . and he's going to kill again.'

Kendall sat forward and rested his elbows on the table, interlacing his fingers together in front of him. He didn't say a word. He simply stared into Mary's eyes so intensely, it was as if he could read her soul.

Mary didn't shy away from his stare.

Still in silence, Kendall got to his feet and walked over to the door. 'For your sake,' he said, as he pulled the door open, 'you better not be lying.'

Ninety-Seven

Detective Kendall parked his Dodge Challenger in the exact same spot where he had parked earlier – just a little to the left of Quaddra and Mary's front door.

Before leaving the station, just about five minutes ago, he got in touch with the hospital at UCSF, where Quaddra had been taken to. To prevent him from entering hypovolemic shock, Quaddra had to be put on a blood drip, and he would have to spend the night in observation, which meant that there was no danger of him coming back to the house before morning.

Back at the station, Kendall had also asked his partner, Detective Derek Choi, what he thought of Mary's story. Choi had been the one sitting on the other side of the two-way mirror, while Kendall talked to Mary.

'She was too rattled up for me to get a good reading on her,' Choi had replied. Derek Choi was an expert when it came to reading and interpreting body language. No one could really lie to him for too long before he started picking up on telltale signs. 'But if she's lying, then she's a great actress.'

'That's what I thought,' Kendall had agreed.

'And also a bit stupid,' Choi had added. 'If this was a murder attempt gone wrong and she was trying to come up with an excuse for it, then the easiest thing to do would be to go with abusive husband. Simple story – he hit her one too many times and she finally fought back. That story would fly, even if it wasn't completely true, but making up a serial killer story?'

'Not only that,' Kendal had countered, 'but also making up a secret room – 007-style. If that room and those photographs aren't there, she's going down for first-degree attempted murder. In California, that's life inside.'

Both detectives agreed that Mary was right – they couldn't really let her story slide without at least checking it out.

'Office to the right of the stairwells, right?' Choi asked, as he closed the passenger door behind him.

'That's what she said,' Kendall confirmed.

They entered the house and slowly crossed the living room, heading towards the stairs. Choi hit every light switch he found on the way. At the stairwell, they veered right, and at the door to Quaddra's office they found the first full droplets of blood on the floor. This wasn't where any of the stabbing wounds had occurred – both detectives knew that – there was no blood splatter on the walls or on the door. These were merely blood drops from an already open wound – somebody had walked in or out of that office, dripping blood.

On the floor, in the living room, they had also encountered a faint blood trail, but those weren't droplets – they weren't left there by a bleeder – those were blood smears, left there via transference.

'This is the office,' Kendall said, pushing the door open.

Choi hit the light switch.

More blood droplets on the floor, and funnily enough, they seemed to be coming from the file cabinet pushed up against the south wall.

'Now this is getting interesting,' Kendall said, referring to the blood trail.

'Let's see,' Choi replied, kneeling down by the Victorian chest of drawers to the left of the door. 'Bottom right-hand drawer, right?' He reached for the handle. 'And twist the handle clockwise.'

Click.

Both detectives looked right, in the direction of the cabinet.

'I'll be rubbed with salt and laid on the grill,' Choi said, straightening up his body. 'It's a fucking secret door. Just like she said.'

'Uh-huh.' Kendall nodded.

They approached the cabinet and pulled it open. The light on the stairwell and downstairs activated. More blood droplets on the steps.

'Well, fuck me!' Kendall said before he and Choi pulled out their service weapons at the same time.

'SFPD,' Kendall called in a loud and firm voice. 'Is anyone down there?'

No reply.

'San Francisco Police Department,' Choi, this time. 'Is there anyone in the basement?'

Silence.

They nodded at each other and began taking the steps down one at a time and very slowly – Kendall ahead of Choi. As the stairwell snaked right on itself, Kendall stopped and called again.

'SFPD. We're coming into the basement. Is anyone here?'

Not a peep.

Kendall signaled Choi that he was about to have a look.

Choi got ready.

In a very quick dip-in movement, Kendall stuck his head around to look at the basement before dipping out again. He shook his head at Choi. 'It looks clear, but I'll look again.'

He repeated the movement, keeping his head in the 'dip-in' position for a little longer this time. He couldn't see anything. He nodded at Choi and both detectives carried on taking the steps down. As they finally reached the basement, Kendall quickly veered sharp right and Choi sharp left, checking the walls to the right and left of the stairs. There were no other hiding places in that basement.

'Clear,' Kendall called.

'Clear,' Choi replied.

They both holstered their weapons before focusing their attention on the wall directly in front of them.

'Holy fucking shit!'

Ninety-Eight

At 6:00 a.m., Mary was given a breakfast tray containing a bowl of oatmeal porridge, some coffee, and a small bottle of water.

At 8:00 a.m., a police officer asked her if she wanted to make use of her phone call.

'Detective Kendall,' she asked back, instead of answering the question. 'Is he in?'

'I haven't seen him this morning,' the officer replied.

'What the fuck is going on?' Mary asked herself, trying to figure out why Detective Kendall hadn't come back to her first, apologize for arresting her, and, second, to thank her for leading him to a serial killer who they had no idea existed. She came up with only two answers to that question – either Detective Kendall had bullshitted her about going back to the house to check for the basement, or they were still there, with CSI . . . FBI . . . DA's office . . . the lot . . . trying to understand the hell-room that they had just stumbled upon.

'Do you want to use your phone call or not?' the officer tried again.

'Yes,' Mary replied. She had no idea what was going on, but it was better to have someone by her side than not.

The officer guided Mary back to the same room where she had been fingerprinted and photographed.

'You can make *one* call.' He indicated a wall phone. 'Five

minutes.' The officer didn't leave the room. He simply stepped back and leaned, shoulder first, against the wall.

Mary picked up the receiver and brought it to her ear. She didn't have her cellphone with her and by heart, she only knew three numbers – Quaddra's private number, Denise's burner cell and Dr. Fox's personal number. She dialed Dr. Fox's.

'Hello?' Dr. Fox picked up after the second ring.

'Dr. Fox? It's Mary . . . Mary Smith.' Mary had never given Dr. Fox her new married name. 'I need your help.' The urgency and desperation in her tone was almost palpable.

'Mary, are you OK? What's going on? How can I help? Is this to do with your friend? The one with the photos in the basement?'

'Yes,' Mary replied, as she felt a rush of chemicals wash over her body. 'Did you have a chance to look inside the package that I gave you yesterday?'

'I did.' Dr. Fox's voice tensed up. *'You should've come clean about your husband earlier, Mary. I could've helped you.'*

'I know,' Mary interrupted her. 'I just thought that this time it would be different, you know?' She lied again. 'I really wanted it to be different, but after I found that basement, I just knew it wouldn't be.'

'Hold on a sec, Mary.' Dr. Fox's tone went from tense to anxious. *'Are you telling me that that basement with the photographs is in YOUR house? The friend you mentioned . . . that's – YOUR husband?'*

'Yes.'

'Jesus Christ, Mary. Are you OK? Are you hurt? Are you in the house right now?'

'That's why I need your help, Doc.' Mary proceeded to tell Dr. Fox everything that had happened since last night, followed by where she was at the moment. 'Could you please contact a lawyer for me. Don't worry about the fees. I can afford it. Just please get someone with tons of experience.'

'Yes . . . of course.'

'And could you please bring that package over to the station. I think that they will want to see those Polaroids and listen to those Dictaphone tapes.'

'You don't have a backup?' Dr. Fox sounded surprised.

'No,' Mary told her. 'That's why they are Polaroid photos and analog tapes, Doc. Their format alone testifies to their veracity.'

'I understand . . . and of course I can bring them to you. I can be there in an hour . . . an hour and a half . . . tops.'

'Thank you, Doc. I really owe you for this one.' Mary disconnected from the call.

Ninety-Nine

Another half an hour went by before another officer opened the door to Mary's holding cell once again.

'Let's go,' he said, gesturing for her to stand up and follow him.

'Where am I going this time?'

'Back to the interrogation room,' the officer told her. 'A couple of detectives want to speak to you again.'

'Fucking finally.'

This time, Detective Kendall was already in the interrogation room, waiting for Mary. Sitting to his left was a much shorter man – Korean descendancy – with a number four crew cut and an ill-fitting dark suit. They both looked tired, their eyes bloodshot, as if they'd been up all night.

'Mrs. Buckner,' Kendall said, as soon as the officer guided Mary into the room. He didn't stand up. 'Please have a seat.' He indicated the chair across the table from him. 'This is my partner, Detective Derek Choi.'

Choi also didn't stand.

'Did you find the basement?' Mary asked, even before taking her seat.

'Oh, we found it, alright,' Choi replied, and the way his eyes pinged to Kendall for a millisecond made Mary frown at them.

'So, you found the photos and the computer?' She sat down and allowed her gaze to skip between the two detectives for an instant.

'We did,' Kendall confirmed, his stare moving to the large manila envelope on the table, sitting between him and Choi. 'I'm sorry it took us so long to get back to you – there was a lot that needed checking out first.'

Mary let go of the biggest relief breath she'd ever held, before slumping back on her chair. 'Oh, thank God.' She locked Kendall in a 'I told you so' stare. 'And you're welcome.'

'Are you on any medication?' Choi asked.

Mary looked back at him completely confused. 'Excuse me . . . what?'

'Medication,' Choi repeated it. 'Are you on any? Something that you should've been taking, but you've been skipping it for a while?'

'What? No.' Mary addressed Kendall. 'What the hell is he talking about?'

Kendall sat forward, placing his arms on the table. 'The man you stabbed,' he began. 'You said that he is your husband, right?'

'I didn't just say it.' Irritation was clearly grabbing hold of Mary. 'He *is* my husband . . . for now.'

Kendall nodded. 'And you said his name is Quaddra Buckner, is that correct?'

'What is this bullshit?' Mary's eyes were still bouncing between the two detectives.

'Hey!' Kendall's voice was almost a shout, and it startled Mary. 'You asked us to go to the house and check the basement. We did. We did what you asked, so now, the least you can do is return the favor and answer our questions, because we've got plenty of them.'

Mary was starting to feel scared again.

'Are you on any medication?' Choi asked again.

'No . . . none.'

'And the man who you stabbed in the kitchen,' Kendall jumped in. 'That's your husband?'

'Yes . . . and his name is Quaddra – Quaddra Buckner.'

'So, if he's your husband,' Kendall carried on, 'then you must know what he does for a living, right?'

Mary sat still, staring at the detectives.

Kendall's eyebrows lifted at her as if asking "Well?"

'Yes, of course I know what he does for a living.'

'And what *does* he do?' Choi again.

'He's an entrepreneur . . .an investor. He's got businesses everywhere.'

'In Los Angeles?' Kendall asked.

'Yes.' Mary nodded. 'He's got a couple of movie production companies down in Los Angeles.'

Choi threw his hands up in the air, in a victory gesture. 'Finally, we seem to be getting somewhere.'

'What the hell does that mean?' Right then, Mary seemed to be made of confusion.

Kendall reached for the manila envelope on the table. 'What that means, Mary, is that we seem to have a big problem.'

One Hundred

Mary sat completely still, except for her eyes, which first narrowed at Detective Kendall, before bouncing over to Detective Choi, and finally to the manila envelope on the table.

'What problem?'

Kendall retrieved a photograph from inside the envelope and placed it on the table in front of Mary. It was a Polaroid photo of a woman – a facial shot. Her eyes were open, and all that Mary could really see in them was fear. She had seen that same Polaroid photo before – on the wall down in Quaddra's basement.

'Do you know this woman?' Kendall asked.

'No,' Mary shook her head. 'I don't, but I'm sure that she was one of the women on the wall down in that basement. Just like I told you.'

'She was,' Choi confirmed.

'So, what's the problem?' Mary asked, her eyes wide, her head shaking ever so slightly.

Kendall retrieved several other Polaroid photos from the envelope, placing them all on the table in front of Mary. They all followed the exact same pattern as the columns in Quaddra's wall – three facial close-ups, to start, then photos of the hands, body, bare feet and, finally, another facial close-up – the cadaver shot.

'Yes,' Mary said firmly. 'That was exactly what I told you – the photos displayed in columns – each column representing a different woman . . . a different victim.'

'And you have no idea who she is?' Choi, this time.

'No. I've never seen her before. The first time I saw her was in these photos, on the wall down in that fucking basement.'

Kendall retrieved another photo from the envelope. This one, Mary had never seen before. It wasn't a Polaroid. It was a headshot – the type used by casting companies, model agencies and movie studios. The woman on the photo was the same woman from the Polaroids.

'What the hell is this?' Mary asked, frowning at the photo.

'You haven't seen this photo before?' Kendall asked.

'No.'

'It was on the wall,' Choi informed Mary. 'Together with all the Polaroids. This was the very first photo right at the top of the columns you mentioned. Every column had one.'

'What?'

The two detectives exchanged a concerned look.

'So, you're telling me that you saw all the Polaroids on that wall,' Choi pressed. 'But you didn't see this?'

Mary felt a shiver grab hold of her. 'No, that photo was *not* on that wall. And what are you talking about – every column had one.'

'Her name is Elena Muñoz,' Kendall took over. 'She's an actress based in Los Angeles.'

Confusion seemed to form an aura around Mary.

'We spoke to her about an hour or so ago,' Choi tipped in. 'She's alive and well.'

'You guys are kidding, right?'

'Do we look like we're kidding?' Choi asked.

Kendall grabbed another set of Polaroids from the envelope – same exact pattern – face, hands, body, bare feet and face again. 'How about her? Do you know her?'

'No.' The word came out with a deflated breath.

Kendall placed another model agency headshot on the table – the same woman as the Polaroids. 'Kaitlin Morse,' he told Mary. 'Also an actress based in LA. Also very alive and well. You didn't see this picture on the wall either?'

Tears welled up in Mary's eyes. 'No. That wasn't on that wall.'

Kendall retrieved a third set from the envelope – exactly the same as the previous two, followed by another headshot. 'Amanda Carrillo,' he said. 'Another actress from LA, who's living the dream down there. Emphasis on "living".' He fixed Mary with a laser stare. 'Shall I continue? Because I've got sixteen more in here?'

'I . . .' Mary stuttered. 'I don't understand.'

'These women,' Choi tried to explain. 'All of them. All nineteen women showing on the wall in that basement.' He tapped the envelope with his right hand. 'All of these women . . . they're actresses . . . and they're all alive and well.' He gave Mary a few seconds so that his words could sink in. 'Do you know what your "husband's" production company's main source of income is?' He used his fingers to draw air quotes when he mentioned the word husband. 'I mean, what type of movies they produce the most?'

Mary had never really talked to Quaddra about that. She had never really talked to Quaddra about any of his businesses. 'No,' she replied, her voice faltering. 'As a rule, we never talked about work at home.'

'That's a good rule,' Choi agreed. 'Pretty convenient too.'

'Horror films,' Kendall offered in explanation. 'B-type movies, slasher movies, silly gore . . . that kind of stuff.'

Mary heard the words, but her brain was having a hard time understanding them.

'All the photos on that wall,' Choi continued. 'Were test shots for one of the company's productions – a serial killer TV series – eight episodes. The production company, or your "husband" . . .'

He drew air quotes again. '... needed a different actress for each episode – eight in total – in case you forgot how to count. The photos were splashed over the wall in that basement to ease the selection process for your "husband".' Air quotes again.

'But he confessed,' Mary blurted out, her tone dripping anxiety. 'Quaddra confessed to murdering all of those women.' She pointed at the envelope. 'Did you hear the 911 call? It's all there. He said it loud and clear while we were in the kitchen. He said that he had to kill them all, in the same way that he would have to kill me.'

Kendall and Choi exchanged a new look that Mary wasn't able to decipher.

'Did you hear the 911 call?' Mary asked again, her voice reaching a new octave.

'We did,' Kendall confirmed, while reaching inside his jacket pocket for his cellphone. 'We actually have it here.' He called up an application on his phone, placed it on the table, and hit the "play" button. 'Have a listen.'

> *'Nine-one-one, what's your emergency?'* The dispatch operator's voice came through the tiny speakers at the bottom of the phone.
>
> 'There's an intruder in my house,' a desperate male voice replied – Quaddra's voice. 'A woman ... she's gone mad. She's trying to kill me. Please help.'

'*What?*' If disbelief had a human form, it would be Mary right at that moment.

Kendall lifted a hand at her, indicating that there was more.

> *'What's your address, sir?'*
>
> Quaddra rattled the address in a shaky voice.
>
> *'Are you in the house right now?'*

'Yes. I'm hiding. I'm in the kitchen. But she's going to find me.'

'OK, I need you to stay hidden and stay on the line with me, OK? Units are on their way to you right now. They'll be there in less than five minutes. Are you hurt?'

'Yes. I walked in on her in my office, and she slammed me across the face with something. I'm bleeding, badly, and I feel really dizzy. My eyes are completely out of focus. I can't . . . Oh fuck, she's here. She's got a knife. Arghhh, arghhh, arghhh . . .'

A loud noise followed, as if the phone had been smashed against the ground.

Kendall stopped the recording. 'The call was placed at 12:38 a.m.' He informed Mary. 'Five minutes before uniforms showed up in response.'

'There's no other 911 call for that address?' Mary asked, her voice weak.

'Nope,' Choi replied. 'This was the only recorded call.'

In the kitchen, last night, Mary had dropped the phone just as she had dialed 911 . . . just as Quaddra had gotten to the kitchen. She had hoped that the call had connected, and she was pretty certain that it had once she saw the flashing police lights outside, but they weren't there because of her call. They were there because of his. Her call had never connected.

'That's not right,' Mary said, shaking her head at both detectives. 'That was a fake call.'

'It sounds pretty legit to us,' Choi said. 'Especially because that was exactly what several SFPD officers encountered as they arrived at the house – you, covered in the caller's blood, holding the knife that you had used to stab him with.'

To Mary nothing made sense anymore. She could understand that Quaddra had weaved a pretty believable story to the detectives to try to get him off the hook – the women on those Polaroids weren't victims . . . they were actresses on test shots for one of his company's productions . . . the same with the video or videos in that computer . . . just test reels – but where had those headshots come from? The detectives had said that they found them on the wall, right at the top of each column, but Mary knew that that wasn't true – those headshots weren't on that wall down in that basement – so how the hell did they get there? There was no way that Quaddra had time to stick nineteen headshots to that wall before he came after Mary in the kitchen. And even if he had somehow miraculously stopped time to add those headshots to that wall, they would've been covered in blood . . . because his hands were covered in blood. And who were the women that the detectives talked to on the phone? They said that they contacted all the actresses on those Polaroids and they were all alive and well. How was that possible?

'My cellphone,' Mary said, her pleading eyes meeting Kendall's stare.

'What?' he asked.

'I threw my cellphone at Quaddra just as he was about to attack me when we were in the basement,' Mary explained. 'Did you find a cellphone on the floor somewhere? I took pictures of that wall before he came after me. I can prove that those headshots weren't there. They weren't at the top of each column like you said they were. And I never stopped recording when we were down there. You'll be able to hear exactly what happened.'

'No cellphone,' Choi replied.

Kendall shook his head. 'No, there was nothing on the floor in that basement except for blood.'

For the second time in less than twenty-four hours, Mary felt hope leave her.

'Look,' Choi took over. 'Why don't you just come clean and save us all a lot of hassle and a lot of shitty hours locked in this room? Tell us why you wanted to kill him? Was he an abusive ex-boyfriend? Someone who dumped you and you wanted your revenge?'

'I was defending myself,' Mary told them again, as tears finally broke through.

'That story won't fly, Mary,' Choi said in return before pointing out the obvious. 'You don't have a scratch on you, while the dude in the hospital is covered in defensive wounds.' He lifted his arms at her, simulating a person trying to defend himself from a knife attack. 'Hands . . . arms . . .shoulders the lot. We have the 911 call with him begging for help and saying that a crazy woman was trying to kill him in his house . . . we have the attack weapon, covered in his blood and *your* fingerprints . . . and we have six police officers who witnessed you exiting the house carrying that weapon.'

'Arms?' Mary asked, her eyes jittering from one detective to another. 'I never touched his arms. And he was reaching for my throat. I got lucky placing the blade between his hand and my throat.'

Choi sniggered. 'Are you saying that you just held the knife up and he *ran* into the blade?'

'I know it sounds crazy . . .'

'Oh, you think?' Choi cut her short. 'Just tell us straight, Mary – you went into that house to kill that guy.'

'Quaddra,' Mary said, her tone a crazy mix of anger and fear. 'I've told you his name a thousand times. And he's not "that guy", he's my husband.'

'You see,' Choi said, as he pressed his lips together and nodded back at Mary. 'This is why I asked you if you were on any medications . . . maybe something anti-psychotic?'

'I'm not psychotic, and I'm not on any medications.' Irritation clearly coming through in Mary's tone.

'So, tell me something,' Kendall said, as he reached for

something else from the envelope before placing it on the table, facing Mary. This time, he retrieved an enlarged photocopy of a California driver's license. 'If you're not psychotic and you're not lying, why do you keep on calling him Quaddra when his name is Thomas – Thomas Cameron.'

One Hundred and One

Mary's surprised and questioning eyes stayed on the driver's license photocopy for several long seconds. All the information about Quaddra was correct – date and city of birth, address, and it was definitely Quaddra on the photograph, except the name read Thomas Cameron . . . not Quaddra Buckner. 'That's fake,' she said, shaking her head at the detectives. 'It's got to be.'

Choi's eyebrows lifted at her.

'You don't understand,' Mary tried to remedy an argument that had already gone sideways yesterday. 'Thomas is just a name that he uses when he doesn't want anyone to know who he is.'

Kendall and Choi looked at each other.

'A name that he uses when he doesn't want anyone to know who he is?' Choi asked. 'In your head, *that* doesn't sound crazy?'

'It's legit,' Kendal said, nodding at the photocopy. 'We've checked it.'

What the fuck is going on here? the voice inside Mary's head asked.

'Shall we talk about all the photos on the other wall?' Kendall took over again, reaching for a second manila envelope, which he had kept on the floor by his chair.

Mary frowned back at him so hard, her eyebrows almost touched at the center of her forehead. 'What photos? And what other wall?'

'The one to the right of the wall with all the test shots for the serial killer series?' Choi replied, pointing at the first manila envelope that contained all the Polaroids they'd just shown Mary.

'What about the wall to the right of it? What photos are you talking about?'

'The ones displayed on it?' Choi's intrigued stare zoomed in on Mary. 'Or are you also trying to tell us that you didn't see those either . . . just like you didn't see the headshots at the head of all those Polaroid columns.'

'There were no photos on the wall to the right of the one with the Polaroids,' Mary said, fighting back tears once again.

'Evidence to the contrary,' Kendall said, placing the second manila envelope on the table.

Mary's attention crawled to it and despite not having a clue what was inside that envelope, fear began spreading to every corner of her body.

Kendall reached into the second envelope and brought out ten new photographs. None of them were Polaroids – these were all A4-sized, colored, portrait photographs, which he placed on the table in two rows – five photos each.

'Do you recognize any of these people?'

Mary's attention returned to the table, and she felt her jaw muscles tightening.

Choi was attentively studying Mary's every reaction, every movement, every expression. He knew that she had recognized at least some of the people on those photos even before she answered the question.

'What the fuck?' Mary said under her breath, as her gaze moved from one photo to the other.

'You recognize them?' Kendall pushed.

'Yes,' Mary finally replied. 'Everyone but these two.' She indicated the last photo on the second row. It was the only photo in the whole group that showed two people in the same photograph, the remaining nine were individual portrait shots. The photo that Mary had indicated was of a couple – a man and a woman together. He was an older gentleman, mid-sixties perhaps, with a clean-shaven head. His ears looked a little odd – too big for his head – as if they'd been glued on. The woman had dark hair, a hawk-style nose, and she looked to be at least fifteen years younger than the 'big ears' gentleman. They did look vaguely familiar, but Mary was too confused by all the other photos to be able to search her memory.

'Who are the people you recognize?' Choi asked, gesturing broadly at the photos. 'Can you tell us?'

Mary started with the top row, moving from left to right. 'Antonia and Gabriela are our housemaids.' She indicated as she spoke. 'Jonas takes care of the garden, the pool and everything else that needs fixing around the house. These are all Quaddra's friends – Brian, Tyler, Richard, Carol, Rachel and Kathy. Kathy and Tyler are married.'

Choi nodded as he jotted down every name Mary mentioned. Neither he nor Kendall seemed to care that she was still insisting on using the name Quaddra instead of Thomas. 'But this couple on the last picture,' Choi asked. 'You have no idea who they are?'

'No.'

'OK,' Kendall collected all the photographs from the table before selecting a brand-new one from the envelope. Once again, this was an A4-sized, colored, portrait photograph. He placed it on the table, in front of Mary.

Her eyes moved to the photo and her heart skipped a beat. 'What is happening here?'

'Do you know this man?' Kendall asked.

'Yes,' Mary said back, blinking and shaking her head as if she was waking up from an odd dream. 'His name is Luke Jenkins. He's a country singer/songwriter who I met in Nashville over two years ago. What is this?'

'Luke Jenkins, you said?' Choi asked, writing down the name.

'Yes.' Mary looked back at the detectives. 'But what does he have to do with any of this?'

Kendall didn't reply. Instead, he reached inside the envelope for a new portrait photograph – also in color . . . also A4 in size – before placing it on the table.

Mary looked down at the photo and frowned. This time, she was looking at a photo of a blonde woman, whose wavy hair just touched her shoulders. Her eyes were blue, but not as blue as Mary's, and they seemed kind and intelligent. Mary was sure that she'd seen her before. She just couldn't remember where, or when.

'Does she look familiar?' Choi asked, reading Mary's reaction.

'Umm . . .' Mary shrugged, still searching her memory. 'She does . . . a little . . . yes, but I can't . . .' All of a sudden, it came back to her. 'Oh my god.' She pointed at the photo. 'Yes. I met her in New Orleans.' She took a pause to properly remember. 'I think it was about two months or so after I met Luke.'

'Do you remember where in New Orleans you met her?' Kendall asked.

'Yes, I met her in a bar called Lafitte's Blacksmith Shop.'

'Lafitte's Blacksmith Shop,' Choi repeated it, as he wrote the name down.

'Yes, this woman . . .' She tapped the photo with her index finger. 'Was also there . . . by herself. Her name is . . .' Mary closed her eyes and searched her memory once again. It took her a few seconds. 'Natálie.' She snapped her fingers and pointed at the photo again. 'Yes, her name is Natálie. She was visiting from London. We shared a table in the bar and had a few drinks together.' Mary paused and lifted a hand at the detectives. 'Why? What do she and Luke have to do with any of this? And how did you get these photos?'

'From the basement that you told us to go look.' The reply

came from Choi. 'These photos were on the wall to the right of the one with all the Polaroids, but apparently, you never saw them.'

'Because they weren't there,' Mary shot back. 'They weren't there last night.'

'So how come they were there when we got back to the house to check the secret basement, like you told us to, just a couple of hours after we arrested you?'

'I don't know.'

'You said that you and Mr. Cameron . . . or Quaddra . . . were the only two people in the house, right?' Choi pushed.

'Yes.'

'So how did these photos come to be on that wall, all neatly spread out into a coherent storyboard and timeline?'

'A what?' A pit opened up at the bottom of Mary's stomach. 'A storyboard and timeline?'

'Just like the ones you see in films,' Kendall confirmed, gesturing as he explained. 'With colored strings linking photos together and all.'

How's that even possible? the voice inside Mary's head asked. *Why would Quaddra have these photos?*

Kendal clearly wasn't done yet, as he, once again, reached inside the envelope for a new photograph.

Mary chuckled nervously, as he placed the picture on the table. This time she didn't need to search her memory for who the person in that photograph was. She was looking at Betsy – Betsy Fletcher – the waitress that she'd met at the Jolt N Bolt bakery in the Dogpatch. The same Betsy who had invited her to the exhibition where she met Quaddra for the first time.

'From your reaction,' Choi said, resting his elbows on the table. 'I take it you know her.'

'Yes, I know her,' Mary confirmed. 'Her name is Betsy Fletcher. She's an artist.'

'From San Francisco?' Kendall asked.

'She used to live here, yes,' Mary replied. 'But she's moved to LA.' She sat back on her chair and once again, raised her hands at Kendall and Choi. 'Look, I'm seriously very confused here. You first show me all the Polaroids I found down in that basement before telling me that all of those women aren't dead . . . they are, in fact, actresses auditioning for a role. Now you're showing me all these photos from completely random people, who I've met sometime in the past two years, telling me that these photos were also down in that basement, arranged in some kind of storyboard. I don't know what's going on here.'

'Don't you?' Choi challenged.

'No. I don't.' Fear was starting to take hold of Mary's tone as well.

'After we left the house,' Kendall took over again, 'we had to drop by the hospital to have a chat with Mr. Cameron – the man you stabbed.'

This time, Mary didn't try to correct him.

'There was a lot that needed clearing up,' Kendall continued. 'The Polaroids . . . the storyboard . . . that basement . . . nothing was really making a lot of sense.'

'That's exactly what I'm saying,' Mary agreed, wondering if either of the detectives had listened to anything she'd said.

'Oh, but it will,' Kendall told her. 'And here's where this story jumps from the crazy to the absolutely fucking insane.'

One Hundred and Two

The pit inside Mary's stomach began turning into an abyss. How could any of this get any more insane?

'There are four more photos I'd like to show you before we move on,' Kendall said, retrieving the four new images from the same envelope and placing them on the table, once again, in a single row. 'These are a bit of a conundrum to us, and we were wondering if maybe you can help us out.'

Mary's confused stare moved to the four new photos on the table, while Choi's analytical eyes moved back to her. She blinked, frowned, bit her bottom lip, then blinked again.

The first photo on the far left was a photo of a CD case – Luke Jenkins' CD – the same CD that he'd handed her back in Nashville . . . the same CD that she'd listened to tens of times.

The second photo was also of Luke's CD case, but the case was open, and it had been picked apart – disk tray pulled from the back cover. In between the disk tray, which was dark in color, and the back cover, Mary could see what looked to be a computer chip, attached to a small, round battery. With the disk tray in place – clicked onto the back cover – the chip and battery would be completely hidden away.

'What is this?' Mary asked, pointing at the chip.

'It's a GPS tracker,' Choi told her.

Mary's eyes shot to him. 'A what?'

'A GPS tracker,' he told her again before explaining. 'It pings out a location signal every few seconds, or minutes . . . it depends on how it's programmed. It sends out the exact location of that CD case twenty-four seven.' Choi shrugged at his partner. 'It must be a one-of-a-kind CD.'

The abyss inside Mary's stomach turned into a supermassive black hole, the color draining from her skin.

The next photo along seemed completely random. It showed a page, which had been torn from a newspaper and folded four times.

Mary stared at it for several long seconds before shaking her head and moving on to the last image, which was a picture of the courthouse in Woburn, Massachusetts, where Nelson's trial had taken place over two years ago.

Inside Mary's head, thoughts began colliding against each other.

'Can you help us understand any of this?' Kendall asked.

Mary pursed her lips, shrugged, then shook her head. 'Unfortunately, I can't.'

'You can't?' Choi asked. 'Or you won't?'

'I can't,' Mary lied. 'I don't know what any of this means.'

Choi held her stare for longer than he needed to. 'Of course you don't.'

'If you don't know, you don't know,' Kendall said, pushing the four conundrum photos to one side before retrieving the same ten photographs that were on the table just moments earlier – Antonia, Gabriela, Jonas, Brian, Tyler, Richard, Carol, Rachel, Kathy, and the couple that Mary had failed to recognize. He, once again, arranged them in two rows, before adding Luke, Natálie and Betsy to the group.

'Are you sure you don't know who these two are?' Kendall tried again, indicating the couple on the photo that Mary hadn't recognized.

'No, I don . . .' Mary paused. The familiarity of their faces was still playing in her mind. Maybe it was the look in the lady's eyes, or the gentleman's ears, which clearly stood out. Mary took a second to search her memory one more time. It took her a little longer than with Natálie, but she did, eventually, remember them.

'Oh my god!' Mary said, her head jerking back from the surprise, her eyes round and wide. 'I've seen them before . . . yes. I never met them, but I've seen them before.'

'Can you remember where?' Kendall asked.

'At an art exhibition,' Mary revealed. 'On the same night that I met Quaddra for the first time. They were there, looking at this painting that was nothing more than just a canvas painted black. We were standing right behind them.'

'And you're sure that that's them?' Choi again.

'Yes, that's them.'

'So,' Kendall said, nodding at the table. 'You have crossed paths with everyone in these photographs in the past what? Two years?'

Mary drew in a deep breath as she studied the photos on the table one last time. 'Give or take . . . yes.'

Choi ran a hand over his mouth, as if he was smoothing an imaginary goatee. 'And you're insisting on saying that you're not on any medication?'

'I'm not on any medication.' Frustration came through in Mary's voice and in her eyes. 'Why? Did Quaddra tell you that I was?'

'Thomas,' Choi reminded her. 'His name is Thomas Cameron.'

Mary was through fighting that battle. 'Whatever. Did he tell you that I was on medication?'

'He doesn't even know who you are,' Choi revealed.

Something lodged itself in Mary's throat. 'What?'

'But I think we do,' Kendall said, placing what looked to be a manuscript on the table, which must've been around one hundred and fifty pages long.

'What is that?' Mary's voice came out shaky.

'It's a script for a new production that Mr. Cameron's company has been working on,' Choi replied.

'A script?' Mary's stare bounced between the two detectives again. To Mary, the more they talked, the less sense everything made.

'That's right,' Kendall confirmed. 'A movie script ... or maybe a TV series. They're not sure yet. And like I said earlier, this is where it goes from crazy to absolutely insane.' He indicated the thirteen photos on the table. 'All these people ... who you've said you've crossed paths with in the past two years – from Antonia, the housemaid, to Betsy, the artist – they are all actors and actresses, working for Thomas Cameron's production company in LA.' He paused to allow Mary to ponder over the implications of what he'd just said before resting his left palm over the manuscript. 'And they're the *cast* for this script.'

Mary could practically feel the ground starting to crack just under her feet.

'And all the names you gave us ...' Choi said, reading from his notes, '... Luke, Betsy, Natálie, Antonia, Gabriella, Jonas, etc ... they're all characters in this script, Mary ... created to fit the story. They aren't real. And you named them all. How's that possible?' He reached for the photos and began turning them over. On the back of each photograph there were two names – the actor or actress' real name and the character that they were playing in the script. An actor named Eddie Cowell was playing Luke Jenkins. Laura Dickens was playing Betsy Fletcher. Manuela Oliver was playing Natálie ...

Mary heard the words, but her brain seemed to reject their meaning. 'Excuse me ... what?'

'We haven't read the script,' Kendall added. 'I'm not much

of a reader myself, but at the hospital, Mr. Cameron was kind enough to summarize the whole story for us, which is based on real facts . . . and the main character, who is not in any of these pictures – she's real, a real-life dirt bag.'

'Mr. Cameron never met her,' Choi took over. 'He'd never seen any photos of her either because there are none around. Apparently, she's a real modern-day legend, and that was why Mr. Cameron decided to write this script. Would you like to know what the story is all about?'

The thoughts inside Mary's head weren't just colliding with each other anymore – they were crashing and burning.

'It's about a con artist,' Kendall told her. 'A female con artist who marries rich men before divorcing them two years later and bleeding them dry.'

'A bit like my ex-wife,' Choi commented with a forced chuckle. 'That bitch took everything.'

What in the world is going on here?

'What a crazy story, don't you think?' Kendall asked.

Mary remained quiet.

'But it gets better,' Kendall added. 'In this story, the con artist goes after a millionaire from Boston called . . .' he looked at Choi, '. . . drum roll, please.'

Choi used both hands on the table, mimicking a drum roll.

'Quaddra Buckner,' Kendall told her. 'Double D. Is that mad or what? And before you ask – yes, we've googled Quaddra Buckner, double "D". There's not a single entry. The man doesn't exist. He's a fictional character.'

Mary felt faint.

'The insane part is that I think that Mr. Cameron is right,' Kendall continued.

'I do too,' Choi agreed.

'What he told us at the hospital,' Kendall explained, 'is that he thinks that *you* are the real-life con woman – the dirt bag that this whole script is based on.' He placed his left palm on the manuscript again. 'And somehow you found out about this production . . . this script . . . and in a desperate attempt to stop this from becoming a blockbuster that would ruin your life and certainly throw you in prison, you turned up at Mr. Cameron's house with the sole intention of ending his life.'

Mary said nothing in return because she knew that there was nothing that she could say. What she needed to do was find time to think, and she couldn't do that while she was in that interrogation room with both detectives. Her last hope of proving that she wasn't trying to kill Quaddra was Dr. Fox. She would be there at any minute now with an attorney and the package that Mary had given her. Once both detectives had talked to Dr. Fox and had a look at the contents of that 'evidence' package, Mary was sure that Kendall and Choi would re-evaluate the story that they were told by Quaddra . . . Thomas . . . whoever the fuck he really was.

'I think I'm done talking until my attorney gets here,' Mary finally said, nodding at the detectives.

'That would be a wise move,' Kendall agreed, signaling whoever was on the other side of the two-way mirror to pause both the voice and the video recording.

A couple of seconds later, the door to the interrogation room was pulled open by a middle-aged police officer.

'The officer will take you back to your cell,' Kendall said, as he gathered all the photos from the table.

Mary got up to follow the officer, but Choi halted her just as she got to the door. 'By the way, they're trying to get Margot Robbie to play Grace-Kelly.'

Mary paused and looked back at him, feeling a panic attack begin to wrap its long fingers around her heart. 'What did you say?'

'That Mr. Cameron told us that they were trying to get

Margot Robbie, the actress, to play the lead in the production – the con woman – in the script, her name is Grace-Kelly Mitchell.'

One Hundred and Three

As soon as the officer locked the holding cell door behind her, Mary ran to the latrine and puked her guts out.

'This can't be fucking happening,' she whispered to herself, as she took a seat on the bed, back pressed against the cold concrete wall, knees bent up against her chest, with her arms tightly hugging her legs. She buried her head into her knees as the tears began rolling down her cheeks.

How?

How could Quaddra know her real name?

Mary had never, not once, used the name Grace-Kelly Mitchell since she'd left England all those years ago, so how the hell could he know that?'

Images began flashing inside her head like some crazy picture show, taking her all the way back to Nelson's trial.

Nothing made sense, but at the same time . . . it all kind of did.

The reason why Quaddra had asked the two detectives to show her all those photos and tell her about that script was because he 'wanted' Mary to put it all together herself . . . he wanted her to realize the mistakes that she'd made along the way . . . but most of all, he wanted her to know that *he* was the one running a con on her . . . not the other way around – a con that seem to have started a full year before she'd even met him.

The puzzle pieces were all there. All she needed to do now was slot them into their correct places – and the first piece had to be the last photo that she was shown – the courthouse in Woburn, Massachusetts – where, over two years ago, Nelson's trial had taken place. That had to be where it all began. That was why Quaddra wanted her to see that photo last. This, somehow, was all Nelson's doing and Quaddra was his revenge.

'Fuck, fuck, fuck,' Mary said through greeted teeth.

Brrrrrrr.

'What the fuck?' Mary's heart practically relocated. Something had vibrated on her bed.

Brrrrrrr.

There it was again, vibrating exactly like a cellphone.

Brrrrrrr.

It seemed to be coming from under the thin pillow at the head of the bed. Mary reached for it and lifted it up. There it was – a smartphone together with a pair of in-ears headphones – Bluetooth.

'What the fuck is going on here?' She looked back at the door – still closed and locked. 'Who the fuck put this here?'

The phone vibrated again – incoming video call. Mary immediately recognized the number as Quaddra's.

It was clear that he wasn't done with her quite yet.

One Hundred and Four

The phone rang one more time before Mary reached for it and rejected the call. She began wondering if this was all a dream, an episode of *Twilight Zone*, or cruel reality.

Silence ruled the cell for the next thirty seconds before the phone pinged once, making its screen come alive to display a text message.

> QUADDRA: Answer the call, Mary. I know that you want answers, and I'm the only one who can give them to you. You might be able to figure most of it out by yourself, but you won't figure out everything . . . and the 'not knowing' will eat you alive, so answer the call because this is the only chance you'll get to finding those answers.

Mary breathed out anger because Quaddra was right – she needed answers. Not only because she wanted to know, but because if she knew exactly how she ended up in that situation, she could, maybe, mount a counterattack.

The phone rang again – incoming video call.

This time, Mary slotted the headphones into her ears and accepted the call. As she did, she laid down flat on her bed, facing the wall, and pulled the thin covers over her head. If anyone looked through the door's peephole, it would look like she was asleep.

The image that materialized on the cellphone screen shocked Mary.

Quaddra was sitting back on an adjustable hospital bed. His right hand was bandaged, together with both of his arms, but it was the state of his face that really surprised Mary. His right eye was practically swollen shut – the dark bruise around it so severe it looked like his nose had been broken. His bottom lip was cut and puffy, and his right cheek had ballooned up, as if he'd been stung by a couple of wasps.

QUADDRA: 'Hello, Mary . . .'

Quaddra waved his bandaged hand at her. Due to his swollen lip and cheeks, it sounded like he was speaking with a hot chestnut in his mouth.

QUADDRA: 'Or shall I call you Grace-Kelly?'

Mary squinted at the screen and spoke in a whisper.

MARY: 'What the actual fuck?'
QUADDRA: 'What? You think you're the only one who can play a role, give yourself bruises and run a long con? The injuries had to be real.'
MARY: 'Who the fuck are you? Really?'
QUADDRA: 'Didn't the detectives tell you? My real name IS Thomas . . . Thomas Cameron.'
MARY: 'So, you're a con artist?'
THOMAS: 'No.'

He gave her a very subtle shake of the head.

THOMAS:'I really am an investor . . . and a billionaire.'

He tried to smile, but with his swollen lip, it came out a lop-sided grimace.

MARY: 'So, what the fuck?'

THOMAS: 'You haven't put it together yet?'

MARY: 'Put what together? That you created that whole "serial killer" set-up down in that secret basement to get me arrested?'

THOMAS: 'You must admit that it was a great set-up . . . and a great sting. You finding the secret basement "by chance" . . . then the Polaroids and the footage on the computer . . . checking the Internet for some of the victims' names . . . believing that I was a serial killer . . . then coming back to the basement to film it all.'

Thomas shook his head disapprovingly.

THOMAS: 'Honestly, I'm a little disappointed on how easy it was to manipulate you, Grace. Everything that I counted on you doing . . . you did.'

MARY: 'Fuck you.'

THOMAS: 'For it all to work, I needed the ultimate alibi. I needed for the cops to witness YOU come running out of my house, covered in my blood, and holding the same knife that YOU used to stab me with.'

He tried smiling again.

THOMAS: 'Last night, in the kitchen, you think that you placed that knife between my hand and you?'

A new shake of the head.

THOMAS: 'I was gunning for the knife, Grace. I needed to get my blood on that knife and on your hands. Painful, but worth it. And since the cops were the ones who found me, all bruised, cut and bleeding on the kitchen floor, it will take a miracle to prevent you serving time for attempted murder.'

MARY: 'Fuck you, you sonofabitch.'

THOMAS: 'Aww, don't be a sore loser, Grace. You were bettered at your own game. Just accept it.'

MARY: 'Stop calling me Grace.'

THOMAS: 'But that's your real name, isn't it? Grace-Kelly Mitchell?'

There was no reply.

THOMAS: 'But if it bothers you, I can call you Mary. I don't mind.'

Mary took a second to calm herself down. She needed answers and getting angry wasn't the way to get them.

MARY: 'So, how did you and Nelson find out about my real name? How could he possibly know?'

Thomas chuckled cynically.

THOMAS: 'Nelson? You think that this has something to do with Nelson Stewart? The guy you conned in Massachusetts?'

Was he joking? Mary thought. Why else would he have wanted her to see the photo of the courthouse in Woburn?

MARY: 'You asked the detectives to show me that photo of the courthouse where Nelson's trial took place. That was the last photo they showed me. It has to be the starting point for this whole charade, right?'

THOMAS: 'Not the starting point. That was just the place where I finally found you.'

MARY: 'Finally found me?'

Instead of answers, Mary was coming up with more questions.

THOMAS: 'I think that it's finally time that I tell you a little story about myself, Mary.'

One Hundred and Five

Thomas readjusted his back against the pillow on the bed, brought his unbandaged hand up and quickly massaged the back of his neck.

THOMAS: 'Are you comfortable?'

MARY: 'Yeah. I'm enjoying my fucking waterbed inside my king-size holding cell. Popcorn and Champagne are on their way. You should join.'

THOMAS: 'I'm glad to hear that you haven't lost your sense of humor.'

Mary waited.

THOMAS: 'When I was a kid, I was truly a "bully magnet". I was skinny and awkward-looking, I dressed for shit, I had no aptitude for sports, and I had no idea how to be social and talk to anyone, never mind girls. I truly was a "Billy No-Mates". The only thing that I had going for me was that I was a great student, in every subject, but I loved numbers and I excelled with computers–'

MARY: 'I don't give a fuck about your life story. Just tell me what you need to tell me.'

THOMAS: 'Oh, you will. Just let me get there.'

Thomas reached for a cup with a straw that was on a tray to his left and had a sideways sip.

THOMAS: 'So . . . because of the way I looked and the way I dressed, I was bullied practically every day . . . in school . . . on the streets . . . it didn't matter where I went . . . it was as if I had a sign on my back and a target on my forehead. One day – I was only twelve years old then – I was coming home after spending a few hours in the town library. This was during wintertime, so it got dark really early. That day, despite it being only four thirty in the afternoon, it was already getting dark. My mom hated when I got home after dark, so to try to gain some time, I decided to cut through the park instead of sticking to the road. Bad decision. That day, this group of dickheads from my school – four of them – were getting drunk on stolen alcohol on that same park.'

MARY: 'I hope they beat the fuck out of you.'

Thomas chuckled and the effort caused him to wince.

THOMAS: 'They sure did. But here is where this story gets interesting, right? So, these four assholes were kicking the living shit out of me. I was on the ground, curled up into a ball, trying my best to protect my head from being kicked in, when this other kid, also twelve years old at the time, came flying out of the bushes and "bam" punched one of them straight in the face. The other three in the group were completely stunned by this kid's action because this kid was as skinny as I was, and just about as awkward too, but once he punched one of them in the face, he turned to the other three and said – "four against one is a fair fight, you fucktarts. How about we try four against two? Let's see how you like those odds".

'The other three stopped kicking me and turned to face this new kid. Let me add here that they were much bigger than him . . . much bigger than me too.'

Thomas brought his unbandaged hand to his face and softly touched his torn bottom lip.

THOMAS: 'Anyway, to make a long story short . . . judging by how arrogant and self-confident this kid was, I was expecting him to be some kind of kung-fu master, or something. Turned out that he was a worse fighter than I was, so that night, we both got the fuck kicked out of us. We had no chance. Once they left, this kid, who I had never seen before, just lay there, on the grass, by my side, all bruised and beat up. I was bleeding from my lip and nose and this kid's eye looked just like mine.'

He pointed at his right eye.

MARY: 'Is this going to take long? I have some very important "fuck all to do" business that I need to get on with.'

Thomas disregarded her sarcasm and continued.

THOMAS: 'So, once the dickheads were gone, this kid turned to me and asked – "So how are you doing?" Which made me laugh. I then asked him who he was and if he really thought that he could've taken on those four guys? He replied – "Fuck, no. I'm shit at fighting".'

Thomas had another attempt at a smile.

'So I asked him why he did it? Why did he jump into a fight that he knew he couldn't win, to help a complete stranger?'

MARY: 'Seriously, is there a point to this shitty story?'

THOMAS: 'Yep. Coming up.'

Thomas had another sip of his drink.

THOMAS: 'So, like I said, I asked this kid why he jumped into a fight that he knew he couldn't win, to help a complete stranger? He shrugged and replied – "Because everyone needs help every now and then. Because life is full of battles and some of them aren't meant to be fought alone. From now on, those assholes know that you're not alone anymore. They know that every time that they come at you, they'll have to deal with me too. Strength in numbers, you know?"'

Thomas chuckled.

THOMAS: 'I told him that there wasn't much strength if the two of us were getting the shit beaten out of us every time. The kid smiled and told me that at least the beating got divided – he got fifty percent of it, and I got the other fifty percent. The way it used to be, he said, I was getting one hundred percent of the beating. Divide and conquer, he said.'

MARY: 'I'm still waiting for the point to this bullshit.'

THOMAS: 'The point is, Mary, that from that day on, this kid and I became the best of friends ... inseparable, really ... the brother I never had. Yes, we got the shit kicked out of us plenty of times after that day, but I never got beaten up alone anymore. He was always there for me ... dividing the beating.'

Another lopsided smile.

THOMAS: 'Weird concept, but it worked.'

Melancholy masked Thomas' face.

THOMAS: 'When we got to high school, we both began muscling up, and by our sophomore year, no one would mess with us anymore. Once we graduated, his parents got divorced and he moved away, but on our last day of school, I promised him that if he ever needed me . . . EVER . . . for anything, all he needed to do was let me know and I'd be there for him – come what may – divide and conquer.'

MARY: 'The fucking point, Quaddra!'

Her brain was still unable to swap names.

MARY: 'Where is it?'

Thomas nodded at his screen.

THOMAS: 'We kind of lost contact after that and I never heard from him again . . . for well over ten years . . . and then, one day, I got a letter – not an email, a letter – that he sent to my parents, who forwarded it to me. The letter had been written from prison. In the letter, he explained that he'd fallen completely in love with this woman, and that he'd gotten married.'

Thomas chuckled again before his voice became overly serious, with a hint of anger.

THOMAS: 'But it turned out that the woman that he'd fallen in love with . . . the woman that he'd gotten married to was a con artist, who had not only stripped him of everything that he'd worked so hard for his entire adult life, but she'd also sent him to prison for domestic violence, abuse, and false imprisonment and captivity – something that he'd never do . . . and I know that because Phillip was the kindest soul I'd ever met. He always cared more for others than he ever did for himself.'

As Thomas mentioned his friend's name, Mary felt her heart freeze inside her.

Thomas read her like a book.

THOMAS: 'That's right, Mary. My friend's name . . . the kid who had jumped into a fight, which he knew he couldn't win, just so that a complete stranger wouldn't get beaten up alone . . . was Phillip Evans. When his parents got divorced, he and his mother moved to London, in the United Kingdom. You must remember him, don't you? He was your first fucking husband.'

One Hundred and Six

Mary felt a shudder gather momentum at the base of her jaw, before it spread like wildfire down to her core. She blinked at the screen, unable to say anything back. After she and Denise had left England, she'd never once heard of Phillip Evans again.

THOMAS: 'Once I got the letter, I jumped straight on a plane and flew to England, but I was too late. He was in prison, serving time for domestic violence and captivity, which made it sound like he was keeping you prisoner down in some dirty basement, while beating you up to his heart's content. While in prison, he was targeted by a group of righteous inmates.'

Thomas tried to laugh again.

THOMAS: 'Sounds hypocritical, doesn't it? You see, Mary, certain offences are considered too low, even by criminals. Paedophiles top that list. Most of them don't actually survive their time inside. Rapists come second, and wife-beaters a close third. Though they might be able to survive their prison time, that time will be made absolute hell by some of the other inmates. By the time I got to England and visited Phillip in prison, he was blind.'

Mary couldn't hide her surprise.

THOMAS: 'That's right. A fellow inmate, whose sister was beaten to death by her scumbag boyfriend, decided to take revenge on Phillip. The way that they look at it, Mary, is that every domestic abuser is the same – they are all scum, and they all deserve what is coming to them. So, this guy, during lunchtime in the canteen, jumped on Phillip and stuck a pencil into both of his eyes.'

Mary stuttered her next comment.

MARY: 'I . . . I didn't know that.'

THOMAS: 'Of course not. Why would you? You were done with him. You took everything away from him and left him to rot. And rot he did. I only managed to talk to him once . . . one visit . . . that's all I got. During that one visit, he told me the whole story – how he met you . . . how he fell in love with you . . . how he believed that you were the one . . . and how shocked he was when he was arrested – for domestic violence and abuse? False imprisonment and captivity? Phillip thought it was all a joke, but he said that your con was pretty watertight. Too much circumstantial evidence against him and there was nothing that he or his lawyers could do . . . just like the evidence is stacked up against you now.'

Mary said nothing because there was nothing that she could say.

THOMAS: 'A week after I saw Phillip, he committed suicide. He cut his own throat inside his cell. I bet you didn't know that either, did you?'

Mary shook her head ever so slightly.

MARY: 'I never meant for any harm to come to him.'
THOMAS: 'Get the fuck out of my face with that bullshit, Mary.'

There was real anger in Thomas' voice.

THOMAS: 'You ripped his life from him. You took all he'd worked so hard for his entire life, but that wasn't enough for you, was it? You had to send him to prison as well – for something that he'd never done – you blood-sucking parasite. You ripped his heart from his chest and took a bite right in front of him, and you're telling me that you didn't want any harm to come to him? Go fuck yourself.'

Thomas had one more sip of his drink.

THOMAS: 'That was when I promised myself that I wouldn't rest until I'd found you and made you pay. You see, Mary, when I talked to Phillip, he told me everything he could about you – your favorite TV series . . . your struggles as a child . . . your favorite film . . . your favorite musical . . . everything you ever told him. Sure, a lot of it was probably a lie – you're a con woman after all – but when people lie professionally, like you do, there are certain rules that they tend to stick to. The most important of them is – don't ever go that far away from the truth. That way, if something goes wrong and years later you get asked again about something you'd lied about, you'd be able to wing it because there are enough similarities with the truth. As the saying goes – the best lies are wrapped in truth. But even knowing everything I could about you, I couldn't find you.'

MARY: 'So, how did you?'

THOMAS: 'The old-fashioned way ... luck. I searched for you for over ten years, and I got absolutely nowhere. I had practically given up, I'm not going to lie. I tried everything, but without a single clue, it was impossible to find you. So, imagine my surprise when, a little over two years ago, I get invited to teach a seminar at MIT, in Boston. After the first day of the seminar, I was hanging around with some students and I saw an article in the university's newspaper, of all places. It was just a corner article, about a trial going on in Woburn, Massachusetts. The plaintiff was a woman named Samantha Stewart. The defendant was a fairly rich guy who went by the name of Nelson Stewart ... her husband. There was a small photo of each, and when I saw your picture, the world stopped moving. I'd only ever seen one picture of you before.'

Thomas once again reached outside the camera shot for something – a photograph. It was an old picture that had been folded in four so many times that the creases crossing the image from top to bottom and left to right had cut into the picture. He lifted the photo so that Mary could see it. It was a photo of Phillip and her on their wedding day.

THOMAS: 'You looked a little different in the newspaper photo. But I knew it was you. The story was almost identical to the one that Phillip had told me. I couldn't believe that you were running the same con again, but this time, all the way over here, in America. So, I cancelled my next seminar class and got my ass to the courthouse in Woburn as fast as I could – and there you were, looking all distraught and battered, as if that poor guy had really beaten you up for years and kept you chained in the bathroom like you said he did. I was sitting at the back of the courtroom, shaking. I had finally found you, after over ten years of searching, . . .and I'd be damned if I was letting you get away from me. And just like that, it was game on.'

One Hundred and Seven

Thomas put down the photo and used his unbandaged hand to wipe something from his good eye. He continued the story, trying hard to keep his composure.

THOMAS: 'That day in court, what I really wanted to do was follow you back to your place, wait until you fell asleep and strangle you to death – happy days – but that would mean that you'd get off too easy, and that just wasn't good enough. The right thing to do was to serve you a full dose of your own medicine. Do to you exactly what you did to Phillip … and God knows how many others. You see, Mary, my con on you started the day that I saw you in that courtroom in Woburn. From there, I had someone follow you twenty-four seven, until I had a workable plan – something that would destroy your life.'

Thomas paused to touch his swollen lip again.

THOMAS: 'Just a few months later, it was time to start implementing it.

Mary took a deep breath as she nodded.

MARY: 'Luke Jenkins.'

Thomas nodded back.

THOMAS: 'His real name is Eddie Cowell. He's an actor who I've cast a few times before in a couple of minor productions. He's also a very accomplished guitar player and singer/songwriter, as I'm sure you found out.'

MARY: 'That doesn't add up.'

Mary challenged him because she was sure that Thomas was keeping something from her.

MARY: 'There were no guarantees that I would've agreed to watch Luke's gig that night. And more to the point – how could you possibly know that I would walk past that bar that night?'

THOMAS: 'Oh, Mary, Mary. I know you're brighter than this.'

He took a breath.

THOMAS: 'It's simple behavior psychology. Humans are creatures of habit, Mary. We love routines. It's comforting to know exactly what we'll be doing, instead of having to create something new every day.'

Mary thought about it for a beat before her jaw tensed. In Nashville, to escape the boredom of sitting at home alone, she had developed an evening walking routine. Almost every evening, she'd walk along the Cumberland River then down the Broadway for at least a couple of blocks. Always the same route, past The Whisky Bent Saloon.

THOMAS: 'All I needed to do was get "Luke" to approach you at the right time.'

Mary shifted uncomfortably on the stiff bed in her cell.

THOMAS: 'The trick was not to have him approach you too soon. During your first few months in Nashville, you were still on high guard – concerned that someone from your ex-husband's camp was looking for you. If a stranger approached you in the middle of the street during your "high guard" phase, preservation instinct would've told you to walk away, no matter how charming or unthreatening that stranger might've looked, but as the months piled up and you saw no threats coming your way, you would've started to get more comfortable . . . more confident that your trail was clean . . . and your guard, inevitably, would start to relax.'

Mary looked angry, but at herself, not at Thomas.

THOMAS: 'Boredom also played a big part here. You've been living in Nashville for five months . . . no friends . . . no job . . . barely spoke to anyone . . . We are also social creatures, Mary – we long for conversations . . . for friendships . . . and for the feeling that we're not alone.'

He shrugged.

THOMAS: 'Luke was an attractive and charming guy, who didn't pose a threat to you because he was simply trying to get people into his gig. The way you saw it, he wasn't targeting you specifically – he was targeting anyone who walked past that bar – a simple diversion trick, but tremendously effective.'

Mary stayed silent, but inside she was screaming murder at herself because she had taken the bait like a hungry child.

MARY: 'How about the guy in the gangster suit? Where does he fit into all this?'

Thomas lifted his left eyebrow.

THOMAS: 'Marlon? He was my backup plan. A private eye based in Boston. He kept an eye on you. He was the one who spotted your walking routine . . . your eating routine . . . everything about you, really. But that night, he made a mistake that almost cost me my whole plan. He got spotted, and by doing so, he spooked you. If it weren't for the fact that by then you already had Luke's CD with you, we would've probably lost you that night because credit where credit is due here – it was a great counter surveillance trick you played on him back in Alabama. He ended up in Milwaukee, and let me tell you – he wasn't best pleased.'

Mary closed her eyes, as she felt a drop of bile spill from her throat into her mouth. That damn CD.

THOMAS: 'But thanks to Luke's CD and the tracker in it, from that day on, we had your location twenty-four seven, which made implementing the next part of the plan a lot easier. But I had to do it fast, before you decided to throw that CD away.'

Mary's voice was now nothing more than a whisper.

MARY: 'New Orleans. Just a few weeks later.'

Thomas attempted another smile.

THOMAS: 'Beautiful New Orleans – a city full of tourists, is it not? All I had to do was plant a new actor or actress in your path.'

A muscle flexed on the left side of Mary's jaw.

MARY: 'Natálie.'
THOMAS: 'Correct again. A very talented actress called Manuela Oliver, but to you, she was just some stranger, who you had shared a few drinks with at a random bar in New Orleans, and who had handed you a piece of paper with her phone number on it. You do the math.'

Mary breathed out pure anger. The first time that she had ever seen the name Quaddra Buckner had been in a newspaper article, talking about a couple of his new acquisitions. But the truth was that Mary hadn't read the article about Quaddra in a newspaper. She'd read it on a 'torn' page from a newspaper – the page that Natálie had scribbled down her number and handed to her.

This was a psychological technique called subliminal manipulation, but con artists and advertisement experts called it 'force feeding' – the subtle art of presenting relevant information to a mark so as to guide that mark, unsuspectingly, down a pre-arranged path. Mary had used that same technique many times in the past. And that was exactly what Natálie had done to her.

THOMAS: 'If there is one thing that every con artist on this planet has in common, it is that regardless of them running small cons for a couple of bucks, or big cons for millions, they are always on the lookout for a possible next target - even if they say that they aren't. And the first rule of con artistry is that if a good opportunity presents itself, you should never walk away from it. All I really did was plant the seed, Mary. The con artist and the greed inside you did the rest.'

Mary couldn't believe that she'd been so naïve.

THOMAS: 'Once "Natálie" handed you the newspaper page, all I had to do was wait.'

Another lopsided smile.

THOMAS: 'That same night, one of our many "Quaddra" fake websites, after being online for over seven months, got its first-ever hit. How coincidental, don't you think?'

Mary now knew why they had chosen the name Quaddra – double 'D' – a very uncommon name that no one searching the Internet would've come across by accident, which made it so much easier for them to track the number of visitors to any of their websites.

THOMAS: 'In the subsequent days, all the sites we created kept on getting hit after hit, which meant that you were doing your research, getting all your info together. Once you moved to San Francisco, I knew that you were hooked and your plan was "go". All I had to do from then on was simple maintenance, just to make sure that you were riding along the correct path.'

MARY: 'Betsy to get me to go to the exhibition. And that weird couple to give you the perfect excuse to approach me.'

THOMAS: 'Betsy would also encourage you to come out with me on that first date, telling you how hot she thought I was and how you just couldn't miss that exhibition. The "friend approval". Subtle, but also very powerful.'

Mary's blood was about to boil in her veins.

THOMAS: 'Rule number two of con artistry – always control the pace of the con. From there, the rest was easy.'

MARY: 'All your friends? Ricky, your business partner? His family?'

THOMAS: 'Actors and actresses . . . all of them . . . and all of them under a very generous contract that stipulated that they were never to set foot in San Francisco, unless I asked them to.'

Of course, Mary thought, as another piece of the puzzle slotted itself into place. Thomas couldn't risk Mary bumping into any of his 'fake friends' while she was out by herself. What if they didn't respond when Mary called out their 'fake names'? What if they didn't recognize her at first?

MARY: 'So, I take it that you're not from San Francisco either, are you?'

THOMAS: 'Bridgeport, Connecticut. Just like Phillip.'

Running such a long con inside his own city would've been too great a risk to take, Mary knew that. Regardless of how much of a private person Thomas really was, the chances of him running into someone who knew who he truly was, while on a night out with Mary, was always there. So, the trick was to move the con to a place where he was almost certain that he would never bump into anyone he knew, or anyone who knew him – another simple rule of con artistry: tip the odds in your favor.

THOMAS: 'It wasn't a perfect plan. I know that. There were many weak spots throughout, but your greed blinded you to them. Your desire to rob "Quaddra" of everything he had was stronger than your logic, creating blind spots along the way.'

MARY: 'The restaurant . . . after we left The Legion, on our first-ever date.'

THOMAS: 'According to you, it wasn't a date, remember?'

If he could've laughed, he would've done.

THOMAS: 'But I'm guessing that you're talking about the credit card incident.'

MARY: 'Yes.'

THOMAS: 'Now that really was a fluke. The original idea was for me simply to leave the credit card on the table and go to the bathroom. I knew that you would check the credit card once I was gone, but the flying credit card mistake worked much better. Much more natural.'

He paused and nodded at his screen.

THOMAS: 'And I'll hand it to you – back at The Legion, the whole running away trick so that I'd come running after you, followed by the argument in the restaurant because of the false name . . . that was genius and so well played.'

Thomas paused for a second.

THOMAS: 'Back at the house, I wasn't exactly ready for you to find that secret basement yet. I was still working on ideas on how I could make you find it without making you suspicious, but you beat me to it, which made the whole thing seem that much more real too. And I'll tell you this – your performance after you discovered the basement was flawless. You would've probably been a great actress if you hadn't decided to waste your life as a con artist.'

MARY: 'Fuck you! You know nothing about my life.'

THOMAS: 'There's nothing to know, Mary.'

The anger was back in Thomas' voice.

THOMAS: 'Other than you are a fucking lowlife who has destroyed the lives of so many others out of pure greed, nothing more, and now it's your turn. Let's see how you like losing everything you have. Let's see how you like going to prison for something you didn't really do. And do you know the real reason why I chose San Francisco? Because in California, first-degree attempted murder carries a life sentence, where you will have to serve at least fifteen years of that sentence before you are eligible for parole.'

His head angled sideways.

THOMAS: 'Still not close enough to avenge Phil, but I'll tell you this – you better watch your back while you're inside because someone might try to put a pencil into your eyes.'

He tried a smile again, and this time he almost managed it.

THOMAS: 'Being a billionaire has its perks, you know? People can be easily bought.'

MARY: 'Fuck you.'

Mary's tone was as angry as Thomas' now.

MARY: 'You really know nothing about me, or my life. This is a fucked-up world where people can only see the decisions you've made, not the choices that you were given.'

THOMAS: 'Everyone has a past, Mary. And you and Denise are not the only ones who've had a rough childhood, who came from an abusive household, who had parents who never loved or cared for them.'

As Mary heard Thomas say Denise's name, her breath caught in her throat.

THOMAS: 'Yes, this is a fucked-up world, but you and Denise aren't the only ones who, from a very early age, had to find out just how fucked-up life can be. True, I don't know the choices that you were given in life, but I'm sure that there were better decisions to be made.'

MARY: 'Where is she?'

THOMAS: 'What?'

MARY: 'Denise. Where is she? If that was all put up … if you're not really a serial killer, then those Polaroids of her are fake, right? So where is she?'

Tears were gathering on the rims of Mary's eyes.

Thomas was staring straight into his cellphone camera, as if trying to read Mary's expression.

THOMAS: 'No idea. She was supposed to meet me in Seattle the day before yesterday, but she never turned up.'

Mary breathed out a huge sigh of relief. That could only mean that the phone call that she'd made to Denise before calling Dr. Fox had reached her in time, and Denise had aborted the whole con and made her escape.

Mary's tears quickly morphed into a bright smile.

MARY: 'She's gone. I guess your plan wasn't that perfect after all, huh?'

Thomas seemed to take a minute to ponder over something.

THOMAS: 'I found *you*, didn't I?'

He paused for effect.

THOMAS: 'I'll find her as well . . . even if it takes me another ten years.'

MARY: 'No, you won't. She's way too smart for you.'

Just then, Mary heard heavy footsteps approaching her cell door and the sound of its latch unlocking. She quickly removed her headphones and stuck her head out from under the thin blanket.

'I guess your lawyer is here to see you,' the police officer said, jerking his head to one side. 'Let's go.'

Finally, Mary thought. *Dr. Fox has finally made it, and she's waiting outside with a lawyer and her 'evidence' package.*

'I need to use the toilet first,' Mary informed the officer.

'Make it quick,' the officer replied, closing the door again.

Mary quickly returned to the call.

MARY: 'I guess it's my turn to have a surprise for you.'

She smiled at Thomas.

THOMAS: 'A surprise?'

He looked curious.

MARY: 'Just a little package detailing all the abuse I've suffered at your hands for the past year and a half. Something that I'm sure the detectives and the DA will love to see.'

THOMAS: 'Abuse?'

MARY: 'Surprise, motherfucker.'

At the other end of the line, Thomas coughed once . . . twice . . . three times before it turned into a coughing frenzy. While coughing, he extended his unbandaged hand, as if asking someone to get him a glass of water. All of a sudden, a hand appeared on the left side of the picture, handing Thomas a new cup with a straw – a friend . . . a nurse . . . his lawyer . . . someone was in that hospital room with Thomas, and it made Mary's whole body freeze, including her heart.

The small camera on Thomas' phone was able to capture a little more than just the hand – it captured part of the forearm as well, where Mary could see a tattoo, a tattoo that she'd seen plenty of times in the past two years. It showed the two main characters from the classic Christmas animation movie – *The Nightmare Before Christmas* – Jack Skellington and his girlfriend, Sally. In the tattoo, Jack and Sally were facing each other. In their hands, they held each other's bleeding hearts.

MARY: 'Who's that?'

Mary's voice faltered.

THOMAS: 'What do you mean? Who's that where?'

The coughing frenzy had all but gone.

MARY: 'Who is that in the room with you? Who handed you the glass of water?'

Mary's tone sounded desperate.

THOMAS: 'Oh . . . that's my sister – Rose. She's been helping me out from the start.'

He turned his phone so that Mary could see her.

Mary's entire world stopped spinning for a second, before it completely collapsed around her. She was looking at Dr. Lillian Fox, standing by Thomas' hospital bed.

ROSE: 'Hi, Mary.'

'Dr. Fox' was waving at her.

THOMAS: 'What? You don't think that you're the only one who has a sister who can help you with a con, do you?'

Another attempted chuckle failed.

THOMAS: 'She was hiding in the house last night, Mary. She got in while we were having sex, up in the bedroom. Who do you think placed all those photos on that second wall, down in the basement? Who do you think added the headshots to the "murder" wall? Who do you think helped me obtain these bruises and the knife wounds to my back? Who do you think cut the phone line before you could make the 911 call? Divide and conquer, remember? This is for Phil.'

Rose winked at Mary before blowing her a kiss.

ROSE: 'Gotcha!'

One Hundred and Eight

Something that Mary had heard plenty of times before was the presumption that a person's entire life would flash before their eyes at the moment of death. She didn't know if that was true or not, but maybe the saying was wrong. It wasn't exactly at the moment of death that a person's life flashed before their eyes, it was at the moment that they lost 'all' hope, because right then, hiding under the thin blanket in her holding cell and staring at the screen of a cellphone, Mary saw her entire life flash before hers.

How could that even be possible?

How could Dr. Lillian Fox, someone who she had found randomly on the Internet, *five months* before she even met 'Quaddra', be 'Quaddra's' sister?

Mary's brain became a whirlwind of thoughts. She could understand the mistakes she had made with Luke and the tracker CD. She could see where she went wrong with 'Natálie' and the unsuspecting phone number on a torn newspaper page, but how could that be true for Dr. Fox? There were literally thousands of therapists in San Francisco and surrounding areas. Mary could've picked any of them, so how the fuck did Thomas get her to . . .

The realization came like a wrecking ball, sending her entire system into panic. Even her heart seemed to be beating in reverse, sucking the blood away from her veins, instead of pumping it into them.

This had been subliminal manipulation at its absolute best – like an extremely well-crafted algorithm. A 'force feed' so subtle that the word 'force' had no business being there.

The first time that Mary had seen the name Dr. Lillian Fox had been on a webpage, as she surfed the net for more information on 'Quaddra' – a sidebar advertisement on the very same page as the article that she was reading. Subsequently, she saw tens of other advertisements for Dr. Fox, all of them online . . . all of them either as a sidebar or an anchor ad, right at the bottom of the page . . . all of them on a webpage where there was an article about 'Quaddra'.

Back then, Mary didn't click on any of the ads. She didn't even pay attention to them . . . but her subconscious did. Every time that one of Dr. Fox's ads appeared on a page, her subconscious would log what her eyes were seeing, but not exactly registering – the sidebar and anchor ads. That would mount to **strength in numbers** – the more Mary read about 'Quaddra', the more logs her subconscious mind made of one Dr. Lillian Fox. As soon as Mary was ready to put her con into motion – and the first step of her con had always been the therapist . . . months before she even met the mark – her subconscious simply paired the word 'therapist' with something that it had seen in abundance in the past few days . . . weeks . . . months – the name Dr. Lillian Fox.

But the 'icing on the cake', the really clever part of Thomas' well-crafted 'algorithm' had been the tattoo on Dr. Fox's right forearm, which Mary now doubted was even real.

Thomas had said that Phillip had told him everything he could about Mary – her favorite TV series . . . her favorite film . . . her favorite musical . . . etc. Mary couldn't exactly remember, but she was sure that she had told Phillip about how much she loved the film *The Nightmare Before Christmas*.

Dr. Fox's forearm tattoo had appeared in a few of the photos that they had used for the sidebar and anchor advertisements that Mary had seen so many times. That was a detail that her unconscious mind would not only log, but also place a star by its side, indicating a subconscious connection that went back years – before Mary became a con artist ... before Dr. Fox became a psychologist.

Very few things connect people better than a childhood love.

Mary picking Dr. Fox as her therapist hadn't been a choice amongst thousands ... it hadn't been a random act either. Her subconscious had been expertly subliminally manipulated to do so ... and it didn't disappoint. Like Thomas had said – she did everything that *he* wanted her to do.

ROSE: 'Rule number three of con artistry, Mary – always control the narrative.'

MARY: 'Fuuuuuuuck!'

Mary screamed at the top of her lungs, as she got up from her cell bed and threw the cellphone in her hand against the wall, as hard as she could, smashing it into smithereens. 'Fuck! Fuck! Fuuuuuuck!'

The door to her cell was pulled open again, the police officer looking back at her with wide eyes.

'Did you just shit pieces of a cellphone?'

One Hundred and Nine

Twenty Days Later

Layana Resort & Spa, Thailand

Denise had another sip of her cocktail and watched as the waves broke against the almost snow-white sands at Koh Lanta beach. This was her third resort in just twenty days.

Denise had been just about ready to leave her house in Los Angeles, heading towards LAX to catch a flight to Seattle, where she would've met Quaddra, or Thomas, as that was the name that he was using with her, when she got the 'abort' message from Mary. That had been the first-ever time that either of them had to use the 'abort' code word, and Mary sounded completely desperate.

Something had definitely gone wrong.

That morning, Denise did go to LAX, but the flight she caught wasn't heading towards Seattle, it was destined for Kuala Lumpur, in Malaysia, where she spent seven days at the St. Regis Langkawi resort. From Malaysia, she flew to Vietnam, where she spent another seven days at the Four Seasons resort. Six days ago, Denise jumped onto another flight, this time heading towards Thailand, where she took temporary residence at the very luxurious Layana Resort & Spa.

Denise still had no real idea of what had happened – why did

Mary have to use the 'abort' word? She did call Mary's burner cellphone once she had landed in Kuala Lumpur, to let her know that she was safe, but she hadn't heard from Mary yet.

She did try searching the Internet, but she didn't find anything about Quaddra Buckner, which was very strange, and Denise was now starting to get a bit anxious.

'Hey, babe, how's the cocktail?' Cheryl asked, bending down to give Denise a peck on the lips.

Cheryl had just come out of the pool, her shoulder-length blonde hair dripping water onto Denise's body, but Denise didn't mind.

'Absolutely delicious,' Denise replied. 'You should get one.'

'What is it?' Cheryl asked.

'A Champagne Piña Colada.'

Cheryl smiled at Denise. 'Sounds ideal.' She used the towel on her lounger to dry herself a little. 'Would you like a new one?' She indicated the bar.

'Fuck it, why not?'

'I'll be right back.' Cheryl kissed Denise again – a little longer this time.

Denise had met Cheryl on her first night in Thailand, at one of the bars inside Layana's Resort. They had chatted for a while and shared quite a few cocktails, before Cheryl ended up in Denise's bed.

They had slept together every night since.

Cheryl was also holidaying alone, after having divorced her wife, back in Texas. The settlement had made Cheryl a millionaire, several times over, and she had decided to blow off a little steam – and some of her newfound fortune – on a super extravagant holiday.

She and Denise had gotten on like a house on fire, and Denise would be lying if she didn't admit that Cheryl was an extremely accomplished lover.

'Here we go,' Cheryl said, handing Denise a new Champagne Piña Colada before kissing her again.

'Thanks, babe,' Denise said, sitting up on her lounger before moving her shades up to her head and allowing her eyes to feast on Cheryl's body for the zillionth time. She really was a gorgeous woman. 'You know?' She finished her first cocktail and had a sip of the new one. 'I love that tattoo so much.' She nodded at Cheryl's forearm. 'It reminds me of my childhood and of my best friend.'

Cheryl twisted her arm to look at her own tattoo. It showed the two main characters from the classic Christmas animation movie – *The Nightmare Before Christmas* – Jack Skellington and his girlfriend, Sally. In the tattoo, Jack and Sally were facing each other. In their hands, they held each other's bleeding hearts.

'It's a great love story, isn't it?' Cheryl said, as she too had a sip of her cocktail.

Denise smiled. 'That's what my friend always used to say.'

I know, Cheryl thought, as she smiled back at Denise. *She told me plenty of times.*

Acknowledgements

I am tremendously grateful to my agent, Darley Anderson, who has believed in me right from the very start, when the idea for this story was just a dream. I'm also very grateful to Georgia Fuller, Rebeka Finch, Francesca Edwards, Ilaria Albani and everyone at the Darley Anderson Literary Agency for their never-ending strive to promote my work anywhere and everywhere possible. Selling a standalone novel isn't as easy as it might seem – believe me.

Always grateful to my amazing editor at Simon & Schuster, Katherine Armstrong, whose comments, suggestions, knowledge and friendship I could never do without.

Everyone at Simon & Schuster for their tremendous support and belief, and for working their socks off on every aspect of the publishing process. You guys truly rock.

And my most sincere thanks goes out to all of my readers around the world, for the most incredible support over so many years. This is a very different story to what all of you are used to from me, but I'll keep my fingers crossed that you all enjoy it.

MURDER ONE

THE NEW HUNTER & GARCIA THRILLER

COMING JULY 2027

READ ALL THE HUNTER & GARCIA NOVELS

FOLLOW CHRIS CARTER

@ChrisCarterBooksOfficial

HAVE YOU READ THEM ALL?

Discover the entire Robert Hunter series . . .

'Carter is now in the Jeffery Deaver class'
Daily Mail

THE CRUCIFIX KILLER

A body is found with a strange double cross carved into the neck: the signature of a psychopath known as the Crucifix Killer. But Detective Robert Hunter knows that's impossible. Because two years ago the Crucifix Killer was caught. Wasn't he?

THE EXECUTIONER

Inside a Los Angeles church lies the blood-soaked body of a priest, the figure 3 scrawled in blood on his chest. At first, Robert Hunter believes that this is a ritualistic killing. But as more bodies surface, he is forced to reassess.

THE NIGHT STALKER

When an unidentified victim is discovered on a slab in an abandoned butcher's shop, the cause of death is unclear. Her body bears no marks; but her lips have been carefully stitched shut. It is only when the full autopsy gets underway that Robert Hunter discovers the true horror.

THE DEATH SCULPTOR

A student nurse has the shock of her life when she discovers her patient, prosecutor Derek Nicholson, brutally murdered in his bed. But what shocks Detective Robert Hunter the most is the calling card the killer left behind.

ONE BY ONE

Detective Robert Hunter receives an anonymous call asking him to go to a specific web address – a private broadcast. Hunter logs on and a horrific show devised for his eyes only immediately begins.

AN EVIL MIND

A freak accident leads to the arrest of a man, but further investigations suggest a much more horrifying discovery – a serial killer who has been kidnapping, torturing and mutilating victims all over the United States for at least twenty-five years. And he will now only speak to Robert Hunter.

I AM DEATH

Seven days after being abducted, the body of a twenty-year-old woman is found. Detective Robert Hunter is assigned the case and almost immediately a second body turns up. Hunter knows he has to be quick, for he is chasing a monster.

THE CALLER

Be careful before answering your next call. It could be the beginning of a nightmare, as Robert Hunter discovers as he chases a killer who stalks victims on social media.

GALLERY OF THE DEAD

Robert Hunter arrives at one of the most shocking crime scenes he has ever attended. Soon, he joins forces with the FBI to track down a serial killer who sees murder as more than just killing – it's an art form.

HUNTING EVIL

Lucien Folter, the most dangerous serial killer the FBI has ever known, has just escaped. Now, he's hunting for Detective Robert Hunter – and he's going to make him pay . . .

WRITTEN IN BLOOD

When Angela Wood gains possession of a book containing horrific descriptions of multiple murders, it becomes clear that a serial killer is on the loose – and even Robert Hunter might not be able to stop him.

GENESIS

Robert Hunter is on the trail of the most vicious and disciplined serial killer he has ever encountered. Their crimes have only one disturbing link – pieces of a poem, left inside the victims' bodies.

THE DEATH WATCHER

When LA Chief Medical Examiner Dr Carolyn Hove discovers some inconsistencies in a routine autopsy, she calls in Detective Robert Hunter, who quickly finds himself on the trail of a twisted and clever killer who hides in plain sight.